HE WANTED TO PROTECT ME.
NO ONE EVER CARED ENOUGH BEFORE
TO TRY AND PROTECT ME.
AND THAT MADE ME EVEN MADDER.

Thor remained silent on the trip back, but I could sense his disapproval. It grated on my nerves until I was ready to scream.

"That's it." I plowed to a stop and swung to face him, hands on my hips. "If you've got something to say, say it and stop emoting at me."

Thor stabbed a finger toward the Dynatec camp, pointed at me, and gave his head one hard shake. Then he crossed his arms over his chest.

"Oh, yeah?" Not exactly my most brilliant comeback, but I was mad. I poked him in the chest. "Listen up, buddy. I can take care of myself. I've been doing it for damn near thirty-two cycles, and I don't need you coming to my rescue now. I'm a GEP, for Luna's sake! My resume would make your hair stand on end."

In my agitation, I began to pace. "Is there any way to get it through that hard head of yours that I'm trying to help your people? There's something on this planet Dynatec wants very badly, even if it means wiping out your entire race to get it. It's up to me to find out what they're after and stop them. But I can't if you keep interfering."

Stopping in front of him, I gazed up at his expression. But my irritation faded away as our eyes met . . .

By Katherine Allred

Alien Affairs
CLOSE ENCOUNTERS

KATHERINE ALLRED

CLOSE ENCOUNTERS

AN ALIEN AFFAIRS NOVEL

An Imprint of HarperCollinsPublishers

This is a work of fiction. Names, characters, places, and incidents are drawn from the author's imagination or are used fictitiously and are not to be construed as real. Any resemblance to actual events, locales, organizations, or persons, living or dead, is entirely coincidental.

EOS
An Imprint of HarperCollins*Publishers*
10 East 53rd Street
New York, New York 10022-5299

Copyright © 2009 by Kathy Allred
Cover art by Don Sipley
ISBN 978-0-06-167242-2
www.eosbooks.com

First Eos paperback printing: April 2009

HarperCollins® and Eos® are registered trademarks of HarperCollins Publishers.

Printed in the U.S.A.

10 9 8 7 6 5 4 3 2 1

First, for my daughter, Amy, who encouraged me
to finish this novel by shoveling on the guilt.
Second, for Gina Ardito, who told me so.
Also, for Jeannette and Martin Ward, who made
up the loudest section in my cheering squad.
And, of course, for Shelby Reed, critique partner
extraordinaire, who always listens when I need
to whine about the rough spots or life in general.

Last, but not least, this is for Larry,
because he waited five years to pour our front
sidewalk and then chose to do it on a day
when the temperature was below freezing.

ACKNOWLEDGMENTS

No man is an island, and no author completes a novel alone. With that in mind, I'd like to acknowledge the invaluable assistance of the following:

Laura Bradford, for her belief in my writing and for all her hard work getting it into the right hands.

Emily Krump, an editor with the patience of Job, who helped me make this novel the best it could be.

The wonderful art and marketing departments at HarperCollins, for creating not one but two gorgeous covers so readers could pick their favorite.

http://hubblesite.org/ whose amazing pictures of Messier 64, otherwise known as the Black Eye Galaxy, inspired parts of this novel.

Wikipedia, for providing information on everything from quartz to the female reproductive system.

And my family, for putting up with me when I was in the zone.

CLOSE
ENCOUNTERS

CHAPTER 1

Arms locked into position, grip tight on the flexisteel rod, I swung into a perfect handstand and poised for a split second, my body a curve in the air. Before gravity could kick in, I jackknifed, reversed my grip on the fly, and let the force of my body hitting the lower bar carry me into a tuck-and-roll somersault, my hands grasping the upper bar on the way down.

I'd watched holovids of the old Olympics, and it always amazed me how well natural humans did on the uneven bars. Too bad the games had died out with the advent of Genetically Engineered Persons. But anything a Natural could do, a GEP could do better and faster. I guess it made the games seem rather pointless.

It had also caused a lot of hard feelings and no small amount of prejudice toward GEPs in the beginning. Theoretically, all that changed when the Galactic Federation Council passed the Equality Edict, but in reality, no law can do away with bigotry. It just goes into hiding.

I know because I've been on the receiving end of some Naturals' intolerance. Not only am I a blonde bombshell,

I'm also one of the luckiest GEPs ever made. My creation was commissioned by the Bureau of Alien Affairs, and my boss, Dr. Jordan Daniels, is a real sweetheart of a Natural. Not only is he an expert at untying the knots of red tape that governments create, he always treats me like a lady.

It's at his insistence that I record the following events in my own words, for posterity, and so historians will have the facts straight from the horse's mouth, so to speak, above and beyond what the official records show. Unfortunately for him, I'm more of a doer than a writer.

The upper bar twanged as I released it and made a two-point landing on the floor mat, arms extended. "How was that?"

From his position on the weight table, Crigo sneered, and then went back to licking his paws.

"Yeah? I'd like to see you try it."

He ignored me, of course. We both knew his lack of opposable thumbs would severely hinder his chances of gripping the bar.

Crigo's a rock cat, so called because his kind inhabits the rocky hills of his home planet. He's been with me since my assignment in the Alpha sector several cycles ago. I've never understood why he decided to come along when I left his world, since our relationship is, at best, an uneasy one. It goes something like this: if I promise not to compromise his dignity by petting him, he promises not to rip my arm off at the elbow. No mild threat, that, since he weighs more than I do and reaches the middle of my thigh in height.

In return for the food he consumes while we're on board Max, my ship, he keeps me humble by following me around, making derogatory feline comments about everything I do, and turning his back when I talk to him. But he's living, breathing company, so I put up with him.

Besides, he's gorgeous, a fact of which he's well aware. His coat is russet colored with black stripes zigzagging down his sides like dark lightning bolts. His eyes are a pale shade of amber that reflects an intelligence unusual in rock cats. Most of them are dumb as posts.

I snagged a towel and headed for the lav, wondering if he'd adopted me because his own species bored him stiff. It was a distinct possibility. Plus, he knows I understand him like no one else can. I'm an empath, an enhancement the boss keeps out of my personnel records, along with a few other things no one needs to know. It's a talent that comes in handy when one of the big trade companies tries to pull a fast one on the sentient species of a planet they're interested in exploiting.

That's my official job. After a new species is located and studied by a team of scientific experts, I go in and make sure they know their rights according to the Equality Edict. I also help them negotiate deals for marketing their resources with the independent trade companies. If the culture is too primitive to understand their rights, I have two options. Taking the scientific reports into consideration and weighing them against my own observations, I can either ask the bureau to set up a protectorate, or I can close the planet to all further commerce until such time as the bureau deems the race capable of handling its own affairs.

It's also my job to root out breaches of the edict and bring the trade companies involved to justice. So, because of me, more than a few have lost their privilege licenses and had their ships impounded, and some owners have even ended up on Inferno, the prison planet.

Or worse.

Needless to say, I'm not the independent companies' favorite person. Occasionally, one of them will get ambitious and put a hit out on me. *Not* the way to get on my good side, as I really *hate* disposing of bodies. Too messy for my tastes, not to mention time consuming.

On the bright side, I promised Crigo he could have the next assassin who comes along. He does *love* new toys.

Thanks to the boss, Max was currently parked dirt side on a small tropical planet with a low population density and lots of sunshine. Dr. Daniels had insisted I take a vacation after my last job, in spite of my protest. So we had a tiny island all to ourselves, with gentle surf, white sand, and lots of weird ocean life for Crigo to pile at Max's entry hatch. We also had tons of fresh water in the form of a mist-shrouded waterfall spilling into a pool near where we were parked.

After two weeks of enforced idleness, I had a great tan, gorgeous white streaks in my light blonde hair, and sand in places I didn't like to think about. Good thing all that fresh water was handy. Showering three times a day can drain a ship's tank real fast, even with recycling.

I was going stir-crazy, and even Crigo was looking a little desperate as each new ocean wave swept in a fresh batch of crawly things. A rock cat can only do so much hunting and pouncing, and he'd reached his limit a week ago. As a result, I spent four hours a day exercising in Max's gym instead of my usual two. It kept Crigo and me from killing each other.

The hot water felt good, so I stayed in the shower longer than usual after my workout on the uneven bars. I was almost asleep on my feet when the water suddenly turned icy cold.

"Max!" With an indignant yelp, I scrambled to exit the shower. "What in the thirteen hells did you do that for?"

"To wake you up." The computer voice was male, smooth and mellow. "Dr. Daniels wants to speak with you."

"Why didn't you say so?" I grabbed my emergency robe and shoved my arms into the sleeves. Having been raised in the crèche, nudity didn't bother me, but I knew Naturals were funny about things like that, and I didn't want to embarrass the boss.

"Transfer the call in here, will you, Max?" I stepped into the exercise room and belted my robe while the boss materialized in front of me. Even Crigo sat up and paid attention. He knew authority when he saw it.

"Kiera, my dear, I didn't intend to interrupt your shower. Max should have waited."

"Max knows I would have dismantled him chip by chip if he had." Hope for a reprieve from my boring vacation bubbled inside me as I pushed a lock of wet hair away from my face. "What's up?"

"As much as it grieves me to cut your vacation short, I have an assignment only my best agent can handle."

Boss was a nice-looking man, even at his advanced age, tall and well built, with silver hair that gave him a distinguished appearance. If he weren't happily married with a dozen or so grandkids, I'd be tempted to jump him. But being an old-fashioned gentleman, he'd no doubt be horrified at my lascivious thoughts, so I respectfully kept them to myself. I tried to let my expression mirror his, a trick GEPs learn early in life. We may not completely understand the taboos and cultural norms of Naturals, but we're damn good actors. Most of the time. "Cool." I couldn't hide my grin.

"Cool?" His brow furrowed in puzzlement. "If you're chilly this can wait until you're dressed."

"No, no, I'm fine. *Cool* is slang for 'excellent.' It's an Old Earth term."

He stuck his hands in his pockets and leaned against the edge of his desk with a sigh. "Sometimes I think you watch entirely too many old vids. It's as if you're speaking another language entirely. As I was saying, a company is invoking Chapter Twenty of the edict."

My eyebrow arched in surprise. I'd been working for

Alien Affairs since I was thirteen cycles, and I'd never heard of a company invoking that particular clause before. In short, it allowed a company to stake a claim to full ownership of a planet if the sentient, indigenous species would die out in a period of no more than one hundred cycles.

A shiver ran over me from the air brushing my wet skin. "Which company?"

"Dynatec."

Woo boy. Dynatec was the largest of the independent trade companies, with fingers in everything from mining to power supply. Rumor had it that they were even into drug smuggling, but no one had proved it yet. I'd been frothing at the mouth to get something on them for cycles.

I parked my butt on the weight bench, ignoring Crigo's growl of warning when I pushed him to one side. Naturals usually can't tell what I'm thinking, but the boss could read me well enough to make me uncomfortable.

His lips curved slightly. "My sentiments, exactly. But I've got a bad feeling about this one, Kiera. They're being too damned cooperative. They've even requested an agent be sent as soon as possible to 'expedite' the matter." He paused. "Their word, not mine."

"Oh, yeah. There's something going on all right." I nodded agreement. "Companies usually turn themselves wrong side out to keep us away from a new species as long as possible. Do we have any details on the aliens?"

"Sketchy ones, at best. I've already downloaded what we know to Max's files. According to Dynatec's report, the native population includes less than seventy members, with an extremely low birthrate. If their reports are correct, there's only been one live birth since the original exploration team discovered the planet ten cycles ago."

"That's bad."

"Yes, it is. I know you aren't usually the one to make

first contact, but we have no choice. Thanks to an unforeseen loophole left by lawmakers, under the provisions of Chapter Twenty, you only have two months to render a decision. There isn't time for a full scientific team to investigate. So part of your job will be to find out why they aren't having children and see if there's anything we can do to reverse their decline."

I nodded, thinking rapidly. "Dynatec obviously doesn't want our scientists on site. They must be awfully sure one lone agent won't have the time or resources to find anything that will negate their claim."

He pulled his hands out of his pockets and straightened. "That's what worries me. Be careful, Kiera. You'll be alone with the Dynatec crew members, all of whom have a stake in any profits the company might make from Orpheus Two."

I stood and saluted. "Yes, sir. You can count on me. Besides," I chuckled. "Max will have all the relevant information we uncover. He'll send it as we find it, even if they hold me hostage."

"Make sure the Dynatec crew knows that, too." He dipped his head and the hologram vanished.

"Max?"

"I have the jump plotted out, Kiera."

"How long—"

"Three days, sixteen hours, and twenty-four minutes. That's if we stop off at the ZT Twelve station for supplies, which I highly recommend if you'd like to continue eating civilized food in the future."

"Smart-ass computer," I mumbled, heading for the front of the ship.

The hop to ZT Twelve, a bustling hub of commerce that served as a way station for this sector of the universe, took approximately three hours. Normally Max and I use space time to immerse ourselves in Old Earth vids from the late twentieth and early twenty-first centuries. We were both addicted to the old movies. Me in particular because almost everything I knew about Naturals I'd learned from the vids. Having been raised in the crèche with other GEPs and then going straight to living on a ship and dealing with alien races, I'd had little opportunity to learn about them in person.

This time, however, I used the hours to wade through info on the Orpheus system, sitting at the command deck near Max's central brain. Crigo curled himself on an antigrav chair and went to sleep, his snores keeping me company while I worked.

The planet on which Dynatec had filed their claim was the second from the sun, a yellow star similar to Earth's Sol. If the planet had been in Earth's system, its orbit would have fallen closer to Earth's than to Mercury's. Oddly enough, there was no tilt to its axis, which meant it would have one season all cycle long. Combine an average temperature of thirty-five degrees Celsius with a relative humidity of 88 percent, and what you got was hot and wet.

No polar ice caps, I mused as I scrolled down the reports that appeared in front of me, and no oceans. But there were hundreds of freshwater lakes, big and small, dotting the surface of the planet. Lots of mountainous regions, but mostly jungle, interspersed with plains near the lakes. And according to the reports, it had an Earth-normal atmosphere.

"Holo?" I questioned Max.

An image popped up that took my breath away. Orpheus Two hung in the black vastness of space like a glowing emerald, the bigger lakes giving it a sheen that made it appear polished. Wisps of silvery-white clouds circled it like gossamer strands of spider silk, enhancing rather than hiding its beauty. It was escorted on its travels by one medium-sized moon.

If Dynatec's claim was legitimate, they could make a fortune off selling colonization chits alone. One look at this holo, and half the galaxy would stampede the Orpheus system. Habitable planets were a dime a dozen, but the Galactic Federation Council used the term *habitable* loosely. If it had breathable air and some form of drinkable water, it was deemed fit for occupation. The majority of them were harsh, deadly places where life hung on by the old tooth-and-nail method of survival.

Unless Dynatec had failed to mention some nasty surprises with the flora and fauna, Orpheus Two looked to be a habitable paradise by comparison. Plus, since it was earth normal, I could expect the Dynatec crew to be comprised of humans. Why spend big bucks paying for a gas-breathing alien's special equipment when you don't have to?

I stared at the image a bit longer, then cleared it and scrolled down to the report on the aliens. This one was a lot shorter than the report on Orpheus itself. The original Dynatec exploration team that discovered the planet ten cycles ago had dubbed the race *Buri*.

"Max, any reference to the word *Buri* in your data bank?"

Immediately another holo appeared, this time a drawing of a man, apparently made of stone. "Buri," Max intoned. "According to Norse legend, he was the male from which the gods originated. Freed from stone by the primeval cow, he was a perfect specimen of man and quite beautiful. He was the father of Bor and grandfather of Odin. The old texts are unclear on his status. He may have been merely a giant, or a god in his own right."

I nodded. There must have been a mythology buff on the exploration crew to come up with a reference that obscure. "Okay, let's take a look at the Buri. Still shot first, please."

Leaving the drawing in place, Max projected another holo beside it and I leaned back in surprise. Not at their appearance, but at their size, although their appearance was something to see, too.

"Record," I snapped in excitement, leaning forward again as the holo revolved slowly. "Senior Agent Kiera Smith, Alien Affairs, ID 64732. Report number one on the sentient species of Orpheus Two, hereafter referred to as Buri."

I stopped to gather my thoughts. Anything I recorded was admissible in the Galactic Federation courts and I was doing this without the benefit of our normal scientific team's report, so I needed to be precise. "The Buri are bipedal hominids, similar to *Homo sapiens* with one major difference apparent on cursory visual examination. Their bone structure seems to be slightly denser, making them both taller and heavier than man. Due to the lack of enlarged mammary glands on the two in *Holo 618*, and with a loincloth hiding the genitalia of both individuals, I'm assuming they are male until further examination can confirm this data. The shorter male is approximately two meters, or six feet, seven inches, and weighs about two hundred thirty pounds or one hundred five kilos, but is perfectly proportioned, with no sign of fat or abnormalities. Both his hair and eyes are a deep auburn color, unusual in that they are the exact same shade. His hair is magnificent, thick and full and hanging to just below his shoulders. Note: I can see why the exploration team called them Buri. Not only are they beautiful, they truly are giants. They could easily pass for very tall, very large humans."

I had the distinct feeling that the guy was very young, the equivalent of a teenager in earth cycles. It was the other one who kept drawing my gaze, and a shiver chased down my spine as I stared at him.

He stood well over two meters, closer to seven feet, six inches tall in Old Earth terms, and like his younger pal, his skin was a deep bronze. Wide gold armbands circled his wrists, and his long, muscular legs were encased in buckskin boots that hit him mid-thigh. There was something about his stance that spoke of absolute confidence, with a good bit of arrogance thrown in for spice. And he was the most beautiful male of any species I'd ever seen. Even his short, thick beard couldn't hide his chiseled jaw or sharp cheekbones, and his ebony eyes sparkled with shrewd intelligence. Hands on his hips, chin high, he stared at me with proud defiance, black hair waving in a gentle breeze.

No, not at me. At whoever had taken the holo. Food for thought, there.

I entered his description into the record and then stretched to loosen my muscles. "What do you think about the hair and eyes being the same color, Max? Are all of them like that?"

"From the exploration team's report, it would appear so. My best guess is that the gene for hair and eye color is the same in their species, instead of two separate genes as they are in humans. Possibly an evolutionary adaptation, although I'm not sure what its purpose would be."

"I agree. Add that to the record and then stamp it with the date and time." With a wave of my hand, the holo image vanished. "Do they have all the Earth normal hair colors?" I was trying to picture a blonde Buri with blond eyes. Now that would be alien indeed.

"No. They seem to range from a light silvery gray to a deep black, with all shades of brown in between. All of the Buri have the same skin tone, though, and the males have shoulder-length hair. The females hair is longer, usually down to the waist, and it appears both sexes use braids for style."

Yeah, I'd noticed the big guy had a single braid anchored at his right temple, but for now I was more fascinated by their hair colors. "So no blonds." I ruminated. With their bronze skin and rippling muscles and long hair they looked like extra-large, very buff, extremely sexy holovid stars.

The hair and braids also gave me some ideas on ways to get closer to the Buri, get them to accept me. "How long until we dock at ZT Twelve, Max?"

"Thirty minutes."

"Okay. I'm going to dress. I'll look at the rest of the reports on the way to Orpheus Two. As soon as we're connected, pipe the station's manifest to my quarters."

Max wasn't big by luxury space liner standards, but my quarters were roomy and comfortable. Alien Affairs treated its field agents well. It had to, since the majority of us lived and worked on our ships. Humans—Naturals or GEPs— were simply not capable of remaining in small, tight spaces for long periods of time. It did funny things to their heads.

As Alien Affairs' senior and most-experienced agent, I was luckier than a lot of their representatives. Max was a top-of-the-line Surge Zephyr, an artificial intelligence with all the bells and whistles the company could install, whose power source was a rare and costly surge crystal. He was also something of a prude, and insisted on closing off all vidports and sound to my quarters on the rare occasions I brought a playmate home for some rest and relaxation.

There would be no fun and games on this trip to ZT Twelve, though. It was strictly business.

I hesitated over my dress uniform, and then opted for standard spacer garb: a plain black jumpsuit with lots of nice pockets and pouches for holding weapons. I wasn't expecting trouble, but if it came, I'd be ready.

Once dressed, I whipped my hair into a braid and tugged a black cap over it, pulling the brim down enough to leave my green eyes shadowed. A quick glance in the mirror assured me I'd blend in with the other spacers on ZT Twelve perfectly.

My perusal was interrupted when Max lit up my vidscreen with the station manifest. Anything that was for sale in the known universe could be found on ZT Twelve. If not legitimately, then through the black market.

I parked my fanny in front of the screen, searching for and ordering certain items to be loaded into Max's cargo hold. It was common practice for an agent to carry wampum when making their initial contact with a new race. It not only smoothed the way, it gave the potential inductees a taste of what being part of the Galactic Federation could mean.

Choosing the correct wampum, an Old Earth AmerInd term for trade goods, was always risky business for an agent. You could never be positive the items presented wouldn't mortally offend some cultural taboo and get you tossed out on your ear. Or worse. But thanks to their long hair, I was pretty sure of my choices for the Buri.

Satisfied that Max would see to the rest of our supplies and make sure everything was loaded and paid for, I left my quarters and walked to the forward hatch. "Standard security, Max," I said, punching in the code that would equalize the air pressure and allow the outer door to open. "Let me know when we're ready to leave."

I didn't even look at Crigo. His first and only trip on station had convinced him that hordes of running, screaming people weren't his cup of tea. We'd almost been banned from ZT Twelve over that escapade. Now he stayed on Max unless we were dirt side.

The air in the corridor smelled metallic as I made my way to the nearest lift, and I could hear the heavy-duty whine of the giant pumps that circulated oxygen through the station. There were only a few people hanging around in the docking area. Mostly some spacers watching servomotors load cargo onto ships and a few mechs with tools spread around them.

I waited beside a pallet of boxes, and when the lift door slid open, stepped inside. "Level six, please."

"Level six," the mechanical voice droned. "Boutiques, bars, pleasure houses, and fine restaurants." On the wall a vidscreen sprang to life advertising individual businesses. I watched them idly until the lift stopped. I already had a destination in mind, but vendors could change rapidly on ZT Twelve and it paid to stay up to date.

As always, the corridors on level six were packed with people. This was the real heart of the station, the place where everyone wound up sooner or later. It was also the place where information could be had for the price of a drink.

Hugging the wall, hand hovering near my weapon, I slid through the crowd, constantly on the alert. Before I reached Jolaria's Jewel, a small bar and whorehouse hidden in a back corridor, I intercepted busy fingers twice, both intent on lifting anything of value from my pockets. With a fatalistic sigh, I dislocated a few joints for the second youngster and pushed my way inside the Jewel, paying no heed to the mewls of pain behind me. If you play, you pay.

The inside of the bar was dim and smoky, but Douggwah, Jolaria's bartender, looked up and watched me make my way to a corner booth in the back. As soon as I was seated, he vanished through a curtained door, reappearing in a second with a slight nod in my direction.

It wasn't long before Jolaria appeared and made her way to my table, already talking before she sat down. "Been while since chew come round, friend. Chew still seeing dat man?"

I grimaced. "I dumped him over a cycle ago. And frankly, I don't know why I let him hang around as long as I did. The man turned out to be a total zorfa's ass."

"Zorfa?" She tilted her head inquisitively.

"Big ugly critter that lives in the swamps on Gartune. They have two purposes in life, to eat and fornicate, and they aren't real particular in either instance. If it doesn't run, it's fair game. I don't know what I was thinking."

"Chew were thinking wit jer heart, not jer brain. Next time, chew use both. So, chew let me buy jer indenture and come work to me, now? In one cycle, chew be free woman and rich to boot. Ze men will love chew."

Jolaria was a Meltanie, a race that stood a willowy six feet tall, all of it a straight shot with no curves to break up the territory. With their platinum hair, white skin, and red eyes, it was nearly impossible to tell the males from the females.

I'd met Jolaria on my first mission, when I'd accidentally stumbled across the Jewel and was rather insistently mistaken for one of her whores. She assisted me in disposing of the body—I wasn't quite used to handling the slower reflexes of Naturals and had done more damage to the spacer than I'd intended—and we'd been friends ever since.

"Thanks for the offer, Jo, but I'm done with men. All I'm after today is info."

Truthfully, I was in no hurry to pay off Alien Affairs' investment in my creation, even though the job had become a little boring. I'd pretty much climbed to the top of the heap on the agent ladder and there was nowhere left to go. I whittled my debt down a bit more every cycle, but it wasn't like I had other things to do or places to be.

Personal wealth didn't hold much appeal for me, either. All things being equal, I was content with my rut and saw no reason to change it.

Jo propped her elbows on the table, the loose sleeves of her red silk robe falling away to expose her thin forearms. "What chew need to know dis time?"

Douggwah interrupted us long enough to slide two glasses of amberberry wine onto the table and then slipped away again. I lifted my glass and sipped. "Are there any rumors floating around about this new planet Dynatec discovered?"

"Ah." She leaned back and toyed with her glass. "Eberbody know dey invoke Chapter Twenty. Big news. Lots of talk, but no fact. Some say Dynatec make big find, kind dat get people dead if dey be too nosy."

"The kind that would be worth killing off an entire race for?" I arched my eyebrow in question.

One thin shoulder lifted in a shrug. "Maybe so, maybe not. Nobody know fer sure, and Dynatec, dey ain't tellin'. Just de news dat dey trying to close legal loopholes is worrisome. Means dey don't want any questions about dis claim. Dat yer next job?"

"Yes. They've requested an agent as soon as possible."

"Dey know Alien Affairs send de best dey got?"

I smiled. "Not yet, but they will in a few days. I'm heading out as soon as Max is loaded."

She studied me a moment, her eyes filled with concern. "Chew be best off givin' dis one to somebody else, girl. Bad vibes eberwhere 'bout dis business."

"You know I can't do that, Jo. It's my job. Besides, I'm not easy to kill."

Her pale hair swung as she shook her head. "Chew too stubborn fer jer own good sometime." Pushing her untouched glass across the table, she stood. "Chew want jer usual?"

"Yes, I'm dying for some real red meat."

"I send it out. And an extra fer dat beast of jers."

"Thanks, Jo. Just bill it to my expense account."

She paused. "Chew be careful, girl. Chew hear me?"

"Yes, ma'am." I touched the brim of my cap in salute, then watched her sway off to the kitchen. Every time I stopped at the Jewel, Jo waged her campaign to hire me. Due to their sexual training, GEPs can make a lot of credits working in pleasure houses. More than a few have bought their freedom.

Of course, those were normal GEPs. Jolaria might stop offering me a job if she discovered the facts of my creation. But only the boss and I knew the truth.

Because, thanks to Simon Gertz, a geneticist with a god complex and my creator, neither of us was sure I was human. In a universe filled with diversity, where all creatures went two by two, I was one of a kind. Superwoman or monster. Either choice made for a very lonely existence.

CHAPTER 2

"Anything yet, Max?" I glanced at Crigo, distracted by his strong feelings of eagerness. He was at the starboard port, staring out at Orpheus Two, the tip of his tail twitching, ears swiveling as though picking up the sound of prey. We were on our fourth orbit, depositing small satellites at regularly spaced intervals, and he'd been in the same position since the planet had come into view.

"I'm sorry, Kiera." It took Max a full minute to respond, a first for him. He usually answered before I could get the entire question out. "The trees aren't helping, and the surface temperature is warm enough to interfere with the infrared scan. It's taken three filters to get a reliable reading, even on the night side of the planet."

"Did you find anything?"

"There's so much life, it's impossible to tell one species from another. There could be a million Buri and we wouldn't know it."

I leaned back and rubbed my forehead. "If there are more Buri than those reported, they have to live someplace. Did anything that looked like a building show up on the ultraviolet frequency?"

"Only the ones the Dynatec crew erected at the edge of that large lake, and a small group of buildings about five miles away in the jungle."

"Buildings?"

"Yes. We're too far away to tell what they're made from, but they are certainly more than huts."

Interesting. The original report had implied the Buri were somewhat primitive. The fact that they were advanced enough to construct buildings meant that although they were short on mechanical assistance, they were definitely way above the primitive level. At the very least, they would be ranked a developing society if not for their low birthrate. But there was no sense speculating until I got to know them better.

"Anything on the geological spectrograph?" I continued.

"Except for a slight anomaly in the mountainous regions near the Buri site, it looks pretty standard."

"An anomaly?" I sat a little straighter, my interest piqued. "What kind of anomaly?"

"Veins of metal that seem to change composition. First they registered as copper, then as zinc, then as iron. It's most unusual."

"Could it be a new type of metal? Maybe that's what Dynatec is after."

"I wouldn't think so," Max answered. "Alloys of those metals have been common for centuries. The anomaly is more likely due to thin veins of those metals overlapping each other."

"Back to square one." I sighed. "What time is it at the Dynatec encampment?"

"Shortly after midday."

Good. That meant I wouldn't be required to eat their food with them. Call me silly, but I don't eat other people's cooking unless I've watched the preparations myself, or unless I really trust the chef. And I don't trust anyone who works for Dynatec.

"Here's the plan. Max, put down at their camp and stay just long enough to let them have a good look at you. Once they get an eyeful, move to the other side of the lake, nearer to the Buri structures. That's where we'll set up our work area. I'll walk over after I get a look at the camp."

Crigo gave a happy chuff and stalked to the hatch, sitting with his back to the room as though staring at the door would make it open faster. He was really getting on my nerves. From the way he was emoting, Orpheus Two was one big dinner plate and he could hardly wait to dig in.

"Listen, cat," I instructed as Max angled in for his descent. "I go out first, you give me a couple minutes, then follow. And stay away from the humans and the Buri. They aren't food or toys. Got that? I don't want the Dynatec crew getting the wrong idea and taking a shot at you."

The only indication he heard me was the slight flattening of his tufted ears, but I knew he'd do as I asked. He wasn't happy about it, but he'd do it.

I'd already dressed in my standard work uniform: a short-sleeved khaki jumpsuit with the Alien Affairs patch on the breast pocket, and my rank on the collar. While Max touched down light as a feather, I tucked my braid under the matching cap and brushed an imaginary speck of lint from my knee.

A hiss of air warned me the hatch was opening, and I straightened just as Crigo looked at me over his shoulder and gave a low grunt.

"Okay, okay. I'm going. Don't get your tail in a knot."

My boots made a hollow sound on the bare metal floor as I slipped through the tube and ducked outside. Stopping on the top step, I took a deep breath of air lush with the scent of exotic flowers and growing things. From all directions my sensitive hearing picked up the whoops, clicks and rumbles of teeming life, and there was so much green it hurt my eyes to look at it.

Nearby, heat waves shimmied above the group of flexi-plast Quonset huts the Dynatec crew had erected. Several people paused to watch me disembark, their faces curious and expectant. Only one looked happy to see me, and she was a tiny thing with café au lait skin.

"Max," I subvocalized. "Who's the woman to my far right, the one who's smiling?"

He took a second to compare her image with the crew's ID list he had on file. "That's Second Lieutenant Claudia Karle. She's in charge of mapping."

I made a mental note to try and talk to her later. Since she was emitting feelings of friendliness, she might be a good source of information.

"Well, well. Senior Agent Smith."

My gaze swung to the man who had spoken as I descended the remaining steps. I'd crossed paths with Frisk before. He was the kind of Natural who thought GEPs were second-class citizens, there only for his entertainment. Especially the females, and the scuttlebutt was that he liked his sex rough and kinky.

He was also part of the crew that had appropriated the assets of the Sematians, a primitive race in the Sema Galaxy, leaving the planet denuded of resources.

I was the agent who'd gone in and cleaned up the mess, and while I hadn't been able to prove Dynatec had broken the law, everyone knew they had. I'd been gunning for them ever since. No people should have to go through what the Sematians had.

The surprise here was that Frisk was in charge of this particular mission. He usually got the smash-and-grab assignments. If a job required finesse and a capacity for thinking, then Frisk needed an extra brain to do the work. I took another look around but didn't see anyone who appeared capable of controlling the man. The day was young, however, and I'd keep an open mind.

"Captain Frisk. Nice place you've got here."

"We think so." He extended a hand, which I ignored. The first self-defense lesson a GEP learns is not to offer a hand unless you want to draw back a bloody stump. It's something the prehistoric men of Old Earth had once known, but present-day Naturals seem to have forgotten. It's also one of the easiest ways to tell a Natural from a GEP, since no GEP will shake hands. Even the GEPs who are trying to pass as Naturals can't bring themselves to participate in this ritual. Not when it's embedded in us from birth that injury to the hands leads to helplessness and death.

Frisk let his hand drop. "I'm honored Alien Affairs would send someone of your caliber for such a small job."

Sure he was. And I'm High Empress Tutti-Frutti, queen of the galaxy.

"We don't consider the potential extinction of an entire race a 'small job,' Captain. As a matter of fact, my first order of business is to discover why the Buri are dying out and see if it can be reversed."

While I was talking, I lowered my shields. Waves of arrogance, certainty, and smugness bombarded me, and I forced myself not to wince. Whatever was going on, Frisk was pretty sure it was under control. He waved one of the watching crew forward. The guy was young, tall and blond, with brilliant green eyes. If I'd had a brother, this is what he would have looked like. But GEPs don't have families. The closest we came was shared genetic material, and the same combination was never used twice.

"Maybe Dr. Redfield can be of some assistance in your research. He's our chief science officer. Doc, this is Kiera Smith, Alien Affairs' best agent."

He nodded at the introduction, his gaze wary, but didn't offer to shake hands. Another GEP. Interesting. Especially when you considered he was probably the only person on the planet who, theoretically, should have come close to matching me in physical strength.

He didn't, of course. If humans can be compared to horses, then Naturals where draft animals while regular GEPs were quarter horses. They were faster, smarter, sleeker and had better reflexes than their creators. They were also created sterile. No way were Natural humans going to take a chance on being bred out of existence.

I, on the other hand, am a supersonic thoroughbred. Because instead of using DNA from Naturals to make me, Gertz illegally used DNA from the best GEPs he could find and then manipulated it even more. Not only am I an empath, my reflexes are so fast that I can pick an insect out of the air like it was sitting still. I am so fast that I can run rings around a normal GEP going at top speed. And my body heals what would normally be fatal wounds in seconds. I am also fully functional, another fact *only* the boss and I knew. After all, what good did it do Gertz to play God if his creation couldn't reproduce?

So, while Redfield was smart enough to be Frisk's puppet master, he was no match for me. However, with Frisk's attitude toward GEPs, I couldn't see him taking orders from the doctor.

"Senior Agent Smith." When Redfield spoke, his gaze was shuttered. "I'll be happy to help in any way I can, and you're more than welcome to avail yourself of our labs and archives."

"Thank you, but that won't be necessary." I gestured at Max. "I have state-of-the-art equipment on my ship."

Frisk's gaze ran over Max, and he frowned. "An artificial intelligence Surge Zephyr? That must have set Alien Affairs back a pretty chit. Seems a little like overkill."

I bared my teeth in a fake smile. "Not at all. If anything happens to an agent, a ship like Max is perfectly capable of completing the mission on his own. That alone makes him indispensable."

Okay, warning given. I turned back to Redfield. "Have you taken DNA samples from the Buri?"

He glanced at Frisk and I detected a short burst of uneasiness before he answered. Even more interesting than his GEP status. Note to self: at some point, cut the doctor away from the herd and see if he's willing to talk.

"No, I'm afraid not." Guilt surged to the forefront of his emotions. "The Buri are too aggressive. They won't let us near them. The only way to obtain samples would be to stun them first, and since there are so few of them I didn't want to risk it."

I caught a movement in my peripheral vision and saw Redfield's eyes widen. "Agent Smith, there's a rock cat coming out of your ship."

I gave him points for his lack of panic. Frisk, on the other hand, had gone rather pale, so I addressed my answer to the doctor. "That's Crigo. If you don't bother him, he won't bother you."

As though to prove my point, Crigo trotted by, nose to the ground as he examined every bush and blade of grass, paying no attention to the Dynatec camp. Behind me, the ship hatch closed, and Max lifted silently from the ground.

"Where's he going?" Frisk was having a hard time watching Max and keeping an eye on Crigo at the same time.

"The ship? He's going to the other side of the lake to set up my work area."

Frisk stiffened. "I thought you'd work out of our camp."

"Sorry, Captain. I need to be close to the Buri, and they obviously don't care much for your crew." I'd already spotted the youngster from the holo, lounging against a tree at the edge of the jungle. "Do they always watch your camp so closely?"

"Always," Redfield answered before Frisk could respond. "And several of them usually follow the mapping team when they go out."

I nodded. "He doesn't seem too excited about a new ship landing."

"We have supply drones come in once a month. They're used to seeing ships land and take off." The doctor made an odd little hand gesture at the end of his comment, kind of a "come here, stay away" movement in abbreviated form. If I weren't so good at reading body language I'd have missed it.

I was contemplating his meaning when Frisk interrupted us. "How long do you expect this to take, Smith?"

"I have two months before I'm required by law to render a decision, Captain, and I expect my research to take every second of that time limit." I smiled. "But even if the Buri really are dying out, you've got a long wait. The ones I saw on the vids looked pretty healthy. Who knows what their natural life span is? You could be looking at another hundred cycles or so before you're allowed to open up the planet for trade and colonization."

"I expect you to keep me updated on any discoveries you make." Waves of dislike oozed from Frisk, and I arched a brow.

"Expect all you want, Frisk. I make my reports to Alien Affairs. What you'll get is my final decision. Now, if you'll excuse me, I'd like to get started."

With a nod to Redfield, I strolled toward the jungle. Crigo fell in beside me, his walk graceful, ears constantly twitching. "Like this place, do you?" I murmured.

He gave a low chuff of agreement, his head swinging curiously in the Buri's direction. The youngster wasn't lounging anymore. He was standing at attention, nervously fingering a spear as we drew nearer, his gaze shifting from me to Crigo.

"I don't think he knows what to make of you," I told Crigo. "Why don't you act like you're heading for Max?"

The rock cat cast a longing glance toward the jungle, then turned left. He wouldn't go far. In spite of his surly attitude, he viewed me as an unruly kitten. One he felt free to discipline when required, but was also obligated to protect.

The youngster watched him go, then turned back to face me. A hundred feet separated us, and I took two slow steps in his direction. On the off chance they were telepathic, I broadcast waves of friendliness, warmth and curiosity. Nothing. He didn't so much as twitch, just stared at me with his big auburn eyes.

"Max," I subvocalized. "Are you recording this?"

"Recording." His voice came from the tiny chip embedded behind my ear. It was both a communication and tracking device, and it allowed Max and I to talk without anyone else being the wiser.

Still emoting, I took another two steps, hands lifted to show I was holding no weapon. This time I got a reaction. The youngster's lips curled back to uncover strong, white teeth, and a low warning sound emerged from between his lips. Taking a tighter two-handed grip on his spear, he shifted it across the front of his body in a defensive stance.

Pausing, I studied the spearhead. There was something familiar about it, as if I'd seen it or another like it before. It was a flat black metal with odd markings etched into its surface.

My musing triggered the memory of a picture I'd once run across of a spear belonging to a giant species called the

Ashwani, which had been extinct long before their planet was discovered. "Max, can you get a clear image of his spear?" I subvocalized.

"Yes. I've taken a holo of it."

"Good. See if you've got anything on a race called the Ashwani and compare the spear's markings to any written language we have for them."

Junior was still grimacing at me, so I took a deep breath and walked closer, hoping I wouldn't have to hurt him. His body tensed, and a growling sound rumbled from his throat.

Staying loose and keeping my weight balanced on the balls of my feet, I took another step. I was only fifty feet from him now, and apparently I crossed some imperceptible barrier. Without further warning, he charged.

On the trip from ZT Twelve to Orpheus, Max and I had run the vids almost constantly, searching for consistencies in the grunts and growls that made up the Buri's language. The first time I'd mimicked the sounds, Crigo had fallen out of the antigrav chair and hissed at me. When I laughed, he stuck his nose in the air and vanished into another part of the ship.

There was only one sound I was reasonably sure about, and only because I'd seen the results when the big guy used it. When Junior charged, I stopped and let out a roar that had the fauna chittering in the trees.

The effect on the youngster was electric. He reacted as though he'd slammed into an invisible wall, staring at me with eyes the size of Max's portholes. I could feel waves of surprise and uncertainty pouring from him.

The bushes at the edge of the jungle rustled, and Junior looked over his shoulder as two more males stepped into sight. One was the big guy from the vids, the obvious leader of the tribe. The other was one I hadn't seen before. He was somewhere between the youngster and the big guy in size, and his hair and eyes were a deep brown. He didn't look happy. A scowl marred his features as he barked at Junior.

When the youngster answered, his tone was low and apologetic. The two new arrivals listened, and then refocused their attention on me. A deep anger and defiance emanated from Brownie, but all I got from the big guy was a vague sense of curiosity and interest as his black eyes moved over me. He stood with his long legs braced apart, arms crossed over his broad chest, while Brownie gestured toward me and grunted ferocious-sounding epithets.

With a distinct air of resignation, the big guy growled a response. Brownie, radiating satisfaction, handed his spear to Junior and started toward me.

Damn. I was hoping to avoid this. But since I couldn't, I was glad it was Brownie. His attitude got on my nerves.

I held my ground until he lunged, then moved to one side. With my faster reflexes, I could have circled him three times, filed my nails, and had lunch before he touched me, but I didn't want to show off. Yet, from his perspective, it must have seemed like I'd vanished. He staggered to a halt and gazed around.

I tapped him on the back. "Looking for me?"

With a roar of fury, he spun and grabbed. This time I didn't dodge. Instead, I bent at the waist and twisted my lower torso into the air. My feet hit his jaw in rapid succession as I spun into the air. His head rocked back, but he didn't go down. His eyes narrowed, studying me as he touched his bleeding lip with one hand.

Flexing my knees, I dropped into a defensive stance and waited. He came at me slower, a calculating gleam in his eyes. Warily, we circled each other, him edging ever closer. It didn't take an empath to understand his plan. He figured if he could only get his hands on me, I wouldn't stand a chance. And if I were a Natural, he'd have been right.

But I wasn't even a normal GEP.

I stopped circling and let him come. With a grunt of triumph, his massive arms fisted around me and lifted me from the ground. Using the edge of my boot, I made contact with his shin, and then jammed my elbow into his throat.

Choking and gasping, he released me to clutch at his neck, and I used the movement to grab his arm and toss him over my hip. He landed on his back with a bone-jarring thud that would have knocked the air out of a lesser creature, and then rolled to his feet.

Before he could take another step toward me, I dropped to the ground and kicked his feet out from under him. Even as he hit the dirt again, I returned to an upright position, but the maneuver had knocked my cap off and my braid spilled down my back.

Instantly, the big guy roared a command that froze Brownie in his tracks. He glowered in his leader's direction while they exchanged a series of grunts and growls, then three sets of eyes lowered to my chest.

"I think they just realized you're female," Max commented in my ear.

With a smile, I propped my hands on my hips and thrust my boobs out so there would be no doubt in their minds. Hey, they might not be my best feature, but I was proud of what I had.

Brownie groaned and shut his eyes, humiliation in every line of his body. Not only had he got his butt whipped, it had been a female who'd done the job.

The big guy snapped another order, and Brownie shot me a hate-filled glare as he retrieved his spear from Junior and slunk off into the jungle. I'd have to do something about that, and soon, I realized. I couldn't afford to have enemies in the Buri tribe.

I glanced back at the two remaining Buri to find them

watching me, the big guy's dark gaze intent, as though he couldn't quite figure me out. Still smiling, I walked slowly forward until I was right in front of him. Junior took a few steps back, but the big guy held his ground.

Normally I wouldn't have to worry about names as our scientific team would have supplied the important ones during introductions on my arrival. This time I was on my own. I'd named Junior because of his age and Brownie based on his color. But it didn't feel right to name the big guy that way for some reason.

"Key-rah," I said, touching my chest. "Key-rah." I moved my fingers to his chest. "What's your name?"

He glanced at my fingers and then lifted his gaze back to mine, his expression inscrutable. I wasn't picking up a single emotion from him, even when I touched him. All I felt was the solid warmth of his skin under my hand.

"Key-rah." I tried again. "My name is Key-rah. Your name?" He captured my wrist in his big hand, holding it gently but firmly so I couldn't pull away. His free hand went around me and lifted my braid.

He studied it for a moment, rubbing it between his fingers, then leaned down and sniffed. Now I was getting something from him. A feeling of . . . expectation? That was the only way I could describe it. Whatever it was, he was pleased.

His lips curved in a smile and he grunted something to Junior as he straightened. Without any warning, he released me and turned back to the jungle, vanishing into the thick brush.

"Same to ya, buddy," I grumbled. "And if you just told him I was a harmless female, you've got a big surprise coming."

Junior watched me warily throughout my remarks, so I gave him my most reassuring smile, then turned toward Max. To my surprise, the young Buri followed me. I brightened.

Apparently the big guy's comment hadn't been derogatory after all. He must have ordered Junior to keep an eye on me. I looked back at the clearing just in time to see another male, this one with dark gray hair, take up the position Junior had vacated.

So I rated my own guard, did I? Well, if Junior thought he was going to spend the rest of the day holding up a tree, he had another thought coming.

It had been my experience that societies with low technology tend to be uncomfortable approaching Max, so when I was on a job, I always set up Quonset huts to live and work in. Since the huts came preprogrammed to erect themselves, the hardest part of this task involved wrestling the boxes onto the antigrav sled for transportation.

By the time we reached Max, the cargo hatch was down, and the hold's conveyor belts had stacked the boxes in the opening. Crigo, who had arrived seconds before Junior and me, was sprawled in the shadows at the edge of the jungle. Giving the rock cat a wide berth, Junior chose his own tree and leaned against it.

They had the right idea, I decided. It was hotter than Inferno in midsummer, so it only made good sense to set the huts up where they would be shaded by the trees. It would also impede any line-of-sight surveillance the Dynatec crew endeavored.

There also didn't seem to be as much flying insect life in the jungle. The plains abounded in the speedy little critters. A swarm went by me doing about 140 kilometers per hour, and I used my superfast reflexes to delicately pluck one of them from the group for a better look.

Yep, they certainly were ugly things. They had long, nasty-looking proboscises and orange eyes. But their bodies were streamlined for speed and they had six wings.

Yetch. I released it in a hurry and went back to what I was doing, wiping my fingers on my leg to divest myself of any leftover bug juice that might be contaminating me.

Retrieving a laser cutter from the cargo bay, I walked a few steps into the jungle and looked around. The brush wasn't quite so thick once you got past the outer edge, and I could see the trees gradually became bigger the farther away they grew from the grassy plain.

A movement in the over-canopy caught my attention, and I glanced up in time to see a tiny creature the size of my hand flit from one flowered vine to another, chittering as it went. It resembled nothing so much as a miniature dragon, but instead of scales, it was covered in jewel-toned feathers.

It landed by gripping the vine with tiny talons and then delicately sipped from a flower. And it wasn't alone. Now that I'd noticed the first one, there seemed to be hundreds of them, filling the trees with flashes of brilliant color that rivaled the flowers for sheer beauty.

A few of them noticed me watching and flitted closer, heads tilting from side to side as they studied me intently. One of my observers, a brilliant iridescent green fellow, dangled upside down from a vine not two feet in front of me and gurgled inquisitively.

I couldn't help smiling at their antics. "Friend," I told them, on the off chance they might understand. It seemed to work. With satisfied cheeps, they went back to flower hopping.

The more I saw of Orpheus Two, the more I liked it, and that worried me. Agents couldn't allow themselves to get too attached to a place or a people. Not only did it lead to bias, which could skew the findings, it caused undue upset and heartache when it was time to leave. And that time always came.

Shaking my head, I went to work clearing a space big

enough for the huts, and making a path through the thicker brush so I could reach Max without having to fight my way out. When I was done, I put the laser cutter away and then motioned for Junior.

His eyes narrowed, but he didn't move. With a sigh, I walked over to him, took his hand, and pulled. He planted both feet and refused to budge.

I glanced at Crigo, who was still sprawled under a nearby tree, front legs crossed as he looked on with amusement. "Hey, I could use a little help getting him moving."

Lazily, Crigo rose and stalked into the jungle. A few seconds later, he let out a roar from right behind Junior that had the dragon birds swooping and fluttering in panic. It also served my purpose, since Junior launched himself a foot into the air at the sound. I used his forward momentum to drag him to the cargo bay while he was still looking apprehensively over his shoulder.

Amazingly enough, it didn't take him long to figure out that I wanted help loading boxes onto the antigrav sled, and he set to work with such enthusiasm that I suspected he'd been bored. Either that, or he was afraid of what Crigo would do if he didn't cooperate.

While we worked, I checked in with Max, using my chip so the conversation wouldn't disturb Junior. "Did you have a chance to scan Dynatec's ship?"

"Yes." Max's voice vibrated in my ear. "It's in good condition, but it's a much older model with a conventional computer. I made sure we're out of its scanner and weapon range."

Odd. Dynatec was a huge company. They could afford the most up-to-date ships and equipment available. So why use such an old one, especially when there was always a danger of pirates targeting lone ships? "What weapons are they carrying?"

"Standard, old-fashioned laser rays, and a few projectile cannons. The type that fires laser-guided missiles."

I nodded, although still puzzled at their use of outdated weapons. Projectile cannons could be devastating when used dirt side, but Max would know the instant their system locked on to a target. Using our orbiting satellites and weapons based on his surge crystal, he could strike with pinpoint accuracy to take out a single weapon, or destroy their entire camp if necessary.

The satellites also allowed Max to record any activity on the planet's surface. And once Max recorded something, it was a permanent part of the ship's log. No tampering could destroy his records, because they weren't stored physically on board. They were beamed directly to a special storage unit in the Alpha Centauri system, where Alien Affairs had its headquarters. Only Max or the boss could access the files, and even they couldn't erase them.

After the mission was completed and the fate of the Buri decided, all the recordings would be released to the Federation Library and Archives to be studied by sociologists and other scientists. They would forever be part of Federation history.

"Set up the usual perimeter," I instructed Max. "If anyone from the Dynatec crew broaches it, let me know immediately. If I'm not here and one of them shows up, use the static shield. I don't want them getting within fifty feet of you or the camp unless I'm aware they're here."

"What about the Buri?"

I shrugged. "I don't think they're capable of hurting you. Just don't let them on board unless it's with me. Other than that, don't interfere with them. The more they hang around the camp, the easier it will be to gather info on them." I paused. "You might want to let me know if Brownie is lurking in the bushes, though. I don't think he likes me much."

"Probably with good reason," Max replied. "There's an area of new skin growth on his left hip. From a close scan of the scar, it would appear to be the remnants of a laser burn."

I mulled that over for a second. So much for Redfield's assertion about not wanting to stun the Buri. Apparently they'd rather kill them. Unless Redfield didn't know everything that was going on. With Frisk's reputation for hating GEPs, it wouldn't surprise me to discover he was withholding info from the doctor.

Well, there was nothing I could do about it right this minute, and I still had a lot of work to complete.

Once the antigrav sled was loaded, we tugged it to the clearing I'd made, and I set the huts to work erecting themselves. The process clearly fascinated Junior, and he watched them go up with a mixture of awe and curiosity.

When they were done, I had two huts side by side, with a connecting partition between them that I used for storage. Each section of hut had a door with a porch roof covering it. Most of the complicated lab work would be done by Max, but the back hut was equipped with instruments so I could work on my own.

The front hut would be my living quarters. It came with its own lav, kitchen, and bedroom, and Max controlled the climate through remotes. When I tried to coax Junior inside for a look around, his eyes widened, and he backed up a step. I suspect he thought that any building that could go up so fast all by itself might come down the same way, and he wasn't going to take any chances on being inside when it did.

But at least he seemed to be over his hesitancy where I was concerned. He helped me unload the rest of my supplies without a quibble and then made himself comfortable near one of the porches.

As a reward for his assistance, I made him dinner after Max did a medic scan and assured me the Buri physiology was compatible with human rations. It took some mimicking on my part, and finally taking a bite myself before he'd try the food. And he didn't seem too fond of the vegetables sautéed in lemon wine, making faces with each swallow. But at his first taste of amberberries covered in chocolate sauce and topped with whipped cream, total rapture lit his features. It didn't take a fluent command of Buri to understand his meaning when he shoved the empty bowl at me and growled.

With a smile, I zapped another packet of the dessert in the heating unit and refilled his bowl. Even when you're dealing with an alien species, the way to a man's heart was apparently through his stomach.

I just hoped it would be this easy with the big guy. If I wanted to be accepted by the Buri, he was the one I had to impress. But I suspected I had my work cut out for me.

CHAPTER 3

My first night on Orpheus Two turned out to be a long one. Junior was still working on his second dessert when his replacement showed up. He gave the new Buri with light gray hair and silvery eyes a meager taste of the sweet, and I ended up fixing yet another bowl. Apparently this earned me Ghost's undying gratitude, because he spent the rest of the night guarding my door, keeping me awake with his shifting and turning.

Crigo had vanished with first dark, but that didn't surprise me. He was itching to explore, and I'd seen him eyeing a herd of grazers that looked like a cross between the buffalo and gazelles I'd seen in the Centaurius Zoo. They were elegantly built with long legs and spiral horns, but furred with a woolly coat of dark brown curls. They also had a hump on their backs, long beards, and broad, heavy faces.

It was during one of Ghost's tossing-and-turning periods that I awakened from a light doze with a strange thought. What if the Buri weren't posted outside my hut as guards? What if they thought they were protecting me from the Dynatec crew?

The idea was so odd I couldn't believe it had even occurred to me. My eyes opened and I blinked twice before sliding out of bed and into a robe. Moving silently, I padded to the front of the hut and gazed through the transparent door at Ghost. Had I picked up something from him?

It didn't seem likely. He was leaning against the wall, head tipped back, gentle snores parting his lips.

Trying not to wake him, I opened the door and stepped outside, letting my gaze scan the surrounding jungle. Something or someone was out there. I could feel a presence in the tingle that ran down my back and lifted the fine hair on my nape.

I was on the verge of querying Max when a slight movement caught my eye. It wasn't much, just a shimmer of moonlight on inky hair, but it was enough to tell me who my watcher was.

The big guy was back.

Shifting slightly to my right, I walked to the edge of the porch. We were within touching distance when I stopped. Close enough that I could pick up the scent of his warm, clean, very male body. I had a clear view of him from this angle.

I'm well above average height for a human female, skimming six feet tall. But he was the largest male of any species I'd ever met. He stood motionless as I stared up at him, and I tightened the belt on my robe nervously.

Which was ridiculous. I never got nervous.

In the distance, the roar of a rock cat after prey split the night, but neither of us so much as twitched. If the emotion I'd picked up earlier had come from him, there was no sign of it now. My shields were completely down and I wasn't getting a thing.

"Shall I record?" Max asked in my ear.

I hesitated. Technically, every meeting with a new race should be recorded, because you never know what you'll miss during a contact that you might pick up on later.

"No," I answered. "Not this time."

As usual, I had subvocalized when talking to Max, but the big guy tilted his head and his gaze became more intense. Slowly, he lifted one hand and touched me just over the chip implanted behind my ear. Immediately I felt a sense of puzzlement coming from him, and I sucked in a deep breath of night air.

No one had ever been aware of my conversations with Max before. Absolutely no one. Either his hearing was better than mine, which was impossible, or he had, at the very least, a rudimentary telepathic talent.

While I was thinking, his interest shifted from my conversation to my hair. I'd left it loose when I prepared for bed, and he spread his fingers to sift through the heavy mass, draping thick locks over my shoulder and wrapping them around his fist.

For the first time in my life, I didn't know what to do next. Nothing in my experience had prepared me for this.

He continued stroking my hair, then his gaze shifted and our eyes met. And as we stared at each other, a buzzing filled my head, a small, pleasant sensation that gave me a warm fuzzy feeling and made me smile.

Suddenly I was picking up more emotion from him than I wanted to, in the form of complete and utter shock. He dropped my hair as though it had burned him and took a step back. A low rumble erupted from deep in his chest as his gaze swept down to take in my bare legs and silk-clad body.

With another growl, he turned and faded into the surrounding darkness, leaving me alone to wonder what in the thirteen hells had just happened.

Had I dreamed the entire encounter?

No, it was no dream. I was on the porch wearing nothing but my robe, and Ghost was still snoring from his spot against the wall. And I'd just had a deeply physical reaction to a male from an alien species.

Oh, no. There was no way I'd allow this to continue. I was finished with men, regardless of what species they belonged to. Damn Gertz. When he was busy taking liberties with my genetic makeup, why hadn't he excised this deep-seated need for love and acceptance I'd been cursed with? It would have made my life so much simpler.

With a sigh, I padded back to bed, my mind still on the big guy. But sleep was a long time coming. I really needed to come up with a name for him, like I had for the others. Blackie was out. He just didn't seem the type for a cutesy nickname.

After an unusual amount of dithering, I settled on Thor. Yeah, that had some dignity to it, and I could picture him as the god of thunder. All he needed was a hammer.

With that decision out of the way, I finally drifted off to sleep, only to have the dragon birds wake me two hours later at the crack of dawn. Apparently they'd decided the huts were a new toy. They covered the roof, their tiny feet sounding like a pouring rain, chattering and inspecting, even swooping down to peer in the Plexiglas windows.

Mumbling under my breath, I dragged myself to the shower, and then forced my eyes open so I could find my clothes and dress. It took two cups of scalding cafftea before I felt semi-normal again. When I was sure my brain was functioning at its usual level, I walked to the door and looked out.

Crigo was stretched out on his side beneath a flowering vine, lazily cleaning his paws. His stomach was rounder, a bulging ball that marred his normally sleek lines, and he was awash in contentment. But that wasn't what made me do a double take.

Including Junior and Ghost, five Buri males squatted in

a half circle around my porch, all looking hopefully at the door.

Normally, Alien Affairs tries to limit first contact with a low technology group to simple observation for a few cycles by trained xenologists so as not to influence or disrupt their culture. Unfortunately, we didn't have that luxury with the Buri. Time was a limited commodity if we wanted to save them, and my need for information necessitated getting as close to them as possible as quickly as I could manage. Disturbing their culture was small potatoes when compared with losing the entire species.

I sighed. "Max, how much of the amberberries in chocolate sauce is left? I think I've created a monster."

"Not much, Kiera. We are overstocked with Zip Bars, though."

"That will do." I went to the food unit and punched in my request. Zip Bars are high-energy rations. You could live for a month or more eating one a day. It helps that they taste wonderful too. They're made from compressed zipple nuts and amberberries, coated in caramel and covered in chocolate. All of which hides the taste of the super nutrients mingled with the other ingredients.

I scooped up the individually wrapped bars and carried them to the porch, handing one to each Buri. In unison, they lifted the bars to their noses and sniffed. Thanks to my reflexes, I managed to stop them before they took a bite, wrapper and all.

Patiently, I showed a Buri with white streaks in his dark brown hair how to unwrap the bar before he ate it. The others watched, then mimicked the action, their eyes closing in bliss while they chewed.

As they ate, I covertly studied the male with the streaks. He appeared to be in good physical condition, but he had an aura of age about him, so I dubbed him Elder.

He caught me sneaking glances at him and grinned, holding out the Zip Bar and nodding in what I assumed was thanks.

I was waiting for them to finish, and mulling over my plans for the day, when Max interrupted me. "Kiera, one of the Dynatec crew is approaching."

"Who is it?" I straightened and turned toward the path.

"Second Lieutenant Claudia Karle, the woman you asked about yesterday."

"Is she armed?"

"Only with a hand laser and belt knife. And I detect no recording equipment on her person."

"Okay. Let her through."

The Buri were just finishing off the Zip Bars when the bushes at the head of the path rattled and Lieutenant Karle stepped into view. At the sound, all five males lurched to their feet, spears at the ready, lips curled back from their teeth.

Karle plowed to a stop and raised her hands. "Whoa. Didn't realize you'd have company. Maybe I'll just come back later."

"No, it's okay." I pushed my way between Junior and Ghost, and started forward. I hadn't taken two steps before Junior's hand clamped down on my shoulder, bringing me to a halt.

I turned to face him, smiling and radiating tranquility and calm. "She's not going to hurt me," I assured him with a serene tone. "She couldn't, even if she wanted to."

He hesitated, glanced at Elder, and then dropped his hand. All the Buri moved away to take up positions at the edges of the clearing, watching Karle with suspicion.

"Whew." Karle wiped imaginary sweat from her forehead. "They had me worried for a second there. You sure didn't waste any time making friends with them."

"They like my cooking," I said. "What can I do for you, Lieutenant?"

"I have a few minutes before my team is ready to go, and thought I'd drop by and introduce myself." She grimaced. "There are only six females in the crew, and one of them is attached to Frisk at the hip. I figure the rest of us women need to stick together."

My shields were down and I was picking up overtures of friendliness from her. For the moment, I accepted her at face value. Even if she were somehow masking her true emotions, she'd piqued my interest with that comment about Frisk.

I gestured toward the hut. "Do you have time for a cup of cafftea?"

I'd noted she was tiny the day before, but now I saw she was downright petite, with hazel eyes, café au lait skin and a dark cap of short hair curling around her face. When she smiled, her eyes sparkled. "I'll make time."

"Then please, come in."

Junior looked vaguely alarmed when she followed me to the hut, but I smiled assurance at him and he settled down.

"Have you been working with Frisk long?" I asked as I punched the button for two caffteas.

She straddled one of the bench seats at the table. "Six months now. Dynatec replaced our regular captain and our chief science officer at the last minute. None of the crew were too happy about it. Captain Morgan was a great guy, a real jewel to work with." She shrugged as I slid a cup in front of her. "Not that we had a choice. You take what you get with Dynatec. Frisk can be a real ass, but I've seen worse. At least he stays busy romping with Quilla and leaves us alone to do our job."

"Quilla?" I tried to sound casual. That name wasn't included on the ship roster I'd received, a sure sign Dynatec didn't want us to know about her. Chances were good I'd just found Frisk's superior.

"Yeah, Quilla Dorn." She sipped from her cup. "She's the other new crew member, although we've yet to figure out exactly what her job is. She came on board at the very last second, and spends all her time entertaining Frisk."

Oh, yeah. She was the one, all right. "Max?"

"Checking," he responded.

I nodded. "How's the mapping going, Lieutenant?"

"Slowly. It's a big planet and we have to cover most of it on foot." She smiled. "And please, call me Claudia."

"Claudia. I'm Kiera." I cradled my cup in my hands and settled my elbows on the table. "Doesn't Dynatec provide you with mapping drones?"

A frown flickered across her face. "Not this trip."

Apparently I wasn't the only one puzzled by Dynatec's refusal to take advantage of modern technology. "It doesn't look like you'd get much of the planet mapped if you have to walk to a new location each day."

"Oh, we don't walk. We take a sled to the last place we marked and start from there."

"Redfield said the Buri always follow you. Don't they have trouble keeping up with a sled?"

She laughed. "They don't try. It only took them one day to figure out how we operate. Now the two assigned to my team just stay at our last location until we come back the next day. Gorgeous, aren't they, though? Any one of them could make a fortune as a holovid star. Especially wearing nothing but those loincloths and thigh-high boots. Not to mention the gold bracelets. There's nothing sexier than a well-muscled arm highlighted by hot jewelry." She fanned her face with one hand. "I hope you find a way to save them."

I arched an eyebrow. "Won't that cut into your profit?"

"Of course. But I'm not so mercenary that I could still

sleep well at night knowing I'd gotten rich off the extinction of an entire race. And I'll get my usual pay no matter what your decision is. I can live with that."

She drank from her cup, her gaze going to the door. "You know, if this place is ever opened up for colonization, I wouldn't mind settling here permanently."

"If the decision goes against the Buri, that could be a long time happening. Colonization won't be allowed until the last surviving member is gone."

"I know." Her smile turned wistful. "That's another reason I want you to find a way to help them."

I really hoped Claudia was on the level, because in spite of her employer, I couldn't help but like her. And I could always use an ally in the enemy camp, so to speak.

I'd been created to be flexible, to make snap assessments and rely on my own judgment. In other words, be a doer. Abruptly, I made an executive decision. "Claudia, Dynatec is up to something big. I don't know what it is they're after yet, but I'm pretty sure they won't hesitate to wipe out the Buri to get it. If I'm going to stop them, I'll need all the information I can get."

She started to speak, but I raised a hand to stop her. "Before you say anything, I want you to know this could be very dangerous. If they're willing to kill an entire race, they won't quibble over doing away with one woman. At the very least it would probably mean the end of your career with Dynatec."

Her gaze met mine steadily, and I could feel her weighing the pros and cons against her personal code of honor. Finally, a sigh lifted her chest and she took a sip of cafftea before answering. "I'd never be able to live with myself if it turns out you're right and I stood by and did nothing. What do you need?"

"Since you're head of mapping, I'm assuming you have access to the computers?"

"Yes." She nodded. "And I'm good with computers. I input our data every evening as soon as we return."

"Okay, I want you to look for files on the Buri and Orpheus Two, or anything that looks unusual or suspicious. Try to be careful, but if you need help head for Max. He'll protect you."

I gave her a comm unit code that Dynatec wouldn't be able to monitor. "Use that to contact Max if you find anything or want to get in touch with me."

I reached across the table and touched her hand. "And Claudia, I promise you'll have an even better job with Alien Affairs when this is over."

"Thanks." She put her cup down and stood. "Well, I need to get back before my team comes looking for me."

Guilt tickled my stomach as I escorted her to the path and watched as she headed around the lake toward the Dynatec camp. I really hoped this turned out well, that I hadn't made a big mistake.

I pushed the feeling away and thought again of the Dorn woman. "Max—"

"Nothing on Dorn yet, Kiera. I'm still checking."

"Okay, let me know the second you find anything." I turned to follow the path back to my huts and promptly collided with a solid wall of warm, clean-smelling, very muscular male.

Either I'd been concentrating so hard that my supersensitive ears hadn't heard his arrival, or the big guy moved with preternatural quiet for someone so large. For some reason I thought it was the latter. I also felt an almost overwhelming certainty that, my GEP status notwithstanding, he was nearly as strong as I was.

The idea was a bit disconcerting, to say the least. I'd never before met anyone who came even remotely close to matching my abilities.

Getting a grip on my wandering thoughts, I stepped back and smiled as I waved one hand in greeting. "Hi there. Looking for me?"

With no discernible expression, he studied me for a full minute, then motioned with one hand and headed off in a westerly direction. Apparently I was supposed to follow.

Curiosity running rampant, I trotted to catch up with his long-legged stride. We were moving parallel to my camp and away from Dynatec, staying inside the tree line. None of my guards came with us, but a few dragon birds tagged along, watching our every move with interest.

Five minutes later he found what he was looking for. We stopped on the sandy bank of a small rill. The dragon birds promptly moved upstream a bit and dived into the water, splashing for all they were worth.

I was looking around, wondering what we were doing here, when Thor squatted and brushed the debris away to clear a wide swath of sand. Picking up a small stick, he drew an oval and put a stylized, intertwined *DT* in the center.

Surprise ran through me as I recognized Dynatec's corporate symbol. It was on the crew's uniforms and on their ships, so apparently he was familiar enough with the logo to reproduce it.

When he was done, he pointed at the drawing, pointed toward the Dynatec encampment, and then gestured at me, his brow arched in question. There was no doubt in my mind that he was asking if I were a part of their group.

I shook my head in denial, then took his stick, knelt next to him, and made my own drawing, this one far away from the Dynatec symbol. It was the same Alien Affairs logo that was on my pocket, depicting the three suns of Alpha Centauri, and I drew a wall between the two sketches.

After giving him a second to study the drawing, I tapped him on the shoulder and waited until I was sure I had his undivided attention. Keeping my movements abrupt, almost angry, to indicate decisiveness, I tapped the Dynatec logo, jabbed the stick toward their camp, then did the same with the Alien Affairs logo. Only this time, I pointed toward my pocket, and when I was done, made a slicing gesture with my hands and broke the stick in half. Then I flung the two parts in opposite directions and looked at him expectantly.

He watched intently and then turned his gaze back to the drawing. I could literally feel his thoughts turning rapidly as he processed the information I'd given him. When he looked back up, he was smiling and a feeling of relief flowed from him.

Not only did he get that I wasn't allied with Dynatec, he believed me. And I was more than a little stunned at how important that was to me.

I was mentally backpedaling, reminding myself of my vow to stay away from males when he rose lithely to his feet and extended a broad well-formed hand to me.

Dear Goddess, was I blushing? I'd never had anyone but the boss treat me with such chivalry before.

Grimly, I took his hand and rose, then pulled away and dusted off my knees to give myself a second. When I was done, he grabbed my hand again, gave it a gentle tug, and pointed toward the Buri village. His invitation to visit couldn't be plainer, but I needed some equipment before I could take him up on it.

Once more I shook my head, this time pointing back toward my huts. "I really want to visit your village, but I have to go back to my camp first."

He watched my lips moving and then raised his gaze to meet mine. Immediately the same buzzing I'd felt last night started, and I couldn't stop my smile. Instead of reacting with shock as he had the first time, I picked up a sense of acceptance mixed with an underlying excitement, almost a feeling of fulfillment.

Slowly he lifted a hand and two long, strong fingers ran gently over my cheek in a sensual caress.

And then he was gone, leaving me in stunned confusion, wondering what had just happened.

As soon as I got back to camp, I went into the storage section of the hut and filled a couple of knapsacks. Now that I had an invitation, it was time I paid a visit to the Buri village.

All my buddies were standing at attention when I stepped outside, as if they knew what I had planned. Even Crigo rose to his feet. When I headed northeast, toward the Buri village, they all fell in behind me, including a large flock of dragon birds, but only Junior dared to get within spitting distance of the rock cat at my side.

We'd been walking a few minutes when Junior gestured at Crigo and growled something at me.

"Crigo." I touched the cat's head. "His name is Crigo. He's a rock cat."

I stopped and took Junior's hand, pulling it down to Crigo's nose. "Behave yourself, damn it," I said when the rock cat's ears flattened and a low growl rumbled in his chest. "Pretend you're a bunny rabbit."

He rolled his eyes at me, but politely sniffed Junior's hand and then allowed the young Buri to stroke his coat. A murmur of excited voices erupted from the other males, and to Crigo's disgust, they all had to take turns gingerly touching him.

When we finally got started again, they moved in closer, some going in front of me this time. "Here." I slid one of the heavy knapsacks off my shoulder and handed it to Junior. "Make yourself useful."

He hefted it in his left hand, keeping his right free for the spear that was never far away, and motioned toward Elder. The senior Buri angled to the left, leading us to one of the small streams that emptied into the lake Max had settled near. Since the banks were free of brush, the going was much easier and my thoughts wandered to the reactions the villagers would have to my presence. I needed to be ready for anything up to and including an attack. Since I didn't dare injure any of them, my actions would have to be defensive and evasive, although I didn't think being attacked was likely, given the basically friendly nature of my escort and the big guy's invitation. On the other hand, the rest of the tribe hadn't tried my cooking.

The Buri village sat at the very base of the largest mountain range on Orpheus Two. No gentle rise to higher elevations, this, but an abrupt transition from jungle to towering peaks.

The stream opened out into a small, rocky clearing where a waterfall spilled from a huge granite bluff, bounced off an outcropping halfway down, and ended in a crystal-clear pool. Dragon birds dove in and out of the water with playful splashes, then landed on the multihued vines that decorated the rocks beside the water. As soon as my flock spotted them, they dived into the fun with a vengeance, both groups warbling enthusiastic greetings like they were long lost friends, reunited at last.

I paused to watch, fascinated by the small creatures, and then glanced around at the buildings dotted here and there under the trees that circled the pool. Thanks to Max, I wasn't expecting grass huts, but the buildings were even better than I'd imagined. What I found were dwellings that resembled the old single-story adobe homes of the Pueblo Indians. Altogether I counted about thirty of them, all one room, ranging in size from 16 meters to 5 meters. The windows and doors were covered in some type of cloth material that had been pulled aside to let air circulate. Pretty advanced for a developing society, I decided. There was more going on here than met the eye.

There was something else odd about the buildings, something that took me a second to put my finger on. They looked new.

"Max, can you date the Buri homes?"

"According to my carbon dating scans, the oldest are approximately ten cycles. Some are more recent than that. While carbon dating isn't very accurate beyond ten cycles, there's one that still hasn't dried completely. It can't be more than two or three months old."

"The Dynatec exploration team discovered the planet ten cycles ago. And because I don't believe in coincidences, it would seem the Buri built this place because of the exploration team."

"It is possible."

"Wonder where they lived before that."

"I saw no indication of other structures, Kiera."

"Okay, we'll worry about it later. For now, begin recording."

Elder strode to the center of the clearing and raised his voice in a loud string of growls and grunts. Before he was finished, Buri poured out of the jungle and the buildings, all of them tall enough to make me feel tiny by comparison, a condition that would take some getting used to.

Thor immediately caught my attention when he stepped out of one of the larger buildings, followed by a smaller Buri. Smaller, I realized, because it was a female, the first I'd seen among the Buri.

I examined her closely as the tribe gathered around Elder to stare at me. Her hair was as inky as Thor's, and hung nearly to her waist in the back. Her face was exquisite by any standard of beauty. Lacking the facial hair of the males, her high cheekbones, full lips, and well-formed brow were clearly apparent.

His mate? A pang of disappointment went through me at

the thought. My gaze shifted between them. No, the resemblance was too strong. They had to be related. He didn't look old enough to be her father, so she was probably a sibling.

Relieved in spite of myself, I made a quick scan of the rest of the group, looking for more females. They were easy to pick out, although there were shockingly few of them. Like the males, they were bare from the waist up, but instead of the leather loincloths and thigh-high boots, the women had ankle-high moccasin-type footwear and a band of material low around their hips. Through this strip was threaded a long rectangle of colored cloth that went between their legs and hung to their knees in the front and back. The females also wore gold bands, but instead of bracelets, theirs were worn around the upper part of the arms.

"Max, do you have a total population yet?"

"Counting the Buri who are guarding the Dynatec crew, sixty-nine. Eighteen females, fifty-one males."

Damn. A population of fifty was considered the bare minimum for a healthy genetic pool, but I'd feel much better about their chances if the females equaled or outnumbered the males. And one of the women looked to be well beyond childbearing age.

Plus, there was another slight problem. According to the records the boss had given me, there were seventy Buri. What had happened to the one that was missing? Was it dead? It was the only explanation I could come up with at the moment. If it were anywhere in the area, Max would have found it.

My thoughts were interrupted as my contingent of Buri surrounded me while Elder gestured and made a speech to the rest of the tribe. Crigo, supremely unconcerned with the proceedings, bounded onto a rock beside the pool, yawned and curled up to sleep off his late-night snack.

Occasionally, one of my group growled an agreement

with whatever Elder was telling them, and then quieted to listen. When he finished, they all turned to look at Thor.

The big guy seemed to be caught in indecision, because he continued to stare at me until the female next to him tugged at his arm and growled a question. His answer was short and to the point, and her eyes rounded as a gasp ran through the crowd.

She growled another question, and his response was a sharp nod. Even from several arms' lengths away and surrounded by other Buri, I caught a wisp of his emotion. He was feeling very smug, but there were overtones of vindication mixed in with it, all of which he was trying hard not to show.

With only a brief hesitation, the female let go of his arm and walked across the clearing to face me.

I had no idea what had just transpired, so I braced myself for anything. Anything but her lips curving into a smile of welcome as she gently stroked my cheek. When I cautiously mimicked the gesture, Thor nodded in satisfaction and crossed his arms over his chest while the rest of the tribe relaxed tensed muscles.

As though it were a signal, I was suddenly surrounded by grunting, smiling females, all of them vying for my notice. Somehow in the melee, my cap got knocked off, provoking another round of excited chatter as they touched my blonde hair and rubbed the material of my jumpsuit between their fingers.

Things settled down when Thor's sister took my chin in her hand and made me look at her again. Once she was sure she had my undivided attention, she touched her chest and made a soft noise that started in the back of her throat and sort of rolled between her lips. I tried to repeat it, but the best I could do was *Churka*. She nodded, then touched my chest.

"Key-rah," I pronounced slowly. "Key-rah."

She watched my mouth closely, then pursed her lips. What came out sounded more like a growled *Kuyya* than *Kiera*, but I nodded. She repeated it, then took my hand and led me to Thor. Touching his shoulder while he stared impassively down at us, she growled a string of syllables a mile long.

I must have looked blank, because she repeated it. Shaking my head in frustration, I touched his arm. "Thor."

With a sideways glance at his sister, he shrugged.

"Thor," I said again, smiling and stroking his skin. His dark eyes met mine, and the same odd buzzing filled my head.

Which is why I didn't notice there was a problem until Thor stiffened and yanked his gaze from mine. I glanced in the direction he was staring and then spun to face the threat.

Brownie stood at the edge of the clearing, hands fisted at his sides, anger radiating from him in heavy waves. Thor growled, but it only seemed to increase the other Buri's agitation.

Well, this was one of the reasons I'd come to the village today. I only hoped it worked.

I still had one of the knapsacks slung across my shoulder. With my right hand, I unfastened a side compartment and pulled out a cloth-wrapped bundle. Doing my level best to emit admiration and appreciation, I held the gift reverently on my extended palms as I crossed the clearing to him, Thor close by.

When I reached him, I bowed once and then extended my offering.

Anger unabated, his gaze shifted from me, to my hands, to Thor, and I got the impression Brownie's ire was directed as much at the Buri leader as it was toward me. Seemingly unaffected by the other Buri's animosity except for a touch of resignation, the big guy gave me a slight smile, and I got the impression he knew I was trying to tell Brownie that I admired his strength, and was honored he'd condescended to fight me.

His voice low, Thor talked to Brownie for a few minutes, the longest speech I'd ever heard him make. When he finished, Brownie looked at me guardedly. His anger hadn't ebbed, but it was temporarily buried.

Warily, he took the bundle from my hands and unwrapped the cloth, his eyes going big and round when he saw what was inside.

It was a knife, one of the very best in my stores. Made of chromium and platinum, it had an eight-inch blade that was scalpel sharp and would never dull, rust or wear. The hilt was textured to insure a tighter grip, and decorated with engravings of strange and fantastic animals.

When Brownie looked at me again, his eyes held a warning. He might accept the gift, but this wasn't over yet, and he wanted me to know it. When I nodded, he held the knife up so everyone could see it.

All of the males except Thor gathered around, admiring his gift, when a small streak of bronze with chocolate-colored hair pushed through the group and ran toward Brownie. One of the females made a grab but missed. The child lunged for Brownie's leg, hanging on while he chattered in a high-pitched voice.

Keeping an eye on me, Brownie leaned down and scooped the little boy into his arms while the other adults moved protectively closer.

The child wrapped his arms around Brownie's neck and then stared at me with unblinking chocolate eyes.

I was so delighted I laughed, and he smiled in return. Even one living child meant there was hope for the Buri. I had a chance to save them.

Reaching back into my knapsack, I pulled out a Zip Bar,

unwrapped it, and offered it to the little boy. He looked at Brownie questioningly, but all of my personal guards were smiling and nodding. When Brownie hesitated, I broke off a piece and popped it in my mouth. He watched me closely for a second before giving his permission, and the child reached eagerly for the bar.

I waited long enough to see his expression of joy, and then handed Zip Bars out to the rest of the adults. All but Thor. When I offered him one, he shook his head, a feeling of sadness coming from him as he watched Brownie. But the movement pushed his hair away from his right ear, and that's when I noticed he was wearing two earrings.

Curious, I stepped closer and went up on my tiptoes. The metal piercing his right lobe was one I couldn't readily identify by sight alone. It was a dull gray and could have been anything from tin to unpolished silver. Each earring had one link on the end with a black stone attached. It resembled obsidian, but had enough clarity to let me see it was faceted. I'd never seen anything quite like it.

"Max, can you tell what kind of stone this is?"

"I'm sorry, Kiera. Not without doing a full spectrogram."

Thor stood still during my examination, but when I reached up to touch the stones, he grabbed my wrist and shook his head, his earlier feelings replaced by amusement. Curious.

With a shrug, I dropped my hand. Where there were two stones, there were bound to be more. I'd just have to be on the lookout for a specimen that Max could analyze. For all I knew, there could be huge veins of the stuff lying around. The ship needed to do some more in-depth geological testing, and I quickly reminded him of that fact.

In the meantime, I was determined to find some wampum that would pique Thor's interest. If food wouldn't do it, I needed to bring out the big guns.

Letting my knapsack slide to the ground, I knelt and rummaged through the contents, coming up with several of the items I'd purchased on ZT Twelve. When I stood, I grabbed his hand and tugged him toward the pool.

"Come on, big boy. I've got a nice little surprise for you. You're going to like it, I promise," I told him in a lighthearted tone.

He resisted for a second, then gave in and followed me as an expectant hush fell over the tribe. All eyes were locked on me as I put the bottle of biodegradable body soap and shampoo on a rock.

Please, please, please don't let them have a nudity taboo, I begged silently as I pulled off my boots, unfastened my jumpsuit and let it slide down my shoulders.

CHAPTER 4

To my undying relief, the Buri seemed more curious over my blonde hair, pink skin and green eyes than offended by my nudity. Undoubtedly, I was the first naked human they'd seen, and they all took advantage of the situation by looking their fill. Thor in particular appeared fascinated by my anatomy, moving a step back so his gaze could slide from the top of my head to my toes.

At least he didn't growl. By the time his eyes made it back to my face, the corners of his lips curved in a half smile, and I didn't need to pick up his emotions to know he was pleased by what he saw.

Okay, enough was enough. I didn't have a modest bone in my body, but I wasn't an exhibitionist, either.

Turning, I picked up the bottle of soap and stepped to the edge of the pool. Crigo opened one eye, saw what I doing, and went back to sleep. Being a member of the cat family, he couldn't understand why I immersed myself in water so often. The first time I'd taken a shower after he joined me on board Max, he'd tried to save me by dragging me out from under the spray with one big paw. It had taken a lot of talking to convince him I'd done it deliberately.

I hesitated as I stared down at the pool. It was so clear I could see the rocks on the bottom, sparkling in the sunlight. What if the Buri were like cats and hated the water? With a glance over my shoulder at Thor, I did a mental headshake. They were too clean, and smelled too good. The only way to maintain that level of hygiene was frequent bathing.

Gathering my courage, I waded out until the water was waist deep. It was pleasantly cool, but not icy enough to turn my skin blue. Stopping, I motioned for Thor to join me. I have to admit, I was really hoping he'd lose the loincloth before he entered the water, but no such luck.

Hands on his hips, he glanced around at the tribe. They were all holding their breath, waiting for his reaction. Lowering his hands, he deliberately pulled his boots off, stepped into the pool and walked out to me, the water barely reaching the tops of his thighs when he stopped.

With gestures and a gentle push, I indicated I wanted him to duck under the water. The tribe stood frozen, their gazes swinging from me to Thor. Even the little boy was silent and wide-eyed. The dragon birds had settled onto vines at our approach and watched with interest. The only sound now was the thundering of the falls behind me.

Thor slowly obeyed my request, then rose from the water like the god of the seas. Maybe I should have named him Neptune, I thought fuzzily, my gaze moving over his body. The water trickled over thick, well-defined chest muscles, and highlighted his trim waist. It dripped from his hair onto a perfectly shaped forehead and slid sinuously over prominent cheekbones.

Not even his facial hair could hide the sudden softening of his lips, and I felt a familiar stirring inside. It took an effort, but I forced it away. This was no time to get overly friendly with the natives, even if the idea was tempting. I glanced at the enthralled tribe. Maybe another day, when we wouldn't be turning sex into a spectator sport. I may be a promiscuous gal, but I'm a private one.

Keeping a tight rein on my libido, I moved around him, spritzing him with the soap. It was concentrated and self-activating, so a little went a long way. As soon as it hit his hair and skin, it foamed up into a wealth of lather.

Technically, no scrubbing was required, but I couldn't resist getting my hands on that wonderful expanse of hot, male territory. I started on his back, sliding my fingers over long corded muscles that flexed under my touch, and then moved on to his front.

Thor's eyes were closed, his nostrils flaring as though he wanted to catch every scent and imprint it on his consciousness forever. The shampoo did smell good. It wasn't the loud floral type, but more like the clean earthy scent that fills the air after a thunderstorm.

When I put my palms on his chest, his eyes opened, heavy-lidded and intense, and his head dipped to watch my movements.

The close contact gave me greater access to his emotions, and he was radiating even more than he normally did. I was almost bowled over by his feelings of pleasure, his desire to take the proceedings to the next level. In reaction, and despite my best intentions, the scrubbing turned into a caress.

All my nerve endings went on alert, and time seemed to stand still. Even the small islands of lather drifting on the water slowed to a stop, and the buzzing in my head swelled to a roar.

"Kiera." I was barely aware that Max had spoken and I didn't respond, my attention focused solely on Thor.

"Kiera!"

It was the tinge of panic in Max's voice that snapped me back to the here and now. Panic? Max? I dropped my hands, stepped back, and time began to flow again.

"What's wrong, Max?"

He sounded a bit calmer when he answered me. "Your heart rate was entering the dangerous zone, and your blood pressure was rising. But it seems to be dropping now."

I rolled my eyes. Damn medic scanner bracelet. I'd worn it so Max could gather more in-depth information on the Buri physiology, but now he was using it against me. How do you explain the body's natural preparations for inter-course to an intelligence whose only body is a spaceship? You don't. And prude that he was, it would only embarrass him if I tried.

"I'm fine, Max. It must have been a momentary aberration." One that I wasn't about to let happen again. I had no idea why I seemed to be so attracted to the big guy when I'd sworn off men, but I needed to be very careful around this particular male.

Thor was still standing in front of me covered in lather, but the spell had been broken for him, too. Before I could tell him to rinse, he dove into the water and came up free of the suds.

But I wasn't quite done with him yet.

Once we were out of the pool, I motioned him down onto a rock, and then retrieved my knapsack. The first thing I took out was a stiff bristled brush. It was oval-shaped with a strap across the back to slide your hand through.

I set to work on his hair and discovered something surprising. Their hair and skin must have evolved to repel rain, because he shed water like a duck. One swipe of the brush, and the hair behind it was dry, silky and glistening with blue-white glimmers in the bright sun. It left me rather envious, and wishing my hair had the same ability.

He sat still and allowed my ministrations, his eyes cutting sideways to keep me in sight as I moved around him. By the time I finished, he was all but purring.

"Like that, do you?" I murmured, giving his hair a final stroke. "One more thing and we'll be done."

I was reaching back into my knapsack when Brownie caught my attention. His anger had returned full force. Was he jealous of the special attention Thor was getting? No. Narrowing my eyes I studied him a bit more intently, shields completely down. His anger wasn't due to jealousy. It was because Thor was accepting my ministrations, accepting me as . . .

Damn, I'd lost the mental thread.

Frustrated by my inability to clarify his thoughts, I gave up temporarily, went back to what I was doing and pulled a hair clip out of my knapsack. I'd bought over fifty boxes of the clips on ZT Twelve along with lots of brushes, enough for an entire population of Buri. They were relatively inexpensive when bought in bulk, functional and lovely to look at. But the one I held now was special. Not only was it one of a kind, I'd known the second I saw it that it was made for the big guy. Maybe even on ZT Twelve I'd had his name floating in the back of my mind.

The band was solid silver, polished to a high sheen. Emblazoned on its surface was a lightning bolt made of reddish-gold metal that seemed to glow from within. Around it radiated blue lines of static electricity.

I held it down where Thor could see it, and he took it from my hand, examining the clip minutely. He wasn't even alarmed when it closed around his finger, just mildly curious.

With a nod, he handed it back. Using the brush again, I pulled his hair into a queue and let the clip fasten around it. He looked gorgeous, the colors standing out with stunning clarity against his ebony tresses.

Smiling, I faced him and lifted my hands palms up. "All done."

The raucous cheers that erupted made me jump and spin to face the tribe. I'd been so intent on what I was doing, and they were so quiet, I'd forgotten they were there.

So had Crigo. At the first yell, he leaped into the air, and then had to scramble to keep from falling into the pool, his claws digging at the rock for purchase. Once he was back on solid ground, his ears flattened and he glared at the Buri, tail twitching in a frenzy of ire.

"Max, any idea why they're cheering?"

"There is a thirty percent probability that you performed a ritual honoring their leader."

"Thirty percent isn't too high."

"It's the best I can do without more data."

I'd swear I heard a sniff in his answer, and I smiled. Sometimes I think he's more human than I am. But his response did remind me that I'd asked him to check on Junior's spear markings for me.

"Have you found anything in your files about the Ashwani?" There was a second of silence before he answered, and I knew he was locating whatever he'd found.

"There's only one mention about their size, along with a notation that the Ashwani's hair and eye color are the same. For more information we're directed to the Federation archives."

Yeah, the hair and eye color, added to the spears the Buri carried were what made me think of the Ashwani in the first place. "Okay, when you get a chance, connect to the archives and get me everything you can find."

While I dressed, the Buri tribe gathered around Thor to examine his hair and the clip. A few checked out the oddly shaped brush. Choosing a broad, flat rock, I upended the contents of both knapsacks, spreading them out so the Buri could see them clearly.

Turning to invite the tribe to help themselves to the goodies, I was just in time to see a male Buri with light brown hair and eyes spritz the soap into his mouth. His eyes widened in alarm when it activated, filling his mouth with bubbles until he looked like he had a case of old-fashioned rabies.

Thor joined me as I laughed until my sides hurt, a grin wide enough to show strong white teeth curving his lips. Together we watched the Buri spit frantically and then dive into the pool to rinse his mouth. Soon, all the males were in the water, passing the shampoo back and forth between them.

The women ignored their antics in favor of the loot I'd put out, and there was a distinct air of celebration among the tribe.

It was when the women began using the hair clips and barrettes that I noticed Thor wasn't the only one wearing the black-stoned earrings. But there seemed to be no rhyme or reason to their dispersal. Some of the females wore a single earring in their left ear, and others wore none at all.

I glanced at the males. Junior had no earrings, Elder had one, and, like Thor, Ghost had two, both on the right lobe. Most curious. I didn't think they were symbols of rank, because if that were the case, only the highest-ranking males would wear two. Ghost obviously wasn't a leader among his people, or he wouldn't have been relegated to guard duty.

It was at times like these when I really wished technology had come up with a reliable translator. There were many out there, but unfortunately, they tended to do more harm than good. The problem wasn't in the languages; it was in the inflection of the spoken words. Say a word one way, and it got you smiles. Say it another way, and it got you dead for insulting someone's mother.

Even the most sophisticated machine couldn't tell the difference, and an artificial intelligence like Max was too expensive to waste on such a small task. Given enough time and exposure to the Buri, he would eventually be able to communicate with them on a basic level, but that didn't help me now. I would simply have to rely on my own ability to extrapolate word meanings from actions and body language and hope I got it right.

With a sigh, I parked myself on a dry rock and watched the Buri play, glancing occasionally at Thor, who stood beside me, hands on his hips. Damn, he smelled good. It took an effort to stop sniffing and keep my attention on the rest of the Buri.

The females were having a grand old time, brushing each other's hair and putting on as many clips as they could grab. The older woman was the ringleader, snatching a clip from one female and giving it to another, all the while issuing orders like one of the martial-arts instructors from my crèche days. Auntie Em, I decided, smiling.

No one paid the least bit of attention when I stood, picked up a knapsack, and began gathering samples of hair from the brushes. I was careful to keep them separate, placing each in its own little packet until I had specimens from every individual present. DNA testing was going to keep me busy for the next week.

"Max, are you finished with the medical scans?"

"Yes, Kiera."

"Okay, I'm heading back to the hut now."

After a brief hesitation, I moved to face Thor. "I have to leave," I told him, projecting sorrow while I gestured in the direction of my hut.

His brows lowered and he barked out a word, pointing toward one of the smaller buildings.

I shook my head. "I can't stay. All my equipment is at the hut. But I promise, I'll be back when I can."

He studied my face as though trying to read my lips, and his expression cleared. Very gently, he lifted a hand and let his fingers slide down my cheek, then turned and snapped an order at Ghost and Junior. Both Buri stopped playing and grabbed their spears before flanking me, a distinct air of pride emanating from them that hadn't been there before. Apparently, I'd gone up in status, probably due to the gifts.

With a last look around the village, I turned and walked into the jungle, my Buri honor guard sticking close, with Crigo and my flock of dragon birds bringing up the rear.

Leaning back in my chair, I glanced out the lab door to see the first rays of sunlight filtering through leaves, giving the morning a greenish-gold cast. It took the full week to process the Buri DNA, but as the results began to come in, I spent more and more time in the lab, stunned at what I'd found.

I hit the button that sent the files to Max's database and on to his archives, then yawned. Cafftea wasn't going to cut it this time. I needed at least eight hours of uninterrupted sleep.

Somehow, I didn't think I was going to get it.

"Did you double-check the data, Kiera?" Max's question came as I walked into my living quarters.

"Of course I did. There's no way to get around the facts. As impossible as it sounds, none of the Buri are related to each other except for Thor and his sister, and the little boy to Brownie and his mate. Brownie and Thor also share a few common alleles, so at a guess I'd say Brownie's distantly related to Thor and Churka. Second cousins, maybe."

"Nothing is impossible. We simply haven't discovered the reason for this anomaly yet."

I scowled as I ordered a double-strength cafftea from the food unit. There's nothing like a philosophical AI to make a bad mood even worse. Especially first thing in the morning when you're suffering from sleep deprivation.

Blowing steam from the cup, I carried it to the table and

collapsed on a bench. "The good news is, I found no genetic mutations that would prevent the Buri from reproducing at a normal rate, or giving birth to viable offspring."

I took a sip from the cup, burning my tongue in the process. Good thing I healed fast. "Have you finished analyzing their medicals yet?"

"Yesterday. I didn't want to disturb you."

"And?" I glanced longingly at the lav. Maybe after I got the cafftea down I'd have enough energy to take a shower.

"Other than a few minor anomalies, all the Buri are extremely healthy, and their physiology is almost identical to that of humans. I found no signs of illness or deformity, and no foreign substances in their blood, except in one instance. There's nothing physical to keep them from reproducing as far as I can tell, and one female is, in fact, gestating. It was in her blood that I found traces of an unknown element that bears a slight resemblance to estrogen."

I brightened. A pregnancy was very good news. "How far along is she?"

"Approximately three months. And the fetus seems to be fully developed and healthy. It's another male."

I scratched a bump on my arm while I tried to think. Orpheus Two had the expected number of insects for a jungle planet, but the majority of them appeared to dislike the taste of humans. Unfortunately, the one that did had found me. Fortunately, my own immune system would take care of the reaction almost immediately. I glanced at the bump and watched it fade away to nothing before responding. "Do you think Dynatec falsified their reports?"

"It could be," Max responded. "But the fact is, the Buri are a healthy, vital species. They should have a much higher number of offspring, and yet there's only one living child in the village."

"Damn. I was hoping this would be easy." I finished off

the cafftea and carried the cup to the recycling unit. "Anything on this Quilla Dorn person yet?"

"Very little. She's the daughter of a man named Zander Dorn, deceased, who was something of a recluse. Her planet of birth is Furthman Four. She spent three cycles attending a university on Alpha Centauri, but jumped from subject to subject, and never received a degree in one discipline. After that, there's no record of her until she signed on with Dynatec ten cycles ago."

Ten cycles ago. Everything about this mission seemed to revolve around that time period. What in the thirteen hells had that exploration team found? And what did Dorn have to do with it?

"Signed on as what?" I stood and headed for the lav, stripping as I went.

"Her personnel records only indicate she's an executive-level employee."

I mulled that over as I showered. Executive level could mean anything from CEO to head of personnel. Looked like I needed to pay a visit to the Dynatec crew and meet this Dorn woman. Later. Sleep came first.

"Wake me in eight hours, Max." I toweled off and was on the verge of climbing into bed when Max interrupted me.

"The Buri females are approaching, Kiera."

A groan escaped my lips. Every day for the last week, Churka, Thor's sister, had shown up at the hut bearing gifts. Nothing major, just dishes of food or bunches of flowers. But she gave off such an air of happiness when I accepted them that I didn't want to risk offending her by refusing the items.

She was always accompanied by another female, usually Auntie Em, and at least two Buri males. They never stayed long, and like the males, the women were uneasy about entering my quarters, looking with vague feelings of suspicion at all the gizmos the hut contained.

All of them except Auntie Em, that is. She seemed fascinated by the hut's contents. I had to keep the doors to the storage room and lab locked when she was on the premises. During her first visit, she'd punched so many buttons on the food unit that it jammed. It took me the better part of two hours to repair it.

She was a fast learner, though. The last time she was here she'd discovered the combination that produced Panga ale, a beerlike drink that could curl the hair of a confirmed lush with one small glass. And she drank it like water, smacking her lips with glee and exhibiting no effects from the liquor.

I'd love to take her to Jolaria's Jewel on ZT Twelve someday and make a few wagers on her drinking capacity. I could probably pay off my indenture with the winnings.

"Is Auntie Em with Churka this time?" I asked Max.

"Yes. I've already locked the inner doors."

"Thank you."

I slipped into my robe and went to open the front door for them. Though half asleep, I noticed the way Junior perked up when Churka appeared. She pretty much ignored him, but it was obvious the boy had a bad case of puppy love, his gaze following her with such longing that I felt sorry for him. Even without her amazing beauty, being one of only fifteen females meant she could have her pick of the available Buri males. Poor Junior probably didn't stand a chance.

Although I'd never experienced it personally, I'd heard young love among Naturals could be quite crushing. GEPs are raised to believe sex is simply another biological function, a lot more fun than using the lav, but nothing to get in a dither about. We're taught from the beginning that for most of us, there's no chance of a lifelong commitment, and my last disastrous affair had certainly proved that theory true.

Not that there's any law preventing GEPs from marrying,

but Naturals either can't cope with our superior skills and makeup, or they become obsessed with them to the point of worship. Neither option makes for a good marriage, and the few GEPs that have tried ended up divorced.

As for marriages between GEPs, it isn't financially or spatially feasible. Each of us is created with a specific job in mind, and the company who orders us pays dearly for our creation. Until that debt is repaid, we live where the company puts us, and go where they tell us to go. It's our job, one we've been designed for and love doing. So, there's not much sense in marrying when your partner is likely to be stationed on the other side of the universe.

While we may not enjoy our solitary status, we learn to live with it. Which is why I could empathize with Junior.

Churka smiled as she slipped by me into the hut. Auntie Em made a beeline for the food unit and punched up the Panga ale. I couldn't help but grimace as I watched her take a long drink. It was barely daylight and the woman was already guzzling alcohol. She must have had a stomach of tempered steel.

After making two more cups of cafftea, I carried them to the table and handed one to Churka. She sipped delicately, then put the cup on the table and removed a leather bag that was fastened at her waist.

Since Auntie Em had co-opted one side of the table, I joined Churka on the other side, smiling as she handed me the bag. Both women went still as I examined it, a look of uncertainty on their faces. Whatever was in the bag was important to them.

There was a metallic clink as I turned it in my hands, but for now, the bag itself held my attention. It was the finest leather I'd ever seen, soft as velvet and cured to a creamy eggshell white. The seams were hand-sewn instead of chemically fused, the stitches tight and even. The workmanship was excellent. On ZT Twelve, handmade items like this bag would send the fashion industry into a feeding frenzy.

Churka fidgeted anxiously on the bench, and I gave her a reassuring smile as I opened the drawstring and let the contents slide onto the table. My gasp was involuntary as I saw what she'd brought.

Two armlets of beaten gold lay in front of me, shooting sparks of sunlight to dance in prisms of color from the ceiling. Like the ones the female Buri wore, each was over an inch wide and designed to fit the upper arm.

But that was where the similarity stopped, because these were decorated to a fare-thee-well.

Gingerly—almost afraid to breathe—I picked one up. Dragon birds, etched in bold relief, danced across the surface. They were intertwined with clusters of flowers whose petals were an inlay of what looked like mother-of-pearl in a golden-tan shade. The center of each flower was the same shade of green as my eyes.

Stunned, I glanced at Churka. "These are for me?"

"Choorr," she growled. The Buri had trouble with "Ts", but I knew what she meant.

"Thor sent them?" Sudden nerves had my palms clammy. In other low-tech cultures I'd dealt with, a gift like this usually implied commitment. Since I lacked the benefit of several cycles' worth of xenologists' findings, I wasn't sure what it meant to the Buri or how to react.

"Max, any idea why Thor would be giving me a gift like these armlets?"

"Since all the Buri wear them, there is a sixty-one percent probability that they're adopting you into the tribe."

Frustration filled Churka's eyes at my apparent hesitation. Before I could move, she reached out and placed her fingertips against my temples. Lines of strain formed around her mouth, and abruptly I was receiving images. Not emotions—images. Fuzzy ones to be sure, but there was no doubt what was happening.

In my mind, I saw myself fasten the silver clip in Thor's hair. From there, the picture changed to Thor alone, hammer in his hand as he worked on the armlets.

The images stopped the instant Churka dropped her hands. Her skin was pale and sweat beaded her forehead, but she looked satisfied.

Great goddess of the fifth hell, she was telepathic! The number of races discovered to have psi talents were so slim I could count them on one hand and have fingers left over. I was so excited I almost forgot what she'd shown me.

Thor, slaving away over the armlets he'd made just for me. I blinked, then looked down at them. By all rights, I shouldn't keep the jewelry. Their value far outweighed the silver hair clip I'd given him, and I wasn't sure it was fair to let them adopt me when I'd only be here, at most, two months.

I opened my mouth to tell her I couldn't take the gift, and then closed it again. Damn it, I wanted those armlets, no matter how wrong it was. Thor had made them for me, and I'd never really belonged anywhere before. The idea of being adopted by the Buri was strangely appealing. Plus, I really didn't want to risk insulting them by refusing to accept the bands.

Slowly, I picked them up and slid them onto my arms.

Churka let out a squeal of excitement and pounced on me, hugging the breath right out of me before kissing both my cheeks. Auntie Em growled something at her, and Churka flushed.

Releasing me, she rose to her feet, gave me a short, formal bow and made a speech I couldn't understand.

Weird.

But the armlets felt right on my arms, picking up the

warmth from my skin like they were a living part of me. And my acceptance of them certainly seemed to make Churka's day. Even Auntie Em was smiling and nodding as she gulped down the last of her drink.

They didn't stay long after that. Churka, especially, appeared to be in a hurry to return home. As soon as they were gone, I shed my robe and stepped to the mirror that covered one wall of the lav.

Turning this way and that to highlight the armlets, I admired my reflection. The petals on the flowers were the exact color of my hair, I realized.

GEPs tend not to get sentimental about material things. After all, we have no family antiques that have been handed down from generation to generation, and there would be no one to leave such items to if we acquired them, since normal GEPs can't have children. And things are, after all, just things. Easily lost, easily replaced. But I knew I would keep these armlets forever.

With a sigh, I climbed into bed. Sleep eluded me, however. I couldn't stop thinking about Churka's use of telepathy. It had obviously required a lot of effort on her part, and yet that she could do it at all was amazing. Humans were one of the only species that had shown any shred of psi talent.

I'd suspected from the beginning that Thor was picking up my emotions, and Churka was his sibling. So, did that mean the talent ran in families, or could all the Buri do it?

It was one more mystery among the dozens I was trying to unravel, and probably the least important. But I couldn't help hoping. If I could communicate with Thor, really communicate, it might help solve all the other problems.

A sound distracted me, and I shifted to watch Crigo enter the hut through the bottom door panel. From the odor that preceded him, he'd been out hunting again last night.

Nose to the floor, he followed the Buri's scent around the

table, then came toward the bed to see if I was still in one piece. Starting at my feet, he sniffed his way up my length until he came to the new armbands.

Abruptly, his ears flattened and a low snarl issued from his curled-up lips.

"What's your problem?" I asked him. "These are just an adoption gift from the Buri. Thor made them."

Before I could dodge, he raised a huge paw and swatted the bands so hard one of them flew from my arm. Luckily, he kept his claws sheathed.

"Hey!" I jumped up and scrambled after the band, examining it closely to make sure it wasn't damaged while the cat glared at me. A sigh of relief escaped me when I discovered it was still in one piece, and I slid it carefully back on my arm before turning to Crigo.

"Okay, what's going on? Why don't you like the armlets? They're just jewelry."

He continued to glare, his gaze shifting from me to the gold bands and back again. Frustration and—I frowned. Worry? Anxiety? Whichever it was, the emotion poured off him in waves.

Puzzled, I tilted my head and studied him. "Max, any theories on why he doesn't want me wearing the armlets?"

"Nothing statistically valid, Kiera. Maybe he's picking up a scent on them he doesn't like. Or maybe he's simply jealous of the Buri and wants to keep you to himself. He could see the gift as a threat to his ownership."

"Huh." I knelt in front of him and took his face in my hands so we were eye to eye. "Listen up, cat. It doesn't matter if the Buri adopt me. You're still my family, and nothing is going to change that."

He stared at me a second longer, his feelings changing to disgust, then flopped to the floor and stretched out, effectively shutting me off.

Once again, I studied an armlet as I returned to my bunk. Not even the zorfa's ass had ever given me a gift, and we'd been together almost a cycle. That Thor had done so warmed a place deep inside me, even if it was part of some adoption ritual. "Max?"

"Yes, Kiera?"

"What do you think this mother-of-pearl stuff is?"

"It appears to be from the shells of the crustaceans my cameras have picked up at the edge of the lake. I've seen hundreds of different colors, but in structure they are similar to clams."

"And the green stones in the center of the flowers?"

"Quartz. Of good quality, and sliced extremely thin, but in and of itself, not valuable. This planet seems to have an overabundance of it. The gold, however, is of a very high grade. Combined with the workmanship, I'd say they are worth a fortune."

I let my eyes drift shut. "They aren't for sale," I murmured. Letting the images Churka had shown me play through my head, I smiled. Well, I'll be damned. Thor had a hammer after all. It was my last thought before sleep claimed me.

CHAPTER 5

I only managed six hours of sleep, but when Max woke me mid-afternoon, I felt rested, refreshed and starved. My stomach rumbled loudly as I climbed out of bed and headed for the food unit. I was determined to visit the Dynatec camp today, but my innards came first.

While my prime rib cooked, I moved to the other end of the hut to dress, pausing as I caught sight of the armlets. I didn't want anyone on the Dynatec crew to see them, and yet I didn't want to take them off, either. Long sleeves looked like my best option, in spite of the heat.

It only took a few minutes to don a lightweight syntec khaki jumpsuit, and by then my food was ready. The aroma made my mouth water. In celebration of finishing the DNA studies on the Buri, I allowed myself a glass of wine.

I had been too tired that morning for the implications of the tests to really sink in, but now I could think of little else. I mulled the problem over in my mind as I mopped up the last bite of gravy with a thick slice of fresh bread and popped it into my mouth. "Okay, Max. We'd better talk about this DNA stuff." I leaned back and picked up my glass, swirling the deep red wine in the bottom of the flute. "The Buri didn't simply materialize full grown. They had to come from families, from mothers and fathers."

"You didn't."

I scowled. "Not funny. But even if you're right and they were created in a lab, where are their makers? Where are the geneticists and the labs? Where did the original genetic material come from that made them?" I shook my head. "It wouldn't make sense to create seventy individuals and then drop them on a planet for no reason, especially with the ratio of males to females being *so* uneven."

"It's only one theory."

"And not a very good one." I sipped the wine. "Can't you do better than that?"

"Well, I do have another, but I must warn you, there is insufficient data to prove its validity."

"Spill it." I finished the wine, then stood and carried my dishes to the recycler.

"An epidemic."

I stopped, my head tilted to one side as I considered the possibilities. "It would have to be deadly to wipe out all but seventy Buri. And, since none of our bunch are related to each other, their population would have needed to be fairly high to start with. But we've seen no signs of buildings, except the new ones in the Buri village."

"It's possible they burned any buildings where deaths occurred, and then the survivors moved to a new location. Over a ten-cycle period, the jungle would have reclaimed the scarred areas, making them impossible to find. And it would also explain the age of the current dwellings."

"Well, at least that one sounds logical." I resumed my seat at the table. "But I still think the age of their buildings has a direct correlation to the arrival of Dynatec's exploration team. Did you mention an anomaly in their physiology this morning, or was I so tired I imagined it?"

"You didn't imagine it. And that brings me to our third possibility."

"I'm listening."

"The Buri may not have originated on Orpheus Two."

I dropped my forehead to my hands and groaned. "Come on, Max! You said it yourself. These people are low tech. I'll admit their ability to maintain a culture and a high quality of living indicates a great level of evolution, but they still use spears, for Luna's sakes. Now you want me to believe they built a spaceship and arrived here from another planet?"

"Hear me out before you dismiss this idea. During my tests on the Buri, it occurred to me that their size and denser bone structure would seem to indicate that they evolved on a planet with a heavier gravity than Orpheus Two. Otherwise, there's no evolutionary reason for their massive scale. And you mentioned their resemblance to the Ashwani, yourself."

"Uh-huh. And their spears are really magic wands that allow them to move through space with a single wave."

"Don't be facetious," he reprimanded. "We both know a lack of technology doesn't mean a race is primitive. Their lifestyle could well be a choice they've made for reasons that are unknown to us. Besides, I didn't mean to imply they landed ten cycles ago. What if a group of Buri arrived on Orpheus Two hundreds of cycles ago, and for some reason couldn't leave again?"

"You mean like a crash, or a disabled ship?" I dropped my hand to the table and drummed my nails on the surface. "Then where's the ship?" But my mind was working at high speed now, and I didn't wait for an answer.

"Suppose the ship never landed on the planet? The early colonization ships from Old Earth weren't designed to land. They were too big." I jumped up and paced the length of the hut, excitement curling in my chest.

"This could be it, Max." I waved one hand. "Okay, here's the scenario. The Buri are on a colonization ship from Ashwan. When they're near the Orpheus system, something goes wrong. People have to flee in rescue pods. At least one pod makes it to Orpheus Two, stranding the survivors. Maybe the colonization ship is pulled into the sun, leaving no trace of its existence. The survivors would have to scavenge the pod they arrived in to make it through the first few cycles, and thus, there's no pod left to find. And with no technology available, their descendants would be reduced to starting all over again, even if they kept some higher-level skills."

I stopped pacing and sighed. "But that still doesn't explain why none of the Buri are related."

"It might if you combined it with my second theory."

"The plague one?"

"Yes. It's common knowledge that simple viruses can become deadly if a race with no immunity is exposed to them. There are even examples in the history of Old Earth. Measles, for instance. The disease was a common childhood ailment among Europeans, and yet it wiped out thousands of Native Americans when the Anglo Saxons first brought it to the Americas. And then there's the last plague, which wiped out the entire population of Old Earth. Scientists believe it was a mutated form of avian flu."

"Okay, I see where you're going with this." I lifted a hand to rub my temple. "So, the Buri survivors were doing fine. Orpheus Two has everything they needed to live. Food and water are abundant. They reproduce, and eventually reach the stage where they can once again work metal and build adobe dwellings. The population increases. Then, whammo. A little over ten cycles ago, an Orpheus bug grabs them and wipes out ninety-five percent of the race, leaving only seventy Buri to carry on."

I plunked down heavily on the bench, my legs suddenly weak. "Did you find any common antibodies in their systems?"

"Yes, but there's no way to determine what the antibodies are fighting. It could be anything."

"Did the little boy and the fetus have them too?" I held my breath.

"Yes."

My eyes closed in relief. "The parents are passing the immunity down. The Buri will make it."

The relief was replaced with anger as the implications hit me. "That means Dynatec is responsible for the Buri that went missing. Max, I want you to transmit this information to your archives immediately, and send the boss a red alert. I want him to see this as soon as possible."

"Kiera, this is only a theory. We can't prove its validity."

"No, and I don't believe it happened exactly the way we've outlined. That would be too easy. But when you take the pieces we *can* prove, parts of the theory start to add up. Especially the part that says the Buri may not be native to Orpheus Two. That's major, especially if they *are* descended from the Ashwani. And in the event that something happens to us, it will put the next agent Alien Affairs sends ahead of the game."

"Do you really believe Dynatec would arrange an accident knowing the repercussions of such an event?"

Max, being only two cycles old, is a mere babe in AI terms, and tends to be a bit naïve when it comes to humans. "Take my word for it. Whatever they've found is so important they're willing to kill off an entire race to get their hands on it. They aren't going to quibble over one agent and her ship."

"Sending."

I gave a curt nod. "And while you're at it, see if the boss

can get his hands on the original log from the Dynatec exploration team. The company may not have realized what they had right away. I'd like to see if there are any hints we can pick up from it."

"Yes, Kiera. Anything else?"

I hesitated. "Is Second Lieutenant Karle at the camp? I'd like to check in with her, see if she's found anything that might indicate what the company is after on Orpheus Two."

"No, she left this morning with the mapping team."

"Okay, I'll wait until she gets back before I head over there. Where's Redfield?"

"He went into the jungle several hours ago."

"Alone?"

"He appeared to be alone at the time he left, but Captain Frisk and the Dorn woman are also missing."

I checked my weapons. "Point me in the right direction, Max. It's time I had a little chat with Redfield."

Crigo had left the hut while I was sleeping, but he hadn't gone far. He was squeezed under a bush, ears flattened in annoyance as two dragon birds threw sticks and berries at him from just out of reach.

"It's your own fault," I told him, as the gorgeous creatures left him to chirp happy greetings in my direction. Every time I walked out the door, there was a contingent waiting for me, usually led by the iridescent green lad. He was getting braver, too, coming closer and closer by the day. "If you'd stop stalking them, they'd leave you alone."

When I walked to the edge of the clearing, the cat rose and followed. "Okay, Max, which way?"

"If you travel northeast at an eighty degree angle, you should intercept the path he was on."

"Thanks."

Junior and Ghost were watching, and as soon as I started

off, they fell in beside me. I would have preferred to confront Redfield alone, but the only way to rid myself of my honor guard was to outrun them. Since I didn't want to get them in trouble by outrunning them, I'd have to put up with the duo and hope they didn't interfere.

It took the better part of an hour to locate Redfield's trail, and then another fifteen minutes to find the man himself. It had rained earlier, as it did nearly every day, and the jungle dripped around us in glistening drops of moisture. With every step we made, the scent of rich, damp soil and growing things filled the air.

There was so much life, I didn't know where to look first. In one tree, I spotted a creature that looked like a long-legged, long-tailed koala bear. It watched us pass with unblinking dark eyes that were nearly buried in the folds of fat around its face.

Another time, we disturbed a catlike animal half Crigo's size, with long, shaggy fur in shades of light tan, black and white that made it resemble a large dust mop. It hissed at us when Ghost stepped in front of me and raised his spear, then turned and fled into the brush.

Crigo watched it with interest, then thoroughly sniffed the area where it had lain, his lips curling back from his teeth as he inhaled. Without a glance in my direction, he bounded into the jungle to give chase.

Great. All I needed was a bunch of half-breed rock cats running loose on Orpheus Two. Nothing like screwing up the ecology in a big way. On the other hand, I didn't want to wrestle with a hot and bothered rock cat either, so Orpheus Two would simply have to make room for a potential new species.

We weren't making any effort to move silently, so Redfield had plenty of warning that he had company. I spotted him through the trees, facing us, a knapsack at his feet.

My gaze dropped to the hand resting on the butt of his laser.

"Expecting trouble, Redfield?"

His glance shifted from Ghost to Junior before he swung his upper body to nervously to scan the surrounding jungle. "It pays to stay prepared for anything on this planet. Make them stay back."

"Sorry, I don't speak their language. But I do know they won't hurt you unless you threaten them. If I were you, I'd take my hand off that laser."

Behind Redfield, the bushes rattled and another Buri stepped into view. This one had dark auburn hair, and he looked as tense and ready as my escorts.

Redfield hesitated, then slowly removed his hand from the laser, his gaze going again to an area off to our right, and I picked up a feeling of tense awareness from him, like he knew something I didn't. "What do you want, Smith?"

I smiled. "Want? Nothing in particular. I was out for a stroll and ran across your trail. Thought I'd be sociable, since we're the only GEPs around." I lowered my shields further, and was almost bowled over by the frustration he generated. He wanted desperately to talk with me, but something was stopping him, and until I knew what it was, I couldn't risk saying anything.

"Beautiful day, isn't it?" I moved closer and gestured at the knapsack. "What are you collecting?"

"Botanical specimens." He relaxed just the tiniest bit and gave me a "wait until later" signal.

Surprised, I dipped my head in an almost imperceptible nod. "Find anything interesting?"

Again, he hesitated, then shrugged. "Yes, I did." He pointed to the plant near his foot. "Take a look at this."

I leaned down and studied the flowers he'd indicated. They were about the size of a large orchid, as inky black as

Thor's hair, and shaped like a trumpet. A cloyingly sweet aroma rose from the petals. Redfield stopped me before I could touch them.

"You don't want to do that. They're carnivorous."

I yanked my hand back. They couldn't have hurt me, but Redfield didn't know that. He had no idea I'd been created by a monster. Besides, reflexes are reflexes, even when you're less prone to injury than the average GEP, and my reaction was spontaneous. "Really?"

"Watch." He removed a probe from his pocket, squatted, and lightly touched the edge of a petal. Instantly, the filaments I had taken for stamens snapped out, grabbed the metal probe, and tried to pull it down into the flower.

Gently, he disentangled the probe, then stood and pulled out a square of gauze. He used it to wipe down the probe, and then held the material out for me to see. Small bubbles boiled on the surface, and the threads parted, eaten away by the liquid.

"Acid," he said. "They use it to liquefy their prey. And just look at their color. They aren't simply a dark purple, they're really a true black. Do you know how rare that is? And that's not all. They exhibit some unusual properties in the lab. I'm convinced they could have a real use in the medical field."

He was so enthusiastic about the plant that he'd forgotten his frustration. Good. I wanted him relaxed and friendly.

"Sounds like you know your stuff. I take it you were created for botany?"

"For all the life sciences, but botany is my favorite." He was still studying the flower.

I nodded. "It's obvious. Dynatec must be happy with their investment."

He glanced at me, and then returned the probe to his pocket. "Dynatec didn't commission my creation. A small drug company in the Cygnus sector was my original indenture holder."

"Isn't that unusual?" I arched a brow. "For them to sell your indenture, I mean. They must have invested a lot of time and money in you."

"I guess Frisk made it worth their while."

A surge of horror washed over me at his statement and I forgot his reluctance to speak candidly. "Frisk bought your indenture, not Dynatec?"

His gaze turned wary and he took another quick look over his shoulder. "That's right."

I could barely breathe. According to my records, Redfield was very young, only twenty cycles. He'd been out of the crèche five cycles, and most of that time had probably been spent in the rarefied atmosphere of a research and development unit. There was no way he could have been prepared for someone like Frisk.

It also introduced yet another problem. Where in the thirteen hells had Frisk gotten enough credit to buy an indenture? Dynatec paid its captains well, but even with frequent bonuses, it didn't pay *that* much.

"Listen to me, Redfield." I gripped his arm, my voice low and urgent. "It's no secret how Frisk feels about GEPs. But there are laws to protect you, even from your indenture holder. He can't force you to commit any illegal acts, and he can't touch you physically. If he's tried, I can help you. You don't have to put up with his perversions."

"I don't know what you're talking about."

He struggled to get away from me, but I hung on. The contact allowed me clearer reception of his emotions, and he was on the verge of a full-blown panic, which seemed to be focused on the section of jungle he'd kept glancing at.

"Don't you?" I knew my fingers were digging into his arm, but I had to get through to him somehow. "A Buri is missing, and several of the males have scars from laser burns. Are you going to tell me you don't know how they got them?"

With a spurt of adrenaline, he wrenched his arm from my grasp, shoving me back so that I had to fight to keep my balance. His eyes were wild, and his hand hovered over his laser.

Around us, the three Buri guards sprang into action, lifting their spears to shoulder level, the deadly tips aimed at Redfield's chest. Before I could move to stop them, a roar of rage split the jungle, halting the other noises as though someone had turned off a switch. Without quite knowing how he got there, I saw that Thor was now positioned between Redfield and me. And he didn't look happy. His fists were clenched at his side, and a low, continuous growl rumbled in his chest as he advanced.

It was enough to send Redfield over the edge. He backed away hurriedly, nearly tripping over his own feet as he yanked the laser from his utility belt. "It wasn't our fault! They attacked us. We had to protect ourselves!"

I peered around Thor's arm, my mind spinning with this new information. Maybe I hadn't been around them long, but I knew the Buri wouldn't have attacked men armed with lasers without a damn good reason. "Why did they attack you?"

"I don't know, they just did." All the blood had drained from his face, leaving his skin pale and clammy with sweat.

He was lying. I could feel the deceit oozing in his veins like blood. But there was something else there with it. Guilt. Self-disgust. And fear, always the fear.

But again the fear wasn't toward me or the Buri, which left me with only one conclusion.

I grabbed Thor's arm and hung on, forcing him to stop while I stepped up beside him. "Redfield, you don't have to do whatever Frisk is forcing you to do. I can help you, protect you."

He motioned at Thor. "Then call him off. I'm as strong as you are. I can hurt him."

The bicep under my hand rippled with muscle, and I glanced from it to Redfield. "I wouldn't be too sure about that if I were you. And even if you manage to get through him, you'd never beat me. I'm ten cycles older than you, and I've had ten times the training in hand-to-hand combat. I can break your arm in three places before you can pull the trigger. Now drop the laser and let's talk about it."

"Kiera," Max murmured in my ear. "Frisk and the Dorn woman are listening. From the heat signature, it would appear they've been behind that group of trees to your right for the last ten minutes or so."

Ah, no wonder Redfield was frustrated and scared! He'd known the two were in the area, keeping an eye on him. "Geesh, Max, thanks for telling me. Any Buri with them?"

"Two. They are circling around to make their presence known."

I nodded and glanced at the trees. "You can come out now, Frisk."

Redfield's eyes closed briefly in relief, and he inhaled a deep sigh. Acting as if lurking behind trees was everyday fare, Frisk strolled into sight, the Dorn woman beside him.

"What's going on here? Redfield, put that laser away." He glared at the doctor, and I saw Redfield's hand tremble as he slid the weapon back into its holster. From the way he was emoting, he'd much rather use it on Frisk than the Buri.

"Just a slight misunderstanding," I told Frisk calmly. "The Buri thought Redfield was threatening me. He pulled the laser in self-defense." I didn't think Frisk had heard anything but the last few comments. They were too far away and we weren't speaking loudly until Redfield panicked. At least I hoped that was the case. I didn't want to get the other GEP into even more trouble since I still planned to get him alone long enough at some point that he could tell me what was going on.

To take the attention off the doctor, I turned to the woman. "I don't believe we've met. I'm Senior Agent Kiera Smith."

She was average height, but that was the only thing average about her. Her eyes were crystal blue, and her hair was long and dark, curling to the middle of her back. She had the kind of figure that sent men into temporary comas. But in spite of the languid sex-kitten façade she projected, I could feel an underlying razor-sharp intelligence. There was no doubt left in my mind. Standing before me was the brains behind this operation. As I'd suspected, Frisk was little more than hired muscle.

By now, there were six very tense Buri circling us, all with their spears ready, but Quilla Dorn treated them like they were tree trunks. She walked toward me, her stride confident and about as sexually muted as a super nova, and held out a hand.

"Agent Smith. I've heard so much about you. It's a pleasure to finally meet. I hope Tommy hasn't caused you any problems with the Buri."

I ignored the hand and glanced at Redfield. *Tommy?* A red flush covered his cheeks, and his gaze was locked on Dorn worshipfully. It made me want to curse. Or pray he was a damn fine actor.

And it wasn't helping matters that Thor was trying to shove me behind him.

I shifted slightly and gave him a good hard glare so he'd get the message. He returned the sentiments with a fierce glower of his own and a determined look in his dark eyes. Dorn lowered her hand as I turned to face her again.

"Leave the Buri to me. Unfortunately, I can't say I've

heard much about you. You aren't listed on the Dynatec roster as a crew member."

"No, it was a last minute decision and there wasn't time to do the paperwork. I'm sure the company will rectify the matter shortly if they haven't yet."

"Uh-huh." I grabbed Thor's hand and held it still. "Exactly what is your job on this assignment?"

Her full, crimson lips curved into a smile. "Officially, I'm the quartermaster, but just between us, Jon suggested I come along as a kind of vacation. They really don't need anyone to handle the supplies. Isn't that right, Jon?" She glanced at Frisk over her shoulder.

He wasn't nearly as casual about the Buri as she appeared to be, and stayed where he was, eyeing Thor uneasily. "That's right. Quilla and I go back a long way."

"So you suggested she vacation on an unexplored world? Kind of dangerous, isn't it, Frisk?"

"Oh, no," Dorn interjected. "Jon knows I'm an avid explorer. The trouble is, I rarely get the chance to indulge. He did me a huge favor, bringing me along. I'm even getting paid for it." She shot a hundred-watt smile at Frisk, and then gazed around at the Buri. "Looks like you've got a fan club. None of us has been able to get that close to them."

It was on the tip of my tongue to tell her that the Buri would be a lot friendlier if the Dynatec crew hadn't shot at, and possibly killed, one of them, but I restrained myself. "I think they realize I'm trying to help."

She nodded. "Could be. They certainly are gorgeous, aren't they?" Her gaze lingered on Ghost, reminding me of the carnivorous plant Redfield had found.

Did all human females have that reaction to the Buri? I was beginning to think so. Claudia Karle had, and I'd certainly proven I wasn't immune. Now Dorn looked as if she wanted to swallow Ghost whole.

I ignored her comment and brought the subject back to her presence on Orpheus Two. "As an agent for the Bureau of Alien Affairs, I'll have to report your inclusion on the Dynatec crew."

"Of course." She tore her gaze away from Ghost and smiled at me. "Although I'm sure Dynatec reported the alteration to the proper authorities when they were notified of the change."

When Dynatec was *notified* of the change? Just who in the fifth hell was this woman that she could issue orders to a company as big as Dynatec? She'd have to own the company, lock stock and barrel before they'd listen to her. I made a mental note to have Max trace the corporate ownership right to its source, but I was already pretty sure of what he'd find.

"If they have, there won't be a problem." I dipped my head in a brief nod. "Now, if you'll excuse me, I'll let you get back to whatever you were doing."

"Have you found anything yet, Smith?" Frisk called as I turned away.

"No, not yet," I lied as I continued walking. Thor went with me after issuing a growled command to the other Buri.

Ghost and Junior stayed in place, guarding our backs, until we put some distance between us and the Dynatec people, and then jogged to catch up. Instead of taking the same path I'd used to reach Redfield, Thor headed toward my camp in a straight line.

All three Buri remained silent on the trip, but I could sense the disapproval coming from Thor. It set my teeth on edge and grated on my nerves until I was ready to scream from the tension wafting in the air. My shields weren't helping, and I was already in a tizzy about everything I'd learned. I couldn't take any more.

"That's it." I plowed to a stop and swung to face Thor, hands on my hips. "If you've got something to say, say it and stop emoting at me." My frustration at our inability to actually talk had reached critical mass. I wanted to hit something and Thor was looking like a pretty good target.

With one gesture of his hand, he sent Ghost and Junior on ahead of us, but I was too wound up to give much notice to that little detail. All my attention was focused on the Buri leader. He stabbed a finger toward the Dynatec camp, pointed at me, and gave his head one hard shake. Then he crossed his arms over his chest. End of subject. The great one had spoken.

I bristled, every nerve in my body going into high gear. There was only one person in the universe who had the right to give me orders, and that was the boss. It was time to set Thor straight on a few issues.

"Oh, yeah?" Okay, not exactly my most brilliant comeback, but I was mad. And if I were being truthful, I'd have to admit his protectiveness was kind of nice. No one had ever cared enough before to try and protect me. And that made me even madder, made me react more strongly than I normally would have.

I poked him in the chest with one finger. "Listen up, buddy. You don't own me. For your information, I can take care of myself. I've been doing it for damn near thirty-two cycles, and I don't need you coming to my rescue now. The very idea is ludicrous. I'm a GEP, for Luna's sake! My resume would make your hair stand on end." I eyed his long, thick locks, trying to picture the heavy mass standing out from his skull. Maybe that wasn't the best analogy in the world, but it was the only thing I could come up with in my current state of mind.

In my agitation, I began to pace up and down, ignoring the stoic expression he wore. "Do you think there's any way to get it through that hard head of yours that I'm trying to help your people? It's my job. It's what I'm here for."

I reached the apex of my circuit, spun, and started back, hands waving wildly. "There's something on this planet Dynatec wants very badly, even if means wiping out your entire race to get it. It's up to me to find out what they're after and stop them. But I can't get the information I need from the crew members if you keep interfering. Damn, I wish there was a way we could communicate."

Stopping in front of him, I gazed up at his expression, my irritation fading away like water in a sieve as our eyes met and the buzzing filled my head. Each time it seemed to get louder, a little more intense. I tried to break the contact, tried to tear my gaze from his and take a step back, but my feet weren't cooperating.

Around us, the world slowed to a crawl. The sun froze in its descent, and the breeze that had set broad-leaved plants rustling, stilled. There was no movement, no noise anywhere.

Abruptly, I felt a dizzying sense of displacement, as though I were spinning through a dark tunnel with no light at the end. And Thor was my only anchor. His hands, gently cupping my face, the only reality in this endless blackness.

Unafraid but curious, I watched his face loom larger in my vision until he blocked out all external stimulation. Slowly, so very slowly, his lips, warm and firm, touched mine.

CHAPTER 6

Mating rituals vary wildly from race to race, but kissing is one of those odd practices that cross every societal boundary. Any species with lips—and there are a few without them—does it in one form or another.

Thor did it *very* well, indeed.

His kiss shouldn't have surprised me. There had been a spark between us since the beginning, and I'm not an innocent by any means. I'd been kissed more times than I could count. But nothing that had gone before prepared me for my reaction to Thor.

At the first touch of his lips, prisms of deep, rich light shot across the landscape behind my closed eyes, increasing the dizzying sense that I wasn't in Kansas anymore, Toto. And it didn't matter. I only knew Thor's arms were around me, his mouth devouring mine.

His lips were hot, demanding, and my arms snaked around his neck, pulling him even more tightly to me as I went up on tiptoe to reach him. With a mind of their own, my hands buried themselves in his hair, and my tongue tentatively touched his before plunging into the exercise wholeheartedly. Electricity jolted through me, tightening my muscles, turning my stomach inside out and making me ache in places where I hadn't ached before.

He tasted so wonderful that I moaned. The jolt turned into a power blowout as he slanted his head to reach me better, his lips moving on mine, luring me to further abandon all thought and simply react. I'd gone through the standard sexual training in the crèche, and considered myself reasonably sophisticated. Sex was fun, something to be enjoyed whenever possible. The only time I'd had a problem with sex was the one time I'd tried to turn the act into something more. But even then, staying in control hadn't been a problem for me. That appeared to have changed, and in a big way.

For a timeless age, I drifted in a place where nothing existed except Thor. His scent, so warm and erotic and male, enfolded me, turned my legs to jelly. If he hadn't been holding me up, I would have collapsed.

The buzzing in my head became a chorus of musical chimes, a symphony of epic proportions. And for a split second, I caught a glimpse of something I couldn't explain. On a mental plain, a hexagonal building made of faceted black crystal floated above a lush green paradise. Sunlight sparked off its surfaces, creating a rainbow effect on the surrounding foliage, and I was filled with a longing so intense it was painful. This was where I belonged, a place where I'd never be alone again. It was beautiful and safe and perfect. Something to be desired with every fiber of my being. Mentally, I reached for it, desperate to touch it, to hold onto it at all costs. It was so close . . .

Abruptly, Thor pulled back, his breath coming in ragged gasps. "Kuyya," he rumbled the Buri version of my name, his voice rich and husky, and then dropped his forehead to mine.

It was hard to determine which of us shook harder. But

mixed with the overwhelming passion was a feeling of grief and loss so strong that my eyes filled with tears. The building was gone.

What in the thirteen hells was wrong with me? Maybe I should have Max check my hormone levels? At the very least, I needed to put some space between me and Thor.

It wasn't until I tried to step back that I realized my feet were dangling a foot off the ground. At some point, Thor had straightened, taking me with him. Probably didn't want to get a crick in his neck, I thought a tad hysterically. "You can put me down, now." My voice came out a whispered croak.

He grinned at me, white teeth flashing. And then he shook his head.

"No?" I glared at him suspiciously. "Do you understand what I'm saying?"

One shoulder lifted in a shrug, and he loosened his grip, allowing me to slide down his body. I was temporarily distracted from the conversation when I noticed Thor's state of arousal. At least, I hoped to the goddess of the fifth hell he was aroused. Because if he wasn't, I was going to be in Big Trouble when he got that way. It said a lot about my state of mind that I never doubted we would eventually make love.

Keeping my gaze away from his loincloth, I forced my mind back to the subject of communication. "Please, if you understand me, I need to know. This whole thing could be settled in a matter of hours, and your people safe." I grasped his arm. "Is there a way we can talk?"

He lifted his hand and cupped my cheek, his expression indecipherable.

Soon.

The word floated across my mind like a gentle ripple on the surface of a still pond, leaving me to wonder if I'd imagined it. After all, anyone who saw floating crystal buildings while they were being kissed senseless could have a severe reality problem. Maybe I'd accidentally come into contact with a hallucinogen.

Before I could decide, Thor took my hand and tugged me toward my hut. He was still holding it when we entered the clearing and I came to a screeching halt.

Junior and Ghost were stacking my belongings in a neat pile outside the door. Junior must have conquered his fear of the hut, because even as I watched, he headed back inside for another load in spite of the protests coming from a large flock of dragon birds. They were diving and swooping and screeching as though they thought the Buri were robbing me blind. As soon as the tiny creatures spotted me, they settled to the roof of the hut, looking smug and tossing you're gonna-get-it-now chirps at Ghost and Junior.

I yanked my hand from Thor's grip and strode forward. "Hold it right there."

Both Buri ignored me, Ghost actually walking around me to put another crate of supplies on the ground. I would have sworn the dragon birds gave a collective gasp at this rudeness.

I propped my hands on my hips. "Max!"

"Yes, Kiera?"

"Why didn't you stop them?"

His tone was injured when he answered. "You told me not to interfere with the Buri unless they tried to board me."

"That didn't mean you should allow them to ransack the hut." I actually forgot myself to the point where I was speaking aloud instead of subvocalizing, and the Buri gave me odd looks.

Fortunately, they still couldn't hear Max. I wasn't sure how they'd react to his disembodied voice floating through the air.

"They aren't hurting any of the equipment. They haven't even entered the lab. I think their intent is to move you to the

Buri village, and you've always spent time living with the races you've been assigned to. You said the only way to really know a species is to live with them, learn their culture."

"You don't have to quote me, damn it. I know what I said." Smart-ass ship. It didn't help that he was right. But for some reason, I was uneasy about moving to the Buri village. I glanced at Thor to check his reaction, and discovered he was emanating a palpable air of satisfaction.

With a sigh and a deep sense of resignation, I went to the storage room and pulled out the antigrav sled. Junior's eyes lit up, and he immediately began transferring everything to the pallet. Not only did they load my clothes, they loaded everything from the supply section of the hut. Only the lab and kitchen units remained. Max could supply power remotely if I chose to move the entire setup, but living in one of the Buri buildings would make me more accessible to the clan. And I could always come back anytime I needed to use the lab.

With the sled loaded, they wasted no time heading back to the village, several flocks of dragon birds trailing along in our wake. Junior and Ghost took the lead, tugging the sled behind them, occasionally exchanging comments and laughing. Thor, back to his dignified silence, stayed at my side, occasionally allowing our arms to brush as we walked, each contact sending nearly visible sparks between us. I needed to get my mind off the sexual vibrations he was sending in my direction. "Max, where's Crigo?"

"He's—busy."

I rolled my eyes at the tinge of embarrassment in his voice. "Well, I guess if he comes back to the hut and I'm not there, he'll figure out where I've gone. If he can't, I'm sure a dragon bird will inform him." I was being sarcastic, but to my surprise, two of the little birds immediately took off, headed in the direction of where I'd last seen Crigo. Could it be?

Nah, just my imagination.

We were near the village when Max spoke again. "Kiera, one of my satellites is receiving a transmission from the Federation Archives."

"Any idea what it is?"

"From the size, it's probably the information you requested on the Ashwani."

Thor scowled at me, but I paid him no attention. "Let me know when you have the data downloaded."

"I estimate it will take approximately twenty-four hours to sort through it for relevance."

"Okay."

The truth was, I didn't care much about the Ashwani at the moment. All I wanted was some time alone to try and sort out what had happened when Thor kissed me. My reaction to the crystal building had me worried. Even now, there was a dull, hollow ache in my middle that felt suspiciously like homesickness, an emotion I'd read about but never experienced. Max was the closest thing to a home I'd ever had, and where I went, he went.

Dammit, maybe Thor's kiss had triggered the one major flaw Gertz left in my psyche. A need to belong, to be part of a larger whole.

And somehow that need manifested as an image of a crystal building?

I shook my head in disgust. Even for me, that was reaching, and all it proved was my desperate desire to find a logical explanation. The situation on Orpheus Two was dangerous enough without getting sidetracked by an emotional meltdown. It was imperative that I stay mentally healthy and alert.

Squaring my shoulders, I pushed the inner turmoil aside and concentrated on the Buri. There were some changes in the village since I'd been there a week earlier, and I looked around in surprise when we entered the clearing.

Two new buildings were going up, the smaller of the two nearing completion. It sat nestled among the inner circle of older structures, and when completed would look very much like its neighbors.

The larger building was a different story altogether. It was situated away from the other dwellings and looked about ten times the normal size for a Buri home. And that wasn't the only anomaly. Instead of adobe, they were using natural stone to erect the walls.

Considering they'd only had a week, the construction was going amazingly fast. The walls were almost finished, and I could see flat stone floors inside. When completed, it would be a magnificent structure, proving yet again that the Buri were advanced enough to be considered a developing society.

The building's lines were graceful, with large, arched windows and doors to allow for air circulation. Thick pillars already stood in place, support for an overhanging roof that would create wide porches on all sides to block out the hot sun.

Could it be a religious edifice? Did the Buri even worship a higher power? Most races did have some form of organized religion, and they ran the gamut from worshiping blades of grass to messy, bloody sacrifices. There was even one planet in the far reaches of the universe that required men to worship their mothers-in-law. Which was probably the reason their males all had such nasty tempers.

GEPs were pretty much left to decide the issue for themselves, since training in religion wasn't required for most jobs. The more religious Naturals, however, were of the opinion that since GEPs are man-made, we have no souls. I could have argued with them, but I figured it was a waste of valuable time.

I'd seen no sign of worship among the Buri. Still, except

for my honor guard, I hadn't been around them much, and it did make sense that the building was some sort of religious edifice. I made a mental note to check into it. You could tell a lot about a species from the gods they worshipped.

"Max, any idea where they're getting the stone?" I was back to subvocalizing again. While the Buri working in the area had taken note of my arrival, none of them seemed surprised that I was moving in, and I didn't want to disturb them by carrying on a one-sided conversation.

"There's a quarry at the other end of the mountain. The stone is coming from there. It would appear they've been cutting it for some time now. They have a large amount stockpiled."

"How are they moving it?"

"By hand."

Involuntarily, my eyes widened. Each block was approximately one foot square and ten inches thick. It must have taken every Buri in the village, working twelve hours a day, to carry that many bricks.

Well, that was one problem I could solve, if Thor would allow it. I turned, only to discover that he was looking at me expectantly. "What?" I arched a brow in question.

He gestured toward the building.

Did he want my approval? Strange. But then, he had a right to be proud of the new construction. It was gorgeous.

With a smile, I nodded. "It's beautiful, Thor. I love it." I moved closer to him, lifted my hands to his temples, and visualized Buri loading blocks onto the antigrav sled. There was no way to be sure it would work, but I figured it was worth a shot. I'd realized that touch appeared to play a part in our communication. Every time he'd reacted to what I was thinking, we'd been in close physical contact.

"It would make hauling the stone easier," I said, in case he really did understand me. "And faster."

His lips curved into a smile, and he nodded before motioning one of the females forward. Her hair was a dark gray and I remembered her from my last trip. She was obviously young, but older than Junior and Churka. She smiled at me as Thor growled a question, then answered him and pointed at a small building beside the one I'd seen him emerge from that first day.

He gave a curt nod and rumbled a few orders at Junior and Ghost to get them moving toward the dwelling. So Thor had ordered a house prepared for me, had he? That meant he'd started out this morning with the intention of bringing me here. He wasn't doing it because of our run-in with Frisk and company; he was doing it because he wanted me near. The knowledge made me feel much happier about relocating to the village.

It also made me want to grab Thor and snuggle up in those strong arms. And that was scary. I didn't understand what was happening to me, but it had to stop. Sooner or later I would have to leave Orpheus Two and Thor behind. Until my indenture was paid off, there was absolutely no choice in the matter. And why was I even thinking about it?

To take my mind off the subject, I turned to the female and touched my chest. "Kiera."

She mimicked the gesture. "Lurran." Her voice was soft and lyrical, and she had the same exotic beauty I'd found in all the Buri. I was pleased to note her hair was pulled back on one side with a clip I'd brought, one adorned with royal blue stones that complemented her dark gray hair and eyes perfectly. They even matched the skirt she wore in the Buri style. The strip of lightweight blue material, threaded through her belt, left both sides open to expose a long stretch of smooth bronze leg and slender hips.

Why would any Buri male, especially one like Thor, pay attention to pink, blonde me with someone like her around? It boggled the mind.

With the introductions out of the way, she took my arm and led me to my new living quarters. Thor followed us. He didn't make a sound, but I felt his presence in every pore along my back. Remember the zorfa's ass, I told myself. Certainly didn't want a repeat of that fiasco. The boss would disown me. Yes, I really needed to put a stop to whatever was going on between us. Soon.

I loved my new quarters immediately. It was only one room, but the size made it feel cozy instead of confining. There was nothing inside that would pass for conventional furniture, just lots of colorful cushions in warm tones of yellows, oranges, and browns, scattered here and there on braided rugs. Both the rugs and cushions matched the window coverings, which were pulled back to let in light and air. And apparently dragon birds, since the contingent that had followed me from my base camp were now taking up every inch of space on the ledge, peering around the quarters inquisitively. Neither Thor nor Lurran seemed to find the little creatures' actions unusual, so I turned to survey the rest of the room.

Against one wall was what appeared to be a Buri-sized sleeping platform made from adobe. It rose approximately six inches from the floor and was covered with a large, comfortable-looking mat and more cushions. Compared to the cot I'd used in my hut, it was positively decadent.

Between the windows, pegs were driven into the walls, each set holding a wooden shelf bearing pottery jars and bowls of different sizes and shapes. Together, they formed an artistic whole that was functional as well as beautiful.

Thor supervised the unloading of my things, directing Junior and Ghost to stack the crates of supplies behind the building, under the eave to keep them out of the rain. Only my personal items and clothing were brought inside, and even that was probably unnecessary. A wide selection of

Buri skirts and belts were draped over pegs near the sleeping platform.

By the time the three males left me alone with Lurran, the sun was low behind the trees. The female Buri seemed determined to get me into traditional dress as soon as possible. She took a green skirt from one of the pegs, laid it across the platform, and motioned for me to strip. Once assured that I was obeying orders, she pointed to the skirt and began my education in the Buri language.

"Kechic." The sound came from the back of her throat and was clipped at the end. It took me three tries to get it right, but she finally nodded in satisfaction and moved on to the bowls, lifting pieces of fruit to tell me what they were called.

I was doing pretty well until the construction of the kechic belt distracted me. It was actually three layers of material, sewn together on the sides but separated in the front and back to make slots. On one end was a round wooden object with a bar across the middle, through which the end of the material was woven. It had to be a clasp, but I couldn't figure out how it worked. Lurran noticed my confusion and came to the rescue.

She settled the belt low on my hips, and then pulled the loose end through the wooden clasp, winding it over the other material to make a flat knot. Although comfortable, it didn't look all that secure. While she picked up the kechic, I wiggled experimentally, but the belt stayed snugly fastened. Good. I'd really hate for my clothes to fall off the first time I walked through the village.

In front of me, Lurran made sure I was watching, and then pulled the end of the material through the slot closest to my skin. When the length was right, she tucked it through the outer slot and turned the belt so the material hung down behind me. Ah, so that's how they did it.

Nodding my understanding, I pulled the material between my legs and repeated the process in front. It felt a little odd, like I was wearing thicker-than-usual skivvies, but I liked the way the hem swirled around my knees. There was no mirror to check, but with the armlets and bare feet, I must have looked like a harem girl from *Harum Scarum*. Max loved Elvis Presley, so we had a vid of every movie he'd made in our files. Not an image I wanted to project to the Dynatec crew, but for everyday wear in the village, it suited me fine.

Lurran stepped back, checked me out, then retrieved a pair of the moccasin-like boots and handed them to me. The buckskin was buttery soft and formed around my feet snugly, providing comfort as well as protection. When I had them on, she smiled and motioned toward the door. Guess now that I was properly attired, it was okay to appear in public. The thought struck me as funny, and I chuckled as I walked outside.

My laughter died a hard death as two things hit me simultaneously. Four Buri were trying out the antigrav sled. They had it piled so high with blocks I was surprised they could move it.

Which brings me to the second thing I noticed. Apparently none of them had ever heard of Isaac Newton, or his first law of motion. A body in motion tends to remain in motion at a constant speed in a straight line unless acted on by an outside force. It's basic physics. The antigrav sled negates the weight of objects placed on it, but it doesn't do squat for the mass. And in this case, the outside force that was about to act on the sled was the new building the Buri were erecting.

Unfortunately, a Buri male was currently standing between the sled and the solid stone wall. Since the effort it took to get the sled moving while loaded with blocks was directly proportional to the effort it would take to get it stopped, the job required the strength of four, fully grown male Buri. Or me.

Adrenaline exploded through my body, sending me into overdrive. In less than the blink of an eye, I crossed the clearing, braced my feet, and planted my palms against the front of the sled. Teeth grinding and every muscle tight with strain, I shoved with all my strength. The sled halted as though it really had slammed into the stone wall, leaving the endangered Buri gaping at me in surprise.

Immediately I wilted to the ground, my breath coming in hard, short gasps, sweat dripping from my skin. Newton's third law. For every action there is an equal and opposite reaction, and now I'd pay for the massive amount of energy I had expended. I desperately needed food and liquids to replenish that energy.

It seemed to take forever for the Buri to reach me, and I didn't realize I was hurt until Lurran, babbling hysterically, tried to soak up the blood streaming down my leg with the edge of her skirt. I must have cut it on the corner of the sled.

"It's okay, really." I did my best to calm her, but to no avail. She continued screeching until the entire population of the village surrounded me.

Damn, damn, damn. Tears filled my eyes. I'd so hoped that the Buri would accept me fully before they discovered I wasn't "normal." Now there wasn't a chance in the thirteen hells. Even as Thor pushed through the crowd and scooped me into his arms, the deeply torn, jagged flesh on my thigh was healing, the sides knitting together with a speed that couldn't be mistaken.

Shouting orders, Thor took me to the building that served as a communal kitchen and dining room and placed me gently on the low table, hovering over me protectively. Auntie Em was waiting with a bowl of water and a clean cloth. She pushed Thor aside, swabbed the blood away and then blinked at my leg as a resonating silence fell over the Buri.

Instead of the gaping wound they were expecting, there was only a thin pink scar. In an hour, even the scar would be gone. The truth is, only a direct shot to my head or heart will kill me. Anyplace else, and my body will heal itself before the shooter gets a second chance.

Along with empathy, superfast reflexes and immunity to diseases, my body's ability to repair itself is one of the "improvements" we were sure Gertz, the rogue geneticist, had made when he created me. Other less certain alterations lay in wait, ready to pounce on me like a villain in a horror vid.

"It was just a scratch, honest," I lied. "Nothing to worry about."

You could have heard a leaf hit the ground, it was so quiet.

From the back of the crowd, a whisper erupted, soon joined by another, and yet another. The sound swept over the Buri until it took on the cadence of a chant. One word stood out above all the others. It sounded like *shushanna*, but I didn't have time to worry about it. Sweat poured from my body to pool on the surface of the table. If I didn't get food and liquids fast, I'd go into shock.

Pushing Thor's hands away, I sat up and reached for the bowl nearest me. It contained several types of fruit, and I grabbed the first one my hand touched. It was round and red and juicy, and I ate it in two bites, then picked up another one. With my free hand, I mimed drinking, and someone shoved a cup in my direction.

The relief was immediate. I could feel strength flowing back into my body, and sighed. Another minute and I'd be back to normal. Well, normal for me, anyway, although I was still hungry enough to eat an entire herdbeast in one sitting.

Scooting to the edge of the table, I put the cup down, stood and dusted off my hands, a big smile plastered on my face. "See? Good as new."

Lurran paused in her frantic narrative, and the silence de-

scended again. As one, every Buri in the room bowed from
the waist, and I heard *Shushanna* murmured again. Only Thor
was still upright, and I turned to him. "What's a Shushanna?"

One corner of his lips twitched in a half smile, and he
caressed my cheek with one strong finger. "Shushanna." He
was feeling so smug and vindicated that I scowled.

"Me? I'm a Shushanna?" Maybe it was Buri for "GEP." I
glanced back at the group, despair curling in my stomach. I
should have known they would find out. But why were they
bowing? It would make more sense if they threw me out of
the village.

On the other hand, Thor didn't seem too upset by the rev-
elation. What if I was reading the situation wrong and they
were merely grateful I'd saved the male's life?

I waggled my hand at the bowing Buri. "Make them stop,
okay? It's a little distracting."

He issued a command, and then promptly pulled me back
against his chest, his warm arms folding around me as the
other Buri straightened and rushed toward me. They sure
were talking now, and each one seemed determined to touch
me. I kept my smile in place until things finally calmed
down, then glanced at Thor over my shoulder. "Can we eat
now? I'm starved."

With a full-fledged grin, he sat in front of the table and
pulled me down beside him. Churka took up the space on
my other side, and Lurran sat across from us as several of
the females carried trays of food to the table. There was everything from stew to slices of roast meat, and vegetables
and fruit. The aroma was wonderful, but I barely tasted what
went into my mouth. Everything within reach was fair game,
and I ate until I could barely move. For once I didn't even
worry about who had prepared the food or what was in it. I
needed the nourishment too much to quibble. By the time I
was finished, my eyelids drooped with exhaustion.

It had been a long day, and if nothing else, I'd awed the Buri with my ability to pack away the groceries. They were probably wondering how in the thirteen hells they were going to keep me fed.

Suppressing a yawn, I leaned in to Thor and closed my eyes as he draped an arm over my shoulders and pulled me closer. I felt strangely safe with him, unlike other experiences I'd had. Not until someone lowered me to the cushions on the sleeping platform in my quarters did I stir again. When I opened my eyes, Thor was silhouetted in the light of a small oil lantern on the shelf above me. He sat on the side of the platform, watching me. With a serious, intent look, he brushed the hair away from my face, then touched the armlets and murmured something with husky overtones. I got the impression he was telling me how much he liked seeing me wearing them.

"Thank you for making them, even though you didn't have to repay me for the clasp," I whispered. "I've never owned anything so beautiful."

My response satisfied him, and he rose, hesitating a moment as he gazed at me.

"Good night, Thor," I said.

His chest lifted on a deep breath filled with longing, then he walked out the door, pulling the curtain closed behind him.

I was almost asleep when Max jarred me into full awareness.

"Kiera, we have a problem. I tried to tell you earlier, but you weren't responding."

"I was asleep." Swinging my legs over the edge of the platform, I sat up. "What's wrong?"

"There are three strange Buri in the village, two females and a male, and I don't know where they came from."

CHAPTER 7

"What do you mean, there are three new Buri? That's impossible." I stood and rummaged in a knapsack, looking for my prism torch. "And don't you dare tell me nothing is impossible or I'll have to hurt you."

"Kiera, I scanned the entire planet. All the Buri that were here when we landed are accounted for, and their medical information stored. These three have arrived since the first day you visited the village."

I pounced on the torch, adjusted it to its weakest setting, and flicked it on. The dim glow filled the shadowed corners of the room, and by its light, I pulled out two Zip Bars. Unbelievably, I was hungry again.

Mouth full, I paced the confines of the room. "So what you're telling me, Max, is that three full-grown Buri fell out of the sky. Or maybe they popped out of a hole in the ground." I swallowed and took another bite. "You must have miscounted."

He sniffed. "I didn't miscount."

"Okay, then the only other explanation is that they were somewhere else and you mistook them for another species.

You said yourself, there's so much life on Orpheus Two and the climate is so hot, it's hard to get an accurate thermal reading."

There was a moment of silence before he answered. "I suppose it's possible."

"It's the only thing that makes sense. And if there were three we didn't find, there could be hundreds more."

"I'll start another scan immediately, on the night side of the planet. If they're there, I'll find them."

I popped the last half of the second Zip Bar into my mouth and walked back to the sleeping platform. "Good. Let me know if anything shows up. I'll be back tomorrow to look over the information on the Ashwani."

Knowing Max, it would take him three or four days to do the scan. He really hated missing something and would be extra thorough this time around. Unfortunately, I had a feeling he wouldn't find a thing. There was more going on here than Dynatec's larceny. The Buri were up to something too, and I had a sneaky suspicion Thor wouldn't tell me what it was even if we could understand each other. Not yet, at any rate. He might be attracted to me, but I was still a member of the enemy species.

Maybe he'd trust me in time, but I couldn't wait. The longer I was here, the more nervous Frisk and Dorn would become. They were counting heavily on the two-month time limit to keep me from doing any in-depth studies. And Frisk in particular was just stupid enough to try something desperate if he thought I was close to discovering the truth.

Stripping off my kechic, I doused the torch and settled back onto the sleeping platform. Did Dynatec know what was going on, or were Frisk and the Dorn woman working alone? I really needed to speak with Claudia Karle again, but it had to be where no one on the Dynatec crew would know. I didn't want to put her in any more danger than necessary.

With a yawn, I stretched, tendons popping as I pointed my toes, then relaxed and closed my eyes. Tomorrow, when I wasn't so sleepy, I'd figure out a way to get her alone. Right now, I was too tired to think anymore.

I only woke one more time that night, when Crigo slipped into my quarters. He made sure it was me on the platform, and then flopped onto his back, paws splayed as snoring erupted. I could feel his repletion all the way across the room.

Damn. It was bad when you were jealous of a rock cat. If he ever found out, he'd gloat for weeks.

Forcing my eyes closed again, I did some deep breathing exercises to relax. And when sleep claimed me once more, I dreamed.

Thor was standing beside the black crystal building, beckoning me closer, and I knew the two were inexplicably linked. Yearning swept over me, painful in its intensity. Everything I'd ever wanted was there, waiting for me to take it. I tried to walk toward him, but my feet refused to move.

Tears trickled down my cheeks as I struggled ineffectively. Suddenly the boss was in front of me, blocking Thor from my sight. His expression was one of ineffable sadness. "I'm sorry, Kiera. We can't let you go. We need you too much. You've never appreciated exactly how unique you are."

"But I don't want to be unique!" The anguished words were torn from deep inside me. "I just want to be normal."

"No, my dear." His voice, full of sympathy, dropped a level. "You want to be happy as you are. There is a difference, Kiera. You won't find what you truly seek until you can accept yourself."

Before my startled gaze, the boss transformed into a dragon bird and shot away into the trees. I turned my attention back to the clearing too late. Both Thor and the crystal building were gone, and I was left alone with a hollow ache in my middle.

*   *   *

The sound of childish laughter woke me, and I sat up and reached for my jumpsuit. Early-morning sunlight beat down on the window coverings, but it was still relatively cool inside the adobe building.

"How's it going, Max?" I asked as I dressed.

"Nothing yet." He sounded preoccupied. "I've finished downloading the information on the Ashwani, but it will take me a few hours to go over it and prepare the highlights for you."

"Okay. That will give me time to take care of a few things here first." Like unpacking. I finished the job quickly, making use of the shelves that lined the walls, then combed and braided my hair.

The laughter came again, piquing my curiosity. Selecting a piece of fruit from a bowl, I strolled to the door and stepped outside. Brownie and the Buri I'd saved from the sled stood nearby, Brownie's hand resting on the hilt of the knife I'd given him.

I followed the direction of his stare and smiled. Crigo was sprawled under a tree, Brownie's little boy clambering all over him. At my appearance, the rock cat rolled his eyes and his side lifted on a deeply indrawn breath of disgust, but the show was strictly for my benefit. The damn cat was actually enjoying the attention.

When I glanced back at Brownie, his hand tightened on the knife and he shot a heated glare in my direction. Apparently his attitude hadn't softened toward me yet. With a gesture to the Buri standing beside him followed by a low growl, he turned his back and ignored me.

I widened my smile and nodded at his pal, who was staring at me in awe. "Hello there."

The newcomer had different-colored hair from any Buri I'd seen so far. It wasn't the rich auburn shade that

Junior boasted, or the deep chocolate color of Brownie's. It was somewhere in between. Dusty, I decided. The name suited him.

His smile was shy as he extended a handful of flowers. "Shushanna."

They were brilliant red, veined with gold in a lovely filigree pattern, and a heavenly scent rose from the petals as I took them.

"For me?" I buried my face in the bouquet and inhaled. A perfume made from these flowers would cost a fortune in the civilized portions of the Federation. Not to mention, any horticulturist worth his salt would kill to add a specimen to his collection. It seemed everywhere I looked, there was a potential source of trade on Orpheus Two. If the planet were ever opened to commerce, the Buri would be one rich group of people. At least, they'd be rich if they were lucky enough to have an honest, intelligent director to oversee their interests. One who cared more about the Buri than his or her own credit balance.

I sighed. "They're lovely. Thank you."

He bowed, murmured something to Brownie, and headed across the clearing toward the new building. Brownie gingerly collected his son from Crigo's back and departed in the opposite direction.

"Max, that wouldn't be one of the new Buri, would it?"

"Yes. The only male. The other two are female. I saw them go into the communal kitchen earlier."

Munching on my fruit, I watched as Dusty reached the edifice and delivered what sounded like a few curt orders. The other Buri immediately got to work on the structure. It didn't take long to figure out that Dusty was a master when it came to building with stone. Which led me to only one conclusion.

Wherever he'd been, he had returned to oversee the

new construction. I arched my brows. How in the thirteen hells had he become a master stonemason when there were no stone buildings in the Buri village except the one he was working on now, and no sign that there had ever been any?

Giving a mental sigh, I took the flowers inside my quarters and put them in water, then went behind the building and sorted through the crates of supplies. Selecting two that contained easily prepared foodstuffs, I stacked them on top of each other and hoisted them in my arms.

The weight didn't bother me, but I was having trouble seeing around them, stumbling over tree roots several times before I made it to the front of my quarters. It came as a relief when someone plucked the top crate off, and I smiled as Ghost growled a question.

"The kitchen." I tilted my head toward the building.

He led the way, and I looked around curiously as we entered. I was in no condition to pay attention to my surroundings the evening before, and other than the new stone structure, this was the largest of the Buri buildings.

Six long tables were situated in rows on my right, running from the front of the room to the back, with just enough space to move comfortably between them. Elder sat at one of them, a cup in his hands.

On the end wall was the cooking area. It comprised a fireplace—flames banked low under a large iron grille on which rested several pots—and four ovens set into the wall, two on either side.

A group of Buri females looked up and smiled at me from some smaller tables where they prepared food. Lurran and Auntie Em were with them and I carried my crate to the older woman and deposited it on the floor.

While Ghost put his crate next to mine and stepped back, I pulled the top off and extracted a sealed packet. The con-

tents looked like nothing so much as dried dung, and all of
the Buri watched me warily.

Taking out my knife, I slit the packet open and moved to
the fireplace to peer into the pots. Good. One of them contained boiling water.

I returned my knife to its sheath and upended the parcel
into the water, then stood back as the Buri females gaped
in surprise. The dehydrated food soaked up the water and
swelled until it filled the pot, the delicious aroma of fruit
compote pervading the room.

When it was done, a matter of a few seconds only, I took
an implement from a table, dipped it into the compote, and
spread it on a chunk of the round Buri bread. Before anyone
else could move, Auntie Em lifted it from my hand and took
a bite. A slow smile spread across her face, and she nodded.
Immediately, the others dove in. There was a wide variety
of food in the crates, all with pictures on the front of the
packets. I hoped they would at least be able to get an idea of
what was inside.

I left them to it and turned toward the other side of the
room. Since there were so few females in the village, it was
easy for me to recognize all the ones I'd met on my first trip.
I'd never seen the two who were sitting at an odd-looking
contraption, watching me while they worked levers and ped-
als. They both smiled and gave me the short bow when I approached, but they never slowed in their movements.

The darker-haired woman was operating something that
reminded me of a spinning wheel. But instead of sitting and
winding thread around a spool, she was feeding it to the
wooden frame the other female was working. It was a loom,
I realized, as I stared down at the material growing under her
hands, the exact length and width of a kechic. Only the cloth
was like none I'd ever seen before.

It resembled silk, but was finer, almost gauzy in appearance, as though they'd taken the webs from a thousand spiders and woven them into a fabric that was blinding in its beauty. The piece in the loom danced from shades of indigo to emerald and to amethyst in the sunlight streaming through the windows.

I reached out to touch it when a flash of brilliant red drew my gaze to the table beside them. Half a dozen kechics made from the shiny material, complete with belts, were neatly folded on its surface. They ranged in color from vibrant yellows to deepest purples, but it was the red one that held pride of place.

Awestruck, I gently lifted it and felt it slither in my hands as though it were sentient. Like a living flame, it shifted colors from red to orange to yellow, then back again. It was with a sense of regret that I refolded it and put it back on the table.

Yep, something was going on. First Dusty shows up to erect a huge stone edifice unlike any the Buri had built before. Then we have these two new females who were busily creating clothing that no woman with an ounce of estrogen in her bloodstream would wear for everyday.

Was it possible the Buri were preparing for a party? Maybe a dedication ceremony for the new building.

"Kiera, the information on the Ashwani will be ready by the time you reach my location," Max said, knowing my need for more information.

"Okay, on my way." With a smile and a nod at the two new females, I walked toward the door, Ghost following closely on my heels.

Other than the males working on the new building, the village seemed deserted as I walked through it. "Max, where are all the Buri?"

"Most of them are in the fields, tending crops, but some

of the males are practicing warfare skills in a cleared area behind the village."

I stopped so fast Ghost bumped into me. "Warfare skills?"

"So it seems."

This, I had to see. Turning right, I made my way between two buildings. It didn't take long to find them. The grunts and growls were audible even over the racket the dragon birds made.

The males were divided into two groups, one doing target practice with their spears, the other engaged in hand-to-hand combat. Thor stood to one side, hands on his hips as he watched a Buri with light brown hair square off with Junior.

Hesitating at the edge of the clearing, I watched as Junior sailed over his teacher's shoulder to land on the ground. The Buri pulled him to his feet, growled at him for a second, then acted out the move he wanted Junior to accomplish.

For the second time, Junior flew through the air. Well, of course he did, I thought in disgust. His instructor was going about teaching him the maneuver all wrong. Junior was both shorter and lighter than the adult male, which made his center of gravity different.

The Buri was growling at him again when I interrupted. "Mind if I make a few suggestions?" I didn't wait for an agreement, but turned to face Junior. Holding my arms straight out from my shoulders, I twisted from side to side. "Try this."

They all looked at me blankly, and I cursed. How could I teach them the right way if they didn't understand a thing I said?

I thought hard for a second, then picked up two short sticks and gestured the Buri closer. All of them gathered around except Brownie, who marched off in a huff of temper.

Ignoring his exit, I held one stick out, horizontal to the ground, and then tried to balance the second stick on it.

Only, instead of placing it so its middle was poised on the first stick, I moved it toward its end. Naturally it fell off.

The group looked even more puzzled, so I held up a finger. Wait. Retrieving the fallen stick, I placed it on the horizontal one again, only this time I put it in the exact spot that would allow it to balance perfectly. I pointed at that spot, then at my own center, then at Junior's.

They got it. All of them were smiling and nodding, and gesturing for me to show them how to find the spot again. I obliged them and then motioned for Junior to try it.

Junior shot a glance at Thor, and then complied with my request. It only took once for me to locate his center. I placed my hand just above the rim of his loincloth. "This is where your leverage needs to come from, not your stomach. See?" I replaced my hand with his, then had him lean front-to-back and side-to-side. "Feel that? It's the point your whole body revolves around, the place your balance comes from."

By the time I motioned for his instructor, all the Buri were smiling at me. Teacher moved closer, and I glanced at Junior. "Now, I'm going to do this slowly, and I want you to pay close attention to this part right here." I patted my abdomen. "Don't watch the moves, watch what my body does."

Grasping the instructor's forearm, I turned my back to him and pulled his arm over my shoulder, sliding both hands down to grip his wrist. Then I hooked my right leg around his, pulled his foot out from under him, and very gently flipped him over my hip to the ground.

I brushed off my hands and placed them on hips as I smiled at Junior.

Junior watched the whole thing intently, a smile on his lips. When I finished, he nodded in reply, and I stepped back.

Teacher had regained his feet. He gave me a bow and then, with no perceptible warning, rushed Junior. The youngster was ready for him, though. In one smooth move, he grabbed, turned and flipped.

"Excellent!" I laughed and applauded. "I think you've got it."

Thor had moved to my side, and we watched as all the males twisted and turned, trying to find their center of gravity. It looked rather like an aerobics class on Primus Centauri Four, with the participants in desperate need of some good spandex body suits.

I smiled at Thor, only to discover he was frowning at my jumpsuit. "I'm on my way to my ship," I explained, pointing in Max's direction while sending Thor a visual image. "I'll change into the kechic when I'm through there."

His gaze lifted to mine. He studied me for a second, then growled something at Brownie and picked up his spear. Okay. It looked like he was going to tag along with me and Ghost.

"Max, we may have company on board. Thor is with me, and I don't know if he'll come inside or not. Better lock up everything you don't want damaged, just in case."

"Yes, Kiera."

To my surprise, Thor followed me up the ramp as though he'd done it all his life, while Ghost remained at the bottom, eyes alert as he scanned the horizon. I went straight to my terminal, already preoccupied with the information Max had prepared. "Make yourself at home." I waved vaguely toward the back of the ship as I sat down, and heard Thor move away.

"Okay, Max, what do we have?"

A holo came to life in front of me. It was a planet, but hard to see because it was surrounded by darkness. "Ashwan," Max announced. "The world was discovered two hundred and fifty cycles ago by a scientific exploration team that was doing research on dead stars. When they realized the planet had once been inhabited, they called in a group of archeologists."

"Good." A sound came from the back of the ship, and I paused. "What's Thor doing?"

"Trying to figure out how the saniflush works. He also seems rather taken with the mirror."

I grinned. If I were male and looked like he did, I'd be taken with the mirror too. "Print me out the plans for an old-fashioned gravity flush sanitary, will you, Max?"

On the other side of the cabin, three or four sheets of tough laminate paper ejected from a slot.

"Thanks. Now back to Ashwan. What did the archeologist find?"

"Not much at first. The environmental conditions were extremely harsh. The planet's atmosphere was gone, and it was covered in a thick layer of ice. The only reason they knew it had it once supported life was because the very top of one building protruded from the ice."

"Did they do a spectral analysis?" I glanced around as Thor came back into the cabin. He grunted and gestured toward the hatch. Guess now that his curiosity had been satisfied, he was ready to leave.

I shook my head. "I'm not finished here. Have a seat." I pointed at the other command chair, and mimicked sitting.

He approached it gingerly, and eased his bulk onto the seat. Then promptly grabbed the arms and growled when it automatically adjusted to his size and weight.

"Max, run *Holovid 101* for him. That should keep him occupied for a while."

Holovid 101 was the standard introductory vid for new races. There was no narration, only images that depicted the history of the human race. It started with a shot of Old Earth taken from the moon, went through all the evolutionary stages of man, continued through our first meetings with other species and the exodus into space, and ended with Alien Affairs helping other races to join the Galactic Federation.

When the first image materialized in front of him, Thor jumped, then slowly lifted his hand to poke it with one finger. His hand went completely through the holo, and he yanked it back. But it didn't take long until he was absorbed in what he was seeing, and I returned to the information on Ashwan.

"Spectral analysis," I reminded Max.

"Yes, they did several." The holo changed to a vid of the surface, floodlights illuminating the terrain. The scientist had erected a biodome near the building they'd discovered. It was both living quarters and a place where they could work without the pressure suits that supplied oxygen and protection from the cold.

Max continued as the vid camera panned left to show the rim of a stone structure, the blue-white lights casting eerie shadows on its crevices and ridges. "The spectral analysis showed that beneath the ice lay the remnants of a huge stone edifice. Most of it was destroyed by the weight of the ice bearing down on its walls. Only the tower remained intact. It took them almost two cycles to gain entry, but when they did, it was well worth the effort."

The view changed again, this time to a room inside the tower. It looked as though the occupant had just stepped out and was due back any second.

"The cold preserved everything in perfect condition," Max said. "And the scientists learned quite a bit from what they found."

"Such as?" I prompted.

"The Ashwani had a feudal culture, similar to that found on Old Earth during the medieval era. Large areas of land were ruled over by a king, with a nobility swearing fealty to him. In turn, they were allowed portions of the kingdom, with peasants to work the land. But unlike Old Earth's feudal structure, the dividing line between the nobility and the peasants was almost nonexistent. From the drawings they found, everyone did what they were good at. One showed a king's daughter going to work in the fields, and another, a nobleman baking bread."

"Interesting," I commented. "How about weaponry?"

"The most advanced they've found are swords, and only the soldiers used those."

"So they did have warfare?"

"No sign of hostilities were found, but with their societal structure it would have been inevitable. Especially after their star began to die. Once the exploration team knew what to look for, fifteen other castles were discovered under the ice, and even now, scientists aren't sure they've found them all. Land for crops to feed everyone would have been at a premium with their world dying around them."

I nodded. "Any images of their weapons?"

The view changed to what looked like a small arsenal. Shields hung on one wall interspersed with spears and swords. Leaning forward, I peered a bit closer at the spears. Bingo. The Buri's spears had triggered my memories of the Ashwani, and I was staring at the reason why. I'd seen these images before, and the spears were flat black metal with odd markings inscribed on them, just like the Buri's.

A feeling of satisfaction flooded through me as a piece of the puzzle clicked into place. All my instincts were telling me that the Buri were descended from, or related to, the Ashwani. Now I had to prove it. Not to mention figure out a few incidentals like how they got to Orpheus Two and how long they'd been here.

I chewed on my lip for a second before addressing Max again. "What about their clothing? They didn't wear kechics and loincloths, did they?"

"No. The climate was far too cold at the end. The garments the archeologists found were heavy and warm."

"Any bodies?" I crossed my fingers. DNA samples of the

Ashwani could very well link them to the Buri and prove they were the same species.

"None, but you have to remember, the Ashwan star died long before the planet was discovered. The population probably starved to death many cycles before the end."

A sigh expanded my chest. "Damn. I guess that blows any chance of proving the Buri were a colonization party sent out by the Ashwani. At least for now." I glanced at Thor. He was riveted by an animated holovid of *Australopithecus africanus*, one of the first apelike men to use tools and walk erect.

"Given the level of technology the Ashwani achieved, it's not likely they were capable of space travel anyway," Max responded.

I leaned forward and propped my elbows on the console. "Did they find *anything* that would give us a clue to the Ashwani's physiology?"

"Oh, yes. Numerous things. Their clothing and tools indicate they were larger than humans. And since the planet is twice the size of Earth, the gravity would have been greater, making their bones denser. Dried plants and herbs were also found in sealed jars, and after extensive testing, it was concluded they all had medicinal properties compatible with human physiology."

An idea hit me, and I straightened abruptly. "They have the DNA for these plants?"

"Yes, of course."

"The Buri have crops. Max, what if they brought seeds from their home world? That would make sense, wouldn't it? I can gather samples of the Buri plants and run DNA tests on them to see if they match the ones on Ashwan. That would help prove our theory."

"I'll have to request the DNA analysis from the archives."

"Do it, and put a rush on the order."

Max hesitated. "Kiera, the probability that the Ashwani and the Buri are related is extremely low, in spite of the similarities."

"How else do you explain those similarities? Haven't I taught you there's no such thing as coincidences?"

"It could be parallel evolution. I know it's very rare, but it has happened before."

I shook my head. "Not this time, Max. I've got a gut feeling about the Buri. I don't know how or when, but they're descended from the Ashwani. I'd stake my reputation on it."

"And lose it if you insist on making this part of the record without proof."

"Oh, I'll find proof. If it takes me the entire two-month time limit, I'll find it." I leaned back. "But first, I have to find out what Dynatec is after and why the Buri aren't reproducing in higher numbers."

That statement reminded me of Claudia Karle. "Max, is Second Lieutenant Karle keeping her comm unit with her at all times when she's in the field like I asked her to do?"

"Yes, as do all the members of her mapping party."

"Okay, here's what I want you to do. Wait until she's out of hearing range from the others and then change the frequency on her unit remotely. Tell her I need to speak with her privately, and ask her to join me for dinner at the Buri village the first opportunity she has."

"Yes, Kiera."

A tingle of satisfaction went through me with that problem out of the way. "Now, let's see some of those drawings of the Ashwani you mentioned."

"There is one particularly vivid tapestry they found that you might be interested in."

The image in front of me vanished, only to be replaced

by a holo of a large wall hanging. It depicted a table loaded with food, around which a dozen or more Ashwani gathered, eating, drinking and laughing.

The Ashwani in the center of the group was an elderly male, his dark hair streaked with white. Around his forehead was a circlet of gold. But it was the younger man next to him that made me gasp aloud. Except for a wider brow and a scar on one cheek, it could have been Thor.

Before my brain had time to really register what I was seeing, Thor moved. With a deep growl, he lunged out of his chair and grabbed at the image. When his hand passed through it, he flung his head back and let out a roar so full of anguish that it froze me in place.

I was still sitting there as he spun to face me. His fists were clenched so tightly he was in danger of snapping his spear in half. And from the expression on his face, I was in danger of having that spear used on me. Eyes narrowed to glittering slits, he stared at me for what felt like an eternity, then turned and stepped through the hatch.

Finally, I started to breathe again. "Max, did you see that?"

"It was rather hard to miss."

"Damn it, there was something about that tapestry he recognized!"

"Or maybe he was reacting to what he perceived as the presence of another, threatening male."

"I don't think so. It may not be incontrovertible scientific proof, but it's good enough for me. The Buri are descended from the Ashwani, and what's more, Thor knows it somehow." I jumped to my feet and headed for the hatch. "I have to find him."

But by the time I reached the bottom of the ramp, he was gone, the only sign he'd been there the swaying of a few branches at the edge of the jungle.

CHAPTER 8

Ghost stood at the bottom of the ramp, a perplexed look on his face as he stared in the direction Thor had gone. I touched his arm, and he swung his gaze to me. "Do you know where Thor is going?"

He didn't understand me, but he knew who I was talking about. After a few phrases in Buri, he shrugged and shook his head.

Frustration consumed me. "Max, do you see him?"

"Yes. He's moving toward the village. Quite rapidly for someone who is not enhanced, I might add."

Well, at least Thor wasn't running away from his people. Only from me. But he wasn't getting rid of me that easily. I would clean up Dynatec's mess if it killed both of us.

Making a brief detour to grab the sanitary plans Max had printed out, I jogged toward the village, Ghost one step behind.

Thor wasn't hard to spot. He stood outside the new building, hands on his hips and a fierce scowl on his gorgeous face. Brownie and Churka were with him, Churka talking a mile a minute, her voice tinged with desperation. They all glanced at me when I approached, then Churka touched Thor's arm and her tone turned pleading. The only thing I understood was the word *Shushanna*, repeated several times.

With a snarl, Thor yanked his arm away from her, shot a glare in my direction, and walked into the jungle. My stomach sank all the way to my toes. He was even more upset than I'd first thought, and I didn't know how to get through to him, to make him understand. I had to try, though. His reaction to that tapestry was too important.

Dusty stood near the doorway of the new building, observing the proceedings, and I took a second to shove the plans into his hand before starting after Thor. I'd only taken two steps when Brownie blocked my path. Considering the mood I was in, this was not a good thing. Brownie and I had tolerated each other after I'd given him the knife, but it was an uneasy peace at best. He wasn't about to welcome me with open arms, and right now he was feeling distinctly vindicated, as though I'd finally proved him right.

At this point, I didn't much care if he hated me.

"Move." My voice came out low and threatening, and I instinctively assumed a loose-jointed fighting stance.

Brownie lowered his chin and shifted his spear to a two-handed grip, holding it point-up across his body, ready to move rapidly in any direction. A menacing rumble came from deep in his chest.

"I don't want to hurt you, but I will if you don't get out of my way." My gaze stayed locked on his, waiting for him to telegraph his intentions as I took another step. Adrenaline flooded my system and my heart pounded in reaction.

But I had forgotten Churka. Before Brownie could move, she threw herself between us, her back to me as she faced him down, her body vibrating from the force of her emotions.

Damn, I'd really wanted to hit someone. However, Churka's anger was quite impressive. Seeing it was almost worth giving up the chance to pound on Brownie. Especially when it was accompanied by a spate of spitting and snarling that had him looking for the nearest exit.

When she was through shredding him, she turned, patted my arm, and with a final glare at the rapidly retreating Buri, gestured in the direction Thor had gone. It was all the encouragement I needed, and I headed for the jungle at a fast jog.

"Max?"

"He's approximately two hundred yards beyond the communal kitchen."

"Is he still moving away from the village?"

"No, he seems to be pacing."

Exhaling one long breath, I slowed to a walk and tried to calm down. It wasn't easy. I still had all that excess adrenaline pumping through me from the encounter with Brownie. But I didn't want to make Thor think I was charging him, either.

Maybe a peace offering was in order. I stopped and searched the jungle around me. There. A gorgeous white flower dangled from a smaller cluster on a nearby tree. Swirls of black and gold made up its veins, the colors running together in the interior. Black and gold. Symbols for me and Thor? Maybe.

By the time I reached him, he'd stopped pacing. He was standing between two trees in a shaft of sunlight that had been filtered to a pale golden hue by the leaves above. Dust motes drifted in the rays, and a mothlike creature danced in and out of the light above his head, a winged attendant to his dilemma.

And there was no doubt he was a man in a quandary. His shoulders were slumped, eyes closed as he lifted both hands to rub his jaw.

He was in profile to me, so I studied him covertly. I had

no idea how to get through to him, to find out why the tapestry had upset him so much. The subject was a little too complicated for the fingers-on-the-temples trick I'd used before. Showing him an image of the tapestry might set him off all over again, and I didn't want to risk that happening.

The frustration of being unable to communicate almost overwhelmed me again before I got it under control. It was imperative that I come to a decision, and I did it instinctively. Getting back in Thor's good graces was more important right now than anything else I might discover. Not to me, personally, I assured myself, but to the mission.

Okay, maybe it was a tiny bit important to me. There was no other explanation for this sick feeling in the pit of my stomach, or the sudden case of nerves I'd developed. And no explanation for this certainty that there was a lot more at stake here than the mission.

I don't know if I made a noise, or if he simply sensed my presence, but he dropped his hands and spun to face me. His shoulders went back, body straightening as he wiped all emotion from his expression. It felt as if he'd slammed a mental door in my face, and that hurt. More than it should have, damn it.

"I'm sorry." I took a tentative step forward, holding out the flower, bombarding him with all the emotions streaking through me. Confusion, regret, humility—that one was a stretch, but I managed—and most of all, the fear that something special had been damaged beyond repair.

He blinked once, his forehead furrowing, but I saw some of the tension leave his muscles as he took the flower.

I moved closer.

"Please, don't shut me out," I whispered, flattening my palm against his chest. To my absolute horror, tears misted my eyes. But the sad truth was, no one had ever treated me the way he did, like I belonged, like I was a real person and

not a freak created under a molecular microscope. Even with
the boss, who had never been anything but kind, my nature
was always an issue. Considering the uncertainty of my creation, it had to be.

"I think I know why that tapestry distressed you so much,"
I continued. "But it wasn't intentional, I swear. The Ashwani
are your progenitors, aren't they? I don't know how your
people got here, or when, but you recognized the Ashwani in
that tapestry as being the same species as the Buri."

His eyes shut, and a shudder went through him. Then,
in the space of a single breath, his arms closed around
me, pulled me tightly to his body. I lost all track of time
as we stood there, his cheek resting on my hair, hanging
on to each other as though our lives depended on it. And
gradually, the buzzing in my head returned. Only then did
I realized that it had been with me since the first night I'd
encountered Thor outside my hut, low and constant, always
in the background. At least, it had been there until Thor
spotted the tapestry.

Relief nearly buckled my knees because I had it back,
and it was all I could do to keep from soaking him with sobs
of joy.

That's when the truth jumped up and bit me on the ass.

I was falling in love with the big guy.

"Check my hormone level," I ordered Max as I paced outside the open hatch.

"I've already checked it twice, and it was normal both
times."

"It can't be love," I wailed aloud. "It's got to be lust."

When Thor and I had returned to the village, Dusty was
waiting, scratching his head in confusion as he gazed down
at the plans I'd shoved into his hand. I'd been fine until
Thor released my hand and went into the new building

with the other Buri, both of them pouring over the simple drawings.

As I watched him vanish inside, panic had set in. My feet barely touched the ground, I'd headed for Max so fast. It had taken Junior and Ghost completely by surprise, although I expected one or both of them to show up any second now.

"I'm a GEP, Max. Alien Affairs owns my service and loyalty. I have to leave when my job is done. Plus, I learned my lesson with love. There's never going to be a happily ever after for me. I'm just too damn different." I reached the end of the trail I was blazing in the grass, spun and marched back in the other direction, mentally cursing Gertz. The man had given me all these built-in *needs*, and then insured I'd never fulfill them, by making me a freak.

Crigo was sprawled on his side in the shade Max cast, taking halfhearted swipes at my ankles whenever my path brought me within reach. "This simply cannot be happening." I threw my hands into the air. "Maybe it's a virus."

"You're immune to viruses," Max pointed out. "Do your palms become sweaty every time you're near him?"

I rolled my eyes. "Max, its thirty-nine point four degrees Celsius even at night. I sweat all over."

What he was doing was obvious. He was going through our extensive library of old holovids, looking for anything that might give us a clue as to whether or not I was truly falling in love with Thor. Not only were the vids good entertainment, they served as our main reference on the life and times of Naturals. I had little personal experience with Naturals, having been raised in a crèche. And since leaving the crèche I'd spent 60 percent of my time with only Max and Crigo for company. The other 40 percent had been spent with alien species, so that was no help.

"Good point," he said. "Would you die for him?"

"Of course. It's my job to save him and his people. I'd die for any of them. I wouldn't enjoy it, but I'd do it."

You could almost hear his awesome brain shuffling info. "Do you have an insatiable craving for turnips?"

I plowed to a stop, almost stepping on Crigo's extended paw. "Turnips?"

"Gone With the Wind."

My eyes closed in exasperation, and I dropped my forehead to my hands, not sure whether to laugh or cry. "Max, the turnips didn't have anything to do with Scarlett being in love with Rhett."

"Are you sure?"

"Positive."

My pacing resumed when another thought occurred to me. "You aren't recording this, are you?"

There was a split second of silence, then in a small voice, "End recording."

Hands on my hips, I turned to glare at the ship. "Don't you dare send that to the archives. The boss would haul me in for a full psych exam."

"I'm sorry, Kiera. You know everything goes straight to the ship's log."

"Great. Absolutely wonderful. That's all I needed to really make my day."

My mutterings were interrupted when Junior staggered out of the jungle, sweat dripping from his chin, his chest rising and falling in hard gasps. He shot me an accusatory look, then collapsed full-length in the shade near Crigo. A contingent of dragon birds had followed him. They settled on Max's hull and promptly fell to scolding me for leaving them behind. It seemed every time I turned around lately the beautiful little creatures were there.

"Okay, Kiera," I coached myself. "Deep breath. You've handled things a lot worse than this. People fall in and out of love all the time. Goddess knows you've proved that. It doesn't have to be permanent. I'll simply think of it as a temporary affliction, like . . . like . . ."

"Insanity?" Max prompted.

"Right." I nodded vigorously. "Like temporary insanity. That's a perfectly acceptable defense. And worrying about it isn't going to help, so I'll just concentrate on my job." I glanced across the lake toward the Dynatec encampment. "Did you contact Claudia Karle yet?"

"Yes. She sounded worried. But all she said was to tell you she has the day after tomorrow off, and will be happy to meet you that evening."

"Good. Anything from the boss?"

"The original report from the exploration team that discovered Orpheus Two came in. And Dr. Daniels said to inform you that he has three of his best investigators working to uncover information on Quilla Dorn. He'll let you know what they find."

"Anything unusual about the exploration report?"

"Two things, actually. First, they only counted twenty Buri, all males. But then, they weren't really doing an indepth study, and it's possible they simply didn't see the others."

"Either that, or the others were in hiding. There's a ton of caves in the mountains. Okay, what's the second thing?"

"According to Dr. Daniels, of the original five-man team, four are deceased, and the fifth has vanished."

"Natural deaths?" I started up the ramp.

"Accidental."

The boss wouldn't have included that tidbit if he hadn't thought it was suspicious. I agreed with him. Having one or two deaths over a ten-cycle span might be expected, but an entire crew individually wiped out? It stretched believability to the breaking point.

"I'll take my remote terminal and look the report over later today. Goddess knows, as much sunlight as there is on this planet, it should be easy to keep charged. Anything else that comes in, you can send to me directly."

I picked up the palm-sized terminal, slipped it into my pocket, and headed back to the village, trying to convince myself that I could maintain my relationship with Thor without endangering the very fabric of my existence.

The rest of the day dragged along at the speed of mud, and Thor seemed to go out of his way to keep my attention centered on him. "Lust," I chanted for the hundredth time as he casually hoisted a block to another Buri on top of the building, muscles flexing and relaxing with each movement. "Its just lust. If I ever sleep with him, I'll be back to normal."

For some reason, construction on the building had swung into high gear. All the Buri not busy with other jobs were now focused on completing the edifice. At the rate they were going, it would be done sometime tomorrow, and my curiosity was killing me. Twice now I'd tried to go in and look the place over, and both times Thor had stopped me from entering. Even trickery didn't succeed in getting me inside. When I'd calmly picked up a block and strolled nonchalantly toward the door, Thor had just as calmly taken it away from me and gently pushed me to one side. It didn't help that he smiled each time, or that several of the females went into giggling fits whenever he blocked my entrance. Easy for them to laugh. They weren't the one being kept out. It was really getting on my nerves.

Nose in the air, I retired to my quarters to pout and work with the remote terminal. Unfortunately, its solar panels needed direct sunlight to stay charged, so I ended up outside, leaning back against the wall of my building. Which meant Thor was always in my line of sight.

When I realized I was staring at him again, and he was staring back, his gaze hot, I hastily lowered my eyes to the information projected in front of me. The original report from the exploration team was huge, and most of it I'd seen before. To save time, I'd had Max separate the parts that hadn't appeared in the report we'd received. As I scrolled through them for the third time, I shook my head.

"This doesn't make any sense, Max. Why would they leave out the metallurgic and mineral findings? They had to know we'd check those ourselves as soon as we arrived."

"The readings for both are quite a bit higher than what's normally found on a planet. Especially the iron, zinc, sodium and aluminum. There's even a larger-than-usual amount of silicon dioxide. The planet is riddled with it."

I chewed that over for a second. Silicon dioxide was a fancy term for quartz, and while quartz crystals were pretty, their abundance made them cheaper than dirt.

"What about the metals? Is there enough to make Orpheus Two a viable mining operation?"

"Not really." Max sounded a little preoccupied. "It would be easier and more profitable to mine asteroids, where there are greater amounts of these metals and minerals, and less obstacles to overcome."

I rubbed my forehead and scrolled further down the list. "Okay, what about the rays the sun is emitting? For a yellow star, there seems to be a pretty wide spectrum. More gamma, more beta, and way more ultraviolet. If I didn't know better, I'd say it was newly created. But that's impossible. Everything I've seen on this planet indicates it's been around a long time."

"Instead of taking each fact separately, maybe we should be looking at them as a whole."

"What do you mean?" I stretched to ease tight muscles in my back.

"You're right about the sun. It is a relatively new star. I did an analysis when we first arrived."

"Why didn't you tell me?"

"It didn't seem relevant to the mission."

"Okay, so it's a young star. What about the planet's age?"

"It does appear older than its sun. The very diversity of plant life indicates a time span long enough for species to branch away from each other. Billions of cycles, instead of the millions the sun has existed."

There was only one logical explanation. "So, the planet must have been a wanderer that was captured by this star's gravitational field when it came too close."

"Exactly." We both ruminated a second before he spoke again. "Do you remember Messier 64?"

"The star system that resulted when two galaxies collided?"

"Yes. The collision left M64 with some rather bizarre internal motion. All of its stars are rotating in the usual clockwise manner, but it has a dark band of gas on its outer edge that rotates in the opposite direction. This is believed to be the remnants of the satellite galaxy that was destroyed when the two collided. And where the oppositely rotating gases meet, new stars are being formed."

I raised my hand, palm up. "And this is important to us because . . . ?"

"There are indications that a similar event occurred to the galaxy Orpheus is a part of."

Brownie caught my attention for a second. He was talking and gesturing angrily at three other Buri he'd waylaid leaving the new building, but I was too caught up in this new theory to worry about it. "So, hypothetically, this planet could have been part of one of the galaxies, and lost its star in the collision. Then, when Orpheus was formed, it became part of the new solar system."

"Can you imagine what the planet's surface underwent when its star collided with another?"

I could, barely. It was nothing short of a miracle that even one seed or spore had survived. Anything above ground would have been incinerated instantly. "Horrific," I responded.

"Which leads me to my next theory concerning what Dynatec may be after. Silicone dioxide is quartz. The minerals and metals found on Orpheus Two would make different-colored quartz. But more importantly, there's a type of quartz that's formed under intense heat and pressure. It's called *coesite*, and it forms so quickly that it doesn't have time to construct the usual crystal formation found in normal quartz. When you consider the extreme heat and pressure Orpheus Two was under, added to the radiation from the collision, what we may have here is a new type of quartz."

He paused for a second. "It could also explain how some of the plant life survived. The first wave of the blast would have blown the atmosphere away and possibly driven seeds and spores deep into the ground or into caves. Then the heat would have liquefied the silicone dioxide, and there's enough of it that most of the planet would have been covered. After the collision, with no atmosphere and no sun to heat it, the cooldown would have been fast. Then as the coesite quartz cooled and cracked, the seeds that were deeply buried and protected were released, and stayed dormant until the planet was captured by the Orpheus system's sun."

I straightened abruptly, a tingle of suppressed excitement quivering in my chest, and sent the image in front of me to the very end of the document.

And there it was, staring up at me from the information Max had gathered. Not one, but two crew members, both now deceased, had inventoried quartz samples on the manifest, neither of which was mentioned in the report Dynatec had sent Alien Affairs.

"Eureka!" I leaped to my feet and grabbed Junior, who had stuck to me like we were chemically bonded since I'd outrun him earlier that day. "I found it," I yelled, bouncing on my toes.

He cast a rather desperate look in Thor's direction, and I realized two things simultaneously. All the Buri were gaping at me, and I'd had no response from Max. To Junior's obvious relief, I released him.

"Max?"

"Kiera, I think we have a problem."

All my muscles went taut, my senses heightened to the point where I could detect Junior's heart thumping away beneath his well-muscled chest. Max wasn't an alarmist. If he thought we had a problem, we had one. "What's wrong?"

"It's Frisk. He's sneaking around your Quonset hut. I think he may have tried the back door of the living section."

"Has he approached you?"

"Not yet, but he keeps looking in this direction. My static shields are up and the hatch is closed, so he can't get near me. That's not the problem. Crigo is stalking him, and he looks very serious. I don't think he's playing, Kiera."

Adrenaline flooded my body. There were times when Crigo seemed to be endowed with psychic radar when it came to a human's intentions. He didn't disobey my orders often, but on the occasions he had, I'd always discovered later that he was right. And while I, personally, would be thrilled to get rid of Frisk, the boss would frown on turning him into prey before we discovered what Dynatec was up to.

Junior whimpered as I took off at a dead run, but I didn't dare slow down. Foliage whipped by in a green-hued blur, leaves and branches reaching out to slap at me as my feet kicked up clods of damp vegetation from the jungle floor. "Can you stop him?"

"Not without chancing permanent neural damage. Rock cats are extremely sensitive to stunners. I could fire in front of him, but Frisk is armed. If I draw attention to Crigo, the captain might kill him."

"If you have to stun anyone, stun Frisk. But wait until there's no choice left."

There was no need to tell Max I was on my way. He knew, so I saved my breath for running. Thank the Goddess I hadn't changed back into a kechic. Even for a fast healer like me, charging through a jungle half naked is no fun.

The distance from my hut to the village usually took fifteen minutes at a normal walk. I made it in three, dodging trees and leaping over bushes in the twilight gloom beneath the canopy. From all around me came the frenzied clicking and whistles of dragon birds and other life forms, disturbed by my dash through their territory.

"Location," I snapped as I neared the edge of the clearing.

"Frisk is to the left of the hut, center way, facing me. Crigo is at the edge of the jungle, five yards behind Frisk. The angle of attack will be northeast to southwest."

"Cover Frisk. I'll handle Crigo."

The light gradually brightened without the leaves to block the sun's last rays, and I spotted Crigo the instant I cleared the trees. He was crouched low to the ground, ears flattened and lips curled back to expose wicked-looking teeth. His powerful hindquarters were bunched, his intent amber gaze locked on Frisk.

My brain had just registered the scenario when he sprang. I went into overdrive and time slowed to a crawl as I launched myself at Crigo. His tightly muscled body expanded as he rose into the air. Reached with his front paws, claws visibly extended.

I slammed into him at the very apex of his leap, a mere second before he reached Frisk, the hot scent of pissed-off rock cat assailing my nostrils. Part of my consciousness noted Frisk turning, pulling out his laser. And then our momentum carried us into him, knocked the gun from his hand and sent it flying.

All three of us crashed into the side of the hut. I heard a loud crack, then time resumed its normal pace and I was busy trying to contain a spitting, snarling rock cat. It wasn't easy, but at least he recognized me and retracted his claws.

When the dust cleared, Crigo and I were facing each other, his tail lashing in annoyance and frustration as he glared at me. I glared right back, hands on my hips as I drew in a deep cleansing breath. "Go cool off," I told him. "I'll handle it."

With a final sneer in Frisk's direction, he turned his back and started grooming his paws.

Frisk was climbing to his feet, so the crack I'd heard must not have been bone. I positioned myself between him and his laser before I spoke. "Want to explain what you're doing sneaking around my hut?"

"Looking for you." He dusted off his clothing, avoiding a wet spot on the pocket adorning his right leg.

"Oh?" I didn't believe him for a minute. Unless he was a lot more stupid than I knew him to be, he was well aware that I now resided at the Buri village.

"Someone saw you here earlier. I thought maybe I'd catch you before you left."

I crossed my arms. "Now, what could we possibly have to talk about, Frisk? I told you the day I arrived, you'll have my report when I've concluded my investigation."

"That's kind of what I wanted to talk to you about." He glanced at Crigo and I could feel a combination of fear and anger erupt before he looked back at me. "Dynatec would like to buy your indenture from Alien Affairs. Our company is always looking for new talent, and you're one of the best."

My interest immediately skyrocketed. No one had ever tried to bribe me before. It proved how desperate Dynatec was to hang on to this planet. "You know Alien Affairs won't sell a GEP's indenture."

"No, but they'll let you buy your freedom." He glanced nervously at Crigo. "Dynatec will provide the funds, and in return you'll sign a contract to work for them until you pay the loan off. Plus, they're willing to pay you a handsome salary above the cost of your indenture."

"Is that how you acquired Redfield?"

His eyes narrowed. "Something similar."

I pretended to think it over. A tactic like this could stall the investigation drastically. Alien Affairs would have to send another agent, and that someone would have to be brought up to snuff on what was happening. They also might not be as thorough as I was, especially since the two-month time limit that started the second I landed would still be in effect. Just to see how he'd react, I voiced part of my thoughts to Frisk.

"If a new agent is brought in, they'll have to cover the same ground I've gone over, and do it faster. Remember, the time limit is nearly half over."

"Dynatec is willing to accept a slight delay while a new agent is briefed," he responded.

I just bet they were. And while they waited, maybe they could kill off a few more Buri. "Max, are you monitoring his vital signs?"

"Yes."

Good. It was time for a little digging. "Sorry, Frisk, but I'm not interested. I like my job. It can be real exciting. Why, in the next few days, I'm going to be doing all kinds of mining. Never know what you'll find on a new planet."

"His blood pressure just spiked," Max whispered in my ear.

Bingo. I was definitely on the right track.

"I thought your job was to investigate the Buri." He did his best to keep his expression clear, but his eyes gave him away. He was worried.

"Oh, it is. But if the Buri aren't dying out, we'll need to know what types of resources they have available for future Federation trade."

"You don't really believe the Buri are going to survive, do you?" He started to put his hands in his pockets, changed his mind, and propped them on his hips. "Come on, Smith. There are only a handful of them left, and only one child."

"Funny thing about that." I bared my teeth in a smile. "One of the females is pregnant, and I can't find a single reason, medically speaking, why they shouldn't continue to procreate very nicely. Is there something you'd like to share with me as to why you don't think they will?"

"I'm no scientist. But just because a female is pregnant doesn't mean she'll have a viable infant."

"Kiera," Max spoke softly. "There is a seventy-six percent probability that the liquid staining Frisk's leg is a fast-acting poison."

A chill went through me. If someone really wanted to do me in stealthily, a fast-acting poison was the way to go. Even my souped-up body couldn't work quickly enough to save me from its effects. Slip it into the cafftea reservoir on my food preparation unit, and it would be over before I knew what hit me. Which explained why Frisk had tried my door, and why Crigo had disobeyed my orders. Guess I owed the cat an apology. Again.

I gestured toward his pants. "Looks like you had an accident."

He looked down as though he'd only then noticed the wet spot. "Oh, yeah. Almost forgot. When Redfield found out I was coming to speak with you, he asked me to bring you a sample of some weird plant he's been studying. Guess it broke when I hit your hut. I better get back to our camp and change. No telling what was in the stuff." He lowered his hands. "Keep our offer in mind, Smith. It could be the best career move you've ever made."

I watched Frisk walk away and wondered if Dorn knew what he was up to, or if he'd acted on his own. He gave Crigo a wide berth, pausing only to scoop up his laser before heading toward the Dynatec camp. As excuses went, the one the captain had offered was pretty good.

"Max?"

"He was lying."

"Yeah, I thought so."

"And Second Lieutenant Karle reported in right before Frisk showed up."

I hadn't expected to hear from Claudia again until we met for dinner on her day off, so the fact that she'd contacted Max surprised me. "What did she say?"

"First, she thinks she may be onto something but isn't sure what yet. She'll keep trying. And second, Dr. Redfield asked her to pass on a message. He apologizes for what happened in the jungle the day he showed you the black flower and hopes you didn't misunderstand his intent. He needs to speak with you desperately, but either Frisk or Dorn is always watching him."

"Okay." The communication from Redfield was worrisome. It meant Dorn and Frisk no longer trusted him, and that he was in danger. Unfortunately, the laws concerning GEPs and their indenture holders were complicated. I couldn't march into Dynatec's camp and drag him out even though I might want to. In a court of law that could be considered coercion of testimony. To make any charges of indenture abuse against Frisk stick, the doctor needed to find a way to ditch his followers and come to me so he could legally request sanctuary. "Keep an eye on him, and if it looks like he's ever out alone, let me know. I can at least try to put myself in his path."

Crigo still had his back to me, but he'd stopped grooming to watch Frisk leave the area. I went to him and knelt. "Thank you. You may have saved my life. But I couldn't let you kill him yet. I'm making you a promise, though. If it ever becomes necessary, he's yours."

He licked his lips, his amber eyes glowing with anticipation, and I could swear he grinned. I had a feeling that in Crigo's book, Frisk's termination was already deemed necessary.

"You can't have him until I say so," I warned. "Next time you think he's up to something, come get me."

His ears went back and he lifted his nose with an air of hauteur before he focused on something over my shoulder. I shifted to see what he was looking at, and abruptly lurched to my feet.

Eight Buri, all armed with those evilly sharp spears, were arrayed in a semicircle at the edge of the jungle. Thor stood in the middle, a two-handed grip on his weapon, glaring daggers at me.

I lifted one hand in a tiny wave, and gave him a weak smile. "Hi. Looking for me?"

CHAPTER 9

The next morning I awoke with a feeling of well-being so foreign that I had to study it before I climbed from my sleeping platform. It sprang, I finally decided, from Thor's I'm-the-leader, you-will-obey attitude.

An odd thing to get happy about, but considering who and what I am, maybe it was to be expected. Normally, I'm the one people come to for protection, the one in charge. Even the zorfa's ass had constantly deferred to me on the occasions when we were together, which was enormously frustrating. But Thor had demonstrated repeatedly that not only was he determined to protect me, he considered me very soft and feminine in a good kind of way.

Also, as senior agent for Alien Affairs, I'm usually the first official representative of the Federation that most species come in contact with after the scientists leave. This generates a certain amount of awe from native populations. After all, I hold their future in my hands.

But Thor didn't know about the Federation, and I had a sneaky suspicion he wouldn't care even if I spelled it out in plain Buri. He just didn't strike me as the kowtowing type.

And then there was the personal side of things. I'd finally

found a male I didn't have to worry about breaking if things got . . . intense. Take my word for it, to a GEP, Naturals are very delicate creatures. This makes it a little hard to let go and *really* enjoy yourself. Mainly due to the fact that part of your mind is always focused on not doing permanent physical damage to your partner during a moment of ecstasy.

We had made quite a picture yesterday, eight fierce-looking Buri warriors marching silently back to the village. Me, upended over Thor's shoulder, grinning like an idiot. Even the indignity of being treated like a sack of grain couldn't quell my happiness.

It also hadn't hurt that he'd kept me by his side the rest of the evening. I figured that was more because he wanted to make sure I stayed put than it was for the joy of my company, though. He'd even escorted me back to my quarters after we'd shared the evening meal, and made sure I was safely tucked away for the night.

There was only one dark spot in my mood. He hadn't touched me. At least, not like I wanted him to. Was I being too subtle? Had it somehow escaped his attention that I was ready, willing and avid to make love?

I knew damn well he wanted me. I could see it every time he looked at me, could feel it floating in the air around him like static electricity whenever we were within a yard of each other. So *what* was he waiting for? Could it be that I was lacking some come-hither cue that Buri females performed to entice their males into a sexual romp?

Too bad Max's cameras couldn't see through walls. Some footage of Buri mating rituals would really come in handy right about now. I'd never been a voyeur, but if it helped me snag Thor, I was willing to make an exception.

I climbed off the sleeping platform and took a jumpsuit from one of the pegs on the wall, still thinking about Thor as I pulled it on. I'd give him a few more days, and if he hadn't made his move by then, I'd take matters into my own hands. Literally. I could have that loincloth off him in two seconds flat.

That image had me smiling as I pushed the curtain aside and stepped outside. Then I came to a rapid halt, blinking in surprise. I'd overslept. The sun was already high, nearly noon from the looks of it.

My gaze was drawn to the new building. It was finished, rising sturdy and proud in front of the cliffs, and my compulsion to go inside was climbing steadily with every hour I spent in the thing's proximity. It was strange, but I could swear the thing was calling me.

I blinked and refocused on a stream of Buri, both male and female, carrying goods inside. Some of the items were identifiable as curtains and floor coverings, but others were concealed in wrappings. All of the Buri seemed in very good spirits, laughing and talking as they passed each other going in and out.

For that matter, the entire village was abuzz with activity. To one side of the communal kitchen, four males were digging two long pits. From behind Thor's house, I could hear the steady bang of metal on metal. Since the forge was located back there, and he was the only one I'd ever seen use it, I had to assume he was working again.

Near the pool, in the shade of the cliff, Junior sat on a flat rock, legs crossed tailor fashion. Elder was with him, and the youngster listened raptly to every word the older Buri spoke. Even though I couldn't understand the language, it was clear he was giving Junior important instructions.

A movement caught my eye, and I glanced around in time to see Auntie Em emerge from the jungle. Her right arm was curved around a large wooden bowl that rested against her hip.

When she saw me, she smiled and motioned me toward

the kitchen. Once inside, she put the bowl on a table and poured a clay cup full of something that simmered in a pot over the fire, and then pushed it into my hands.

I took a tentative sip, then a larger one as I realized the liquid contained caffeine. It wasn't cafftea, but it was the next best thing—kind of the consistency of hot chocolate, but with a spicy tang to it. Even the fact that it was the color of tomato juice didn't slow me down. Thanks to Frisk and his intention to poison me, the food-preparation unit in the hut now felt haunted. I'd replace it the first chance I got, but until then, I only considered the one on board Max to be 100 percent safe.

While I finished that cup and poured myself another, I watched Auntie Em work. The bowl contained three or four gnarled roots, bits of dirt still clinging to them. She rinsed them thoroughly in a separate bowl of water, then peeled and cut them in half. That done, she brought out what looked to be a large mortar and pestle. Placing the roots inside, she pounded until they broke down into a pale bluish-white liquid.

Midway through the process, Churka came in and took a seat beside her, watching in obvious fascination. Auntie Em spoke to her several times, and Churka would nod. When the roots were reduced to stringy pulp and liquid, Churka stood and went to one of the shelves near the fireplace. When she came back, she was carrying a jug with a wooden stopper.

Auntie Em removed the pestle from the bowl and gestured while she gave instructions. Churka nodded, removed the stopper, and poured part of the jug's contents into the root mixture. Even from across the table I could smell alcohol mixed with a fruity aroma that made me think they were concocting some type of wine. This was good, I decided. Exotic alcoholic beverages were always in big demand, and this one smelled downright sinful.

I didn't get a chance to find out for sure if that's what it was, though. After a quick stir, Auntie Em covered the bowl with a cloth and set it to one side; then, with a smile in my direction, she and Churka left the building.

Wondering if I dared swipe a sample for Max to analyze, I finished my drink and took a fast look around the room. Nope. Too many Buri were coming and going. One of them would spot me for sure. Oh, well, maybe later. Now that I'd had my daily quota of caffeine, I was ready to do a little mining.

Since the episode with Frisk yesterday evening, I'd been assigned two full-time guards. Ghost was still with me, but my other protector was new to the job. We were behind my quarters, going through my supplies, and I studied him from under my lashes as I packed a laser drill, axe, shovel and some specimen containers in a knapsack.

He wasn't a total stranger. I'd noticed him several times around the village, mostly because, in a race of strikingly beautiful people, he was the exception. His hair was a few shades lighter than Brownie's, and was also shorter. It curled in tight ringlets that looked like coils of wire. His beard was fuller and bushier than what the other Buri males sported. Lips so thick they were in a permanent pout protruded below a bulbous nose with a well-defined crook in the middle. Combined with the beard, it gave him a real wild-man look.

It was his size that had me worried, though. Other than Thor, he was the biggest Buri I'd seen so far. But where Thor was all sleek lines and tight, sexy muscle, this guy could compete with a mountain and win.

I didn't doubt I could take him if the necessity arose, but it would be no rapid victory. His weight alone would be enough to slow me down, keep me pinned in place. Especially if I didn't want to hurt him in the effort.

Which made it pretty obvious what Thor was doing. At the first sign I was about to take off like an out-of-control rocket, mountain man would hang on to me until the troops arrived. Thor wasn't taking any chances that I'd outrun my guards again.

Oh, well, if I was stuck with the living mountain, might as well give him a name. I mentally shuffled through all the monikers of mountain men that I could remember, and discarded every one. They didn't seem to fit him somehow.

When I straightened and slung the knapsack over my shoulder, I casually took a step closer to him and lowered my shield. Surprise had me gaping at him in wonder. Around a core of solid steel flowed waves of such gentleness, such sweetness, that I was stunned.

This man would do what needed to be done, but he would do it his way. He was the type who would starve to death in a herd of bunnies because he couldn't stand hurting them. Inside that rough exterior was the soul of a poet.

With no hesitation now, I reached out and patted his massive chest. "Poet," I told him.

He glanced at Ghost in puzzlement, and the other Buri gave him a brief explanation. He listened solemnly and then looked back at me, his head tilted.

"Poet," I repeated.

"Poe." His voice was so cavernous and rough, it sounded like it rumbled from inside a bottomless hole. Rather ironic that his version was the name of an Old Earth poet, and a scary one too.

I smiled and nodded. "Poe."

While I'd studied my new guard, the pounding of Thor's hammer had been replaced with male Buri voices near the stone building. Voices that were now getting louder and angrier with every word. Curious, I stepped around my quarters to see what was going on.

Thor stood outside the main entrance, a wrought-iron object in his arms. His way was blocked by Brownie, a fierce scowl on the Buri's face as he spoke rapidly, gesturing emphatically at my quarters.

Alarm replaced my curiosity. Whatever was going on obviously concerned me, and I didn't like Brownie's tone. Dropping my knapsack at the corner of my building, I headed toward them, but Elder, Auntie Em and Churka beat me to the two males.

Both females were trying to outtalk each other by the time I reached the group, but Elder stopped them with a slashing motion of one hand. When they fell silent, he took over reasoning with Brownie.

There were so many emotions coming at me, it was hard to tell who was feeling what. Thor, I decided, was busy trying to suppress his anger and remain objective. Brownie was frustrated and angry because no one was paying attention to what he thought. A sense of profound loyalty was coming from Churka and was aimed at Thor. Elder was trying to be fair, to see both sides of whatever they were arguing about. Auntie Em just felt a deep certainty.

Normally I wouldn't have interfered with the clan's business any more than I would have allowed Thor to interfere with my mission. But this seemed to concern me. Puzzled, my gaze went back and forth between the participants, trying to ferret out what the problem was. Until Brownie said *Shushanna* and made a chopping motion in my direction with his hand. That's when I finally got it.

"Hey, if he doesn't want me to be Shushanna that's fine with me." They all stopped talking and looked at me politely, so I kept going. "It's not like I lobbied for the position or even know what it is. And you'll just have to find someone to replace me when I leave anyway. Might as well pick another person right off, especially if it will save you from an argument."

As soon as I shut up, Thor spoke to Brownie in a low, calm voice, completely ignoring everything I'd said. Of course, they hadn't understood a word of my oration, but I'd hoped Thor might pick up the emotions behind it. Either he hadn't picked up a thing, or he chose not to listen. Midway through his speech, he lifted a strand of my hair and held it up like it was Exhibit A in a murder trial. Then he pointed at the spot on my thigh where I'd been cut, and continued speaking. Auntie Em and Elder were nodding their agreement.

When he was finished, he did the arms-crossed-over-his-chest thing, the iron gadget dangling from one hand, and gave a decisive nod. The leader had spoken.

I narrowed my eyes at him, prepared to take issue with the action. But Brownie wasn't done yet. He talked for a few minutes and then pointed at one of the smaller buildings. I recognized it as the home of the female Buri who was pregnant.

Did Brownie want her to be Shushanna? I had no idea, but he was clearly determined to get his point across.

Thor remained stoic throughout and refused to respond. Instead, Auntie Em took up the cause, and she was even more determined than Brownie. Her speech culminated when she jabbed a finger at me and said, "Shushanna," in a very emphatic tone.

Well, guess that settled that argument.

Apparently Brownie thought so too. After shooting me a glare filled with ire, he turned his back and stalked off. Thor watched him go, shook his head in disgust and then continued into the building. Auntie Em and Elder both dispersed, each going in their own direction. Churka stayed long enough to smile, pat me on the arm and declare me Shushanna again, then she followed Auntie Em.

I watched them go, then sighed. This Shushanna deal was making me more nervous with every passing hour. It might have been a good thing for me if Brownie had won the dispute. Unfortunately, without knowing exactly what a Shushanna was I couldn't really argue the point.

With a shrug, I went and picked up my knapsack. Ghost and Poe were waiting patiently, and I still had a job to do. I turned to face the mountains. Which way to go? Northwest; but I'd barely taken a step in that direction when Poe stopped me and pointed northeast.

Good thing I wasn't picky. With a shrug to resettle my knapsack, I headed northeast, skirting the edge of the cliffs. Poe stayed right by my side and Ghost brought up the rear. And of course, we were escorted by the usual contingent of dragon birds. They flitted from tree to tree, pausing occasionally at a flower, and then chittering in annoyance when they had to hurry to catch up.

Gradually, the sheer face of the cliff gave way to sloping inclines strewn with boulders and rubble as we left the jungle. I wasn't an expert at geology, but I'd had some training, and something struck me as decidedly odd about the terrain.

Pausing halfway up a steep hill, I turned in a complete circle, this time really looking at the surrounding area.

That's when it hit me.

There was no plant growth on the slopes.

Oh, there were patches of straggly grass here and there, but no trees. It looked like someone had drawn a line of demarcation, and everything on this side had been chopped off. The trees marched in a straight-edged, unnaturally even border for as far as I could see.

Stooping, I carefully examined the ground. Most of the rocks showed evidence of great heat, some to the point of having been melted.

"Interesting, isn't it?"

The sound of a voice speaking Galactic Standard sent the dragon birds still with us diving for cover and had me spinning around to stare at the woman leaning casually against a boulder. Quilla Dorn.

Ghost and Poe must have spotted her the instant she came into view. They were standing protectively between us, watching her warily.

She continued as though it were the most natural thing in the world for her to be there. "I noticed it the first time I came up here. My theory is that in the not-so-distant past, a meteor mowed a path across the edge of the jungle. Since no impact crater showed up on the initial scans, it would have come in at a very low angle from that direction." Pushing away from the boulder, she tilted her head toward the east. "It probably stayed just above the surface until it buried itself in the side of that mountain." She gestured in the general direction of the cliffs above the Buri settlement.

"There's an eighty percent probability that her theory is correct," Max whispered in my ear.

Which raised some interesting possibilities. Could this be what had wiped out most of the Buri? It was something to think about. Later. Right now I had more pressing questions that needed answering.

"What are you doing out here, Quilla?"

"Waiting for you." She stepped over a pile of rubble and made her way down to my level, ignoring the Buri. "Jon mentioned you were going to do some mining today, so I thought I'd offer my services as a guide. I've got a six-month head start on exploring these mountains, so I know them quite well."

Translation: There were places they didn't want me nosing around, and she was here to make sure I wouldn't stumble across them. Well, I could learn a lot from where she *didn't* steer me.

"Works for me." I adjusted the weight of the knapsack. "But out of curiosity, how did you know I'd be heading this way?"

Her gaze shifted to the Buri, and she smiled. "It's the only way they'd let you go. I've made several attempts to go farther to the northwest, and no matter how I approach, they always stop me."

That caught my attention, since she was right. "Max, do you see anything to the northwest of the village that the Buri might want to protect?" I spoke aloud this time so Dorn would understand that I was in constant contact with my ship, and any funny business on her part would be noted.

"Not really. There's nothing but a few fields and more mountains."

"He says only fields. Maybe they don't want anyone trampling their crops." And maybe I had an even better idea of what they were hiding that I wasn't going to share with Dorn. After all, those extra Buri had to come from somewhere, and there were plenty of caves in that direction.

"Possibly."

"Well, lead on." I raised a hand to indicate she should go first.

She glanced over her shoulder as she started up the hill. "What are you looking for?"

"Random samples of ore and minerals." My shields were all the way down, and the only thing I picked up from her was a mild curiosity. If there was something she wanted desperately to keep me away from, she was doing a great job of hiding it.

"There's a warren of caves about a mile to the north of here." She moved without effort in spite of the increasing rise of the hill. "Or, if you'd prefer, we can go due east. There are some interesting canyons in that direction."

Okay, the woman was obviously smarter than I'd given her credit for. By leaving the choice to me, she had effectively shut off any information I might have gleaned from where she led me. "The caves will be fine."

"This way."

I spent the walk watching Dorn as we made idle chitchat. There was something about her that bothered me, a niggling at the back of my mind. But I couldn't figure out what it was.

Poe wasn't helping my concentration. He stayed so close to me that our arms brushed with every step I took. Even in the places where the path was so steep and narrow that we had to go single file, he never let more than two inches separate us.

Ghost was almost as bad. He didn't crowd me, but he made sure he was always between Dorn and me. By the time we reached the caves, both his face and Poe's were filmed with sweat and their breath came in short puffs.

We'd climbed steadily the whole way, so our elevation was well above sea level, and it showed. The canyon, its walls riddled with dark fissures, was a rocky place, the ground dry. A few scraggly trees clung to its walls, their foliage limp in the arid heat.

A scurrying sound caught my attention, and I glanced at a pile of rocks in time to see a neon-red reptile dart into the shade, change colors, and vanish into a hole.

"They're harmless," Dorn said. "And almost as plentiful up here as those odd little birds are in the jungle. Have you noticed that most of the life on this planet seems to be reptilian?" Her gaze shifted to Ghost. "Except the Buri and those grazers out on the plains."

I thought about the feline Crigo had shown an interest in. "Not all of it. I've seen other mammals, too." Of course, I hadn't examined the creature, so I couldn't be positive it wasn't a hairy reptile. Wouldn't it put Crigo's nose out of joint to discover he'd been mating with a lizard? I caught my snort of laughter at the last second.

Either way, I wasn't going to share my theory about the

Buri being descendants of an Ashwani colonization effort. If it were true, Chapter Twenty of the Equality Edict would be null and void. When it came to the colonization of a planet with no sentient species in residence, it was finder's keepers, and the Buri had been here first.

"But not in the same proportion that you do on other planets," she said.

"Maybe not. I'm sure the scientists will work it all out." I selected an opening partway up the canyon and headed toward it, Dorn following.

"Yes, our scientists are chomping at the bit to get started."

"Assuming Dynatec's claim is valid." I dropped my knapsack in the cave entrance, knelt and pushed the flap aside.

"Of course." She chose a boulder to the left of the entry and sat down, watching as I took out my equipment. "Can I ask you a question?"

Stepping just inside the opening, I made a few quick cuts in the cave wall with the laser drill, and deposited the results in specimen containers. "You can ask, but I can't promise to answer."

"What was it like growing up in a government crèche?"

Surprised, I took a second to label the containers before I responded. "I really don't have anything to compare it with. They didn't beat us or starve us, if that's what you mean."

"But were they kind to you?"

"Kind?" What a strange conversation, one I'd never experienced before. Government crèches were so regulated it was a miracle they worked at all. But they did, and most Naturals had at least some knowledge of their operation. "I suppose it depends on your definition of *kind*. They employ the best psychologists in the world, and they kept us busy developing our bodies and our minds. We didn't have time to be unhappy. Why do you ask?"

"Curiosity. I was raised by my father, you know, and he was overly protective of me. I saw a documentary on the crèches once when I was young. In a way, I envied your freedom from parental influence. It looked as though you had the best of all worlds."

"It had its drawbacks." I shrugged. "Is anyone ever really one hundred percent happy with the way they grew up?"

"If they are, I haven't met them." She smiled. "Don't you think it's a bit hypocritical for the government to sanction their own creation of GEPs but ban cloning?"

I arched a brow at the comment and paused to put another sample of stone in the container I was holding. "Totally different proposition. With GEPs, you aren't making a copy of another person, you're making an entirely new being, so it's less of an ethical dilemma. Besides, there wasn't much choice. After the plague wiped out the population of Old Earth ninety cycles into the space colonization program, manpower on Alpha Centauri reached a critical shortage. With no replacements available from Earth, specialized workers were needed to fill jobs that were crucial for continued prosperity. And since GEPs mature faster than Naturals, and can be made resistant to the ailments Naturals suffer, it was cost effective for the government to set up the program."

"Of course." She nodded and rose to her feet. Immediately, Ghost and Poe moved between us again. "I seem to be making your escorts nervous. Now that you know where the caves are, I'll be heading back to our camp."

I nodded. "Thanks for the help."

"Anytime."

The two Buri kept a close eye on the direction she'd gone, and didn't relax until fifteen or twenty minutes had elapsed. I used the time to continue gathering samples from the other caves. One in particular interested me, since large traces of quartz showed in the rock.

But I couldn't get Dorn out of my mind. What was she up to? It had to be something. Putting away the last of the samples, I stepped out of the cave. "Max, have we heard anything from the boss about Quilla Dorn?"

"Not yet, Kiera."

"Contact him and see if he can light a fire under his operatives. I want everything they can find on her, up to and including the color she paints her toenails. There's something about her that gives me chills."

"Did you pick up anything unusual from her?"

I lifted the knapsack to my shoulder. "No, and that's one of the things bothering me. I didn't pick up anything except a stray wisp of curiosity. It's like she feels nothing at all."

"Dr. Daniels always tells you to trust your instincts."

"Oh, I trust them. I only wish I knew what they were trying to show me. I've met people I didn't like, but this is different. She's different. It's . . ." I hesitated.

"What?"

My hands lifted helplessly. "Unnatural. She feels unnatural. I don't know how else to put it."

A second of silence passed before Max responded. "I'll contact Dr. Daniels."

"Good." I glanced at the sheared-off jungle as we descended. "Any idea when that meteor might have come through here?"

"From the new growth, I estimate it happened ten to twenty cycles ago. Long enough that there's no sign of burning left, but not long enough for the trees to reforest the area."

"And if a Buri village were in its path, there wouldn't be much left of it. That could be what happened to the Buri's families, Max."

"It's possible, but not probable. Unless the meteor landed on top of them, there would still be some signs of the buildings, even if only a few ruins. Stone and adobe, both of which the Buri are proficient in using, don't burn easily."

"Maybe it did land on them." I was reaching for straws, and we both knew it. "Okay, forget it for now. I'll drop these samples off for you to analyze before I head back to the village."

"Speaking of the village . . ."

"Yes?"

"There is a ninety percent probability that they are preparing for a celebration of some type."

Since I'd reached the same conclusion earlier, I smiled as the Buri and I reached the edge of the jungle. The dragon birds met us, scolding loudly because they'd been left behind. "What led you to this supposition?"

"The level of activity for one thing, It's increased dramatically. As has the amount of food being brought to the village. Several Buri have been fishing in the nearby lake most of the day."

"Are they catching anything?"

"Yes, a fishy-looking creature with legs and big eyes."

I made a mental note not to try any of those. "Where's Crigo? He's not getting in their way, is he?"

"On the contrary. He helped a group of hunters bring down two of the herdbeasts. They seem very pleased with him."

"Well, there's a first time for everything." I glanced at Ghost and Poe. My conversation with Max had been on a subvocal level again, but somehow, the Buri always knew. Ghost was used to it and paid no attention. Poe continued to give me wary looks from the corners of his eyes.

I shot him my biggest grin. "Gentlemen, let's drop off these samples and go party. But I'm warning you now, I don't know how to waltz."

CHAPTER 10

To my disappointment, the fun and games didn't start that night. Instead, the Buri decided to torture me. Since I'd slept through breakfast, and only had a few cups of the red stuff for lunch, my stomach was eagerly looking forward to the evening feast. What I got was a bowl of weak broth and a tiny glass of something fruity. Neither my attempts at looking pitiful nor the loud rumbling of my stomach garnered me more victuals. My only consolation was that Thor and Junior were in the same predicament.

The three of us sat sequestered at one end of a table, guarded by Elder and Auntie Em, and watched the rest of the tribe nibble at an unusually light meal. But at least they got meat and bread, and my stomach growled ominously at the scent drifting from the other end of the table. Thank the Goddess I had my stash of supplies back at my quarters. I'd just wait until the village was asleep and then sneak a few snacks to hold me over.

Resigned to a few more hours of starvation, I glanced at Thor. He sat to my right, the heat from his big body warming my side. Junior was to Thor's right, and Elder was next to Junior. Auntie Em sat to my left, watching every move I made, and I had the distinct impression she was waiting for me to commit a faux pas so she'd have an excuse to pounce. Only it turned out to be Thor who drew her wrath.

He'd finished off his broth in two swallows, and then occupied himself by chatting with Elder and Junior. But when I glanced at him, he turned to look down at me, and our gazes locked. A wave of dizziness washed over me, and the buzzing in my head increased to a roar. I was barely aware of Thor's hand lifting, sliding under my braid to cup my nape. When my stomach clenched, it had nothing to do with hunger.

My lips were trying to issue an invitation to go for a stroll in the jungle when Auntie Em brought the proceedings to a crashing halt. She did it by the simple expedient of reaching around me and whacking Thor upside his head. Then she delivered a tirade that had Junior and Elder grinning, and Thor scowling. After that he avoided direct eye contact with me as though his life depended on it. And from the glares Auntie Em was giving him, maybe it did.

Damn.

Was I really as desperate to jump Thor as I felt? Oh, yeah. And for some odd reason, either lack of food or something in the juice we were drinking seemed to amplify our mental connection. I could feel his desire like a tangible thing, and it increased my own. Between us, out of Auntie Em's sight, our hands touched and I broke out in a light sheen of sweat.

I was in the process of frantically devising plans that would get me alone with Thor at the soonest possible moment when Auntie Em stood and pulled me up with her. Thor hastily let go of my hand. The other Buri took her movement as a signal. All conversation stopped, and everyone rose to their feet. The females slowly gathered around me and Auntie Em while the males joined Thor, Junior and Elder.

All the males except Brownie. I hadn't noticed his absence until he suddenly appeared in the doorway, a spear held menacingly in his hands, his bulk blocking the exit. The determination he'd felt this morning had doubled and was now flavored with desperation.

Around me the Buri froze into immobile statues, a feeling of dismay rising from the group as they stared intently at Brownie.

Slowly he straightened, his chin rising in a gesture of defiance. Before I had time to blink, he drew his arm back and let the spear fly. It landed in the floor at Thor's feet, the deadly point buried in wood, the shaft quivering from the force of the throw. Sounding very formal, Brownie uttered a short phrase.

Thor answered in the same tone and added a regal nod to the mix. He hadn't flinched or even blinked as the spear landed inches from his buckskin-clad toes. As soon as he finished speaking, Brownie turned and left the building, the other Buri rushing to follow, taking me along in their wake.

I had a horrible feeling that something violent was about to occur.

As soon as we reached the clearing in the center of the buildings, the Buri formed a loose circle with Thor and Brownie in the middle. Pushing my way to the front, I chewed my lip in worry, wishing I could do something to stop the battle that was coming, knowing I couldn't. The tension between Thor and Brownie had obviously been brewing for a while now. Even if I did interfere, it would only delay the inevitable. "Max, record," I told the ship.

"Recording."

The late-evening sun sent a shaft of brilliance to spark off the gold bracelets both males wore as silence descended, broken only by the inquisitive *cheep* of a dragon bird. But even that was cut off abruptly as they began to close the distance between them.

Unconsciously, my muscles tensed in sympathetic readiness, and my breath caught in my lungs.

With minimal warning, Brownie rushed Thor, jamming his shoulder into Thor's chest and driving him back several steps before he caught his balance.

The clench continued for an agonizing second before Thor threw him off. Then, with blinding speed, he retaliated. In a blur of motion, Thor hit Brownie, lifted him from his feet and slammed him to the ground. Before Brownie could move, Thor was on top of him, pinning him to the clearing floor.

A grunt of approval came from beside me, and I cut my eyes sideways to see Poe watching the action, a feeling of vindication coming from him. For that matter, all of the Buri around me were feeling the same thing.

They wanted Thor to best Brownie once and for all.

The waves of emotion radiating from the group suddenly made me realize this wasn't merely about Brownie objecting to Thor's acceptance of my presence. This had been a long time coming, and it was more than just a personal quarrel. Brownie was challenging Thor for leadership of the Buri.

I turned back to the action, heart in my throat, just in time to see Brownie's torso heave and toss Thor to the side. There was no doubt in my mind what would happen if Brownie won. I'd be banished from the tribe, which would result in failing to save the Buri from both Dynatec and their low birthrate.

As though sensing my turmoil, Poe reached over and patted my shoulder. His faith in Thor was absolute, and reinforced my own. Of course Thor would win, I thought, just as Brownie got him in a headlock and fell backward, taking Thor with him. And if by some quirk of fate Thor was badly hurt, I'd kill Brownie myself. I wasn't done with the big guy yet and didn't appreciate the idea that he might be put out of commission for the fun and games I was plotting.

Frowning, I watched the muscles bulge in Thor's arms as he pried Brownie loose. They weren't using fists, I realized, as the two males rolled on the ground. Squeaks erupted from the few females on the other side of the circle when their feet were almost swept from under them by the furiously rolling bodies.

The wrestling match seemed to go on forever, with first Thor on top, then Brownie, and my admiration for the Buri, especially Thor, increased with every passing minute. Their strength was awesome and their beauty without match. And their stamina was nothing to sneeze at, either. Natural human males would have collapsed in exhaustion by now.

Abruptly, Thor surged to his feet. Brownie rose in front of him and I could see the desperation in his eyes. He was losing the challenge and he knew it. He hadn't come close to pinning Thor.

Not good. Desperation made you reckless, made you take stupid risks.

Accompanied by gasps from the horrified tribe, Brownie clenched his fist and swung at Thor's jaw. But Thor wasn't there. In a blur of speed that took me by surprise, Brownie was suddenly flat on the ground with Thor holding his shoulders down. The big guy murmured something, and Brownie nodded, his eyes closed in defeat.

While the tribe cheered, Thor stood and held his hand out to Brownie, pulling him erect when the other Buri accepted the gesture. For a minute longer, Thor held on to him, talking to Brownie in a low intent voice. A feeling of resignation settled over him, and he finally acknowledged whatever Thor was telling him, but I knew he still didn't like it. When they were finished, Thor thumped him on the shoulder in a friendly gesture and then turned to the others and gave a short command.

Every womanly instinct I had was screaming at me to go check Thor for injuries even through I could see he was fine, but the females immediately moved to surround me as the males clustered around Thor. With the division of the sexes once again established, my entourage exited the clearing, taking me with them as I cast longing glances over my shoulder at Thor. Not only was he sexy and gorgeous, he was honorable, and my traitorous heart went pitter-patter just looking at him.

But whatever was happening to me was happening to him, too. The much larger contingent of males escorted him from the clearing in a different direction from where the females were ushering me. Not until he was out of sight did I finally start paying attention to my surroundings and my still empty tummy.

In the last rays of the setting sun, the women led me north, into the jungle. More than a few of them carried bundles, and Auntie Em carried a sheaf of torches. Okay, looked like we were going someplace dark.

We walked for almost an hour, paralleling the cliff face. By the time we reached an opening in the solid wall, night was upon us.

"Max, mark this location. There's a cave, and I might want to come back later."

"Yes, Kiera." He sounded distant, as though most of his attention was focused elsewhere.

"Something wrong?"

"A minor problem. One of my satellites on the far side of the planet is experiencing a technical glitch. I'm afraid a sensor is going out."

"Can you fix it?" I watched Auntie Em light a torch from a small fire that burned near the opening of the cave and then distribute more torches to the others.

"I'm trying, but I'm not sure yet. The images it's sending are flickering in and out. I may need to replace it."

Max's satellites were his eyes. If any of them went out, it left him with a blind spot, something that made us both very nervous.

"Okay. We're going into the cave now. If we get very far from the entrance, you and I won't be able to communicate, but I'll give you a report when I get out."

I wasn't thrilled about taking a stroll through a cave when time was running out. There were only six weeks left to learn about the Buri culture and figure out why they weren't reproducing, so this seemed like a waste of valuable time. On the other hand, you never know what small thing might be the turning point for completing the mission before the two months were up, so I'd go along with the side trip.

Before I could follow Auntie Em inside, Lurran shoved a torch in my hand and gestured to the fire. "If I'd known we were going spelunking, I would have brought my prism torch," I told her. "It gives off a lot more light than these things."

She merely shooed me inside as though I hadn't spoken. Come to think about it, none of the females were indulging in their usual chatter. There was an air of solemnity about them that made me sit up and take notice. Whatever we were doing was very important to the Buri. Could this be the cave others of the race were hiding in? Was I going to meet them? Or would I have to jump through a few more hoops first?

The group paused in the entrance, waiting until all the females held lit torches, then Auntie Em headed deeper into the cave. With Churka on one side and Lurran on the other, I tagged along, observing how the wavering fires created moving shadows on the rough walls. A natural cave, then, as opposed to man-made.

We traveled approximately one hundred yards before the

tunnel branched. Taking the left-hand passage, my group continued onward. At the next branch, we went right and I observed a subtle alteration in the atmosphere.

All my experience with caves to the contrary, the deeper we went, the warmer it got. The rise in temperature wasn't uncomfortable, but it was noticeable. At the same time, the humidity increased and the air took on a slightly astringent quality that stung my nose. Five more steps and my skin began to tingle as though I'd stepped into a field of static electricity. When I glanced down, the fine hair on my arms was standing erect.

Okay, this was just not a good example of hidden living quarters for a bunch of Buri. That hair-on-end thing would get annoying really fast. I couldn't picture having to put up with it for ten or more cycles.

I'd barely registered this phenomenon when Auntie Em stopped and placed her torch in a bracket mounted on the cavern wall. The flames lit a fissure just big enough to allow one person at a time to pass through, and even then it would be a tight fit.

Before I could move, she took my arm and tugged me to her side, then gestured to the other females. Churka went first, picking her way delicately through the opening. Midway, she began an atonal chant that sent chills racing down my spine.

One by one, the others followed her, each repeating her actions, until only Auntie Em and I were left in the tunnel. When the last female had cleared the opening, Auntie Em pushed me forward. Tentatively, holding my torch high, I walked into the fissure, sending up a small request to the Goddess that they wouldn't expect me to sing. The sad truth is that the geneticist who spliced and diced me hadn't considered a pleasant singing voice necessary to my job qualifications. As a result, I couldn't carry a tune in a stasis box.

Sure enough, halfway through Auntie Em poked me in the back. With a wince, I sorted desperately through my mental archives and came up with something that might work. "Ohm," I intoned. It seemed to satisfy her, because she stopped poking me.

I kept it up until I reached the end of the fissure, ducking to clear the shorter exit. My lips rounded to emit another hum as I straightened, but the sound never made it out. Instead I plowed to a halt, my jaw dropping.

Holy shit! What I'd entered was the biggest freaking geode in the universe. Or at least the biggest I'd ever heard of. My stunned gaze ran up the walls to the domed top, eyes blinking as the light from the torches reflected from millions of crystals in every shape and color known to man. It was like being inside a rainbow.

Good grief. I could have saved myself a long walk and Quilla Dorn's dubious company if I'd known about this place earlier. My eyes narrowed. The subtle electrical influence I'd felt in the tunnel was stronger here, and I'd swear it was coming from the crystals.

A surge of excitement slammed into me, nearly lifted me off my feet. Had I finally discovered what Dynatec was after? I'd be willing to take bets on it. Now I needed a sample for Max to analyze. I was pretty damn sure I knew what those crystals were, but I needed proof.

I was still gawking when Auntie Em urged me forward, and I saw that the other females had formed a loose circle around a pool in the middle of the geode. The astringent smell I'd noticed was emanating from the water, so strong now that it made my eyes tear up.

After taking my torch and placing in a wall bracket near the entry, she led me to the head of the circle. At some unseen signal, all the females removed their kechics, placed them on the cavern floor, and then sat down on them. Hastily, I followed suit, covertly studying the Buri's anatomy. It was the first time I'd seen any of them naked, and I'm happy to report there were no surprises in that area. It boded well for a male Buri-human female relationship when the female equipment in question appeared identical to that of the indigenous population.

Curiosity satisfied, I slapped down my hormones and checked to see what we were doing next. Not much, apparently. The others were sitting still, eyes closed, chanting away. As insurance against being poked again, I shut my eyes and let out another "Ohm" while my thoughts drifted.

I really wished there was a way Max could record this event. Our social anthropologists would go into raptures of delight over a ceremony like this one. Did it have religious overtones? I thought it did, even suspected it was some kind of purification ritual to prepare us for a rite that would take place tomorrow.

But why was I being singled out, along with Thor and Junior, for special treatment? Because I was a guest? I mulled that over for a second. Maybe this was my official adoption into the tribe, I decided happily. It would certainly explain why Brownie challenged Thor's leadership when he did. Yeah, that had to be it. The fight was a last-ditch attempt to stop Thor from bringing me into the tribe and making me Shushanna. Nothing else made sense.

Having solved that dilemma to my own satisfaction, my mind shifted to more mundane concerns, like my empty stomach. More time passed, and gradually my breathing evened out, my heart beating in rhythm with the chanting. A strange lassitude stole over me, held me in its grip, and on some level I was aware of power being amplified, gathered and focused.

And aimed at me.

Alarmed, I struggled uselessly, unable to so much as twitch a finger.

Peace.

The voice, oddly like Auntie Em's, whispered in my head, so calm and serene that I immediately relaxed. There was nothing here to be afraid of. I had probably fallen asleep and was dreaming the entire thing anyway. Even when the voice came again, I accepted it without a single qualm.

Bless this female. Purify and consecrate her to your purpose. Open the pathways that she might meet her destiny.

Okay, things were getting a little out of hand here. With a supreme effort of will, I grabbed what consciousness I had left and forced my eyes open, watching Auntie Em suspiciously from beneath my lashes. As far as I could tell, she hadn't moved. Neither had the other females. The chanting continued in the same, low monotonous thread, and no one paid undue attention to me.

Slowly, I faced forward again and let my eyes close once more. And that's the last thing I remember until Churka and Lurran led me out of the water.

My head felt funny. Kind of fuzzy, as though I'd slept too long and too hard. And there was a dull ache that made me wince when Lurran ran a comb through my hair and efficiently rebraided it. When had it been loosened? My head hurt too much to figure it out.

We were still inside the geode, but everyone was talking and laughing now, happily dressing in the fancy, colorful kechics I'd seen the two new women weaving. Something silky moved against my skin, and I looked down in time to see Churka settle a kechic belt low around my hips. It was the red one. The one that looked like living flame.

Instead of the usual wooden clasp, this one was gold. It matched the armlets that already encircled my upper arm.

And the skirt, once in place and adjusted to Churka's satisfaction, went all the way to my ankles, leaving the sides of both legs and my hips bare.

When she and Lurran were finished with me, they stepped back and silence fell over the gathering as the women turned in my direction. In unison, they bowed, and I couldn't even muster up enough curiosity to wonder why. Slowly, with a great deal of effort, I dipped my head in return. The movement made the walls spin lazily, and I must have swayed, because Lurran and Churka each took an arm to steady me.

I was only minimally aware of being led from the geode and through the tunnels, all my concentration focused on putting one foot in front of the other. It was as if I were moving through sludge, like time had slowed to a crawl.

Only when we neared the entrance did I gradually become more responsive, and I credit that more to concern over Crigo than myself. His low, anxious growls echoed off the cavern walls in a steady rumble, and I pulled away from my escorts and stepped outside.

The sun was so bright it hurt my eyes, and I blinked for a second, then looked around. The foliage in front of the cave had been trampled flat from Crigo's pacing. He must have been there all night from the looks of things.

When he saw me, his growl changed to a roar and he bounded toward me. Then came to an abrupt halt a foot away, his nose wrinkled to the point where his fangs were visible. Gingerly, almost as if he weren't sure it was me, he extended his neck and sniffed. And then he did the strangest thing.

He rubbed up against my legs, a loud purr erupting from his chest.

Hesitantly, I dropped my hand to his head, ready to snatch it back if he objected, but the purr only got deeper.

"Kiera?"

Max. My forehead wrinkled. Wasn't there something I wanted to tell him? Something vitally important? Whatever it was, I'd forgotten. Oh, well. It would come to me sooner or later.

"Kiera, are you okay? You've been in that cave all night and half the day. It's after noon."

"I'm fine, Max." I smiled serenely as I stroked Crigo's warm fur.

"What happened in there?"

"I think I slept most of the time. And then they gave me a bath." The other females were out of the cave now, and we headed toward the village. Every time my hand moved away from Crigo's head, he'd nudge it back into place.

"You *think*?" Max's alarmed tone washed over me without ruffling my calm. For the first time in my life, I literally felt it when he used one of his satellites to scan me. Satellites. Something about a satellite . . .

"How's your satellite?" I asked him.

"It's operational again. Kiera, you aren't fine. There's something odd about your brain's electrical activity. You need to come back immediately and let me do a full neural workup."

"I've just got a small headache. That's probably what you're picking up. Honest, it's nothing to get excited about."

"You never get headaches."

I thought that over. "I think maybe it has to do with those crystals."

"Crystals?"

Oh, yeah. That was it. The crystals. "You should have seen them, Max. They're so beautiful. Did you by any chance check the planet for surge crystals during your original scans?"

"No, of course not. Surge crystals are only found on one

planetary system in the universe. Scientists believe the planets were formed during the collision of the system's double suns—" His words broke off suddenly, and I knew he had made the connection. If two galaxies collided, it was almost certain that stars within those galaxies did the same.

"Scanning."

We were almost at the village when he spoke again, a touch of disgust in his voice. "Orpheus Two is riddled with quartz. It's everywhere. But I'm detecting nothing different about it other than the fact it's coesite quartz. It certainly is not surge crystals."

"I'm not sure any mechanical test could pick up the difference, Max. The crystals aren't emitting on the same frequency that normal surge crystals do. As a matter of fact, I'm fairly sure they're emitting on a frequency that only an organic brain would pick up. That's probably the reason you haven't noticed anything odd about them before."

The effort of thinking coherently was more than I could manage, except in short bursts. With a sigh, I stopped trying. "Colors," I told him dreamily. "They're all different colors, Max, not just clear, like the usual surge crystals. And so beautiful. They were all around us, singing to me."

"Singing?" He sounded alarmed again. "Kiera, I order you back right now. We have no way of knowing what effect those crystals had on you."

But I'd spotted Thor and Elder waiting at the edge of the village, and my full attention shifted to them. "Later, Max. I have other things to do now."

Thor's gaze locked on me and I could feel a mixture of anticipation and urgency when we reached him. He spoke to Auntie Em, his words echoing in my head in a way they'd never done before. I could almost understand what he was saying, as though it were garbled Galactic Standard, spoken from the other side of a thick wall.

When Auntie Em answered him, her words, too, echoed in my mind, and she radiated smug satisfaction. Thor immediately relaxed, his lips curving into a smile. Without looking away, he reached for my hand.

Which is why I saw him flinch away at the exact same moment that a shaft of pain jolted up my arm from his touch. Keeping his distance, he questioned Auntie Em again. Apparently, whatever she said satisfied him, because he nodded and then turned toward the center of the village. A village that had been transformed into a fantasy wonderland overnight.

Flowers of every shape and color decorated the buildings, hung from trees, lay draped over rocks, and wound around platters and bowls heaping with food on makeshift tables that sat in the clearing. Their perfume filled the warm air until I walked through an ocean of aroma, inhaling with pleasure. I could almost feel the fragrance against my skin as the other females dispersed to join the males.

The only discordant note was the dark blue of a spacers jumpsuit, and I lifted my gaze to see Claudia Karle coming toward me, Ghost at her side.

"When you asked me to meet you today, I didn't know there was going to be a party." She stopped and swept me with a wide-eyed look of amazement. "Dang, woman. All you need is a spear and you'd look like Ziffa, Warrior Queen of the Jungle. It suits you, though. Gives you this weird glow." She squinted and peered closer. "Wow, you really *are* glowing. Are you okay?"

"I'm fine," I assured her with a smile. "I hope you didn't have any trouble with the Buri when you arrived." What had I wanted to talk to her about? I couldn't remember.

"Not a bit. I think this one recognized me." She jerked a thumb at Ghost. "He's not letting me out of his sight."

"You're more than welcome to join us. Would you like to borrow a kechic?" I asked politely.

"Kechic?"

Coming from her, it sounded more like a sneeze than a word. I ran a hand over my skirt. "One of these."

"And run around the jungle half naked? I don't think so, but thanks anyway. So what's going on here today?"

"I think it's some kind of religious ceremony." Auntie Em tugged on my arm, and as I drifted in the direction of a table, I spoke over my shoulder. "Just stay with Ghost. He'll take care of you."

Her presence faded from my awareness like fog in hot sunshine as I took my place at the head of a table. Thor sat across from me at the opposite end, and there was a brief scramble as the other Buri found their seats. When everyone was settled, Elder stood from his position beside Junior at the center right of the table and spoke for a few minutes, all the Buri listening intently. As he finished and sat down, a spontaneous cheer erupted, and I caught many surreptitious grins aimed in my direction.

I sat quietly while the others dived into the food spread before them. There was a hollow ache of emptiness in my middle, but the aroma coming from the food made me slightly nauseous. Neither Thor nor Junior had touched the food either, I noticed.

My fingers curled into Crigo's fur as I waited, the rise and fall of his purr keeping time with his breathing, the rhythmic quality of the sound making me drowsy. My gaze wandered to the new stone building, drawn by an irresistible urge. There was an odd glimmer near the back that rippled and wavered as I watched. It fascinated me, called to me in a way I'd never experienced before.

My attention was yanked back to the Buri when several of the males broke out instruments and began to play an eerily pitched, wavering melody. I was mildly startled to realize enough time had passed for the tribe to finish eating.

At the first note, the majority of females rose, moved away from the tables, and formed a circle facing outward. An equal number of males joined them, making a larger circle outside the first. I felt Thor's gaze on me, and when I glanced at him, he tilted his head toward the dancers. With a return nod, I stood.

Churka smiled as I approached, then squeezed over to make room for me. Junior was across from her in the outer circle, a slightly dazed expression on his face. When I took my place and turned, it came as no surprise to find Thor waiting for me.

Luckily for me, the dance was a slow stately affair. A good two foot of space separated the inner female circle from the outer males. Arms remained at the sides, bodies straight and eyes downcast. Only the feet and legs moved, and mine fell into the rhythm as if they had a mind of their own. I don't know who was leading, but my movements and Thor's mirrored each other exactly.

I was vaguely aware of people leaving the circles periodically, to be replaced by others. At one point, Claudia Karle danced beside me, radiating waves of self-consciousness at Ghost, who partnered her. There was no impression of hours slipping away, no sensation of tiredness, but I could feel Max scanning me every few minutes with what I can only describe as anxiety.

When the music trailed off with a few discordant notes, I stumbled, caught myself, and then checked to see what everyone was looking at. Elder and Auntie Em stood solemnly in front of the pool, the last rays of the sun creating long shadows that stretched eastward. He held a cloth-covered tray bearing several objects I couldn't make out, she held another tray on which three cups rested.

The Buri silently gathered around them in a half circle, taking me with them. When everyone in the village was accounted for, Elder motioned Junior forward. He went nervously, and stood, shifting his weight from one foot to another, in front of them.

Elder eyed him for a second, then barked a command. Instantly, Junior snapped to attention, head up, back rigid. The older Buri nodded in satisfaction. With a smile, Auntie Em lifted a cup from her tray and handed it to Junior. Holding it in both hands, he tilted it to his lips and drank deeply, not stopping until the cup was empty. He blinked twice, swayed, and then pulled himself together enough to resume his stance.

Auntie Em retrieved the cup from his grasp and put it back on the tray while Elder stepped forward. He lifted an object from the white cloth and handed the tray to another Buri, who was positioned near his elbow. After a few words, the older Buri reached up, grasped Junior's right earlobe, and punctured it twice. Junior didn't so much as flinch when the needle pierced his flesh, but when the two black-stoned earrings were pushed through the holes, his eyes closed and his knees buckled.

Apparently, his reaction was expected. Brownie and Dusty caught him before he hit the ground, and half carried, half dragged him into one of the huts. A few minutes later, Dusty returned alone and took up his former position.

Somehow, I knew it was my turn. Without waiting for Auntie Em to beckon, I moved forward. Thor stayed at my side, waves of pride and excitement pouring from him. My skin felt hypersensitive, the silky softness of the kechic almost painfully abrasive as it swung around my legs.

Auntie Em, looking pleased at my initiative, handed me one of the remaining cups and gave the other to Thor. We shifted to face each other, and I slowly lifted the cup. The fruity aroma that assailed my nose was familiar, and I recognized it as the concoction that Auntie Em and Churka had made from the roots.

"Kiera! Wait!" Max's voice had overtones of panic. "The liquid has unknown properties. We don't know how it will affect you. Don't drink it."

"I have to," I told him with a certainty that sent a tingle of surprise through me. "It will cure my headache."

He was still protesting when the rim touched my lips. As Junior had done, I drained the cup, lowering it at the same instant Thor lowered his. The liquid had a smooth, musky taste, not at all unpleasant. It slid down my throat and pooled in my empty stomach to generate a warm glow.

Max had fallen silent, but he was scanning me continuously as I waited for something else to happen. It didn't take long.

Abruptly, the warm glow inside me exploded, heat lightning streaking along my nerves to encompass every molecule of my body. Behind my unconsciously closed eyelids, fireworks erupted, and I swayed before forcing myself still again.

Someone called out my name, and I opened my eyes. Thor's image wavered in front of me, obscured by the detonation of lights occurring in my head, lights that were reaching, seeking.

There was a movement to my left, and a small stinging sensation in my earlobe. But instead of taking an earring from his tray, Elder moved to Thor's side and removed one of his.

Understanding how quickly I healed, the older Buri hurried back to my side and thrust the earring through my lobe.

And the lights finally found what they were searching for.

Images spun through my mind, too rapidly for me to grasp as the light coalesced around the black stone, shot across the space that separated me from Thor, and bound us together with a vibrant black cord of radiance.

With the last of my consciousness, I felt two strong arms close around me and lift, cradle me close to a warm muscular chest as one word with very masculine overtones reverberated in my head.

"Mine."

CHAPTER 11

I came to as I was being lowered onto a sleeping platform, a feeling of lethargy pervading my senses. Where the hell was I, and what was going on? And why did my ear feel funny?

You wear my rellanti.

Rellanti? An image of the earring with the black stone floated through my mind. Oh, that was right. Elder had pierced my ear.

Something tugged on my kechic, pulled the belt loose, and I forced my heavy eyelids to rise enough that I could see what was happening. There was a vague sense of disorientation when I realized I was inside my adobe hut. And an even greater one when I realized it was Thor removing my kechic.

Now wasn't this just wonderful? He finally decides to make whoopee, and I was too damn tired to move.

Male amusement touched my mind. *It is not required that you move.*

"But I'm trained at this stuff," I told him. "Really, I could make your eyes roll back in your head. Just let me . . ." A frown furrowed my brow as I tried to lift a hand to assist him. My arm felt like it weighted a ton. "Am I drunk? What *was* that stuff Auntie Em gave me?"

It is given to facilitate the forming of the bond.

"Okay." Still frowning, I tried to force my fuzzy brain to function. "Does that mean we aren't going to make love?"

Penetration must be achieved for the completion of the bond.

"So you're going to handle the penetration and I don't have to move?"

Correct.

Huh, so I could relax and enjoy. This should be a novel experience. I'm usually the one who does all the work.

Thor's big callused hand skimmed slowly down my body, pulling a purr of delight from deep inside my chest. The sound seemed to spur him on, because suddenly his weight covered me. There was a brief feeling of pressure between my legs, and then nothing.

Kiera.

I snapped awake, heart pounding, mouth dry, and stared around at a lush green paradise. It was my dream again, and I turned, already knowing what I'd see. A black hexagonal building made from crystal, floating just above the ground.

Well, hell. Thor was probably boffing my brains out back in the real world, and I was sleeping through it. But if I had to miss the fun and games, I was damn well going to get inside that building, and this time, nothing would stop me.

Back straight and chin lifted, I moved forward, the hip-high grass brushing my bare skin as I walked, the sweet scent of growing things perfuming the air. Disturbed by my passage, thousands of yellow butterflies rose to flutter around me, their delicate wings tickling my arms and shoulders like fairy's breath. Enthralled by their beauty, I lifted a hand and several lit on my fingers, clinging briefly before rejoining the others to dance along the rays of warm sunlight.

Distracted by their joyful gyrations, I reached the hexagon sooner than expected. It loomed over me, prisms of color sparking from its many facets. An ache of longing filled me, so intense my eyes welled with moisture as I stared at the crystalline surface. It was mine, created just for me, and I wanted it the way I'd never wanted anything before.

What if it vanished again, or I woke up too soon? The thought sent a shaft of fear straight through my middle.

Trembling inside, hands shaking, I reached to touch it. But instead of resting on a cool, solid surface, my hand passed through the crystal as if there were nothing there. Startled, I yanked back, wiggling my fingers to make sure they still worked. Everything seemed to be in order. And this was, after all, just in my head. Nothing here could hurt me.

Taking a deep breath, I stepped up and forward, into the crystal. Immediately, the buzzing in my head rose to a crescendo, a billion wind chimes pealing a rhapsodic welcome. A feeling of such peace settled over me that I staggered my way through the stygian darkness and stumbled out the other side, tears streaking my cheeks. And came to rest in a place that couldn't possibly exist on Orpheus Two, a place I'd never seen before. It was like being caught in a snow globe, a scene of wondrous beauty contained within the confines of the crystal.

Giant, oddly shaped conifers rimed in ice surrounded me. High in the sky hung a huge red sun, its pale rays casting brownish shadows on the snow-covered ground. In the distance rose a magnificent castle, its towers and minarets reaching into the heavens. The chilly breeze that lifted my hair and brushed my bare skin carried the crisp scent of winter, and yet I felt no cold.

"Why do you weep?"

I turned to look at Thor. He was sitting on the ground, one knee drawn up, his back resting against a massive trunk.

Slowly, I shook my head. "I don't know. It's just that I've never . . ." Again, I shook my head. "I'm not sure I *can* explain." I paused. "What is this place?"

His gaze swept the horizon before returning to me. "All that I am."

"It's so beautiful." Another tear made its way down my cheek and I reached up to swipe it away.

"This is why you weep? From the beauty?" His voice was deep and dusky, the gruff overtones giving it a resonance that vibrated deep inside me.

"Partly. But there are other reasons too."

"Come." He held out a hand. "Tell me these reasons so I might understand."

What the heck. It wasn't like I'd be sharing my innermost yearnings with a real person. This was dream Thor. I could safely tell him anything I wanted.

When I took his hand, he pulled me down onto his lap and curled one arm around my waist. I snuggled until the fit was right, and then faced him. The tenderness in his ebony eyes damn near did me in. No one had ever looked at me that way before, and my explanation froze on my lips.

"Tell me." A lock of hair had escaped my braid, and his strong fingers gently brushed it away from my face.

I swallowed hard, and forced myself to speak about what I'd never shared with another living creature. "I've been alone my whole life. There's no other like me, and there never will be again." I looked down, unable to meet his gaze. "I've never belonged before. Until now. Here, in this place, inside the crystal, I feel like I've found something I didn't even know I was searching for. A part of me that was missing. It's as if this place was created just for me, to make me whole."

He was silent for so long that I finally looked up to gauge his reaction. His expression was thoughtful, but not fearful, and I knew he hadn't understood. How could he when I barely understood myself? I had to try again.

"There are two kinds of humans, Thor. Naturals and GEPs. Naturals are people who are born of two parents, a male and a female. GEPs are created in a lab. DNA is taken from any number of Naturals based on their superior talents and intellect, and then it's patched together and improvements are made. The end result is a human that's stronger, faster and smarter than a Natural."

A frown wrinkled his brow. "You are one of these 'made' people?"

"More so than most GEPs." I took a deep breath, gathered my courage, and continued. "There are very strict laws that govern the creation of GEPs. For instance, a GEP can't be created unless they've been commissioned by a government-sanctioned business or institution. That's why I was made. The Bureau of Alien Affairs paid an extremely high price for my creation because they wanted a special agent, one who was an empath. A GEP with psi abilities had never been made before, and the geneticist who fashioned me went a little overboard."

I picked up the end of my braid and toyed with it so I wouldn't have to look at him during this next part. "Instead of taking DNA from Naturals as he should have, Dr. Gertz, the geneticist, illegally took it from other GEPs. And then he manipulated that DNA in ways only the Goddess knows. As a result, the Bureau got more than they bargained for. They got me. A fully functional female with a psi ability, who's faster and stronger than any GEP ever created, with a metabolism capable of healing near fatal wounds in record time.

"The boss was furious when he realized what Gertz had done. He went after him. But Gertz knew he'd been caught, and he killed himself before the boss could arrest him." I shrugged. "Unfortunately, Gertz destroyed all his records, so no one else knows precisely what he did to me. You see, I'm not a Natural, but I'm not exactly a normal GEP either. Neither the boss nor I know what I am, or what I'm capable of."

Thor's hand moved in slow stroking motions on my skin, and when he spoke I heard puzzlement in his voice. "This is bad, to be better?"

"It's not bad to be better, it's bad to be different. And I was . . . am. Even the other GEPs in my crèche sensed it somehow, though I tried very hard to hide it."

"I am different from you. Does this make me bad?"

"No, of course not." I looked up at him earnestly. "You're exactly what nature intended you to be. Strong, beautiful and healthy."

"You are strong and beautiful and healthy," he said. "Does the way it happened matter so very much when the results are the same?"

With a sigh, I leaned against his chest and let my head rest on his shoulder. "You sound like the boss. He keeps telling me that I'm probably what humans will evolve into, given time. But neither of you can grasp how it feels to know that you're the only member of your species, that you'll never look into another face and find traces of yourself there, because no other exists. Or know what it's like to be so alone among thousands of other people and races."

"I know what it is like to be alone." He rested his chin on the top of my head and rubbed it gently back and forth.

"You? You aren't alone. You have your clan, your sibling."

"Yes, but there are ways of being alone even among others. I am their . . ."

The word he spoke was in Buri, and I frowned. That was certainly odd. This was my dream and I didn't speak Buri.

Shouldn't my dream Thor speak only Galactic Standard? I pushed away from him so I could see his face. "You're their what? Leader?"

He seemed to struggle with the word for a moment, then nodded. "Their leader. Each day I make decisions that affect the welfare of my people. They trust me to protect them, to do what is necessary even when they don't like or agree with my decisions. It is my responsibility, and no one can take it from my shoulders. This has held me separate from my people, and so I, too, know what it is to be alone. Until now." He put a finger under my chin and lifted until our eyes met. "Now, neither of us will ever be alone again."

"We won't?" My voice came out in a wistful puff of air, and his lips curved in a smile.

"Never again."

"It sounds so wonderful. I only wish it were real."

His smile faded abruptly. "Why should it not be real?"

"Because this is a dream." I lifted a hand to cup his cheek. "And because I'm not free. The Bureau needs me. I'm the best agent they have, plus they own my indenture. Until it's paid off, I go where they tell me to go, and do what they tell me to do."

He looked horrified, and I rushed to clarify what I'd said. "The Bureau doesn't own *me*, Thor. Not in the sense you're thinking. I have the same rights as any other citizen. But they did invest a lot of money in my creation. I have a moral and legal obligation to repay that debt. But that's not the only reason."

I hesitated, then spoke again. "This is what I was created for. Without my job, I have no purpose, no reason for being."

The concept of a "job" seemed to give him problems for a second, and I studied him in perplexity. If this were a dream, he should know everything I did. Unless my subconscious didn't want him to know for some weird reason. Maybe I should go along with it and see where it led me.

"This 'job' is why you came here?"

"Yes."

"Explain to me your purpose."

I rested against his upraised knee and hooked one arm around his thickly muscled thigh. "The other humans who are here work for a trade company called Dynatec. They want to claim this planet as their own so they can derive material gain from its resources. Our laws allow them to do this if the planet isn't occupied by a sentient species, or if the sentient species in residence is dying out. That last one is what they're claiming about your people. There are only a few of you left, and your birthrate is almost nonexistent. Dynatec believes that in a hundred cycles, none of your people will be left."

"But you do not work for these humans." He had the most inscrutable look on his face I'd ever seen, almost as if he knew something I didn't.

"No, I work for our government. It's my job to protect species from companies like Dynatec, to make sure they aren't taken advantage of. And if a company breaks the law, I see to it they're brought to justice. But that's only part of what I do. The main reason I'm here is to find out why your clan is dwindling away, and hopefully, reverse it."

He stared at me, his gaze hooded. "I see. And when this 'job' is done, when you've saved my people, you will leave."

"Yes."

Ice-covered branches tinkled in the breeze as he turned his head to look at the distant castle. "How long will this take?"

"I'm not having much luck so far. There doesn't seem to

be any physical reason for your low birthrate. Unfortunately, by law, I only have two months to complete my mission and render a decision."

"Why only two months?" His gaze shifted back to me.

"Because the people who wrote the law never envisioned a scenario quite like this one. Normally an entire team of specialists would have cycles to study the problem before I was called in."

Another second ticked by in silence, then he precipitously changed the subject. "Why do you call me this name, Thor? It is very small."

"Unlike you?" I grinned. "It's because you remind me of him. On Old Earth, the planet where my species originated, Thor was the Norse god of thunder. He was second only to Odin, his father. He has a beard like yours, and a hammer called Mjolnir that he uses to create the thunder. He was known for his immense strength."

He stretched out his leg, depriving me of my backrest, and then lowered me gently to the ground before coming to rest at my side. "I like this *Thor*. It is a good name. You may continue to use it."

"Thank you, your high-and-mighty-ness. I'm glad you approve." He looked so smug I couldn't help laughing. "Especially since I couldn't say your real name correctly under threat of torture."

"Enough talk," he said imperiously. "Time grows short and there are other things we must do."

"Oh? Like what?"

"This." He leaned over me, his dark hair forming a shield around us, and let his lips cover mine. Like the man who gave it, the kiss was demanding, heated by the flavor of passion too long withheld.

It's about time, I thought as desire roared through my veins. His, mine, they tumbled together to form a rapturous whole that was greater than the sum of its parts. My fingers took on a life of their own, touching, exploring, as his hands slid down my body on a mission of their own.

My eyes drifted closed as the last vestiges of restraint fled and I savored the experience of letting someone else take control. This was Thor, the person I'd plotted to be alone with for what felt like ages. Finally, it was happening, and I didn't care if it were a dream or not. I twisted in his arms until my breasts were against his chest, my arms coiled around his neck. My lips parted under his, offering myself to him in a way I'd never done with any male before.

A low growl sounded deep in his throat, and I trembled at the need expressed in the noise. He moved without warning and I found myself on my back again, the upper part of Thor's body pinning me to the ground, his mouth demanding on mine. I felt his desire shimmering and dancing throughout my body, creating an answering echo that set my nerves tingling.

The enchantment began, hot and sweet, as his kiss gentled and I felt tenderness fill him. "I need you," I murmured, giving him my complete surrender as well as my body.

Fire erupted through him at my words, at my touch, raging through him like a conflagration, out of control and devastating everything in its path. I was shaken to the core as he captured my mouth and I felt his lips move against mine, softly at first, until his tongue slipped between my lips. And with it, what little control I had left plunged into nonexistence. My hands buried themselves in the silken mass of his hair, holding his mouth captive.

"Kiera." My name was forced from him in a shaky breath.

Instantly, my nipples hardened against him and he shifted to cover them with his hand, rolling them between his fingers as I arched to meet him. Pulling his mouth from mine, he trailed it down my neck, fighting desperately to control his need to simply take me.

For just a second, I hesitated, surprised at how clearly I picked up his feelings. But the thought was swamped by the tide of emotions flowing from him. Even Thor was stunned at the depth of his own desire. At his need to possess me, make me his so completely that we would be forever one. And when his lips closed over a nipple, his tongue lathing it taut, I stopped thinking and only felt. And he felt with me. Felt the sharp jab of need that shot through me from his mouth to the center of my legs. Felt the hunger that coiled in my belly, more than a match for his.

Seemingly with a will of its own, his hand slid down to cover that center, his touch soft and slow, tantalizing. I whimpered as his fingers caressed, stoked the flames until I was ready to scream with frustration. It wasn't enough. He wanted more, wanted to taste.

He slid down, his mouth and tongue leaving a damp path down my stomach. With his eyes on my face he let his breath touch me.

"What—"

Before I could even form the question, his mouth covered me, caressing, tasting, and teasing. My head went back as my hands buried themselves in his hair once again.

"Oh, sweet Goddess!" My cry was choked, feverish, as my hips involuntarily thrust upward, begging for more. And he gave it to me until I was writhing beneath him, out of control. When I was on the edge of climax, he shifted.

On his knees, he pushed his erection against me and paused. "Kiera." His voice was barely a whisper as I watched him through eyes heavy with desire. "Let the bond be complete." With one hard thrust, he was inside, filling me in a way I'd never experienced before.

Abruptly, I was dizzy, the trees seeming to spin and

swoop as a wave of shimmering light swept over us, and something inside me clicked into place. He froze, waiting for the shimmering to subside, and then sighed when it was gone.

Then my hands flexed on his back, my lips touched his chest, and Thor was lost. Teeth clamped together, he withdrew and drove into me again. At the same instant, I felt our minds touch, meld as firmly as our bodies were joined. Startled, I tried to pull away but he held on.

Stay. The plea was wordless, impossible to tell if it came from him or me, so closely were we joined. Our bodies seemed to move of their own accord, withdrawing and plunging again as though they couldn't bear to be apart.

And I surrendered, let him sink into me mentally and physically, be enfolded until we became one entity, our desire burning together. I could hardly breathe.

Yes.

You're mine. The thought was fiercely protective.

Yes, came the soft reply. *We are one.*

Thought came to a stop as emotions exploded. Hips moved, tongues brushed, fingers twined together, every feeling sending an echo through the other. The climax was a whirlwind of sensation that turned us into a supernova, the heat of our passion burning us clean of everything but each other.

Sanity was slow to return, and when it did I was lethargic and replete in a way I'd never been before. For that matter, so was Thor. I could feel him, all smug and satisfied as he rolled to the side, taking me with him and curling his warm body around mine. My hair had come loose, covering half my face, and he brushed it back, his lips stroking my temple. "Sleep now," he murmured. "All is well accomplished."

I smiled as my eyes drifted closed. What a funny way to put the most earth-shattering experience of my life. Well accomplished. Yes, I suppose you could say that. Except after what had just occurred, it felt as though he were part of me.

That should worry me, I realized, just before sleep pulled me away. It should worry me a lot.

"Kiera!"

I bolted upright on the sleeping platform, hands gripping my head to keep my skull bones from vibrating loose with the force of Max's yell. "What!"

"You're awake." His voice quivered with relief.

"I am now. Why the hell are you yelling?"

"It's the middle of the morning and I've been trying to rouse you all night. You wouldn't respond, and it scared me. I'm sorry, Kiera, but after you drank the unknown liquid, I had to do something."

Suspicion stole over me, but I forced myself to remain calm and collected. "What did you do, Max?"

"I sent an emergency call through to Dr. Daniels," he said meekly. "After watching the vids of the Buri ceremony he agrees with me."

"About what?"

"There is a ninety-eight point nine percent probability that you wed the Buri leader you call Thor."

"What!"

Beside me, something warm and hard and muscled stirred, and I spun around like a dervish to meet Thor's irate gaze. I was still gawking when he spoke.

"Tell this male who speaks in your mind that he must leave now. You belong to me."

I lifted a shaky finger and pointed it at him. "I heard that. Your lips weren't moving, but I heard it."

"Kiera? Who are you talking to?"

"Thor. You can't hear him?"

"No."

Thor's frown deepened. "Tell him to leave." He spoke aloud now, in Buri. But what I *heard* was Galactic Standard.

My hand fell limply to my lap. "He's not a him—sorry, Max. Not in the usual sense. He's my ship, and I can't tell him to leave."

"He wants me to leave?" Max sounded shocked, and I felt like I'd been caught up in a holovid of the old "Who's on First?" routine.

"Just be quiet for a second. He doesn't understand who you are, and I'm trying to explain."

Thor levered himself up on one elbow and stared at me through narrowed eyes. "Ships do not speak this way."

"This one does. He's an artificial intelligence. That means he thinks, feels and has the ability to learn, even though he's a machine. His name is Max and he's very smart."

"Thank you."

"Max, for Goddess's sake, will you shut up?" I glared at Thor. "Besides, how do you know ships don't speak this way?"

"I see the ships the others come in. And I see the images in your mind. None of them speaks."

"Yeah, well, Max is special. Don't say it," I held up a hand in warning before Max could get another thank-you out.

"I would see this ship again." Thor sat up and swung his long legs over the side of the sleeping platform.

"Hold it just a darn minute, there, big boy. I think there are a few other things we need to discuss first."

"What are these things?"

As he spoke, he stood and turned to face me. I blinked. He wasn't wearing a loincloth. He wasn't wearing anything. Yeppers, he'd definitely requested they supersize that order at the old galactic burger drive-thru window.

Instantly I became aware of mild discomfort in the nether regions of my person, a place where there had only been pleasure before. Nervously, I licked my dry lips and forced my gaze upward. "Uh, I had this dream last night . . ." My voice tapered off as his lips curved in a satisfied smile.

Oh, shit. "It wasn't a dream, was it?" I asked weakly.

"No."

"I had a feeling you were going to say that. Just tell me this. Are we married?"

"Married?" He rolled the word over while he reached for his loincloth.

"Mated. As in bound together for life." I scrambled off the sleeping platform, grabbed a jumpsuit, and pulled it on. For some reason, it felt safer to be dressed in my own clothes.

"The bond was sealed. We are mated."

"That's impossible! GEPs don't marry." My legs were wobbling so hard I sank down on the edge of the sleeping platform to keep from falling. For someone who was supposed to be smarter than the average GEP, I sure had screwed up big this time.

"You are GEP. We are mated. Therefore, it is possible. Yelling will not change this truth."

"Kiera."

"Not now, Max. And I wasn't yelling." Much. I shot a glare at Thor as he walked to a shelf and picked up a piece of fruit. "How did this happen?"

He took a bite from the pale yellow globe and chewed thoughtfully for a second. "I felt the connection the first night you were here, as did you. Then, when you came to my village, you groomed me and gave me a gift. I accepted. As you accepted my offering gift in return. The Rellantiim Ceremony is completed. We are bonded." He finished off the fruit in another bite, and then looked around for more.

Come to think about it, I was damn near starved myself. I went to rummage through a knapsack stacked in the corner, and pulled out two Zip Bars. I tossed one to Thor and tore into the other one, speaking with my mouth full. "Are you telling me *I* proposed to *you*?"

"Kiera."

"Later, Max."

Thor sniffed the bar, then took a bite that consumed half of it in one fell swoop. "Proposed?"

"Asked you to be my mate." I swallowed, and reached for my boots with my free hand.

"Yes." He popped the last half of the bar into his mouth and headed for my knapsack. "But even if you hadn't, I would not have let you go."

"Kiera."

"What!" I threw my hands up in exasperation at Max's continued interruptions.

"Dr. Daniels would like to speak with you."

I closed my eyes and swore steadily for three minutes, even calling into question the paternity of the man who'd created faster-than-light communication. It took three days for a ship like Max to warp here from ZT Twelve, but I could talk to the boss as if he were in the next room. Occasionally, technology has its drawbacks.

"When?" I opened my eyes to see Thor staring at me with a great deal of interest, another Zip Bar suspended halfway to his mouth.

"In one hour. The transmission will be beamed into my control room. He doesn't want to disturb the Buri by suddenly appearing in their village."

"Fine, I'll be there."

"As will I," Thor said. "Who is this person that you do not wish to speak with?"

"The man I work for. My leader," I clarified. "Just out

of curiosity, did you understand everything I told you last night?"

"Yes." Even white teeth flashed as he grinned at me. Damn, but he was gorgeous.

"As are you."

"Whoa. Do you hear everything I think?"

He finished off the second Zip Bar, then stretched out on the sleeping platform, back propped against the wall. "Yes. You broadcast very strongly and have not yet learned to shield."

"How?" I shifted to face him, and he lifted a hand and set my new earring swinging. The touch of his finger on the stone was oddly erotic, and I shivered.

"Through the mind bond formed by the rellanti."

I remembered the word from last night, but now I was thinking more clearly. The rellanti was obviously the black stone in the earring. "Why can't I hear your thoughts?"

"You can." His lips weren't moving. *"In time, you will stop fighting the connection and learn to control the bond with more accuracy."*

I ignored the fighting comment and concentrated on the earring. The stone had to have some kind of psychic properties. Hell, maybe all the colored ones had psychic properties. While I'd always been able to detect emotions, I'd never picked up actual words before. Would I be able to hear everyone's thoughts now?

"No. Only mine. When a young male becomes an adult, he is given two rellanti. If he has been prepared correctly, the rellanti gradually attune themselves to his mind. He wears both until he finds the female who is destined to form the mind bond with him."

"What happens if he hasn't been prepared correctly?"

"He dies."

A chill ran over me as I remembered Junior receiving his

rellanti last night. And what about me? Could I have died, too?

"We were all correctly prepared. I would not have risked you otherwise."

"If I was 'correctly' prepared, then why did your touch hurt me when I first returned to the village?"

"The pathways were opened, but you did not yet wear my rellanti. This created a dissonance which caused pain when we touched."

That didn't make me feel a lot better, but I decided to let it pass for now. There was only so much anxiety I could take at one time, and I'd reached my limit. "So, when Elder took the rellanti from you, and put it on me, it what? Became attuned to my mind?"

He thought that over for a second, frowning. "It synchronized the patterns of our minds so they are in accord, and amplified our thoughts. This is why you hear my words in your language, and I hear yours in mine."

"Will I be able to understand the rest of the tribe?"

"If I hear their words, you would understand through me."

"Kiera," Max interrupted. "If you understand what he's saying, we could easily make a language program."

Thor frowned again. "Does this ship read your thoughts?"

"No, although it seems that way sometimes." I picked up his hand and placed his fingers behind my ear. "Feel that?"

He explored for a second, then nodded.

"That's a computer chip. It contains both a listening and tracking device, as well as a tiny speaker. I can stay in contact with Max from almost anywhere on the planet's surface."

His head tilted thoughtfully. "He would protect you?"

"Of course. My protection is his primary directive."

"Then he may stay."

"Gee, thanks."

But I didn't want to talk about Max now. There was more I needed to know about the rellanti. My braid had come undone during the night and Thor was lifting my hair, letting it slide through his fingers. I caught his hand in mine, and held it still. As pleasant as another round of lovemaking might sound, I was desperate for answers, panic creeping along my nerves.

"You said the bond was sealed last night. How was it sealed?"

"When we made love, both here and within the rellanti."

"What would have happened if we hadn't made love?"

His gaze drifted from my hair to my face. "I do not know. No one has ever refused the bond before. It has always been as it was with us, and now it is sealed. You are mine."

My grip on his hand tightened. "Can the bond be broken once it's sealed?"

Suddenly he was very alert, his body tense. "Yes."

"How?"

"If one of us dies, it will be broken."

"That's a little more drastic than I was considering."

He relaxed slightly, but there was still watchfulness in his gaze.

"What's going to happen to this bond when I leave?"

"I do not know."

"Thor, I told you that I'd be leaving when my job is done. You knew I meant it, and yet you sealed the bond anyway. Why?"

He looked down at our joined hands. "I have waited all my life to find my bond mate. A true bond has become very rare among my people. I know of only two others. Most of my people mate now in hopelessness. For them, the Rellant-iim Ceremony is hollow with no true sharing of spirits. This is why I chose to seal our bond."

When he looked up, there was a gleam of determination in his eyes. "The answers you seek will not come easily. When you find a way to restore our fertility, you will change your mind about this 'job.' You will not leave me."

"And how do you plan on changing my mind?" I asked quietly.

"You will have a new purpose, a new reason for being. It has begun." He pulled his hand from mine and stood. "I am still hungry. We will eat now."

I waited until he'd almost reached the door before I spoke again. "Thor, do you know why the Buri birthrate is so low?"

He stopped, but didn't turn around. "Come. There is much to do before we meet this leader your ship spoke of."

A shiver ran over me as I watched him step through the door. I had a bad feeling about this. A very bad feeling.

CHAPTER 12

I braided my hair at high speed, and then ran after Thor, determined to continue our conversation. He was halfway across the village, talking to Auntie Em and Elder, by the time I cleared the threshold. Both of them were smiling, Thor was frowning. They were too far away for me to hear most of what they were saying, but I caught just enough to make me wonder. Auntie Em was asking about "the others" and Elder wanted to wake someone up.

My brow furrowed in puzzlement. What others was Auntie Em talking about? All the Buri seemed to be present and accounted for. Was she asking him about the Dynatec crew? Surely not.

When the three new Buri had shown up in the village, it had occurred to me that maybe an unknown number of Buri were hiding out in one of the caves. I wasn't sure why they thought it was necessary unless it was just to confuse Dynatec, but it would explain why Max hadn't located them. Maybe those were the "others" Auntie Em was talking about.

But why would Thor vehemently refuse Elder's simple request to wake someone up? There had to be a missing bit of information here.

Marriage aside, not to mention my gut-level fear of linked minds, I really needed to learn how this bond thing worked if it would let me make sense of Thor's discussions.

Thor gave his head another emphatic shake, then glanced in my direction, his gaze settling on something to my left. With a final comment to the two Buri facing him that wiped the smiles off their faces, he started toward me.

I was admiring the lithe, sensuous grace of his stride when I noticed the flickers of light. Not with my eyes, but mentally. I paused, trying to find them again, but every time I attempted to focus on the phenomenon, it vanished. A side effect of the mind bond? If so, it was certainly a distracting one.

Frustrated, I returned my gaze to Thor. And saw the flickers again. It was like glimmering strings of opalescence seen only with the peripheral vision of my psi ability. I was trying to examine this marvel without aiming my attention directly at it when Claudia Karle reached me, Ghost dogging her steps.

She was talking before she came to a stop. "That was some party last night. Thanks for inviting me. What was that last ceremony about? It looked intense."

I gave her a weak smile as Thor joined us. "I sort of got married. I don't think it's legal, though."

Actually, I was pretty sure it was legal, but denial had me in a stranglehold. It wasn't that I didn't care for Thor, because I did. We had this magical chemistry going on between us that was like nothing I'd ever experienced, and love was the only word that seemed to fit. If I were going to give up my work for anyone, it would be him. But at the risk of repeating myself, GEPs don't marry. It never works for the regular GEPs, and I was even more of a risk than they were.

"It will work."

"Will you stop that!" I answered his smug response with a mental yell of my own.

Claudia's eyes were wide round circles of awe as she gazed at Thor. "Holy Goddess. You're married to *him*?" She let out a long sigh. "Why don't things like that happen to me?"

As she spoke, Ghost caught my attention. Every few seconds he'd shake his head as though to rid himself of an annoying insect. There was a distinct familiarity about the movement, and eyes narrowed, I turned back to Claudia.

"Is your head buzzing, by any chance?"

She reached up and gingerly rubbed her forehead. "Yeah, I think I drank too much last night."

Seeing where I was headed, Thor abruptly faced Ghost. "Is this female a bond mate for you?"

A surprised expression froze Ghost's face into immobility, then he nodded slowly and took a step closer to Claudia.

"What's going on?" Claudia divided her attention between the three of us like a spectator at a sky ball match.

No way was I going to break the news she'd just gotten engaged. "I think I've just lost one of my guards," I improvised. Come to think about it, Poe wasn't anywhere to be seen, either.

"The bond is in place. They are no longer needed."

Handling multilevel conversations was giving me another headache, so I ignored Thor and forced myself to concentrate on Claudia. "So you wouldn't mind marrying a Buri and staying here?"

She shot a sidelong glance at Ghost from beneath lowered lashes, a red flush tinting her cheeks. "Not if it was the right Buri."

Okay, she was on her own. I had bigger herdbeast to fry. "I'm surprised you haven't gone back to work."

"All that wine knocked me out and I overslept. My crew is already in the field. I was on my way to join them when

I saw you. Figured we needed to talk while we have the chance."

I shifted uneasily, painfully aware that Thor now understood everything I said. Or even thought. It was downright spooky, being on the receiving end for a change, and I finally understood why the boss insisted only the two of us know I was an empath. But there was no help for his eavesdropping. "What have you found?" I asked Claudia.

"Nothing specific, but there's a big chunk of data hidden on the ship's main computer. I found it by checking the available space that's left against the amount of space taken up by the visible files."

I hesitated. "Can you get at it without putting yourself in danger?"

She nodded. "I almost had it last time I tried. And I'll probably be taking you up on that job offer from Alien Affairs. This is going to be my last trip with Dynatec, regardless. I didn't sign on to take orders from Quilla Dorn, no matter how good the pay. Is there anything specific you need when I get in?"

"Research notes. I want anything you can find on a couple of crystals the original exploration team took with them when they left Orpheus Two."

"Crystals? Like this one?" She reached into the front of her jumpsuit and tugged out a chain. At the end dangled a pale green crystal, about an inch long and the size of my little finger in circumference. It was wrapped in thin silver wire to hold it in place.

"Where did you get it?"

"Are you joking? The damn things are everywhere. They're pretty enough, but hell on my location markers. I bet we've bent a good third of our supply trying to drive their shafts through crystal. That's part of the reason our mapping is going slower than usual. Half the time, we can only locate the markers visually instead of letting our equipment home in on them, because we've damaged them trying to get them in the ground."

I couldn't take my eyes off the crystal. To my heightened senses, it seemed to pulse with a faint glow that was nearly overshadowed by the bright sunlight. "Why did you pick that particular color to use as a pendant?"

She looked down at the crystal in her hand. "I don't know. I've never been particularly fond of green, but I fell in love with this one as soon as I saw it. Now I never take it off."

"Claudia, have you ever been tested for psi abilities?"

A flicker of surprise lit her eyes, and then vanished. "No, I've never shown a speck of talent. Getting tested would be a waste of time."

"You'd better reconsider. I think those crystals may be the reason Dynatec filed Chapter Twenty. If I'm right, they enhance psychic abilities. Come by my ship later and he can test you."

"Sure, if you think it's necessary." She didn't look convinced as she tucked the crystal away, and I could sense she was only humoring me. "So, you want me to look for any indication that Dynatec knows the crystals enhance psi abilities?"

"Exactly. I was also going to ask you to find out if there's any mention of an altercation between the Buri and some of the crew, but I think I can get that information from another source now." I glanced at Thor. *You will tell me, won't you.* It wasn't a question, and he gave a slight nod of acknowledgment.

"A fight?" She sounded shocked. "I haven't heard any mention of a fight. Are you sure about this?"

"Yes. Some of the Buri show signs of laser burns. I would like to hear what Redfield has to say about the incident. I don't think he's too comfortable with whatever Dorn and

Frisk are up to. He still hasn't managed to get away from them long enough to talk to me, though."

"I'll see what I can do, although it might take me a few days to get Redfield alone. He's telling the truth about Frisk and Dorn. I've noticed that at least one of them is with him at all times. And it's gotten a lot worse since you arrived. They won't even leave him alone with the other crewmembers. Dorn almost caught us the day he asked me to give you that message about wanting to speak with you."

I nodded my understanding. "Okay. If you need me, just make sure you're outside and set your comm unit to the frequency Max contacted you on before. He'll relay the message to me."

She gave a little wave, cast one last look of longing at Ghost, and then headed in the direction her crew was working. Ghost took a step after her and then hesitated.

Thor seemed to understand his problem. "Go." He gestured at Claudia's retreating form. "But remember, you must not mate with the female until the ceremony has been performed."

Not mate? I grabbed Thor's arm and tugged him around to face me as Ghost hurried after Claudia. "Why can't they mate until the ceremony?"

"The rellanti would try to complete the bond. Without preparation, the female would die."

"Is that why you didn't . . . uh, mate with me before?"

"Yes."

And all this time I'd thought I had bad breath. "But you said the bond is rare. How can your people mate at all? Wouldn't every female die?"

"Only if the possibility of the bond is there, and she is unprepared. Without the potential of the bond, the rellanti does not react to mating."

I narrowed my eyes as an idea occurred to me. "Does this bond have to exist for your people to bear young?"

"No."

"And you have no intention of telling me why they aren't reproducing, do you?"

"No." He grinned.

Damn. Back to square one. I never should have told him I'd be leaving when I found out what the problem was and corrected it.

"Kiera," Max interrupted. "It's almost time."

"On my way. And you," I told Thor, "can tell me all about this battle with the Dynatec crew while we walk. Max can have something ready to eat when we get there." It came as a surprise that I'd picked up his thoughts of food without even trying. Maybe the key to using this bond was to relax and let it work instead of forcing it.

"This ship cooks, too?"

"In a manner of speaking."

He made a slight detour to collect his spear and a wicked-looking knife, and then we entered the dim light of the jungle side by side. The branches closed us off from the village when he spoke again.

"The battle occurred shortly after these others arrived. The mate of Dryggahn went into the jungle to gather fruit, taking her child with her."

When he said *Dryggahn*, I got a mental image of Brownie. It didn't surprise me. I'd suspected it had something to do with him.

"The child wandered a short distance away from his mother and three of your people grabbed him. Alerted by her child's screams, Dryggahn's mate called to him through their bond. A large group of my people stopped the three before they could reach their camp. The child was retrieved unharmed, but several were wounded, and one died. We do not understand why the child was taken."

"I've got a pretty good idea why. They wanted to run tests

on him, to ensure your people really can't reproduce. As long as you're dying out, there's nothing we can do to stop them from claiming this world." A shudder ran over me. "No wonder Brownie hates me."

"He does not hate you, merely distrusts. Our children are so few, those we do have are precious to us."

"There's another female who's expecting a child." I stepped around a nasty-looking plant with saw-toothed blades and glanced at Thor in time to see him smile.

"Yes. We celebrated many days when Sillia shared this joyous news."

"Does this Sillia share the mind bond with her mate?"

"No. They were not so fortunate." He held a branch aside so I could pass. "Dryggahn has convinced himself that Sillia's child will be our Shushanna."

That would explain why Brownie was so opposed to the Buri calling me Shushanna, I thought. "Is that why he challenged you for leadership?"

"Yes, in part. There is also more."

"More?" I arched a brow in question.

He sighed. "When it is time to chose a new ruler, all those eligible from the royal line are considered, and then the people vote for whomever they believe will make the best *Deshunnat*. I was chosen, but Dryggahn felt it should have been him. He also is of the royal line and ten cycles my elder. He truly believes he knows better than I what is best for the tribe and resents that I do not follow his thoughts. He was sure the new Shushanna would be born into the tribe, while I was not."

Holy shit! My mouth had dropped open halfway through that pronouncement and I had trouble closing it now. "You aren't just the Buri leader," I said. "You're the damn king!"

His head tilted thoughtfully. "I do not know this word, *king*."

I waved one hand. "Descended from a royal line, ruler by right of blood."

He nodded. "Then yes, I am king."

Air was having trouble squeezing through my suddenly tight throat. "And since I'm your mate, that would make me . . ."

"The Shushanna," he said with a great deal of satisfaction.

"Is the Shushanna always mated to the king?" I asked, still trying to breathe.

"No, of course not. Although it was so with my sire and dam."

Whew. "So I'm not the queen." When he looked blank I clarified. "A queen is the female who is mated to the king, or sole ruler in her own right."

"If you were ruler, then I suppose you would be this queen," he commented. "But I alone am ruler of my people. You are my mate and the Shushanna."

Okay, I could finally breathe again. Queen was the very last thing I wanted to be. I did want to explore this Shushanna thing in more depth later, but right now I needed to refocus on the bond.

"You said you knew of only two couples who share the bond. Brownie and his mate are one. Who are the others?"

He gave me one of "those" looks, like he was trying to decide whether or not to answer. "My sire and his mate."

"Where are your parents now?" A curl of excitement unfolded inside me. This was one of the things I needed desperately to find out. If a disease had killed the older Buri, it could also have done something to affect the reproduction cycle of those remaining.

His voice was hard when he answered. "Dead."

"What about the rest of your people? Are their parents all dead too?"

"Yes."

We had almost reached the clearing where my hut stood when I stopped and touched his arm. "How? Why did they die?"

He gazed down at me stoically. "By their own choice."

My jaw dropped. Of all the scenarios I'd come up with, this was one I'd never so much as considered. "Are you telling me they committed mass suicide? Why in the thirteen hells would they do that?"

"The reasons were their own. And it did not happen all at once as you are thinking. At first, there were only a few. The numbers increased until the end, when many died every day."

"You just let them do it? Why didn't anyone stop them?"

"It was their right to choose."

"But what about Auntie Em and Elder? They're much older than the rest of you and they didn't die."

"Their knowledge was needed. They chose to live."

Lifting both hands, I rubbed my face. Why did it seem as if the more I found out, the more confused the issues became? At this rate, I was going to need another vacation. Soon. I turned and pushed through the brush at the edge of the clearing.

"What is 'honeymoon'?" Thor asked.

"It's a period of time newly mated couples spend alone so they can get to know each other." I squinted at him. "Where did you hear the word?"

"You were thinking it."

"I most certainly was not!" I spun around, hands on my hips as I glared at him. "And even if I were—which I wasn't—and even if I accept that we're . . . mated—which I don't—a honeymoon never crossed my mind. I've got a job to do. I don't have time to run off and play games with you."

"Why are you upset?" He truly looked confused. Not that I blamed him. I was pretty confused myself. Had I really been thinking about honeymoons? How else would he know the word?

All the zip went out of me. "I'm not upset, damn it. It's just that . . . never mind. I don't think I can explain it."

"You will try."

"Okay. You asked for it." I inhaled sharply and then let the air out in a slow, calming exhale. "People should get married because they love each other and want to spend their lives together. Not because some damn rock decides it can attune their brain waves."

His gaze met mine, and I went all gooey at the warmth reflected in their ebony depths. "You crave love very much, mate. But it is like a seed that must first be sown and nurtured before the plant can bloom. Between us, a seed was sown when first we met. Already it has sprouted. With time and attention, it will come to full flower. This I swear to you."

I blinked away the pesky moisture that clouded my vision and raised my chin. "What? Are you channeling Yoda now?"

He frowned. "What is a 'yoda'?"

"A short, green, very wise little person. I can see I need to introduce you to holovids. Maybe have Max fix some popcorn so you can enjoy the full experience."

His frown deepened, and he lifted a hand to cup my cheek. "It is not necessary to distract me when your feelings make you uncomfortable. I will not allow us to be separated, mate. Even though this is what you seek, it is not what you really want. You are safe with me. The pain you fear will not come to pass."

For a brief instant, I allowed my eyes to close, let myself lean into his warm, strong palm. And I wished with all my heart that it could be as easy as he made it sound. But it wasn't, and I couldn't seem to make him understand that I had no choice. When this job was done, I would be assigned another, far away from Orpheus Two and the Buri regardless of how I might want it to be otherwise.

Forcing a smile, I opened my eyes and reached up to clasp his hand in mine. "Come on. Max is waiting for us."

Luscious smells drifted from Max's open hatch as we climbed the stairs, and I heard the soft *plop* of dishes sliding into the pickup tray just as we reached the cabin. You certainly couldn't fault the ship's timing.

"How long do we have to eat?" I asked Max aloud.

"Dr. Daniels is scheduled to begin transmission in twenty minutes and forty-five seconds."

"Good." I pulled the steaming dishes out and placed them on the small table in front of the food-prep unit before motioning Thor to have a seat across from me. Looked like Max had gone all out, no doubt showing off for Thor. It wasn't often we had a real live guest join us on board for meals.

"Where's Crigo?" I asked, slicing into the grilled chicken covered in mushroom gravy. Thor, hesitant about the strange foods in front of him, took a tiny nibble of a tuber lightly roasted with garlic, then dug in like he hadn't eaten in a week.

"Watching the Dynatec camp from the edge of the jungle."

"Should I be worried?" I could feel the curiosity coming from Thor as I talked to Max, and he kept looking around the cabin as if trying to identify where the voice was coming from.

"I don't believe so. He spends a lot of time watching, but so far, he's only entered the camp once."

I detected an odd note in Max's voice and paused before I could put the chicken in my mouth. "Why did he enter the camp?"

"The Dorn woman left her boots outside on the porch of her hut."

"And?" I waved my fork for him to continue.

"Well, uh . . . Crigo—"

"Spit it out, Max. Crigo what?"

"He urinated on her boots."

I dropped my forehead to the table and rapped it gently on the laminate surface three times. "Please tell me no one saw him."

"No one saw him."

"You're sure?" I sat up hopefully.

"No."

I glowered. "You just said no one saw him."

"You told me to say that. But if anyone did see him, they neglected to mention his actions to Dorn. She was rather surprised at the condition of her footgear, and ended up tossing them in the recycler near the door. And she never so much as glanced in Crigo's direction."

A breath of relief escaped me. "Let me know if he so much as looks like he's going to enter the camp again. While I might agree with his sentiments, I don't want them taking potshots at him."

"You are speaking of your animal?" Thor flashed me an image of Crigo, and I blinked. How the heck did he do that so easily?

"He'd probably object to you calling him mine, but yes. His name is Crigo."

"He does not belong to you?"

"No, he's more like a friend." I reached for my glass, then paused, frowning at the water filling it. "Max, why does Thor have wine and I don't?"

"Because alcohol might skew the results of the physical."

"What physical?" I asked ominously.

"The one Dr. Daniels ordered performed while he's here."

"Damn it, Max! You told him there was something wrong with me, didn't you?" Appetite gone, I dropped my fork and pushed my plate back.

There was a flicker of movement from my right, and abruptly Thor was standing, muscles tensed and ready as he reached for his knife.

Max, the coward, had initiated the call to Dr. Daniels ten minutes early.

"Don't blame Max, my dear. You know one of his imperatives is to keep you healthy." The boss wiped dirt from his hands as he stood. Around him, plants grew in lush recklessness, and I realized Max had caught him at work in his garden. "He was worried about you. Now why don't you introduce me to your young man before he tries to attack my image and hurts himself?"

I sighed in defeat, knowing he was right. Protection of their partners was the most important imperative programmed into an AI. They would self-destruct before violating the rule.

Giving up on that front, I waved a hand. "Dr. Daniels, this is Thor, leader of the Buri. Thor, Dr. Jordan Daniels, my boss."

To my surprise, the boss gave a slight bow and growled a short phrase in Buri. Thor hesitated, then dipped his head in a regal nod, his gaze still locked on the image.

"Since when do you speak Buri?" I asked the boss.

His grin was smug, white teeth flashing. "Max has been recording conversations and running language probability programs. I'm afraid I just exhausted my Buri vocabulary, though."

"Don't worry about it." I waved a hand at Thor. "He understands everything we say. We've got this mind-bond thing going on."

"Yes, Max told me." He put his hands in his pockets.

"I find it very intriguing. You actually read each other's minds?"

I glanced at Thor. He gave his head a slight shake. *"Only when we make love, or when you broadcast."*

Hurriedly, I turned back to the boss, hoping my face wasn't red. "Not exactly. It's more like talking, only on a mental level rather than aloud."

"That should come in handy." He leaned forward slightly to get a better look at me. "And this came about through the exchange of the earring during the marriage ceremony?"

"About that ceremony . . ."

"Later." He gave me his best gimlet-eyed stare and I knew we'd be having a private conversation before this call was over. "First, I have some information for you. My investigators have uncovered a few very interesting details about Ms. Dorn."

"Such as?" I sat up straighter, my curiosity running rampant.

The boss removed one hand from his pocket, plucked a flower from the bush next to him and twirled it idly between his fingers. "Max, put up the first image I sent you."

A hologram appeared in the air above the table and I studied it for a second. "Yeah, that's Quilla, all right."

"Actually, it's not." The boss's lips quirked. "That's Laura Dorn, Zander Dorn's wife. Max, put Ms. Dorn's image next to it."

Another holo appeared, and I swung my gaze between the two. Other than clothing, there was no discernible difference. "They look like identical twins," I murmured.

"The resemblance is even more striking than that. Our facial recognition system insists they are the same woman. Retinal scans confirm it."

Thor remained silent, but I knew he was listening intently. "So, you're saying Quilla is really Laura Dorn?"

"No. Laura Dorn is dead." He paused. "She died three cycles before Quilla was born."

"A clone?" I leaned back in shock. "But cloning is illegal."

"So is creating a GEP without a government license, but we both know that with enough money, black-market geneticists will do it. Zander Dorn was an extremely wealthy man, and from all reports, he was devastated by his wife's death."

"So he had her recreated and passed her off as his daughter? That's sick."

"Very sick. When Quilla was thirteen cycles, she killed Zander Dorn. According to the police reports, it was self-defense. Dorn was molesting her."

A shudder of revulsion ran over me, and Thor reached out to cover my hand with his. The boss's expression turned to one of interest at the gesture, and I spoke quickly before he got any ideas. "What happened to her?"

"The court appointed her a guardian. She was, after all, a rich young lady. There's very little information on her after that."

"If she's so rich, why is she working for Dynatec?" While Thor was busy staring at a bird that had landed behind the boss, I slipped my hand out from under his, trying to make the movement look casual.

"She doesn't." He moved to a pastel pink bench on one side of the white crushed shell path and sat down. "We can't prove it yet, but there's reason to believe she owns the company. The information Max uncovered at your request leads us to think she bought Dynatec approximately ten cycles ago, as you suspected."

"Right after the exploration team returned with the crystals."

"Exactly." He smiled. "And right after several members of that team met with an early demise."

"So, if we've got this right, Quilla somehow found out about the crystals, probably from the exploration team themselves. Then, before Dynatec could discover what they had, she wiped out the original team and bought the company."

"That's the theory we're going on. I'll let you know if we find any proof. Now, why don't we get this physical out of the way so Max can stop fretting?"

My stomach roiled at the very thought, but I knew the boss wasn't going to let me off the hook. "Fine. I'll meet you in sick bay."

Thor touched my arm as I stood, his dark eyes filled with concern. "There is danger in this thing you do not wish to do?"

"No, no danger." I grimaced. "I just don't particularly like seeing images of my insides floating in the air."

It was the truth, but there was more to it than that. Every physical I took just pointed out the differences between me and Naturals, or even other GEPs. Natural humans use very little of their brain, GEPs use a bit more. I, on the other hand, use almost half. It's bad enough knowing I'm different, I don't need the additional proof of my otherness by looking it in the face, so to speak.

Until now, the 50 percent of my gray matter not in use seemed to have no more function than it did in any human. Call me a pessimist, but I had a sneaking suspicion that had changed during my night in the cave.

The boss's call had been transferred to sick bay by the time I stepped through the door, Thor hard on my heels. Wiping suddenly damp palms on my thighs, I sat in the diagnostic chair, sucked in a lungful of air, and nodded. "Okay, Max. Let's get this over with."

There was a soft hum as medical equipment sprang to life. An image of my brain appeared in the air, and the boss stood, moving closer for a better look.

"This is the base image taken a cycle ago," Max said. Another image sprang to life beside the first. "And this is now."

The difference in the two images was stark. In the base image, the ridges of the surface tissue were a flat gray. Only a slightly above average number of sparks indicated my enhanced neural activity. The image Max was taking now looked like a fireworks display on Virgo Nine during their annual mating celebrations. Sparks were shooting everywhere, and even as we watched, the level of activity increased.

Silence reigned for several seconds as we all contemplated this phenomenon, and then a pleased rumble erupted from Thor's chest before he spoke.

"You are indeed the true Shushanna. The pathways are opening."

Fear like I'd never known inundated me. Fear that immediately transformed to anger as I leaped to my feet, hands clenched with the effort not to physically lash out. "What do you mean, 'the pathways are opening'? What have you done to me?"

Thor's eyes narrowed as he took in my stance, but when he spoke, all I heard was Buri. A look of frustration crossed his face before he turned on his heel and walked stiffly away, the sound of his footsteps fading as he left the ship.

"Max? What just happened? I couldn't understand him."

"The probability is strong that anger blocks the bond. Please calm down, Kiera. Your blood pressure is reaching dangerous levels."

"You haven't seen dangerous yet," I ground out through clenched teeth as I faced the boss. "I want this marriage broken. The sooner the better."

Dr. Daniels had his hands in his pockets again and was rocking from heel to toe, a sure sign that he was thinking furiously. "Very well. I'll see what needs to be done."

Just like that, the anger drained away. "Aren't you going to try and talk me out of it?"

"It's your life, my dear. If a divorce is what you really want, I'll do my best to help you obtain one."

I stared at him for a second while I chewed on my bottom lip, then took a deep breath. "Thor says the only way to break the mind bond is if one of us dies."

"Ah." He smiled. "Then you'll have to kill him, of course. That will also save us the necessity of going through legal channels."

I crossed my arms and glared at him. "You're using reverse psychology aren't you? I hate it when you do that."

His smile turned into a low chuckle. "You needed time to calm down. Now that you have, you can think about this rationally."

Okay, I could do rational. Most of the time.

Closing my eyes, I forced each muscle to relax and took a few more deep breaths. When I opened my eyes again, the boss was watching me closely. "Well?"

"You're right. Getting a divorce won't help as long the mind bond exists. And I obviously can't kill him. So, I'll use the bond to find out what I need to know to complete my job, and worry about the rest later."

"Excellent!" Dr. Daniels beamed approval at me. "And by then, you may discover that you rather like being mated with your Buri."

It didn't matter what I liked, I thought glumly. It would have to end. All I could do was make the best of the situation until it did. And pray to all the gods that I'd find a way to sever the bond without hurting Thor or myself.

CHAPTER 13

I hesitated at the bottom of Max's steps, wondering what to do. Now that I'd calmed down a bit, I could literally *feel* Thor at the Buri village, and knew he was also aware of me, but I wasn't ready to face him yet. Those damn glimmers of light at the periphery of my internal vision were getting stronger too. I needed a distraction.

"Max, is Quilla Dorn at the Dynatec camp?"

"Yes, she returned thirty minutes ago, with a full knapsack."

"And I bet I know what it was full of. Crystals. Max, I want you to run every test known to man on those crystals, right down to the molecular level. We've established they aren't surge crystals like the one you run off of, but they do enhance psi ability. There's something important going on with them, even if it's not apparent on a cursory scan."

"I'll get started right away. And don't forget, I need a sample of the Buri's plants for DNA comparison."

"You got the DNA for the Ashwani plants?"

"Yes, it came in while you were asleep."

I started toward the Dynatec camp, strolling as if I were

merely out enjoying the day. "Okay, I'll get the plants to you later today."

As I rounded the end of the lake, a thought occurred to me. *"Thor, if you can hear me, I'm going to the Dynatec camp. I'd rather not have a Buri in attendance. I don't want Dorn distracted."*

"The Crigo will be there?"

His voice was so clear, he could have been standing beside me, and I smiled at his wording. *"His name is Crigo. His species is rock cat. And yes, I'm sure he'll be there."*

"He would protect you if necessary?"

"In a flash. But I'm quite capable of protecting myself."

"As you wish."

I was starting to get the hang of this mind-bond thing, I decided. All I had to do was relax and pretend we were in the same room, talking. Nothing to it.

"We also feel each other's emotions, and always know where the other is," Thor commented.

"Yeah, yeah, whatever." I rolled my eyes, and then jumped when he did something to the bond that felt distinctly like a yank. "Hey, how did you do that?"

"Do not believe you have mastered all aspects of the bond, mate. You still have much to learn."

Well, guess that put me in my place. I ignored him and focused my attention on the Dynatec camp. There were several people in sight, moving around, doing the routine tasks required in any camp. As I headed for a stocky woman working on a piece of machinery, Crigo stood, stretched and moved out of the jungle to intersect my path, a flock of dragon birds keeping him company. Even from a distance of twenty or so yards I could feel his anticipation.

Wonder what he thought I was going to do? For that matter, *I* wondered what I'd do. I had no plan except to follow where my instincts were leading me.

The woman was aware of our approach, although she wasn't obvious about it. She didn't look up until we reached her, and paid no attention to Crigo.

"Agent Smith." Her head dipped in a nod of greeting. "Something I can help you with?"

"I'm here to see Quilla Dorn."

"She's on the other side of the Quonset hut."

"Thanks." I knew Dorn was expecting us now because I'd seen another crew member slide around the hut in question when I stopped. Crigo stayed close as I followed the man's path.

Apparently, life was good at the camp. I found Dorn and Frisk on a plascrete patio complete with an awning, table and chairs. From the sides, fans stirred the air, and the table was laden with fruit, cheese and thinly sliced meat. A bottle of wine was nestled in a bucket of ice.

Frisk was sitting like someone had strapped a rod to his back, but Dorn was the picture of languid repletion. With her booted feet propped on the edge of the table, she lazed in her chair, a crystal flute of wine in her hand.

"Agent Smith. This is a surprise." She waved a hand at the table. "We just finished lunch, but feel free to help yourself."

"Thanks. I already ate." I pulled out a chair and sat down. Crigo positioned himself where he could stare intently at Frisk, his muscles tensed.

"What's wrong with your cat?" Frisk asked, glancing nervously at Crigo.

"Oh, don't mind him." I bared my teeth at Frisk in a grin. "He just takes exception to people who try to poison me. It's been all I can do to keep him from turning you into dinner. Since I'm not always around, better watch your back in the jungle, Frisk."

His level of tension increased as he kept his attention on Crigo, but from Dorn all I got was amusement.

"Jon, what have you been up to? Didn't I tell you Agent Smith isn't your run-of-the-mill GEP?"

I blinked in surprise. Was it possible she knew the truth about me? How could she? Only the boss and I knew, and neither of us was talking.

"I didn't try to poison her." Frisk was pouting like an overindulged child chastised by his mother.

Still a bit uneasy over Dorn's remark, I forced myself to reply to Frisk. "Unfortunately, Crigo can be rather stubborn. He doesn't believe you."

Dorn swirled the wine in her glass, obviously dismissing Frisk's attempt to do me in. "So what prompted this visit to our humble home, Agent Smith?"

Elbows propped on the arms of the chair, I laced my fingers together and tapped them on my chin as if I were thinking. "I guess you could call it curiosity."

"Curiosity?"

"Yes." I gave her one of the grins I normally reserved for Frisk. "I'm wondering what it's like to own a company the size of Dynatec."

Her full lips curved in a smile, and she took a delicate sip of wine before answering. "It has its ups and downs, just like any business. But it's much better to be the boss than an employee, don't you think?"

"I wouldn't know. It is odd, however, that you bought the company right after the exploration team returned from Orpheus Two."

Her direct gaze met mine. "There's nothing odd about it. I was . . . acquainted with one of the team members, and he raved about Orpheus Two, until my interest was piqued. After I acquired the team's official reports and Dynatec's financial statements, I realized it was the investment I'd been looking for."

"Too bad about the exploration team, huh?" I kept my

gaze locked with hers and my barriers completely down. She gave away nothing, not by so much as a flicker of emotion.

"Yes, tragic accidents all. It's almost as if they were cursed."

I arched a brow at her. "I didn't know clones were superstitious. Is it only you, or are all of them the same way?"

Her gaze darkened and her smile faded. She tried to hide it, but I caught a whiff of anger. Bingo. Definitely hit a nerve that time. Maybe if I got her mad enough, she'd slip and give me some information I hadn't uncovered on my own.

I finally got Frisk's attention too. He jerked away from his nervous perusal of Crigo to stare at Dorn. "A clone? Is she lying?"

"What I am is none of your business," she snapped. "It has nothing to do with why we're here."

"Why, exactly, *are* you here?" I casually lifted a piece of fruit from the bowl, examined it, and put it back. "Most company owners stay in their nice, tidy offices and leave the grunt work to the help. Don't trust your pal Frisk, Dorn?"

"Of course I trust him. I'm—" Suddenly she leaned forward, eyes narrowing to slits. "Where did you get that earring?"

"This?" I touched the black stone dangling from my lobe. "One of the Buri gave it to me. It's so unusual, I'm thinking about letting Max run some tests on it."

"I see." She stood abruptly. "If you'll excuse us, Agent Smith, we need to get back to work."

"Sure thing." I pushed my chair away from the table and rose. "It's been an enlightening visit. We should get together and chat more often."

I sauntered away as though I didn't have a care in the world. After one wistful, lip-licking look in Frisk's direction, Crigo followed me.

Still not ready to face the Buri, I headed for Max, thinking furiously. Had I made a mistake letting Dorn know we were investigating the crystals? I didn't think so. It may have pushed her into acting sooner than she'd planned, but I'd much rather she act hastily and make mistakes than wait and be better prepared. And while I believed she'd already planned to wipe out the Buri, I didn't think it had occurred to her that I might figure out the true nature of the crystals.

If not for my night in the cave, she might have been right.

Maybe there really is a reason for everything.

But that would imply I was meant to bond with Thor.

Shaking my head at that melancholy bit of logic, I climbed Max's steps, noting as I did that Crigo was heading back to the jungle, where he could keep an eye on the Dynatec camp.

"Max, increase the security level. I think Dynatec may try something soon."

"Yes, Kiera. Do you have any idea what to expect?"

"Expect anything. And if there's information you haven't sent to the archives yet, do it now, even if it's speculation. I don't want to take chances."

"Sending."

Good. That made me feel a little better. Come to think about it, raising my own security level would make me feel better still. I took out a weapon, checked the charge, and strapped it on. "Oh, and Max, I really need you to put a rush on those crystal tests. Whatever you find, send it to archives even before you tell me. Same with the Buri plant DNA. I'm heading out to collect the samples now."

"I'll start on them as soon as you return."

Grabbing some sample pouches from a storage compartment, I packed them in a spare knapsack and left the ship, headed in a half circle that would bring me to the fields while bypassing the village.

Only a few Buri were present when I reached the cultivated acres, clearing an irrigation channel. They looked up and smiled when I arrived, but kept on working.

Ignoring them, I collected samples from the species of plants that seemed to be the Buri's main crops, and then moved to the smaller fields. The plants here were compact and more pungent. Medicinal? Herbal? Possibly both. I filled my pouches with a leaf or two from each and headed back to Max. Once there, I busied myself sorting them into containers in the lab so Max could access them, but I was running out of excuses for avoiding the village.

With a sigh, I finished the last specimen, brushed my hands off, and walked back to the control room.

Thor was lounging in an antigrav chair, gazing at the control panel as though memorizing it.

Surprised, I came to a screeching halt. "What are you doing here?"

He swung the chair around to face me. "The day grows long. Food is prepared. It is time to return to the village."

"I was on my way."

Gracefully, he rose from the chair. "I will walk with you."

I nodded and started down the steps, Thor behind me. "It wasn't necessary for you to come after me, you know."

"I know." He moved up to walk beside me and took my hand. "But we were only mated last night and have been apart many hours today. Is it so surprising that I wanted to see you?"

Ah, man. Talk about playing dirty. I swallowed the lump in my throat and shook my head. "I'm sorry I got upset earlier."

He tilted his head down to look at me. "And I wish you could have been given a choice. But without the bond there was no way to offer one, no way to explain. Nor did we understand that there was even a choice to be considered. Among my people, Shushannas are born, not made. They grow up knowing what they are, where their duty and destiny will lead. None would consider denying what they are."

"Thor." I looked at him entreatingly. "I don't even know what a Shushanna is. All I know is that you somehow changed me, and it scares me to death. There's so much Dr. Gertz did to me that we don't understand. I'm not sure I can tolerate even more surprises."

We walked in silence for a moment before he answered, as if he were trying to think the explanation through. "We did not change you."

He held a hand up when I started to protest. "We did not change you. As I said, a Shushanna is born, not made. Regardless of whatever else this man did, you were created with the capacity to be a Shushanna. Somehow the ability was blocked in you, but it *was* there. We merely unblocked it."

"How?"

"Through the *Demantti*. They knew what you were and what was wrong. They fixed the problem."

When he said *Demantti*, I heard the word *crystals*. "Do you know how the crystals work?"

"No. Only that they do. The how doesn't matter so much to us."

So much for a quick answer. But we were nearing the village and there was one more question I needed out of the way before we got there. "At least tell me what a Shushanna is."

His brow furrowed. "It is not easy to tell."

"Try."

He took a deep breath, held it, and then let it out slowly. "A Shushanna is the lifeblood of my people, our heart, the very air we breathe. Without a Shushanna we die."

Well, that certainly cleared that right up. That was sarcasm, in case you're wondering. If anything, I was even more confused, and since we'd reached the village, we were out of time to talk.

And suddenly I had something else to worry about. *What* in the thirteen hells were those damn gossamer strands that kept floating on the edges of my mind's eye? They were like a single thread from a spider web, drifting on the breeze, only visible when they passed through a beam of sunlight. But the closer we got to the village, the brighter they became, and I had to resist the urge to rub my physical eyes to see if they'd go away.

Thor tried to tug me toward the communal kitchen, but I barely noticed, all my attention suddenly focused on Poe as I stopped.

He was walking toward us, a spear over his shoulder, heading in the same direction we'd been going. Nothing abnormal about that. Except one of the shining strands was moving with him.

The closer he came, the brighter the strand grew. Then, when he reached me and kept going, the strand shifted from the right side of my internal vision to the left, and gradually dimmed as he moved farther away.

Could it be . . . ?

I let my eyes go unfocused and concentrated. Sure enough, for every Buri moving about the village, a strand moved in conjunction, and they all seemed to be attached to me somehow.

Shaking my head in puzzlement, I let my vision go back to normal. If I was seeing the life force of the Buri, why were there so many of them? Even if I assumed some Buri were staying out of sight in caves, I figured there were less than a hundred Buri surviving on Orpheus Two. More than that, and they would have left signs of their occupation.

But there seemed to be thousands of strands. It made no sense at all.

Admittedly, the majority of the filaments were clumped together, unmoving, so bright it was hard to distinguish individual strands. Maybe it just felt like there were more than there really were. Or maybe the extra Buri actually numbered in the thousands and were all wadded up in a ball, holding still just to fool me, I thought sarcastically.

A thought occurred to me. Could this clump be "the others" Auntie Em had referred to? And what about Elder's request to "wake them up?" A slithery feeling of prescience slid down my spine, but before I could follow that line of reasoning to its conclusion, another phenomenon surprised me into losing my train of thought.

Gossamer strands attached to me somehow. Thor doing something that felt like a yank on our bond. Oh yeah, the pieces were falling into place.

Experimentally I searched for the strand that linked me to Thor. It wasn't hard to find since he was standing right beside me, looking on with interest. Plus, his strand was denser and brighter, more substantial than the others.

I closed my eyes and mentally reached out, careful not to be too harsh or abrupt. It was the oddest feeling, kind of like trying to grasp a slippery eel that wiggled to get away. But I held on, gave it a gentle tug, and was rewarded for my effort when Thor jumped.

I released it and opened my eyes to find him smiling at me.

"You learn fast, mate."

"Yes. I do. So tell me, am I mated to all the Buri?"

His smile faded to a frown. "No. You are my mate alone."

"Then why am I seeing strands that correspond to all the Buri's life force?"

"You are Shushanna."

It was all I could do to keep from screaming in frustration. "Yeah, I got that."

Before I could continue, he changed the subject. "Your talk with the others went well?"

"I suppose you could say that." Reaching out with one hand I touched his arm. "Thor, you need to prepare your people. Dynatec won't let anything stand between them and ownership of this planet. I'm afraid they plan on wiping you out. If you have weapons other than spears, now is the time to start keeping them with you."

He nodded. "I have suspected as much. I will tell those with swords to arm themselves."

"Good."

"Now come." He headed toward the kitchen again. "The food is prepared."

"Is food all you ever think about?" I groused, following him.

He shot me a teasing glance from his ebony eyes. "No."

Well. That sure came across loud and clear. A wave of lust flashed through my body. I suppose being his mate did have *some* perks. And frankly, I could hardly wait to enjoy them. "So why are you walking so slowly? Do we have to stay until everyone has finished eating? I mean, I'd really hate to break some Buri protocol, but . . ."

My voice trailed off as Thor laughed. It was the first time I'd ever heard him laugh aloud, and it gave me a warm melty feeling in my middle. "I'm being too pushy, aren't I?"

He smiled down at me. "I like it that you show what you feel. Especially when it comes to making love."

"Nope, not a shy bone in my body. Are you sure we have to eat first?" Just thinking about dragging him to bed was getting me all worked up. "I mean, we could eat in, say, an hour or two. Three at the most."

A sigh lifted his broad chest. "I must be there to hear reports."

Well, damn. Okay, I could tamp my libido down for a while longer. And anticipation did heighten the pleasure, right? Right. My sigh echoed Thor's. "Let's get this over with."

All the Buri that weren't on guard duty were in the communal kitchen, but they'd left space for Thor and me at the main table. We squeezed in just as the dishes of food began to make the rounds, and I helped myself to something that looked like roast beef and gravy. Thor assisted by dumping a large spoonful of green leaves on my plate, along with some tubers.

I took a tentative bite, realized it was good, and dug in. It never hurt to replenish my strength, after all. Especially since I planned to expend a lot of energy later.

We were nearly finished when Auntie Em leaned across the table and spoke to Thor. "Is she ready to assume her duties yet?"

The bite I'd just taken went down wrong and I almost choked when I realized she was talking about me. He gave me a solid swat on the back before answering her.

"She does not know what her duties are, and we have no other Shushanna to teach her. Have patience. She will learn."

Auntie Em made a harrumphing noise before turning to speak with Churka. I wanted to know what the two females were talking about, but Thor was chatting with a sandy-colored Buri and paying no attention to them.

I'd noticed this particular Buri worked in the fields a lot, and it seemed he was having problems with small, scaled herbivores eating his crops. By the time he got close enough to use his spear, they spotted him and fled. He'd considered a fence, but doubted it would do any good since the creatures were agile climbers. Plus, by the time they built a fence for all the land they'd cultivated, there wouldn't be any crops left to protect.

Both Thor and the other Buri were at a loss as to how the problem should be handled, other than placing guards at strategic locations around the fields at night.

Maybe I could help a little. "Max, do we have bows left from that trip the Cygnus sector?"

"Only three, Kiera, and ten arrows each to go with them."

"Ten arrows each will be enough if they recycle them. Put them near the hold door and I'll pick them up tomorrow."

Thor turned to me, one brow arched in question. "What is a bow?"

"It's a device used to shoot small spears over a greater distance than you can throw your bigger ones." I formed a mental image of a person shooting an arrow from a bow. "It should allow Gardner here, along with two others, to hunt the herbivores without getting close enough to scare them off. But it does take practice to be accurate, and they'll have to be careful not to lose the arrows."

With a nod, he explained everything I'd just told him to Sandy. The Buri gave me a brief smile and dipped his head before leaving.

During the next thirty minutes, four more Buri approached Thor, three males and one female. Since the conversations appeared to be routine reports that I couldn't help with, I finished eating and then just waited.

About the time I got my hopes up for an escape, Churka walked over and sat beside me, then peered around me at Thor. "She can understand me now through the bond?"

"Yes."

To my surprise, she smiled and took my hand. "As eldest female of my family, it is my duty and privilege to welcome you, sister. We" —she gestured around at the other Buri— "knew you would come, but did not realize you would be the mind mate of my brother. I am pleased that it is so."

I returned her smile before what she'd said sunk in. "Whoa! Back up a sentence or two." My glare landed on Thor. "What does she mean, you knew I'd come?"

He returned my gaze calmly. "Our grandsire was descended from a long line of Shushannas and had the gift of foretelling. He said that when our need was greatest, a Shushanna with hair the color of the sun would come to us, and she would be the greatest Shushanna we have ever known."

My mouth gaped for a second, and then closed with a snap. "That's why you decided I was a Shushanna?"

Churka was watching us like a spectator at a spaceball match, a puzzled look on her face. Thor and I both ignored her while he answered me.

"I suspected it when I first saw your hair. My suspicion was proven correct when your leg healed. Only a Shushanna is capable of such a thing, and if it had not been true, the Demantti would have had no effect on you."

Even though my teeth were clenched, I took a deep breath and forced myself to calm down. We'd been over this, after all. He couldn't have told me before because we couldn't communicate. He hadn't withheld the information deliberately. It wasn't his fault.

Forcing a smile, I turned back to Churka. "Thank you. I too am pleased to have a new sister."

At least I didn't lie. It would be kind of nice to have someone around I could claim as family, even if it was only temporary.

Thor nudged me, his gaze warm. *"We are both your family now. All of us are your family, your tribe. We belong*

*to you as much as you belong to us. No matter where you go
or what you do, that will never change."*

At that moment, I could state positively that Naturals who
think GEPs have no souls were wrong. My eyes misted up
and I couldn't speak for the lump in my throat, but my soul
yearned with every fiber of its being, because Thor was offering me something I'd never dared to believe would be
mine. He was offering me the chance to fit in, to be part
of a greater whole than I'd ever been before. Not only did
they accept my strangeness, they embraced and celebrated
it, something I'd never managed to do for myself.

If I hadn't already fallen in love with him, I would have
then. And the surprising thing was, it didn't scare me this
time.

I still didn't see how things could work out in the end, but
at least I was willing to entertain the notion that we might
be able to reach an agreement that would suit everyone. I'd
have to think about it some more.

Thor had finished eating while I mulled that over. Placing his wooden utensil on the table, he turned to me. "The
reports are done. Are you prepared to leave?"

"Yes." I jumped up so fast I almost knocked over the
bench, grabbed his hand and towed him out the door behind
me. But when I headed for my quarters, he pulled me to a
stop.

"No. We will go home." He gestured at the stone edifice.

Home? That's our home? I whipped around to stare at the
graceful structure. The Buri had constructed that magnificent building for Thor and me?

*"I am leader, you are Shushanna, we are bonded. My
people were pleased to so honor us."*

"But it's too much!" My protest was damn near a wail,
and I forced myself to calm down. Max was the closest thing
I'd ever had to a real home, and until now I'd thought it was

enough. I'd been wrong. Because the thought of a real, solid, unmovable dirt-side home filled me with such a deep longing that my eyes stung with the effort not to weep.

"Compared to the hope you have brought my people, this is a small thing."

"What hope?"

He held out his hand. *"Come. We will not be interrupted here. I have explained 'honeymoon' to my people. They agree it is a wise habit to cultivate."*

With a groan, I walked across the clearing with him. That honeymoon thing was coming back to bite me in the butt. But if it bought me time alone with Thor, I'd live with it.

Accepting his offered hand, I followed him inside. "What hope?"

He looked down at me, a smile tilting the corners of his expressive mouth. "Is it not your purpose to find a way for my people to reproduce?"

Suspicious now, I squinted back at him. "Yes. That's part of my job."

"Because we have so few, children are precious to us." He stopped and faced me fully, serious now. "Your purpose brings renewed hope to my people. They know you will give them their hearts' greatest desire."

Oh, sure. Nothing like a little pressure to encourage a girl's fear of failure.

You will not fail.

CHAPTER 14

The room we entered was huge, with arched windows and doors that allowed any stray breeze to wander through. Low wooden tables in different sizes and shapes were strategically placed to make up individual conversation areas. Large colorful cushions were tossed around each table on the polished tile floor, adjusted for maximum comfort and style.

Decorative ironwork was set into the stone on each side of the windows and doors, and I realized they contained oil lamps. Matching lamps sat on the glossy tables beside beautiful flower arrangements.

And that wasn't all. On the most prominent interior wall, water danced and played down the stone to a catch basin near the floor. Flowering vines that filled the air with their perfume framed the marvelous little fall.

Delight rippled through me as I turned in a slow circle. I'd been in palaces on dozens of worlds, lush places that reflected their owners' wealth. But none of them had moved me the way this room did.

"You like it."

I caught feelings of pleasure rolling from Thor, and for a

second was taken aback. In the furor over the mind bond and our marriage, I'd somehow forgotten I could read emotions. Now that I'd remembered, I felt better. It was something familiar to hang on to in my suddenly turbulent world.

"It's beautiful, Thor. How could I not like it?"

"Churka will be pleased."

"Your sibling did this?"

"All contributed items, but she decided what to use where." He took my hand and led me to the table nearest the waterfall, where a tray containing a pitcher and two glasses rested.

"Why wasn't I allowed to come inside while they were working on it?"

He poured the glasses full of a clear golden liquid and handed one to me. "It is tradition for the male to bring his mate inside their home for the first time after the Rellantiim Ceremony is sealed."

"Kind of like carrying the bride over the threshold, huh?" I sniffed the liquid, decided it was fruit juice, and took a cautious sip. Yep, juice. I took a bigger swallow.

"These brides cannot walk?" His head was tilted in puzzlement as he regarded me.

"Of course they can walk." Although, considering I'd had trouble remaining in an upright position after the ceremony, I could see how he might get that idea. "It's an Old Earth superstition. No one knows for sure why it's done, though. One explanation I've heard is that it's bad luck for the female to fall when entering their home for the first time. Another one is that if she steps into the new home with the left foot first it's unlucky. Why press your luck when you can avoid the possibility by being carried? A third explanation is that it was handed down by the remnants of a clan that acquired females by stealing them and carrying them away from the protection of their fathers and brothers."

Thor's eyes glazed over, and I realized I was rambling. Taking a deep breath, I put the glass of juice back on the table. "Why don't you show me the rest of the place?"

"Of course." He took my hand and led me to a wide hall.

On each side were smaller, more intimate rooms decorated much like the room we'd first entered, minus the waterfall. Through the mind bond I picked up a blurry image of Buri meeting with Thor or myself. Kind of like offices, I decided.

Next came sleeping quarters, all beautifully decorated. Some had two sleeping platforms, others had one large one. But my attention kept returning to a curtain-covered opening at the far end of the hall.

Ever since returning from the crystal cave I'd felt a subtle pull toward this building. Now that I was inside, it was getting stronger, and there was no doubt in my mind that the attraction came from whatever was behind that kechic-like curtain.

I ran a sweaty palm down the outside of my thigh and glanced at Thor. Either he wasn't picking up my nervousness, or he was ignoring it. Since he'd picked up on everything else that had so much as flitted through my mind, I figured it was Option B. The question was, why? Did I really want to know?

Nope. No. Sure didn't. Call me the Queen of Denial, but I'd had about all the surprises I could take for a while. The only thing I wanted right now was to find our new sleeping quarters, jump Thor's bones, and then get some rest. It had been a long, unsettling day.

With a distinct gleam in his eyes, Thor tugged on my hand. "Through here."

He led me into a room on the right and I stopped abruptly, my jaw dropping at the sheer beauty in front of me. "This is our sleeping quarters?" I couldn't help the awe in my voice.

"Yes. The design was mine, but I thought you would approve."

"Approve" was an understatement, if I'd ever heard one. I took another step forward, trying to see everything at once.

The sleeping platform to my right was large enough for an orgy of epic proportions, and covered with dozens of pillows in the bright colors the tribe favored. On either side were shelves filled with my clothes and supplies, interspersed with beautiful jars and bowls. Someone, probably Churka, had unpacked for me.

Halfway across the room from the end of the platform was another small table with flowers, lamps, and cushions for sitting.

On the outside wall, arched openings led to a covered terrace, allowing the evening breeze to find its way inside.

But it was the far end that shot trickles of amazement through me. For here the waterfall from the front room was recreated on a much grander scale.

"It is for bathing," Thor told me. "Come, I will show you."

He stopped at the side of a crystal-clear pool and gestured to the fall. "It hits a wide shelf suitable for standing on, so you can let the water shower over you. Then it goes into the pool. There is an opening on the far end that lets water escape, so the pool stays clean. Would you like to bathe now?"

"I'd love to bathe—" My answer was cut off when a dragon bird zipped through one of the arches and hovered in midair, letting loose a startled squawk at our presence before darting back out. I couldn't stop a grin at the creature's antics. "They come inside?"

Thor watched his retreat. "They love to play in water anywhere they find it." With a gleam in his eyes, he turned back to me and reached for the fastening on his loincloth. "We will bathe now."

Sure worked for me. Only problem was I had on more clothes than Thor. As a result, by time I'd divested myself of my jumpsuit, boots and weapon, he was already under the shower. Yanking the tie from my hair, I took a step forward just as he moved out from under the water. And there he was, stark naked, water glistening on his body. My mouth dropped open just as he held out a bowl containing soft, creamy soap.

"Would you mind cleansing my back?" he said mildly. He turned around, waiting.

Mind? Did I mind? I couldn't wait to get my hands on the hard muscles that rippled just under his skin. Or the tight cheeks of his bottom, or the long, full legs. He was so gorgeous it was almost impossible to think. And he knew, damn it. Knew just what I was feeling.

"Come."

Almost as if I were in a trance, I took the soap from his hand and moved onto the ledge. Maybe if I didn't look I could get through this part without drooling all over him. Hastily, I closed my eyes even as my hand reached his back. It didn't help. Even with my eyes closed, I could see every perfect inch of him etched on my eyelids, would probably see him that way till the day I died. Might as well enjoy the show. I opened them again, and damn near stopped breathing. Under my hands, he was warm, slick with the soap. If seeing him naked hadn't been enough to start heat coiling through me, touching him like this would have. His texture was like nothing I'd experienced before. The heat extended to my breasts and then lower, causing a pleasing, resonant throb between my legs.

With a muffled oath, Thor grabbed me and dragged me completely under the shower with him. Hands gripping my elbows, he lifted me to my toes before his mouth crashed down on mine and plundered until I was limp. "Open the bond, feel what you make me feel."

"No." Panic hit me, taking the edge off my pleasure. I was used to sensing my partner's emotions when I made love. But opening up to actually letting *him* feel every touch, experience my every sensation, scared me, made me too vulnerable.

"Do not be afraid, my heart," he whispered, his eyes holding mine. The water hit us both, soaking our hair until it was plastered to our shoulders like a second skin. Slowly, his eyes moved down my body, taking in the erect nipples straining to be touched. My heart pounded frantically against my ribs at the heat in his expression. Gradually, he lifted his head until his gaze came back to mine. "I will protect you. Please, do not deny us this sharing."

"I've never . . . I don't know how." My voice wasn't quite steady, and I looked away.

"The truth." He raised my chin with one hand, forcing me to face him. "Why do you fear the bond?"

My teeth were suddenly chattering in spite of the fact that the water wasn't all that cold. Get out, I told myself. Get out now while you still can. "You." The words slipped from my traitorous mouth. "It's you."

"Why?"

In spite of his solemn tone, I could feel him, hard with arousal, pressing against my stomach. My breath caught on a half sob. "Because I'm afraid of getting even closer to you. If I do, then when I lose you, I don't know how I'll stand it."

"You will never lose me," he murmured. "If you cannot stay with my people, then I will go with you."

My heart was suddenly doing its damnedest to throttle me, clogging my throat until I could barely breathe. "You'd leave your home, your family, tribe, for me?"

"You are my family, my heart. Without you, there is nothing left for me here."

As his lips descended on mine again, I hesitated. Was he telling me the truth, or only telling me what I wanted to hear so I would cooperate? But he wasn't giving me a chance to figure it out. A shiver ran over me as he teased my mouth, gently but firmly forcing my lips apart. And then his tongue slid inside, exploring, searching, savoring. When it touched mine, the heat that had filled me before detonated into raging incandescence.

"I need you," he breathed into my mouth. "Put your arms around me," he commanded softly. "Touch me."

Helpless to disobey, I snaked my arms around his neck briefly while his lips found mine again. This time I needed no urging. My tongue sought his urgently, needing so much more, as I freed my hands to roam over him. Our bodies touched all the way down and I pressed more tightly against him, my erect nipples rubbing the hair on his chest.

Ecstasy. Glorious, wonderful ecstasy. Skin sliding over skin. Even in my wildest dreams I'd never thought it would be like this. I couldn't get close enough to him. He was touching me, holding me. He was making love to me.

He was opening the bond.

Another bolt of fear shot through me, warring with the need to give him what he'd asked of me.

"Kiera," he groaned. "Just relax. Let me do this, please. I know what you need." His lips moved over my face, blindly, desperately. "As much as I want to be inside you, I won't do it. Not until you're ready to fully share through the bond. Without it, this would only be a release, nothing more."

He was telling the truth. I could feel it as though his emotional shields were completely gone. The fear drained away from me, and I didn't even have to tell him. He knew the instant I stopped resisting and opened the bond. I went down without a fight. His tongue traced my lips and then plunged inside, our minds molded together as closely as our bodies. His hands slid up my hips, and then around, cupping my bottom before pulling me more tightly to him, once, twice in a rhythmic motion that had me moaning aloud. I could no more have shut off the bond than I could have cut off my right arm.

"That feels good," he whispered, "but you need more. You need this." His hands cradled my breasts, his thumbs slowly stroking my nipples until I was almost crazy. And the whole time, his mouth stayed on mine. "And this," he breathed. One hand moved lower. "This is what you want, what you need. Hold on tight."

His fingers parted me so gently, touched me, and then moved up slightly. Even with his warning, I wasn't prepared.

"Yes," he groaned. "Right there. Let go, my heart." His fingers caressed me once, and then again, while his tongue caught mine.

Everything I experienced, he shared. What I felt, he felt. And even as my need increased his own desire, his feelings merged with mine and amplified my own.

With a sob, I climaxed, pushing myself harder into his hand. And he was with me. My orgasm triggered his, which in turn intensified mine. My hand closed around him convulsively and he pulsed against my stomach and spilled over, each of us creating an echo of pleasure in the other that seemed to last forever.

Waves of smug satisfaction rippled from Thor as we stood there under the water, snuggled together. And not just from the sex, either. In spite of myself, I smiled without lifting my head from his chest. "Think you're pretty smart, don't you?"

"Yes." I felt a rumble of content under my cheek. "Now

you know the bond will not hurt you. You can stop fighting it."

"What I know is that if we don't get out of the water soon I'm going to look like a prune." I sent him a grossly exaggerated mental picture of the wrinkled fruit and he chuckled.

"We have something similar. It is called a *yapanya*. I do not like them." He pried me gently away. "What did you do with the cleanser?"

I shrugged one shoulder. "Must have dropped it."

He vanished from under the waterfall for a second. When he returned he was holding the bowl of creamy soap. "It floated into the pool."

We did a quick scrub down, and then went out onto the terrace to drip dry. Orpheus's moon was full, a big round orb that limned the night with bluish shadows. Across the clearing, I heard Brownie's little boy jabber something in a high-pitched voice, followed by the soothing tones of his mother.

It all felt so normal, so right. Until Crigo padded onto the terrace, sat down, and glared at me.

"Stop pretending you couldn't find me," I told him. "You keep track of me better than Max does."

Thor slanted me a curious look. "He understands what you say to him?"

"Oh, yeah, he understands every word. And I can pick up his emotions, so we communicate pretty well."

He gazed down at Crigo, who was now ignoring us in favor of staring into the dark toward the Dynatec camp. "Yes, I can feel them through you. Why is he so pleased?"

Uh-oh.

I straightened, a tingle of apprehension knotting my shoulders. "Max, what has Crigo been up to today?"

"After you returned to the village, he went back to watch the Dynatec people from the jungle and stayed for an hour.

There was a small disturbance in the camp, and then he left, heading in the general direction of the mapping party. I thought he might be hunting, and he wasn't near any humans or Buri so I didn't keep track of him."

"Is there any chance he caused the disturbance?" It was my turn to glare.

"I don't think so, Kiera. He never went into the camp, just watched from a distance."

Crigo raised his nose in the air, gave a disdainful sniff, and stalked into the building radiating injured pride.

Oh, this was just great. I'd hurt his feelings. No telling what he'd come up with to punish me.

Thor smiled. "He will survive."

"Yeah, but I may not."

He reached over and ran a hand down my damp hair. "You are tired?"

"Not really. Why? Is there something you want to do?"

An explicit image popped into my head. I sucked in a great lungful of air, nearly choked and then nodded vigorously. "Yes, I think we can manage that."

I grabbed his hand and towed him back inside. And then came to a screeching halt.

Crigo was sprawled in the middle of the sleeping platform, faking snores.

Releasing Thor's hand, I propped my hands on my hips. "Listen cat, that might be a large bed, but it's not big enough for a Buri, a GEP and a rock cat. Now scram."

He stopped snoring and regarded me through narrowly opened eyes, but didn't move.

Okay, time to take more drastic action. Climbing onto the bed, I put both hands against him and shoved. He growled. I stopped pushing. Fast. Just because I heal in the blink of an eye doesn't mean injuries don't hurt.

I glanced at Thor, who was watching with interest, then

back at Crigo. There had to be a solution to this problem. If physical strength wouldn't work, maybe logic would.

"Here's the thing," I told Crigo. "Thor and I are going to have sex, and we're going to have it on this bed whether you're in it or not. So you have a choice. You can stay here and endure our amorous antics, or you can postpone your revenge, save it for another day."

He stared at me, and I sighed. "Would it help if I said I was sorry, and that I'll never ever doubt you again for as long as we live, cross my heart?"

With an air of majesty, he gave a grunt of patent disbelief, climbed down, and stalked off to explore the rest of the building.

I watched him leave and then turned to Thor with a smile.

It was several hours later when Crigo returned. I was curled up beside Thor, his arm around my waist, almost asleep.

The cat slipped softly to the side of the bed, gently butted my hand, and then went to sprawl in the door leading to the terrace. He'd forgiven me.

More content than I'd ever been in my life, I drifted the rest of the way into sleep.

It seemed like only a few minutes later when a horrible din erupted and I bolted upright in bed.

What in the thirteen hells . . . ?

The sun was shining, and from the look of the shadows, had been for several hours. Moreover, I was alone. I searched frantically for the source of the noise and discovered what appeared to be approximately one hundred dragon birds frolicking in the pool and shower, and squabbling over the cleanser we'd left beside the water last night. They were scooping it up in tiny paws, dipping it into the water until it frothed, and then wallowing in the suds.

I had the distinct feeling that sleeping late every day was going to be out of the question in this room. But on the other hand, they *were* amusing. One popped up with a mound of foam on its head that looked like a big top hat, gave a smug *peep*, and used its wings to do a back flip in the water. Others gathered around the sides, preening, and I saw two chattering at each other as if they were old women at a social event, gossiping about the neighbors.

Thor suddenly stepped through the interior door, setting the entire bunch to scolding and squawking. He had to use the bond to talk to me, because there was no way to be heard over the noise.

You are hungry? Churka has brought food.

I'm starved. Give me a minute to dress and I'll be right out. I hopped out of bed, briefly contemplated donning a blue kechic, and then grabbed a clean jumpsuit, pulling it on before sliding my feet into my boots. Wearing the kechic might make Thor happy, but I had no idea what the day might bring. Besides, it just didn't go with my weapon.

Speaking of which . . . I went and retrieved the blaster from a dragon bird who was examining it and my discarded clothes intently. "Take my word for it," I told him. "They're not edible."

This particular creature was one I recognized as part of the flock that had followed me around from my first day on Orpheus Two. He tilted his head to one side, gave me a quizzical *cheep*, and then waddled back to his pals, wings half unfurled. It looked like he was getting braver every day.

After depositing the dirty jumpsuit in a basket near the door, I fastened the weapon around my waist, did a fast job of braiding my hair, and stepped into the hall.

Thor was standing near the front of the building, talking to someone in the smaller sitting room. Churka, I presumed.

I started toward him, then stopped and turned slowly toward the curtained door at the far end of the hall. We hadn't gone through it last night, and I really needed to now.

The walls on either side of me went fuzzy and my vision tunneled. Involuntarily, I took a step toward the curtain.

Abruptly, Thor was in front of me, his hands on my cheeks, forcing my head up so I had to meet his eyes. "Kiera, look at me."

I blinked once, then again before finally focusing on him. "What's in there?" I asked as he tried to steer me back toward the front of the building.

"Nothing."

"Nothing?" I put on the brakes. "If it's nothing, why are you dragging me away from it?"

"You wouldn't be interested in that area."

There was such a stew of emotions coming from him that my curiosity immediately soared. I was picking up hope, regret and the tiniest fear of failure all at the same time.

"What is it? You might as well tell me and get it over with."

He hesitated, glanced at the curtain, and then looked back. "It is the *Shushadeien*. The place where the Shushanna works."

My brows snapped together in reflex. "You're right. I'm not interested."

That was wrong of me, and I knew it. I should be gathering any and every scrap of information that might lead to solving the Buri's problems. But I couldn't do it. Because I still remembered the odd shimmer I'd noticed during the ceremony, coming from the back of this building. I still felt the pull, the urge, to go . . . do something. What, I wasn't sure, but the compulsion was gradually getting stronger, and that scared me down to my toes.

Being scared of something as insignificant as a room was

a foreign sensation, and it didn't sit well. I wasn't a coward, I was the best damn agent Alien Affairs had.

Thor was watching me closely, that infuriatingly inscrutable expression on his face again, and I was picking up no emotions. He was simply waiting patiently, letting me decide for myself. Damn it. Now I had no choice.

With a sigh, I turned back toward the curtain, my feet dragging reluctantly on the cool stone. It didn't take a Freud to figure out why this bothered me so much.

All I'd ever wanted out of life was to be as normal as possible in spite of the weirdness surrounding my creation. Now the Buri not only embraced my otherness, they expected me to ratchet it up a couple of notches. It was enough to make a girl pull her hair out by the roots.

But I could at least look at the room. No danger in that, right? It certainly didn't mean I was agreeing to the plan the Buri had laid out for me. One quick peek, then we could get on with the breakfast Churka had brought.

I mentally checked the status of my stomach. Yep, I could eat.

Concentrating on my internal diversionary tactics, I lifted a hand and pushed the curtain aside. Then blinked in surprise. Whatever horrible thing I'd been expecting, it wasn't this.

It looked like a giant filigreed birdcage. Five metal strips, each three inches wide, rose in equally spaced intervals from the spherical stone floor and then arched to meet a circle of metal way at the top.

At the bottom, the strips divided the stone floor into five pie-shaped wedges, and then swept up in the middle to form a waist-high pedestal aligned directly under the circle at the top.

Each strip was inlaid with a different color crystal. Amethyst, green, amber, blue and red, they climbed each strip individually and then swirled together on the top of the pedestal.

Like the stone in a ring, the biggest damn crystal I'd ever seen sat cradled on the pedestal. It was the size of two human heads and so black it seemed to suck light into its smooth facets.

And it wanted me. As I stood there, frozen in the doorway, I could feel its siren call dance inside my head, urging me forward.

Suddenly, my bond with Thor was small potatoes in the grand scheme of things, and it seemed silly that I'd ever worried about it. Because the power flowing from that crystal scared everything else right out of my head. What if someone evil, like—oh, Dorn and Frisk for instance—got their grubby hands on it?

"If they tried to use it, they would die."

At the sound of Thor's voice, I jumped and dropped the curtain. "Don't sneak up on me like that."

"I did not sneak. I've been with you since you stepped out of the sleeping room," he reminded me.

Oh, yeah. I was so absorbed in the crystal I'd forgotten that little fact. "Why would they die?"

"Anyone not a Shushanna who attempts to use the Limantti will die. Just as in the Rellantiim ceremony. It is attuned to you now. You are the only one who can control it."

That didn't give me a lot of comfort. Especially not with the word *control* tacked on in relation to myself. That the stone needed to be controlled at all scared me. That the Buri expected me to do so made me want to climb on board Max and head for parts unknown. Fast.

"And what if I can't control it?"

Thor gazed down at me, worry clear in his dark eyes. "Then it will control you."

CHAPTER 15

This just kept getting worse and worse. By nature, I'm an independent gal. There's no way I want a hunk of quartz calling the shots for me. If I had to beat the crap out of a gemstone to retain my freedom, then I'd do it, even if it took a laser drill and a sledgehammer to finish it off.

I pulled the curtain aside again and stared at the crystal, thinking hard and fast. When Thor called it the Limantti, I heard "mother stone." "Why *Limantti*?" I asked him.

"We believe it is the first living crystal, the one from which all others came."

From behind us, I heard Churka murmur something to Thor. I hadn't realized she'd followed him until then. He spoke to her quietly, and she hurried away, but once again I focused exclusively on the crystal.

If I were the only one who could control it, then I had to try, because there was a lot more at stake here than just the survival of the Buri, or bringing Dynatec to heel. Somehow I knew, down to the cellular level of my DNA that unleashed, this crystal could cause destruction on a scale unknown before now.

Barely aware of what I was I doing, I took a step into the Shushadeien.

And this time, Thor didn't stop me.

The Limantti was right in front of me, close enough to touch. From deep inside its ebony facets lights glimmered and sparked, urged me onward.

Mesmerized, I slowly lifted my hands and cupped them around the crystal. I had a split second to realize its surface wasn't cool but warm, warm and pulsing with life. Then, that same heat was moving up my arms, suffusing my body.

Startled, I tried to jerk back, but it was too late.

Light exploded inside my head, and the world fell away. A dizzying vertigo gripped me as I spun through space. For what seemed to be eons I watched galaxies form, spin into the distance. Planets were born and died, suns went nova.

Everywhere, there was life. So much life I couldn't take it all in. Carbon based, silicon, gaseous, it didn't matter. Everything was alive. Every tree, every rock, every blade of grass or clod of dirt, sun or planet. They all had a form of consciousness that clamored for my attention. It was alien, true, and in some cases slumberous, but I could feel their contentment when their chosen path was on course, their pain as they sickened and died.

And I knew that with one stray thought, I could destroy it all.

It was too much. I couldn't hold it all, and yet it continued. My skin felt hypersensitive, as though I'd shatter if someone touched me. A scream built in my throat, but my teeth were clamped together so tightly only a whimper escaped.

Please, I begged, *please stop*. Agony blazed through my mind, and for a blessed while, darkness descended and everything went away.

* * *

Kiera? Open your eyes.

No. Mentally, I tried to swat the voice away and pressed my eyes tightly closed in rebellious indignation.

You've been asleep for hours. The sun is high. It's time to wake.

Asleep? Like hell I had. That damn thing had knocked me out and I didn't appreciate it one bit.

Please, do it for me. You must eat.

Well, there was that. I could always find room for food. Experimentally, I cracked my eyes open a mere slit and peered up at Thor through my lashes. He tried to smile, but his face looked haggard, the skin pulled too tightly over his bones.

"Welcome back." His hand brushed gently over my hair and then cradled my cheek.

I opened my eyes all the way. He was sitting on the side of the platform near my hip, leaning over me. "You were afraid for me. Why?"

He hesitated and then glanced to his right. My gaze followed his. We were back in our sleeping quarters and both Auntie Em and Elder stood silently beside the bed.

"For an instant when you fell, I could no longer feel our bond. I thought I'd lost you. However, it is back now."

Warmth suffused me, along with distress that I'd inadvertently caused him pain. Before I could answer, Churka and Lurran bustled into the room, each carrying a tray of food and drinks.

"She's awake." The relief in Churka's voice was evident as she spotted me.

I wasn't asleep, damn it. I wished everyone would stop acting like I'd decided to take a little snooze in the middle of a formal diner for the leader of the Galactic Federation. But I forgave her when I saw the variety of food mounded on the tray.

Eagerly, I pushed myself up on the sleeping platform, surprised at how shaky my arms and legs felt. It was almost like what happened when I rapidly expended great amounts of energy.

Auntie Em piled pillows behind me while Churka deposited her tray on my lap. I dug in with relish, only pausing when it occurred to me that I hadn't heard a peep from Max.

"He was concerned," Thor told me. "The ship asked me to bring you outside so he could see you, and then told me you would be fine. He also said an abundance of food should be prepared for your awakening."

I blinked in confusion. "He talked to you? How?"

"He talked to you. I heard him through the bond."

"Max?"

"Yes, Kiera?"

"Did you scan me?"

"Yes, and there was nothing physically wrong except your body was burning calories a bit faster than usual. I assured your mate you'd be fine, but I don't think he believed me."

"Since when do you understand Buri?"

"At every possible chance I record your conversations and extrapolate the Buri meanings from your response. I'm becoming quite good at understanding them. In another day or two I should be able to complete a learning tape."

With a grimace, I picked up a glass of juice to moisten my dry throat. "Just don't neglect the other tests you're running. They have top priority."

"Yes, Kiera."

The Buri suddenly caught my attention. All five of them were staring at me with emotions ranging from excitement to trepidation. That last one was coming from Thor. "What's wrong?" I asked him. "What aren't you telling me?"

He glanced at Auntie Em again, and she nodded. "Tell her before she notices."

"Notices what?"

Thor took the glass of juice from my hand and set it on the tray. Before I could protest, his fingers curled around my wrist and turned my right hand palm up. Shock ran through me as I looked down.

Covering my entire palm was a black outline of the crystal, every facet depicted in an exact replica of the real thing.

Frantically, I rubbed at it with my fingers even knowing I was wasting my time. This was no smudge, nor was it any kind of ink. Though I doubted it was visible to anyone else, to my sensitive eyesight there was a faint black glow emanating from the lines.

"Does she understand me?"

"Yes." Thor moved aside and let Auntie Em take his place beside me.

"At first we were puzzled," she said. "Never before has a Shushanna been so marked by the Limantti. In order to use it, she had to be in contact with the crystal."

She paused and touched my palm with one finger. "After much thought, we realized that the Limantti has sealed you to its purpose. You will be able to call upon its powers from anywhere, because you carry a part of it with you. It is a great honor."

My stomach clenched, the food I'd just consumed thinking seriously about making a return appearance. I forced it to stay put, shoved the tray aside, and jumped to my feet. "No." I paced across the room, then back. "No, I won't do it. I won't use that thing. Not for the Buri, not for anyone. No one should have access to that much power. It's not right. Do you realize what I could do if I use it? With one stray thought I could accidentally wipe out millions of lives."

Heart pounding, I spun to face the Buri. "It's alive, did you know that? I don't know how, I don't even know what it is, but it's alive."

"I know what it is," Max inserted calmly.

"What?" I turned toward the terrace doors in surprise, as though I could see the ship from here. "You know?"

"Yes. I finished my tests on the quartz crystals several hours ago, but you told me to send the results to my archives before I informed you. I just completed the transmission."

Weak kneed, I sank down on the edge of the sleeping platform. "Tell me."

"As I suspected, the quartz is nothing more than ordinary quartz. It has, however, been infested with a microscopic alien life form that appears to feed on minute amounts of the silicon in the quartz without damaging its structure."

An alien life form. Somehow, I wasn't surprised. "What else?"

"More tests will be needed, but it appears this life form is self-aware to an extent I can't quantify. It exhibits two distinct characteristics. It loosely operates like a hive, with different colonies designated as workers, scouts, soldiers and nurses. Of course, those are merely my labels to explain the disparity between the types of organisms that inhabit each color of crystal."

"If it's a hive, then that damn thing" —I jabbed a finger in the general direction of the Limantti— "is the queen."

"There's a good possibility you're right," Max continued. "You see, it reproduces by spreading like a virus, and the organisms near the Buri village are older than the ones farther out. I would venture to guess that if crystal samples were taken from the far side of Orpheus Two, we would find no trace of the life form as yet."

"But sooner or later there will be."

"Yes. And I'd make it sooner. They spread very fast."

While we were talking, all the Buri except Thor had slipped from the room. I opened my clenched fist and gazed down at my palm. "So what does this mean?" I asked the ship.

"The mark on your palm? It would seem the Limantti has entered into symbiosis with you. Its purpose for doing so is unknown at this time."

"Great. That makes me feel *so* much better. I've always dreamed of being joined at the hip with a weird alien whose motivations I don't understand and who has the power to destroy the known universe." My sarcasm was tinged with a touch of hysteria that Max caught immediately.

"There's no need to panic. You're fine. Better than fine if my scan is any indication."

"How can I be better than fine?"

"Consider your normal condition after you rapidly expend large amounts of energy. You're weak, you sweat profusely, and if you don't refuel quickly, your body will shut down."

"So?" I shrugged. "I was weak this time."

"But not to the extent you normally are, and while you were hungry, you would have survived without the immediate intake of food. That's because the Limantti is transferring small quantities of energy to you on a continuous basis."

"I don't care if it makes me immortal." I stood and glanced at Thor. "I'm sorry. I know you say your people will die without a Shushanna, but I can't do this. It's too dangerous."

He reached out and cupped my shoulders with his hands, rubbing gently. "Kiera, the Limantti has been with my people for thousands and thousands of cycles. Never has it done harm."

"But it never had me before."

His expression became thoughtful. "Is it truly the danger you fear?"

"Of course it is." I stared up at him. "What else would it be?"

"You said it has always been your wish to be normal as possible. From the beginning you fought against becoming the Shushanna because you fear being different. Now we are asking you to become even more unusual than you were. Perhaps the peril you sense in the Limantti is to your dream of being normal, not to others."

There was a ring of truth to his words that I couldn't deny, but I also knew I was right about the power contained in the Limantti. After all, I was the one it had taken on a little universal day trip, not him. And at the moment, I could foresee absolutely nothing that would make me use that damn rock again.

"I'm sorry, Thor." Mentally, I pleaded with him to understand. "If there's any way to save your people without using the Limantti, I'll find it. But I can't be your Shushanna if it means working with that thing. I just can't."

I pulled away from him and walked to the terrace doors. "I'm going to help Max run some tests."

What I was really doing was escaping, and we both knew it. I could feel him watching me with a sense of quiet desperation, overlaid with resignation, but as much as it hurt, I kept walking. I needed to put some distance between me and the Buri right now.

I crossed the village, ignoring the Buri that paused in their work as I went by, except to note the majority of them, both male and female, now wore swords in sheaths that crossed over their back. The ones worn by the females were smaller versions of the thicker, longer swords carried by the males, but still deadly-looking.

The second I was out of sight in the jungle, I stopped and rubbed my temples, wondering what to do next. Max didn't need my help, and I had nowhere else to go.

Feeling more lost and alone than I'd ever felt before, I stood there with my head lowered, the Buri's expectations bearing down on me like a ten-ton weight.

How could I help them when I couldn't even help myself?

"Kiera?"

My head came up and I answered Max eagerly, wanting, needing any form of distraction. "Yes Max?"

"We may have a small problem."

"What?" I started in his direction.

"It appears Lieutenant Karle has vanished."

I came to an abrupt halt. "What do you mean, she's vanished?"

"As you requested, she set up a time with me to be tested for psi abilities. She planned to come by yesterday evening after her mapping party returned. When she didn't show up, I assumed she'd forgotten or had other duties that prevented her from contacting me. But she wasn't with the mapping party this morning, and she's not answering her comm unit. I've scanned the area where they were last working and found no trace of her."

"What about Ghost?"

"He, too, seems to have vanished."

A prescience of anger began to uncurl grasping fingers in my chest. I found the thread that connected me to Thor. *Thor, when was the last time you saw Ghost?* I sent him a mental image of the silver-haired, silver-eyed Buri.

I felt him searching his memory for a moment before he answered. *Yesterday morning when he followed the female.* The thought was suddenly tinged with a trace of worry.

You might want to question everyone to make sure. And it wouldn't hurt to send several people to look for him. Max can't find him or Lieutenant Karle.

He was already in action before I finished, and I turned toward the Dynatec camp. With every step, my fury increased until it hazed my vision.

GEPs don't make friends easily, and we value those we have above all else. In the short time I'd known her, Claudia had become a friend. A friend I had asked to do something potentially dangerous. If Frisk and Dorn had done something to her and Ghost, they were going to pay dearly.

"Kiera, stop. You can't barge into the Dynatec camp in this state of mind."

"Give me one good reason why not," I spat through clenched teeth.

"Because they outnumber you thirty to one, they're all armed, and even if you take out Dorn and Frisk, one of the others will eventually hit something vital."

Okay, maybe he had a point. But I had to find out what was going on, and I really, really needed an outlet for all the pent-up emotions I'd experienced lately. If I couldn't unleash them on Dorn or Frisk, well, there was one more option. "Where's Redfield?" I asked.

"In the jungle, about a mile and a half to your left, heading in the direction of the Buri village," Max replied.

"Alone?" I made an abrupt left turn.

"Yes, it would appear so, and I believe he's looking for you."

By the time I reached Redfield, I'd circled until I was almost back at the Buri village. He was crouched on his heels behind a bush, intently examining his back trail.

Making no attempt to move silently, I marched right up to him and planted both feet. "Where's Lieutenant Karle?"

"Agent Smith!" The relief on his face faded as he rose slowly to face me, his gaze taking in my expression. "I don't know where Lieutenant Karle is. I only know that she's not at camp or with the mapping party."

"Wrong answer, Redfield." My hand shot toward his throat. I'd intended to hold him off the ground and shake him until his teeth rattled, but I'd forgotten one little detail. He was a GEP, too, albeit not of my caliber.

Not only did he block the move, he used my forward momentum to throw me over his shoulder.

I'm ashamed to say I did my best to act like the landing stunned me. There was no doubt at all I could have him pinned in five seconds flat. But the petty, childish, pissed-off part of me was chanting "Fight! Fight! Fight!" with a great deal of glee.

Shaking my head as though dazed, I stood and faced him. He'd assumed a classic martial arts stance taught to all GEPs in the crèche.

My fist went through his guard like a laser through glass and landed on his mouth. Blood spurted, but because I'd pulled the punch, he stayed on his feet.

I have to give the guy credit. He tried. Not that it did him any good, of course. By the time Thor, Poe and Junior crashed through the foliage, all three now adorned with swords, Redfield was bloody, bruised, battered and still swinging.

Poe wrapped his arms around Redfield from behind and held him immobile as Thor stepped between us and glared at me.

"What?" I lifted my hands in question. "Yeah, yeah, I know. You're my mate and it's your right to protect me. Honestly, Thor, do I look like I need protecting?"

"You need no protection, but he does." He tilted his head toward Redfield. "What are you trying to accomplish by this action, his death?"

"No! I just need information." A pout came out of nowhere and settled on my mouth. "Besides, he started it."

Before he could reply, Churka and Lurran burst on the scene with what looked like armfuls of first-aid supplies. Poe gingerly released Redfield and the man slid to the ground.

Churka dropped to her knees next to him and poured water into a wooden bowl. Taking out a piece of cloth, she dunked it into the bowl and then gently swabbed away the blood on his face. "We need to take him back to the village so I can care for him properly." She shot me the same glare Thor had favored me with before getting back to business.

I glanced down at Redfield. He was propped on his elbows, his gaze wavering between Churka and Lurran as if he didn't know what to make of them.

"So much for Frisk and Dorn trying to wipe out the Buri, huh, Redfield? Even knowing that, they want to take you back to their home so they can take care of you. Would the people at Dynatec do the same? Maybe we should just send you on your way and find out."

He squinted up at me through swollen eyes. "I came to you because I needed your help getting away from them. If I go back now, especially looking like this, I'm a dead man. They'll think you beat the truth out of me, and nothing I say will stop them."

I moved a step closer and lowered my shields. "And just what is the truth?"

He hesitated. "As you know very well, I've been trying to reach you since your ship first landed, but they've kept me under constant watch. The only reason I got away from them now is because they're occupied looking for Claudia. So before I say anything, you have to promise you'll protect me from them."

"Are you formally requesting asylum from your indenture holder?" The Buri watched us closely, but none of them interfered.

He struggled to his feet, swayed, and then straightened, shrugging off Churka's steadying hand. "Yes."

"Then you have my word you'll be protected. Max, record please." For Redfield's benefit, I spoke aloud.

"Recording."

"A request for asylum under the Equality Edict has been

made." I kept my eyes on Redfield. This was serious business and I wanted him to understand that. "For the record, state your name and ID number."

"Thomas Redfield, LS46639."

"Senior Agent Kiera Smith, ID number 64732, responding. Do you swear that you're undertaking this action voluntarily without coercion from any party?"

His chin went up a notch. "I do."

"On what basis are you making this request?"

A shudder ran over his body. "Violations of the Equality Edict by Captain Jon Frisk, my indenture holder. These violations include, but are not limited to, physical cruelty and mental abuse, and being forced to act in a manner that goes against the laws of the Federation."

The boy remembered his training. Pleased, I nodded encouragement before continuing. "Do you understand that you may be required to testify against your indenture holder in a court of law?"

"Yes."

"Good. Max, seal it, date it and send it to the boss for immediate action."

"What happens now?" Redfield asked. Churka had stopped her ministrations during the proceedings, but now swabbed something sticky on his cuts while he talked.

"The boss will go to the court and have your indenture to Frisk revoked until a trial can be held. As soon as possible you'll be sent to Alien Affairs' Rehabilitation Center for testing, therapy if needed, and retraining. After that, your future will be up to you."

A deep breath lifted his chest and his eyes closed for a moment as relief, almost painful in its intensity, poured off him. "Thank you."

The words were barely a whisper. I shook my head. "Don't thank me, Thomas. I couldn't have done a thing if you hadn't taken the first step. We do need to assign a Buri to stay with you, though. I don't want to take a chance that Frisk will try to silence you."

Thor spoke to Poe, and the big Buri moved closer to Redfield.

"They'll take you back to the village now. This one is named Poe. He'll be your guard." I pointed. "This is Churka, Lurran and Junior." Placing a hand on Thor's arm, I smiled up at him. "And this is Thor, leader of the Buri and my mate."

Redfield blinked at us for a second, and then nodded. "Somehow that seems right. Tell him I appreciate his help."

"He understands."

Poe put his hand on Redfield's back to steer him toward the village. They'd only taken a few steps when Redfield stopped and turned back to face me.

"Agent Smith? I really don't know where Lieutenant Karle is. No one does. Yesterday, Quilla discovered Claudia had returned to camp and tried to access her private records on the ship's computer. She was furious. She gave orders that Claudia was to be taken into custody the second she was found. Only, Lieutenant Karle never came back. The mapping team returned without her. They said they hadn't seen her for several hours and she hadn't responded to their inquiries."

He was telling me the truth. I didn't even need to ask Max for confirmation. I could feel it.

"She must have found out somehow and gone into hiding." I mulled that over for a second. "Maybe she heard Dorn order her capture on her comm unit."

"No, Quilla forbade all chatter from camp on the comm units until the mapping team returned. She didn't want Claudia to receive any warning. And then, when Claudia didn't come back, she tried to locate her using the signal from her comm unit. If it's still working, something is blocking it, because they couldn't get a signal."

The small party continued on, and I watched until they were hidden by the foliage, mulling over Claudia's mysterious escape. She wasn't psychic, so something or someone must have warned her.

"Who would have known?" Thor asked.

Good question. And I could only think of one answer, but I needed to know for sure. "Max, where is Crigo?"

There was a pause before he answered. "He is in the same area where he hunted yesterday, near where the mapping party worked."

"That's it." I couldn't stop my chuckle. "The damn cat hid them."

Thor stared at me in perplexity. "How do you know this?"

"It's simple logic," I told him. "When Crigo makes a kill, he gorges and then curls up to sleep it off somewhere. But when he showed up last night, he wasn't full. Remember how smug and pleased he was?"

His face cleared and a smile curved his lips. "Yes, he was very satisfied about something."

"He must have overheard Dorn and then went to find Claudia and Ghost. They're probably stashed in a cave, wondering what in thirteen hells is going on."

"We should find them and bring them back to the village."

I considered all the possible scenarios and then shook my head. "No, leave them where they are for now and call the searchers back. They're probably safer where they are. Crigo will take care of them, and it would never occur to Dorn or Frisk to watch the cat. The next time he comes to the village I'll give him a note to Claudia explaining what's going on."

Another thought occurred to me. "What do the markings on your spears mean? I'm assuming it's a written form of your language."

"Of course. They indicate ownership, plus some give their weapons names." He seemed slightly puzzled that I'd had to ask. "Do you not name your weapons?"

I hooked an arm through his just to maintain contact and leaned against him. "No, but then we don't really form an emotional attachment to our blasters. I do know some ancient societies followed the practice of naming swords. What I was getting at is that you can write a note to Ghost, too."

"Yes." He lifted a hand and ran it over my hair. "You are feeling better now."

Surprised, I searched my emotions. He was right. My anger had faded away. The Limantti was still there, tugging at me, always on the edge of my awareness, but I could deal with it. Maybe pounding on Redfield had done me some good.

Speaking of which . . . "Let's go back to the village and see how Redfield is doing. If he's up to it, I've got a couple hundred more questions for him."

CHAPTER 16

We took our time walking back to the village so Churka and Lurran could have Redfield settled in my old quarters before we got there. Thor stopped long enough to send Junior after the Buri searching for Claudia and Ghost. Since it was on his way, I asked the youngster to stop and collect the bows and arrows from Max when he returned.

Redfield looked almost normal when we stepped into the small building. Well, except for a swollen lip and a black eye. Okay, and a tiny little cut on his jaw. Probably wouldn't even leave a decent mark.

More importantly, from the way he was broadcasting, he was really taking pleasure in the attention showered on him by the Buri females. Watching him, I realized for the first time just how good-looking the man was. Especially when he smiled, the way he was doing now.

Thor shot me a glare, and I shrugged. *Just because I admire a fine piece of art doesn't mean I have to own it*, I told him mentally. *Redfield isn't my type.*

What is your type?

Fishing for compliments, huh? I fluttered my eyelashes

at him in my best silent-film actress imitation. *I'm surprised you can ask after last night.*

Before the big guy could respond, Redfield noticed us standing in the doorway and his smile faded.

"Feeling any better?" I asked him.

"Yes. Please tell them I appreciate their help. I'll do anything within my power to return the favor. You don't know what a relief it is to be away from Dorn and Frisk."

Thor tilted his head toward the door and the women left the quarters, taking their first-aid supplies with them. When they were gone, I strolled to the foot of the sleeping platform and sat down facing Redfield. "Tell me about Dorn and Frisk."

He glanced at Thor, who was standing in the middle of the room, arms crossed over his broad chest as he studied Redfield. "He understands what I'm saying?"

"Yes. And since it concerns the survival of his people, I think he has the right to hear whatever you know."

With a sigh, he straightened his back against the pillows propping him up. "I'm afraid it's not much. They didn't trust me. I can tell you Quilla is in charge, not Frisk. And I've overheard enough to know that she's after the crystals on Orpheus Two, although I don't why. They look like ordinary quartz to me."

He'd told me nothing I didn't already know, but I wasn't done yet. "Why did they go to the expense of buying your indenture when they could have hired a Natural science officer for a lot less?"

"They wanted someone they had complete control over." He glanced at Thor. "From the very beginning I've suspected they planned on wiping out his people if they discovered the Buri weren't dying out naturally. I was supposed to find out for sure. If they weren't—if they had to kill the Buri—I think they wanted a science officer who could be forced into swearing the deaths weren't caused by them."

Thor's brows lowered in a fierce scowl. "He tried to take Dryggahn's child."

When I repeated his comment in Galactic Standard, Redfield lowered his face, shame rolling off him.

"Yes. I won't deny it. Three of us were sent into the jungle with the orders to grab him so I could run tests." He looked up at Thor. "But I was also the one who took my time getting him back to the camp, and let him go the minute you showed up. And I caught hell for it later. Frisk thought we should have taken the opportunity to kill as many of you as possible, and keep the child."

"Why didn't you?" I asked. So far, everything he'd told me was the truth.

"Because I didn't want to grab the child in the first place. I knew what they'd do to him, what they'd force me to do. But I couldn't disobey orders or it would have been my hide on the line. When he" —Redfield gestured at Thor— "showed up with the other Buri, it was my chance to keep the kid safe and deflect Frisk's anger at the same time. I took it."

Okay, maybe I had misjudged Redfield. I had to admit he'd been doing some fast thinking that day. If I had been in his situation, I might have done the same thing. But I had one more question for him.

"That day in the jungle when you showed me the black flower, I got the impression you wanted to talk to me. If you really aren't on Frisk and Dorn's side, why didn't you say something then?"

His chin went up a notch as his gaze held mine. "Quilla and Frisk had followed me into the jungle. You see, I faked an interest in botany just so I could get away from them for a while every day, looking for a chance to contact you in private. But they were suspicious."

He lifted a hand to rub his forehead. "I spotted them almost immediately, of course, and went to great lengths to convince them I really was looking at plants. Then you showed up, asking questions, quoting indenture law and offering to save me from Frisk, while I knew he was listening to everything we said. You're damn right I kept quiet. I knew I was going to pay for every word out of your mouth. You have no idea what Frisk is capable of."

He gave me a rueful smile. "Ever since you got here, I've been trying to figure out how to talk to you alone. That's why I was so close to the Buri village today. I just didn't expect you to be looking for a fight."

"You started it." That damn pout was trying to come back, but I squelched it.

"Yeah, I swung first, but I can read body language as well as any GEP. You wanted a fight, and you weren't going to take no for an answer. All I could do was hope you'd listen to me after you worked off some steam." He touched his lip gingerly. "The part where I got beaten to a pulp came as something of a surprise, though. Who the hell taught you to fight? I thought all the crèche training was the same."

"Believe me, it's a long story." I stood and walked to the door, Thor following me. "I'll have Churka bring you something to eat soon. Until then, try to get some rest. We'll talk again later."

"Agent Smith?"

Redfield's questioning voice stopped me and I turned to face him. "Yes?"

"If there's anything I can do to help you bring Dynatec to justice, I'd like to try."

For a moment I studied him intently. Could I trust him? I thought he'd told me the truth, but I needed confirmation.

"Max," I subvocalized. "Have you been analyzing his voice?"

"Yes, and all indications are that he's been completely honest in his answers."

Might as well take the plunge. "I need to figure out why the Buri aren't reproducing in greater numbers," I told Redfield. "And you were created to work in the life sciences. Would you be willing to help me with that?"

His eyes lit up. "Yes, but I'll need a lab."

"No problem." I glanced at Thor to get his permission, and when he nodded, turned back to Redfield. "I don't think it would be smart for you to leave the village, but there's no reason why I can't move my Quonset hut here. It has a state-of-the-art lab, and I already have samples of the Buri's DNA as well as medic scans. You could start tomorrow."

"Perfect." With a satisfied smile, he leaned back and closed his eyes.

As soon as Thor and I had stepped outside, Poe went back in and stationed himself so he could watch the door and windows.

Thor glanced at the lowering sun. "You will move this building now? It is almost time to eat."

Yeah, the scents drifting from the communal kitchen were making my stomach growl with anticipation. "It won't take long."

Plus, going after the Quonset hut had the added benefit of keeping me away from the Limantti for a while longer. Not that distance did anything but give me a false sense of security. It seemed I could now feel the blasted rock anywhere I went. The tone of its emissions had changed, though. Now, instead of urging me closer, it sent feelings of comfort, warmth, love. And those were much more dangerous, because they were harder for me to resist.

And the damn stone knew it.

I turned my back on the building that was now my home,

and its Shushadeien. "Do you know where the antigrav sled is?"

"It is beside my work area. This way." He headed around the adobe hut he'd lived in before we were mated. "Would you like me to go with you?"

"Sure. The Quonset hut will be easier to load on the sled with two of us picking it up. It's not heavy, but it is bulky."

When we got to his work area, I looked around with interest. It was basically a roof set on poles, open on all four sides to let heat escape. At the back was a forge made of hardened adobe, cold now. I spotted an anvil, and on a table to one side, a variety of metal tools. The space was neat and clean, as though he took pride in what he did. A pang of guilt hit me.

"You haven't been able to work much lately, have you? I'm sorry about that."

He shrugged as he pulled out the sled. "It is not your fault. When a metal tool is needed, I will work."

Side by side, we walked through the dappled light of the jungle. An evening breeze had sprung up, cooling the air a bit. After a minute, Thor glanced at me. "You now know what the other humans intend. Can your leader not prevent them?"

"I wish it were that easy. Unfortunately, they haven't broken any laws yet. Until they do, we can't arrest them."

His jaw hardened. "They would destroy my people."

"I know, Thor. But we can't arrest someone for thinking bad things. If we did, everyone alive would be consigned to Inferno. At this point, we can't even get them on conspiracy to commit xenocide, because we have no proof. And we can't use Redfield as a witness, because he never heard them specifically say they intended to wipe you out."

A tendril of anger trickled through the bond. "What good are these laws if you cannot act until my people are dead?"

"Sometimes I wonder the same thing." A sigh escaped my lips. "Then I remind myself that without laws, chaos would rule."

I reached over and touched his arm in reassurance. "Thor, I promise to do everything in my power to stop them."

He stared down at me intently. "That is untrue. You will not accept the Limantti."

My hand dropped to my side. "I said I'd do everything within *my* power. That will have to be good enough."

Silence held sway on the rest of the walk, but I could feel Thor's disappointment. As much as that hurt, I shrugged it off. I couldn't let his feelings influence my instincts where the crystal was concerned.

As soon as we reached the Quonset hut, I pushed a button, and we stood watching it fold itself up. When it was done, we each took an end and lifted it onto the antigrav sled. Before I could grab the handle, Thor finally spoke.

"I'm sorry." His voice was low as he moved to stand in front of me. "It was not my intent to cause you pain, and I have no desire to force you to act against your will. It is simply hard for me to understand your distaste for the Limantti when our Shushanna have used it for so long. But I will try to remember that you know nothing of our ways, and have no reason to trust us or the Limantti."

Wrapping my arms around his waist, I leaned against his strong body, my head on his chest as his warm arms closed around me. "I trust you, Thor."

"Do you?"

I was pondering his question when a familiar noise had me spinning from his arms in surprise to face the plains. Just beyond the line of bushes, Max was lifting off!

Shock held me immobile until Max's voice blared over the outside speakers. "Frisk shot Crigo!"

Fear, raw and hot, arrowed straight into my heart. My feet were moving before I could take a full breath. "Where are they?"

"Near the Dynatec encampment. Follow me!"

Max was flying fast and low, and I was right behind him. As much as I wanted to, I didn't dare go into overdrive. The situation was unknown and it wouldn't do to deplete all my strength when I might need it desperately. From the rear, I could hear the pounding of Thor's feet on the ground as he tried to keep up.

Time seemed to slow until it felt like I was moving through sludge, even though the rational part of my mind knew I wasn't. The gray metal surface of Max's hull, flickering in the sun, took on a menacing façade as he surged forward, straight toward the trees.

Suddenly I had a new worry. Was he going to crash in his efforts to reach Crigo?

Even as the thought occurred to me, the ship slowed. Bushes and small saplings cracked under his weight as Max rapidly settled to earth at the edge of the jungle. From the direction of Dynatec's camp came surprised yells.

Heart pounding, I dodged around Max's bulk to the sound of the cargo bay door sliding open and the ramp lowering. Frisk was standing, blaster in hand, gaping at the three port cannons Max had aimed at his chest. Crigo was sprawled, unmoving, in an ungainly heap at his feet.

Clearing a downed sapling in one bound, I fell to my knees beside the rock cat, frantically searching for blood, for any sign he was still alive. There! His chest moved. Just barely, but it moved. There was still time to save him, if we could get him to Max's sick bay.

Awkwardly, I slid my arms under the cat and stood, cradling his long body. He dangled loosely in my grip, head lolling on my right, hind legs sprawled to my left. As gently as possible, I lowered him to the stretcher Max had extended and then watched as the ship whisked him away.

I wasn't going to cry, damn it. Not now. There were other things to take care of. Things like the bastard who shot my cat.

A roaring filled my head as I spun to face Frisk, fully intending to do him great bodily harm. But Thor had beaten me to it, and I realized the roar had come from him.

In one swift move, he disarmed Frisk, tossed the blaster into the jungle, and plowed a huge fist into the man's stomach. Frisk doubled over, groaning in agony. Thor used the opportunity to land an uppercut that spun Frisk around and nearly took his head off. Before he hit the ground, Thor grabbed him by the back of the neck and lifted until Frisk's feet swung a good foot above the ground.

Holding him in that position, Thor glanced at me, his voice a low, dangerous growl. "Shall I kill him for you?"

He wanted to. And by all that was holy, I wanted to let him. Hell, I wanted to help him, and I wanted it to be gory. Just thinking about it had my fingers clawed in anticipation.

But I couldn't.

Murder was illegal, and by now we had an audience comprising all the Dynatec crew and the Buri who had been standing guard on the camp. Unfortunately, that was way too many witnesses. "Let him go."

He took me literally, simply opened his hand and let Frisk plummet to the ground. The captain landed with a bone-jarring thud and curled into a fetal position, arms clutching his middle, moaning like he was dying.

Ignoring the cannons Max now had pointed at the Dynatec crew, Dorn pushed her way through the crowd and stopped beside Frisk. "What's going on here?"

"He shot Crigo." I angled my chin at Frisk.

"It was self-defense," Frisk whined. "He attacked me."

Hands on my hips, I glared down at the worm. "Max, did Crigo attack him?"

"I doubt it, Kiera." He used his outside speakers so everyone could hear. "Crigo was lying in the shade, watching the camp as usual. Captain Frisk was in the jungle behind him the last time I checked, and Crigo was paying no attention to him."

"But you didn't actually see what happened?" Dorn didn't wait for a response. "Frisk could have stumbled on the cat, which surprised both of them. You did tell him that the cat was out to get him, Agent Smith. It's no wonder the captain reacted defensively."

Sure, blame it on the GEP. I almost snorted in disbelief. We both knew he'd done it deliberately. There was just no way to prove it.

"Get him out of my sight," I told her. "Now. Before I change my mind. And if Crigo dies, Frisk better hope he's somewhere I can't find him."

Dorn pointed at two of her men. "You and you. Take him back to camp."

She moved aside as they hoisted Frisk between them, and mumbled "idiot" under her breath. Then she turned back to me. "I'll make sure he's restricted to camp from now on."

"You do that." I waited until the Dynatec people were headed back to their camp, and then ran for the cargo doors, anxious to reach Crigo. Thor stopped to issue an order to the waiting Buri and then followed me.

The smell in sick bay was sharp and astringent, burning my nose and making my eyes water. Through the resultant blur, I saw Crigo stretched on a bunk, tubes and wires leading from his body to openings in the wall. For a moment I stood there, fighting off the nausea caused by my fear.

"Max?" In spite of my intent to be strong, my voice came out in a raspy whisper.

"He's alive. There are no external wounds. His vitals are extremely weak but stable."

I tiptoed to the side of the bed and gently ran my hand over the broad head lying so still. "Will he make it?"

Max hesitated so long I thought he wasn't going to answer me. "Are you sure you want him to? You know what a blaster set to stun can do to a rock cat. They're very sensitive to even the lowest setting. I don't think Frisk had his weapon set on low. I can keep Crigo's body alive, but his brain may be permanently damaged."

"No." A tremor ran over me and tears trickled down my cheeks, but my answer was fierce. "You do whatever you have to do to keep him alive. He'll be fine. He just needs to rest a while."

"Kiera—"

"No!" I knew I was being unreasonable, but that which is not spoken aloud is not real. At least, that's the way it felt. If I insisted hard enough that Crigo would make it, then he would.

Thor's hands settled on my shoulders and rubbed gently as Max lifted off to move back to his original position on the other side of the lake. "Is there anything I can do to help?"

I swiped away a tear, and shook my head. "All we can do is wait. And if you believe in a higher power, pray."

For a moment longer, he stood there behind me, and then his hands slid from my arms and he turned toward the door.

"You're leaving?" Already I missed the comfort of his presence.

"For now. I will return as soon as possible."

"Where are you going?"

He paused to give me a self-conscious smile. "To pray. Should I send back something for you to eat?"

Touched, I looked down at Crigo to hide the reemergence of my tears. "I don't think I could swallow, but thanks."

After Thor was gone I pulled a chair to the side of the bunk and continued stroking the unconscious cat, murmuring encouragement until my voice was raw. Time crawled forward in small, slow increments. "I'm here," I told him over and over. "I won't leave until you're back on your feet. I promise. You're going to be fine, better than ever. By this time tomorrow, you'll be back bothering the dragon birds and hunting herdbeasts. You can even have my bed if you want."

I choked back a sob and dropped my forehead to his warm, silky side, closing my eyes in exhaustion. It must be close to dawn by now, and I wondered where Thor was, why he hadn't returned.

More for something to occupy my mind than out of curiosity, I sent a seeking tendril through our bond. He was awake, but concentrating so hard on something I couldn't get his attention. And he wasn't alone. Several of the females were with him, trying to help him . . . do something.

Whatever was going on, I couldn't worry about it now. I turned my attention back to Crigo. "Max, is there any change?"

"I'm sorry, Kiera. His vitals are still the same."

With a sigh, I straightened, stretching the muscles in my back, then shook my hand. It tingled as if it had gone to sleep. I flexed my fingers a few times, then leaned over and gently rubbed the dark stripe between the cat's eyes.

There was a whirring sound followed by a soft plop, and I glanced over to see a steaming tray sitting in the sick bay's food-preparation unit.

"Thanks, Max, but I'm still not hungry." Under my hand I felt the slight flick of an ear.

"You really need to eat, Kiera. Starving yourself won't help Crigo."

"I know." Damn, my hand felt like it had bugs crawling

on it, and I pressed it harder against Crigo's head to ease the itch. "But forcing myself to eat when I don't want it will only make me sick. I promise, if I feel the least bit hungry, I'll eat."

"Kiera."

"Don't nag, Max. It's not attractive. I told you, I'll eat later."

"Kiera!"

He'd damn near bellowed, and I gaped in surprise. "Well, if it means that much to you . . ."

"It's Crigo! He's waking up!"

"What!" I jerked my gaze back to the cat just as his side lifted on a deep breath. His ear twitched again, and I realized it was the second time I'd felt it.

"His brain activity is increasing. Fast," Max said excitedly. "I've never seen or heard of anything like this happening before with a stunned rock cat."

I leaned closer, almost nose to nose with the cat, excitement surging through my veins. "Crigo? Can you hear me?"

There was a flicker of eyelids, and then two amber eyes were staring into my own. I caught a wisp of puzzlement from him.

"You're okay," I told him. "Frisk stunned you, but you're fine now."

His head shot up so fast it knocked me back a step, a snarl curling his lips, and Max hastily withdrew all the life support paraphernalia. Gathering his legs under him, Crigo lurched upright, wobbled, and then his butt plopped back to the bunk. His emotions changed from anger to disgust and chagrin as he turned his head to survey his backside like it belonged on someone else.

"You're still weak," I told him, a stupid grin on my face. "The Frisk filet will have to wait a while. Here." I grabbed the food tray Max had fixed for me and shoved it under Crigo's nose. "Eat; you'll get your strength back faster."

He narrowed his eyes at me before lowering his head to sniff the food. Reluctantly, he began to eat.

The Crigo is better now?

Thor's question had my brow furrowing at the tone of utter exhaustion it conveyed. *Yes, he's going to recover completely. Have you been up all night?*

Yes. As you suggested, we have been praying.

Except when he said *praying*, what I heard was "imploring." A sudden uncomfortable suspicion hit me. *Who, exactly, were you imploring to?*

The Limantti.

I was afraid he was going to say that. Doing a good imitation of Crigo's butt, I landed back in my chair. *Let me get this straight. You asked the Limantti to heal Crigo?*

It has never been done by someone not a Shushanna before, he told me. *But I hoped it would understand through the bond I share with you.*

Understand what? I asked weakly.

That the Crigo is not just another animal. He is your family, and his death would cause you great pain.

Slowly I raised my hand and stared down at the black lines etched on my palm. The lines that glowed. The lines that had tingled and itched right before Crigo regained consciousness. The hand I'd been stroking him with.

I think you succeeded. Numb with shock, I continued to stare at my hand a moment longer, then stuck it under my thigh where I couldn't see it.

Shall I bring you food now?

No, Max can fix me something. There was a whir as another tray of food slid out of the unit before I even finished the thought, and I wondered if the ship had fixed it for me or

Crigo. Probably Crigo, since I wasn't speaking aloud. *Why don't you get some rest?*

You also need rest.

I know, but I have to stay until Crigo can function on his own. I'll curl up on the extra bunk here in sick bay.

The mental exchange came to an end, and I knew Thor had gone to sleep. Relieved at the privacy, I contemplated what had just happened. My feelings were ambivalent to say the least.

Retrieving the food, I carried it to Crigo and then got a tray of my own and dug in, hungrier than I'd realized.

Of course, I thanked the Goddess that Crigo was alive and well. On the other hand, the stone had used me to heal him, without my permission or knowledge.

I had to look at this logically, I decided. What would I have done if the stone *had* asked my permission? Stupid question. I'd have sold my soul to the master of the thirteen hells to save Crigo, with no hesitation at all.

Thinking hard and fast, I finished eating, gathered up the empty trays for the disposal, and lay down on the spare bunk so I'd be close if Crigo needed me.

Suddenly, I was faced with the biggest moral dilemma of my life. Because if I'd go to those lengths to save Crigo, why was I quibbling over using the Limantti to save the Buri?

For the next hour, I tried hard to convince myself that it was a totally different proposition. That using the Limantti to save the Buri might endanger the rest of the universe. But even I wasn't buying it.

Maybe Thor had been right when he said I didn't trust him. After all, as he'd pointed out repeatedly, their Shushanna had used the Limantti for centuries with no ill effects. I'd just been too busy panicking to really listen. Or care.

That wasn't like me at all, so maybe he was right about something else, too.

Maybe I *was* resisting the Limantti because of my own personal fears. I'd admitted as much when he'd first broached the subject, but hadn't really thought the matter through.

I thought about the consequences now as I drifted to sleep. How could I, in good conscious, accept the use of the Limantti to save Crigo but not the Buri?

Could I really acknowledge that I was what Gertz had made me, no matter what it was, or was I talking myself into playing God?

I didn't know, and I was too tired to figure it out.

CHAPTER 17

I came awake with a jolt when a huge paw swatted me upside the head. The damn cat wasn't gentle about it, either.
His amber eyes were shooting darts straight at me.

Gingerly, I sat up and rubbed the spot while I tried to get
my sleep-addled brain to focus. "What was that for?"

He stalked to the closed sick bay door and sat down facing it while Max answered. "He wants to leave. I wouldn't
let him until you said it was okay."

"How is he?" I shoved off the bunk and stood surveying
the cat, who was now glaring at me over his shoulder, impa-
tience rolling off him.

"His vitals and brain activity are back to normal."

"No residual weakness?"

"None whatsoever."

"Good." Awake now, I moved to the desk against the far
bulkhead. "Crigo, I don't want you anywhere near the Dynatec camp for now. But if you're going to check on Claudia
and Ghost, I need you to take a message."

He came back and sat beside me while I jotted a brief
explanation of why Crigo had hustled them into hiding, put
it in a flexiplast tube, and handed it to him. Thor's note to

Ghost would have to wait. Maybe Claudia could figure out a way to communicate the details to her guy.

"Be careful," I told the cat. "And this time, watch your back. It might even be a good idea to let Frisk think you're out of action permanently, so stay out of sight as much as you can."

As soon as Max opened the doors, Crigo was through them, disappearing down the hall. I started after him, and then paused. "Max, if Frisk leaves the Dynatec camp, let me know at once. And try to keep an eye on Crigo, see where he goes."

"I'll try, Kiera, but I'm having problems with one of my satellites again."

"The same one as before?"

"Yes. And the one closest to it on the left is flickering occasionally."

That worried me. I didn't like Max having blind spots. "Can you fix them remotely?"

"I'm trying."

I hesitated, feeling the need to do something to help. But there really wasn't anything I *could* do right now. "I have to get back to the village. If you don't have them fixed by tomorrow evening, you'll have to go up and replace them."

"Yes, Kiera."

Once outside, I took a deep breath of the perfumed air and headed toward the Buri village. The antigrav sled was gone, so Thor must have taken it with him the night before. A quick check through the bond told me he was still asleep, so I took my time, enjoying the simple pleasure of walking through a tropical paradise.

The dragon birds were out in full force, taking advantage of the afternoon sun filtering through the trees. One of them landed on a vine near me and cheeped a greeting. It was the same one that had been contemplating eating my weapon yesterday morning. His feathers flashed in shades of iridescence from green to blue to purple as he moved. To my surprise, I picked up a trickle of recognition from the tiny creature. Maybe they were more intelligent than I'd thought.

He escorted me almost all the way to the village, flitting from vine to vine, cheeping conversationally, and then abandoned me for a clump of flowers as big as my fist. If I was here long enough, and got all the other problems sorted out, I'd seriously consider studying the dragon birds a little closer. I had a feeling there was more to them than pretty feathers.

The first thing I noticed when I stepped into the village was the Quonset hut sitting off to one side. It looked out of place beside the adobe buildings of the Buri, kind of like an armadillo pretending to be a butterfly. Redfield must have set it up, and from the sound of movement inside, gone right to work.

I skirted it and headed for my new home. At the moment, all I wanted was a bath and a change of clothes.

Thor was just waking up when I reached the bedroom, and joined me in the bathing pool. That, of course, led to a round of hanky-panky that left me breathless and replete. Having sex available whenever I wanted it was something I'd missed for the last cycle or so. I could really, really get used to it again, I decided.

The sun was skimming the treetops by the time we were dressed again, and Thor left to rustle up some grub. I waited until he went through the outside doors, and then moved silently down the hall to the Shushadeien.

The Limantti sat right where it had been the last time I'd seen it, and I shook my head. What? Was I expecting it to get up and walk around? Do a song-and-dance routine? It was a rock, for the Goddess's sake. But the truth was, nothing that crystal did would surprise me.

I walked forward and stopped in front of it. From deep inside its ebony center came pulsing sparks of light. It had stopped broadcasting its siren call the second I stepped through the curtain. Now it was waiting.

A shiver of apprehension ran over me, but I forced the feeling away. Slowly, I lifted my hands and held them curved around the Limantti, an inch above its glossy black surface. No way was I going to touch that thing again. Not yet, anyway.

But it didn't seem to matter whether I touched it or not. The crystal had so much power the air crackled with it, even when the stone was sitting quiescent.

"Where in the thirteen hells did you come from?" The thought flashed through my mind and out my mouth before I realized I'd spoken.

Instantly, I was overwhelmed with the sense of vast distances, of eons passing slowly in the cold darkness of space. And worse, a feeling of being so alone that it was more than painful. It was a soul wound, a hunger for companionship that left me gasping for breath and trying my damnedest not to collapse in a torrent of tears.

Before I could move, the feelings of sadness were gradually replaced by an intense joy, as the crystal discovered the Buri, tempered by its disappointment at their inability to really share with it on a mental level. It needed me for that, and it had waited so long I was tempted to give in right that second. But I couldn't.

I stood there a moment longer, then lowered my hands to my sides and stepped back, my gaze locked on the crystal. "I can't do this," I told it quietly. "I'm not ready. There are things I need to understand about you first, like your history with the Buri. But I promise to have Thor tell me about your association with his people, and to at least consider the options from all angles. If I decide there's a way to work with you safely, we'll give it a shot, but you have to stop trying to lure me into it. Although I appreciate what you did for Crigo, the decision to join with you has to be mine or this won't go well at all."

The Limantti pulsed once and emitted a shimmering blue light that briefly illuminated the surroundings. Its intelligence was more alien than anything I'd encountered before, but I had no trouble picking up feelings of understanding and patience from it. There was even a hint of pleasure that it had helped Crigo. For that, if nothing else, I couldn't help but like it a bit more. And the truth was, I now felt a bit sorry for it. Its loneliness had struck an answering chord deep inside me.

With a rueful smile at the realization that I was suddenly empathizing with a rock, I turned and went inside to find Thor. We had some talking to do, and this time I wasn't going to take no for an answer.

As it turned out, "no" wasn't even on my list of options at the moment. I'd barely passed our bedroom when Redfield stepped through the front door.

"Agent Smith?"

"Right here, Redfield." I walked to the front of the building to meet him. "What's up?"

"I found something."

Thor appeared in the doorway to the large sitting room. "There is food prepared. Eat while you speak with the Redfield."

With a nod, I gestured Redfield into the room. "We can talk in here. Have you eaten yet?"

He tilted his head as he thought about it. "No, I don't think so. Sometimes when I'm working I forget to eat, or eat and don't remember it."

Okay, that boggled my mind. How could anyone forget to eat? Eating was right up there, with sex, breathing and sleeping, on my list of personal priorities. And the aromas coming from the dishes on the low table near the decorative waterfall had my mouth watering.

All three of us chose pillows, sat down and filled our plates, but I could tell Redfield's mind wasn't on what he was doing. I decided to take mercy on him. "What did you find?"

"Honestly, your ship found it, but neither of you realized the significance. Do you know how the reproduction cycle works in mammals?"

"Sure." I stopped chewing long enough to answer him. "The female releases an egg, it's fertilized by the male sperm, and X number of months later a baby or babies pop out. Elementary."

He smiled and shook his head. "That's the end result, not the process." Pushing his plate to one side, he pulled a pen and notepad out of his pocket. "Here's how it works. Right above the brainstem is the hypothalamus." He drew a crude brain and pointed to one organ.

"The hypothalamus makes a gonadotropin-releasing hormone that tells the anterior pituitary to secrete a follicle-stimulating hormone. Moderate levels of FSH are absolutely necessary for correct reproductive function, but the lack of any FSH indicates a problem with either the hypothalamus or the pituitary. None of the Buri females have FSH, and only one shows any sign of an estrogen-like hormone."

I stopped eating to stare at him. "You're talking about the hormone Max found in the gestating female Buri."

"Exactly. And it means that at some point, she must have had the FSH or she could never have conceived. Now she seems to be the only female producing an estrogen-like hormone, which is nothing short of amazing. You see, they need the FSH to become adult females. Since they've obviously done so, I can only speculate that after going through puberty, their bodies stop making the FSH. Therefore, no pregnancies and no estrogen-like hormone except in the one case where a pregnancy *has* occurred."

"So all we have to do is give them hormones and they'll start to reproduce again?" I glanced at Thor to see how he was taking all this. To my surprise, he didn't seem to be paying much attention.

I know we have few offspring. The why doesn't matter. It's the fixing we need. Only the Shushanna can do that.

Unaware of the mental conversation going on, Redfield continued. "Unfortunately, no; it's not that easy, for several reasons. First, the Buri hormone isn't estrogen. It serves the same purpose, and even resembles it a bit, but there's enough difference in the two that one could never be mistaken for the other.

Second, the main problem appears to lie in the hypothalamus. There's a part of the gland that's atrophied in the female Buri, and it's the part that produces the gonadotropin-releasing hormone. Unless we can find a way to revitalize the atrophied section, the Buri may die out in spite of all our efforts."

I sat a little straighter, thinking fast. "Can't we synthesize the hormone?"

Redfield shrugged and pulled his plate back in front of him. "Possibly. But it could take fifty or sixty cycles to do the research and development. I don't think the Buri have that long."

"No, they don't." Worried now, I mentally reviewed all the facts and hit a stumbling block right off the bat. "Wait. How did this one particular female manage to conceive? And what about Brownie's little boy? His mother must be able to secrete the hormone too, or she could never have given birth."

Redfield was shaking his head before I finished. "She doesn't have it. Her hypothalamus is in the same condition as all the other females. I can only believe that for some reason, it became active again and she conceived. And then when the child was old enough to wean, it went back to being dormant."

I turned to Thor. "Is that what happened?"

He put his fork down and faced me. "I did not understand all the words, but yes. Dryggahn's mate worked many months to become with child, as did Sillia, the female who carries now. Most are not capable of this feat, and the few that are produce only male children."

"How do they do it?" I asked, even though part of me already knew the answer.

"Through the Limantti. They have a small portion of the Shushanna power, just enough to invoke its aid in conceiving."

Redfield was looking from Thor to me and back again. "What did he say?"

I wasn't about to tell Redfield about the Limantti, so I said the first thing that popped into my mind. "He said they appealed to a higher power."

Well, it wasn't a lie. Exactly. "And he also said they only have male children."

"That's understandable."

I glanced back at Redfield. "How is it understandable?"

"Because, I believe the sex of a child is determined by the female in the Buri population. The male's sperm is pretty typical of mammals. Some sperm have the X chromosome, others have the Y. But whether or not the egg allows fertilization by either depends on the amount of hormone the female has released. In the one case we have as an example, only enough of the hormone was present to allow for the conception of a male child."

My eyes narrowed in suspicion. "How did you get a sample of the male sperm?"

A grin flashed across his face. "I didn't. Your ship had done an analysis somehow and he shared it with me."

I was so not going to ask how Max had accomplished that deed. I was afraid I knew. Looked like a little chat with the ship on privacy issues was in order.

On the other hand, it meant Thor was fertile. And that meant at some point in the future, if I stayed with him, he would expect me to have a child. I wasn't quite sure how I felt about that. I mean, actually carry another person inside me? To someone who had been grown in a vat, so to speak, actually giving birth seemed a rather messy way to go about the whole reproduction business.

This would require a lot more thought on my part. And maybe a talk with Brownie's mate and Sillia. I wondered if she'd let me watch when she gave birth. There were lots of vids out there showing the event, but I'd never been interested enough to buy one before.

You will be even more beautiful when you carry our child than you are now.

Yeah?

He sent me an image of myself, glowing like the sun, belly protruding as if I'd swallowed a minisub. I didn't know whether to laugh or blush, so instead, I spoke to Redfield again.

"Thanks for all your help, Thomas."

"I'm glad there was something I could do. Besides, you and your ship did all the work. I only put the pieces together." He finished off his food and stood. "If it's okay with you, I'll keep working. Maybe I can eventually come up with something that will stimulate their hypothalamus."

"I'd appreciate it."

He left by the outside door, and I watched him go, knowing there was nothing he could do. Saving the Buri had once again been dumped squarely on my shoulders, pushing me even closer to using the Limantti. But at least trying would keep him busy.

Wait just a darn minute here. Apparently I *wasn't* the only one who could use the Limantti. Sillia had used it to conceive. So had Brownie's mate. As a matter of fact, she'd been one of the females with Thor last night. The other female with him was . . . Churka.

"Churka." I reached across the table and poked him in the chest with one finger. "You neglected to mention that your sibling has more of this ability to connect with the Limantti than the other females, didn't you? That's how she was able to communicate with me mentally when she brought me your armlets. That's how you managed to reach the Limantti last night and convince it to save Crigo."

"Yes." He caught my hand and lifted it to kiss my fingers. "I was not hiding this from you, as you believe. It merely has no importance to my people. Churka is more gifted than the other females because our dam was the last Shushanna. But she is still not gifted enough to become a Shushanna in her own right. Only you have the ability to do that."

Nonchalantly, I stacked our dishes back on the tray. "Speaking of the Limantti . . ."

My bid for turning the conversation to the Buri's history trailed off as the sandy-colored male in charge of the fields stepped through the outer door. He was looking, with a great deal of puzzlement, at an unstrung bow and a quiver of arrows he held in one hand. Mentally, I said a curse word. I'd completely forgotten that Junior was supposed to pick them up from Max.

When he reached us, he stopped and spoke to Thor. "We do not understand the use of these implements. Are we to throw them at the gergians destroying our fields? Our spears would be better."

With a sigh, I stood and reached for the bow. There was

at least an hour of daylight left; might as well use it. "Tell him I'll show him and the others how to use these weapons correctly."

With Thor acting as interpreter, they followed me outside, where two other Buri, one a female, were waiting, each with a bow and arrows.

"Ask him how close they can usually get to these gergians before they flee."

After Thor repeated my question, Gardner looked around and then pointed to an outcropping of rock about one hundred yards away. Good. The bows were seventy-five-pound weight and could shoot an arrow about three hundred and fifty yards, so that was well within their range.

By the time I'd strung the bow, we had an audience. Looked like the entire village was turning out to watch. I glanced around the clearing, looking for a good target and making sure no one was in front of me. "See that tree? The one with pink spots on the dark green leaves? Keep your eye on the trunk."

The one I'd chosen was at least two hundred yards from where we were standing. I picked up an arrow, notched it, and pulled back the string, sighting down the shaft. The Buri were so quiet you could have heard a falling leaf hit the ground. In the silence, the twang of the bowstring was loud when I released it, as was the thud when the arrow hit the tree.

An excited murmur ran through the Buri, and the two still holding unstrung bows looked down at them with new respect.

While Brownie's little boy ran to retrieve the arrow, I unstrung the bow and gave it back to Gardner, then, with Thor translating, walked him through restringing it. The other two Buri watched closely and mimicked our actions until all three had mastered preparing the bow.

It came as no surprise to me that they were shooting like Robin Hood's merry men in less than an hour. They were so graceful and athletic, I'd figured they would be good at archery. And it wasn't just the original three. After they became proficient, everyone had to take a turn, and the falling darkness was no obstacle. They just started a large bonfire and turned the whole thing into a party.

And without the Limantti consuming my attention, I could finally relax and just enjoy being there. Simply watching the Buri have fun aroused all my protective instincts, along with something I'd never felt before. A feeling of possessiveness.

Whether I'd wanted it to happen or not, the Buri were becoming my people. For a GEP, that was both a scary and comforting proposition. Comforting that I'd finally found a place where I could really belong, scary because I knew I'd have to leave them.

A wave of loneliness washed over me at the thought, reminding me of the Limantti. Maybe the crystal and I had more in common than I'd believed.

I was distracted from my thoughts when two of the Buri, a male and a female, stopped and chattered something at me. Thor, who had just taken a turn with the bow, came over and sat down next to me so I could understand them.

"We would like to know how these instruments are constructed," the female said. "We both work in wood, and yet we have never seen such things. All wish to have one of them, but especially our hunters."

"Sure thing. Hang on for a sec and I'll be right back." I jumped up and headed for the Quonset hut. "Max, send a simple diagram on making bows and arrows to the printer in the lab, please."

"Printing," he responded.

Poe was leaning next to the door, so I knew Redfield was

inside. He was bent over a high-powered molecular microscope when I walked into the hut, but he straightened and
stretched. "Wow, what time is it?"

"About an hour after sunset." I snagged the drawing Max
had sent to the printer. "Why don't you take a break and join
the party?"

"Are you sure the Buri won't mind? I don't think I'm very
high on their favorites list."

"They'll get used to you." I shrugged. "Just stay away
from Brownie. He barely tolerates *me* and I didn't try to steal
his kid."

"Good point."

He and Poe followed me back toward the group, but Thor
stopped me before I reached them and pulled me to one side.
"I do not like this, mate. For hundreds of cycles weapons
that can kill from a distance have been outlawed among my
people, and for a very good reason. It is much harder to kill
face to face than it is to hide and kill like a coward."

I arched a brow. "Are you telling me there's no such thing
as murder among your people?"

"No, but it is so rare, the last time it happened I was a
small child. I would not have that change. I know we need
these weapons to protect the fields, but I do not like the idea
of all my people having the bows and arrows." His forehead
was creased by a frown of worry. "Maybe they should only
go to the hunters."

Immediately I shook my head. "That's a recipe for disas-
ter. If you only give them to the hunters, you're creating an
elite group of warriors. It's happened before with very bad
results, usually for women. The hunter/warriors take over
and demand special treatment or they'll stop protecting and
feeding the tribe. Soon, they're insisting everyone believe
the way they do, and those that don't are punished. By giving the bows to everyone, you keep that from occurring."

"Then maybe we should keep them and only issue them at night to those who tend the fields." He stared down at the drawings I held.

Carefully, I folded the diagram and put it in his hand. "In that case, you take this. If you want to share it, you can. Or you can destroy it. However, before you decide, let me tell you something. I think your belief is honorable and that you have your people's best interest at heart. If it were any other time, I'd even say I agree with you. But if it comes down to a fight with the Dynatec crew, they won't hesitate to use blasters that kill at a much greater distance than the bows."

I reached over and put my hand on his arm. "Thor, as I told you before, Dynatec is up to something, and I'm afraid it won't be much longer before they act. That's why I've started wearing my weapons constantly during the day, and keep them close at night. It's why I suggested your people start arming themselves. Max and I will do everything in our power to protect the Buri, but we can't be everywhere. A bow and arrows are pitiful weapons to go against blasters, but they *are* better than bare hands and spears."

He stared at me intently. "You think they will attack us soon."

It was a statement, not a question. "If they want to file Chapter Twenty, they have to get rid of the Buri before I find a way to make you reproduce in greater numbers. The longer I stay here, the greater the chances are I'll succeed before the two-month time limit is up, and Quilla Dorn won't allow that."

For a moment longer he hesitated, and then handed the diagram back to me. "Show them how to make these weapons. I'll worry about what to do with them afterward."

If there was an afterward. We were both thinking it, but neither of us said it. I really doubted the Buri would have time to make more bows, not when it took days of intensive labor to complete just one. If and when it came down to a battle, we were going to depend an awful lot on Max and his six laser cannons. He was up to the job, but there was a worry niggling at the back of my mind, something I couldn't quite pin down.

A wave of noise from my right caused me to glance toward the rest of the tribe. Well, hell. Could I not catch a break? Brownie was stalking Redfield, a blaze of unholy anger lighting his eyes. Oblivious to his danger, Redfield was standing beside Poe, watching one of the younger males take a turn with a bow.

Okay, since they kept insisting I was their damn Shushanna, I was going to act like one and pull rank.

Shoving the drawing in my pocket, I stomped through the crowd and planted myself firmly between Brownie and Redfield, who had just realized he was in the path of danger. "No," I told the Buri. "I won't have a fight between the two of you."

And to emphasize my point, I located his strand and gave it a none-too-gentle yank. Those little suckers were coming in handy, I decided, pleased when Brownie winced.

Unfortunately, it didn't dissuade him. He straightened to his full height and glared down at me. "This man threatened my child. According to our law, it is my right to call challenge."

"Is he right?" I asked Thor, who had stayed by my side.

"Yes."

I turned back to Brownie. "He's already injured. It wouldn't be a fair fight."

The dark-haired Buri surveyed Redfield's colorful bruises, and then gave a grudging nod. "I will offer a concession."

One brow arched in question, I glanced back to Thor for an interpretation of that statement.

"He offers to do whatever you deem necessary to make the contest equal."

"That's big of him. How do you feel?" I asked Redfield.

"Stiff and sore." He was eyeing Brownie with an air of resignation. "But if he wants a fight, I'll do it. I guess I owe him that much."

"Don't be an idiot," I snapped. "It's not going to satisfy his honor to beat an injured man senseless. It needs to be an equal match."

Which gave me an idea.

Smiling now, I faced Brownie. "The concession I ask is to choose the form the contest takes."

"That is acceptable."

Still smiling, I scanned the crowd until I located Auntie Em, and then motioned her forward. "Bring liquor," I told her through Thor. "And lots of it."

CHAPTER 18

While Auntie Em took two other Buri to collect the liquor, I leaned toward Redfield. "Look, I know GEPs don't get drunk nearly as fast as Naturals, but if Auntie Em is any example, neither do the Buri. Either way, Brownie needs to win this contest, and it can't look like you're throwing the match. His honor is at stake."

"You don't have to worry, Agent Smith. I know how to handle the problem."

"Good." Since Thor was frowning at me, I threw him an innocent smile, but he wasn't buying it.

You would have him lose the contest deliberately?

Would you rather they beat each other to a bloody pulp and put two men out of commission when we may need every able fighter we can get our hands on?

The Redfield would fight with us against his people?

Yes, I think he would. And he's a GEP. Not quite like me, but stronger, and with better combat training than Naturals. There's also the fact that he's armed with a blaster, which will come in handy.

He stared at the ground for a second, and then shook his head. "Bending the law this way is not right. A branch too often bent must soon break. It was the Redfield's right to name the concession, but he must not deliberately let Dryg-gahn win, and you will tell him this."

Redfield had been standing by patiently while Thor and I conducted the mental portion of our conversation. But after Thor spoke aloud, Redfield glanced at me. "What did he say?"

"He said you can't deliberately let Brownie win."

A look of puzzlement crossed Redfield's face. "Why not? Isn't the objective to give him satisfaction and restore his honor?"

"It has something to do with the law and tree branches." I shrugged. "Don't look at me. I've never understood Naturals, and probably never will. And despite being an alien race, the Buri are Naturals right down to their toes. But if he wants you to drink Brownie under the table, then go for it."

"If you say so."

He was still looking doubtful, but I knew he'd follow instructions. And Thor was smiling again, which seemed to matter a lot more to me than it should have.

Of course, he knew exactly what I was feeling. Before I realized it, his arm snaked around my waist, pulling me into his side. My knees did a fantastic imitation of limp noodles and it was all I could do to keep from snuggling into him and staying there forever.

Unfortunately, Auntie Em and the two Buri she'd taken along had returned, loaded down with large clay wine jugs. Much as it pained me, I had to at least *try* and act dignified.

Someone had brought out one of the low tables the Buri favored, and she deposited her jug beside it, then marched over to Thor, a glower on her face. "Whose brilliant idea was this? Our stores of wine will be depleted for several seven-days before these two are done. How happy will everyone be when they have only water to drink with their meals?"

"Tell her I'll replace whatever wine they consume with Panga ale from Max's stores first thing tomorrow," I told Thor.

Her answering smile was so smug I had to wonder if that wasn't what she'd planned from the start of this conversation. She really did love Panga ale, after all. No doubt she'd been scheming ways to get her hands on more since I'd shut down the food unit in the Quonset hut when Frisk attempted to poison me.

"It is time to begin." Thor gestured to where Redfield and Brownie were taking their places across the table from each other.

Cups were placed in front of them and Auntie Em hurried to join Elder. After a brief consultation, Elder moved to the north end of the table, while Auntie Em stood guard at the south. In unison, the Buri each lifted a jug and poured the cups full, while the rest of the tribe gathered around to watch.

Clearing my throat, I stepped forward. "Only two rules, guys. If you toss your cookies, you lose. And the last man conscious wins." I waited until Thor finished translating and then asked him, "What happens if Brownie wins?"

"The Redfield will owe him a tribute, of Dryggahn's choosing. If the Redfield wins, the grudge will be dropped and never spoken of again."

When I gave Redfield the terms, he nodded and picked up his cup. "Cheers." He downed it in three swallows and Brownie followed suit.

By the time they were on the fifth cup with no apparent effects, I was getting bored. Shifting restlessly, I looked around for something else to do. Finally, I leaned into Thor. "I think we should go and get Claudia and Ghost and bring them back to the village."

"Now?" He blinked down at me sleepily, and I realized he was as bored as I was.

"Yes, now. It's dark, and the Dynatec ship doesn't have long-range night sensors. I'd like to know exactly what Claudia found. It must have been important for Dorn to react like she has. Claudia is also armed with a blaster. The more weapons we have, the better I'll feel."

His gaze sharpened. "You know where they are."

"Not exactly. But I know the general location. I'm betting that when I get close to them, I'll be able to distinguish Ghost's strand from the others and find them that way. It's only a few miles from here, so we can be there and back before anyone misses us."

All traces of boredom fell away from him as he straightened. "We will go now. Which way?"

I pointed at a spot that was approximately halfway between Max's location and the mountains to the west. "Somewhere in that direction."

Taking my hand, he led me through the crowd and we slipped away into the darkness under the trees, pausing a second to let our eyes adjust before moving onward. I also loosened my blaster in its holster in case I needed to get it out fast.

No more speaking aloud, I told him. *Just because their ship lacks long-range night vision equipment doesn't mean they won't have people out searching.*

He nodded, but remained silent, which gave me a chance to concentrate on the strands as we walked. The large unmoving clump was right there, a kind of in-your-face glow. Just to the south of that cluster, the Buri's strands were a much smaller and looser group that shimmered and shifted, twisting together and then separating into individuals as they moved around. Thor's was right beside me, thicker and more substantial than any of the others.

I let my consciousness expand until I found the individual Buri who were standing watch on the Dynatec camp. To my surprise, one of them was fairly close, just in front of us and to our left.

There could only be one reason why he was there.

Immediately, I stopped and touched Thor's arm, bringing him to a halt. *Someone from the Dynatec crew is just ahead. We need to move, very quietly, to the right and circle around them.*

He peered through the darkness, then slid sideways between two trees without so much as stirring a leaf, leaving me blinking in admiration at the way he'd vanished. Damn, he was good. Especially when you took his size into consideration. Males who are over seven feet tall aren't usually the picture of grace and agility. Thor was the exception to the rule.

This way, his voice sounded in my head. *There's a stream that will cover any noise we make.*

He meant any noise *I* made, because he sure wasn't making any, and my admiration was tinged with a little envy. My usual method of confronting problems was about as subtle as a thundering herd of pachyderms. But if he could move silently, then I could at least try to do the same. Taking a deep breath, I followed him, paying more attention to where I placed my feet and to the branches that brushed against me.

Moving quietly got easier once we reached the stream. The damp banks padded our steps and the gurgling water hid any other small sound we might make.

Keeping an internal eye on the location of the Dynatec crew member, I let my consciousness expand even further. And in the far upper right of my reach, where Max had last seen Crigo, I found a single shimmering strand of Buri life force. It had to be Ghost.

This way, I told Thor, and moved into the lead. We were now far enough from the Dynatec crew member that I wasn't worried about being discovered, so I picked up the pace.

Gradually, the ground sloped upward and became rockier. Just as the trees thinned until I was afraid we were going to be in clear sight on the plain, a low snarl sounded from above us.

"It's me," I whispered, and the snarl changed to a chuff of welcome as Crigo stood from his crouched position on top of a boulder. He watched intently as we made our way to where he stood guard, then turned and led us to a black opening in the rock wall.

We'd barely taken two steps inside when I was grabbed and nearly bowled over.

"Kiera! Thank the Goddess," Claudia babbled, hanging onto me like her life depended on it. "I've been so scared."

"Didn't you get my note?" I gently disentangled myself from her grip and glanced around. It was a good-sized cave with passages branching off in the back. Someone had started a fire far enough into one of the tunnels that its glow couldn't be seen from outside. A small trickle of water spilled down a rock wall to fill a tiny pool next to one opening. All in all, it wasn't a bad place to hide, even if you did have to sleep on the bare floor.

Ghost chattered excitedly at Thor while Claudia answered my question. "I got it, but all you said was to stay in hiding, that Quilla was hunting me, and to trust Crigo. And not to sleep with Ghost." She frowned at that last one. "Why do you care if I sleep with him?"

"It's a long story. I'll explain everything when we get you back to the Buri village."

"Is that safe? Quilla will know right where to find me."

"Yeah, she'll know, but she won't be able to do anything about it. The hardest part will be getting you there. She has people out looking, so you'll have to be quiet. And leave your comm unit here. They're trying to pick up its signal and use it to locate you, but the cave walls are blocking it."

While Thor and Ghost put out the fire, she unfastened the comm unit and threw it deep into one of the passages. Too bad I didn't have time to hook it to one of the herdbeasts that roamed the plains. That would sure keep Dorn and company busy for the night. As pleasant as that thought was, it would take too long to run one down.

I moved to the cave opening, where Crigo waited and mentally checked the area. The Buri I'd located earlier was moving back toward the Dynatec camp, so we should have a clear path.

When the others joined me, we set out single file with Crigo in the front. We were almost back at the village when he flattened his ears and came to an abrupt halt. A wave of animosity rolled off him as he stared intently into the jungle.

Someone is out there, I told Thor. *Keep Ghost and Claudia back.* Freeing my blaster, I moved up to stand beside Crigo and aimed it at the area he was watching.

"Show yourself, Dorn, or I'll shoot first and ask questions later."

"How did you know it was me?" She stepped out of the darkness into a patch of moonlight.

"Logic. If it had been Frisk, Crigo wouldn't be standing here looking at you, he'd be eating you alive. And if had been one of your crew, a Buri would have been near. I've noticed that you seem to be good at evading the guards." I held the blaster loosely, but was prepared to act in a split second if necessary. "Now, what are you doing here?"

"Waiting." She shrugged. "I knew that sooner or later you'd fetch Claudia, so it made more sense than beating the brush. And you can put the blaster away. I'm not going to attack you."

"Let's just make sure of that, shall we? Max, record," I told the ship as I returned my blaster to its holster.

"Recording."

I crossed my arms and stared at her. "What do you want with Claudia?"

"She's a member of my crew. I'd like to have her back."

Before I could respond, Claudia dodged around Thor and rushed to stand next to me. "Consider this my resignation, Quilla. I don't work for people who plan on killing me."

Dorn's lips curved in a calm smile. "Don't be so dramatic, Claudia. You're a valuable asset to my company. Why would I want to kill you?"

Claudia's chin went up. "Because I know what kind of files you have on your computer."

"Oh?" My interest went several notches. "What files does she have?"

Dorn's smile vanished. "That's proprietary information. I could have her arrested for corporate espionage."

"You could, yes." My own smile turned feral. "But then you'd have to open your files to the courts, wouldn't you? I'm sure they'd love to see them."

A bolt of pure frustration shot from her before she got it under control. "It might be worth it."

"Really? Claudia, what are the files?"

"She has one on the Bureau of Alien Affairs, one on you, one on the Buri, another on the crystals of Orpheus Two, and a really big one on someone named Gertz."

A chill ran through me. How in the thirteen hells had she found out about Dr. Gertz? If the file was as big as Claudia thought, I could no longer assume my secrets were safe. I couldn't even confront her about it, because there was a slim chance she didn't know what she had, and I wasn't about to point her in the right direction. This information had to get to the boss right away.

"Max," I subvocalized, "feed this straight to Dr. Daniels, and put a red alert on it so he sees it immediately."

I had to divert Dorn away from that Gertz file, make her think I wasn't interested in it, so I grasped the first topic that came to mind. "There's no need to hide the crystals, Dorn. I know exactly what they are and what they're capable of doing. The information is already permanently entered into Max's archives. Even as we speak, scientists from all over the universe are studying the information."

"You'd have to be stupid not to know." Her smile was back, smug and condescending. "If there's one thing I know about you, Agent Smith, it's that you aren't stupid. A bit naive, perhaps, but not stupid." She gave another of those negligent little shrugs. "It doesn't matter. When our Chapter Twenty is approved, the planet will legally belong to Dynatec, along with all the crystals. We'll be able to ask any price we want for them. Do you know how much people will pay for a crystal that enhances psi ability? The sky is the limit."

"Aren't you forgetting something?" I gestured toward Thor and Ghost, who had moved up to flank Claudia and me. "Orpheus Two belongs to the Buri."

"For now. But we both know they aren't capable of reproducing in significant numbers. And even you can't change that. Not in the time you have left. What is it, three more weeks? You'd need a miracle."

She didn't know about the Limantti. Relief surged through me, and I grinned. "I wouldn't be too sure of myself if I were you, Dorn. Miracles happen all the time. As a matter of fact, I'm getting closer to saving them every day. Wouldn't surprise me at all if every female Buri on the planet weren't expecting a little bundle of joy soon. Well, except Auntie Em. I suspect she'd be a tiny bit peeved if she ended up pregnant at her age."

A chuckle erupted from Thor at the image he'd picked up from me. Ghost asked him what was so funny, and when Thor told him, both Buri laughed.

Dorn's expression suddenly turned frantic as her gaze cut from me to the two males and back. "You're lying!" Her voice came out shrill and furious.

"Am I? Well, stick around a few more weeks and then you'll know for sure."

Her lips thinned for a minute, then she spun on her heels and stalked away without another word.

"Wow," Claudia breathed. "I've never seen anything ruffle Quilla's feathers before. Not sure I want to be in the area if it happens again, either." She glanced at me. "She's really going to be gunning for you now, Kiera."

"Do I look scared?"

She took a longer look at me and then smiled. "No, you look like you're hoping she gives you an excuse to beat the crap out of her."

"Bingo." I responded to her smile with a broad grin. "Now, let's get you to the village and settled in."

When we started off again, Crigo split away from us to follow Dorn. He didn't trust her any more than I did. I took the opportunity to converse silently with Max.

"Did the boss see the part about the file Dorn has on Gertz?"

"Yes, and he's infuriated," the ship replied. "He says he wants that file and he wants it yesterday."

"Uh-huh. And did he mention exactly how I was supposed to get it? I kind of doubt Dorn will stand by and let me stroll in to make copies. Not unless we want to recreate the shoot-out at the OK Corral first."

"I did bring that point up. He's working on it. Alien Affairs has an entire department of computer experts on staff. Since Dynatec's ship is so old, he's hoping their computer is outdated also. With the proper assistance, I should be able to hack into their system."

My jaw nearly hit the ground. "The boss? The boss wants

you to hack into someone else's computer? We are talking about Dr. Daniels, right?"

"I told you, he is upset."

"Yeah, but . . ." I trailed off and shook my head. I've said it before, I'll say it again. If I live to be eight hundred I'll never understand Naturals. Just when you think you've got one of them pegged, they do something totally out of character.

On the other hand, if the boss wanted to break the law, who was I to stand in his way?

"Be sure to tell him Dorn has an alert of some kind set up. It's the only way she could have known Claudia was rifling through her files."

"He knows."

Of course he did. In my estimation, only the Goddess rivaled the boss in intelligence and the ability to ferret out information. And most of the time, she wasn't paying attention. The boss always was.

My thoughts were interrupted by a horrible cacophony intermingled with laughter as we stepped out of the jungle into the village. It was so bad I was tempted to clap my hands over my ears to protect my hearing.

It didn't take me long to locate the source of the noise.

Redfield was singing. And to make matters worse, Brownie was trying to help him.

Sheesh. We'd only been gone an hour. How drunk could they get in that amount of time?

I eyed the empty jugs littering the area and sighed. Apparently they could get pretty soused in an hour. "Max, how much Panga ale do we have on board?"

"Seventy-five gallons."

"Seventy-five *gallons*?" I repeated in sheer disbelief.

"It was on sale."

There was a distinct sniff in his tone, and I rolled my

eyes. "Well, at least we can replace the wine Redfield and Brownie have consumed. And have enough ale left over to serve all the Galactic Federation troops stationed on Centauri."

"What's going on?" Claudia asked, wincing as Redfield raised the volume. Behind us, Thor and Ghost were chuckling in amusement.

"Brownie has a grudge against Redfield. They're settling it by trying to drink each other under the table."

"Sweet Goddess." She rubbed her forehead. "What is he singing? And I use the term *singing* loosely."

I tilted my head and listened closer. "The tune sounds kind of like 'What Do you Do with a Drunken Sailor', but I don't recognize the words."

"If he doesn't pass out soon, I may help him along. My ears can't take much more of this."

The words were no sooner out of her mouth than Redfield cut off mid-word and slumped sideways, a beatific smile on his face. Brownie continued for another stanza and then stopped to eye his fallen foe. With a grunt of triumph, he slid down until his chin rested on the table. Before he'd taken two breaths, snores were emanating from his throat.

"Brownie wins," I declared.

All the Buri cheered while Auntie Em rounded up some of the males to carry the combatants off to bed.

"This way," I told Claudia, gesturing toward the stone building. "You can stay with Thor and me for now. We have plenty of room."

"That's your home?" Her eyes were big as saucers. "You are *so* lucky."

"Uh, yep. That's where I live, all right." And why did it make me so uncomfortable to refer to the building as home? I truly did love it. If I'd designed a home for myself, it would have looked just like this one.

But deep down I knew why. I was scared silly that I'd get attached to the place and then have to leave it. That would hurt almost more than I could stand. So for now, it would remain merely the stone building to me.

Ghost and Thor followed us inside, then went into the small sitting room while I showed Claudia to the first bedroom on the left. It wasn't as big as the master suite, but it had its own bathing pool.

"You should be comfortable enough here," I told her. "If you want privacy, just shut the curtain over the doorway. Are you hungry?"

"No, thanks. Your cat kept us in meat, and Ghost went out at night and picked some berries." She peered around the room in awe. "This beats my quarters at camp all to hell. That pool looks fantastic. I'd kill for a bath right now."

"No need to get violent. It's all yours." I hesitated. "How do you feel about wearing Buri clothing? I'd offer you my jumpsuits, but they'd swallow you whole."

"You mean those loincloth things?" She looked doubtful for a second. "Do you think they could rig me something for up here?" Her hands bounced in front of her breasts. "I just can't get used to the idea of going half naked in public."

"I'm sure we can figure something out. Might even start a fad." I moved farther into the room and sat down on the sleeping platform. "There's something we need to talk about."

"Oh?" She strolled over and sat down beside me. "What's that?"

"Ghost, and why you can't sleep with him."

A rosy tint climbed into her café au lait cheeks. "I was wondering about that."

I turned toward her a bit more. "See, here's the thing. If you have sex with him, it'll kill you."

Her mouth gaped open. "He's that good?"

An involuntary snort of laughter escaped my lips. "I have no idea. In this case, it's not his technique and experience that causes the problem. Have you noticed the earrings he wears?"

"Sure. Two black stones in the same ear."

"They're called Rellanti, and when Ghost is intimate with a female capable of forming a mind bond with him, the Rellanti try to complete the bond. If the female isn't properly prepared, it will kill her. Once she is, and the marriage ceremony takes place, they'll be mated for life."

She stared at me. "You mean he . . . I . . . we . . . *married*?"

The last word came out a shriek and I grinned. "Exactly."

Thor sent me a questioning thought from down the hall. *The Claudia is in pain?*

No, she's in shock. I just explained to her about the mind bond.

Good. Ghost wishes the ceremony to take place in the next sevenday.

Unaware of our conversation, Claudia continued. "But what if he doesn't want to marry me?"

"Take my word for it. He wants to marry you. The mind bond has become very rare for them. When they find someone capable of sharing it, they hang on with both hands. Ghost is making plans for the ceremony with Thor right this minute. All you have to do is agree."

"Yes. I mean, I agree. When?"

"Sometime in the next week." Joy flowed from her in such intense waves that it was making *me* a little giddy. "Congratulations."

"Thank you." She clapped both hands to her cheeks. "I can't believe this is happening to me. Not only do I get to stay on this beautiful world, I get to marry that gorgeous hunk. I feel like I've won some grand, universal lottery that I didn't even know I'd entered."

"Maybe you have." And I couldn't help being a little envious. It must be nice to be so certain of your future. At the moment, mine was on pretty shaky ground.

With a small sigh I stood and walked to the door. "Why don't you go ahead and slip into the bathing pool while I find you something to wear."

"Okay. And Kiera . . ." Her expression sobered. "Thank you for protecting me from Dorn. Thank you for everything. I won't forget it."

Emotion choked me until I couldn't speak. Hers, mine, it didn't matter which. With a nod of acknowledgment, I pulled the curtain down over the doorway and headed to the front of the building.

Thor stepped out of the sitting room to meet me, a worried look in his eyes. "You are upset."

"No." I smiled at him. "Not upset, just a combination of happy/sad. It's a girl thing. Hormones running wild and all that good stuff." I peered around him into the empty room. "Where's Ghost?"

"He has gone to set the preparations for the mating ceremony in motion."

"Okay. Who's in charge of providing everyday clothes?"

"Lurran."

I took his hand. "In that case, I need you to come with me so you can translate. Claudia needs something to wear, and she's too modest for a regular kechic."

We were almost out the door when Max stopped me.

"Kiera?"

"Yes, Max?"

"I've finished the DNA analysis on the Buri plants."

"And?"

"Of the twenty-five varieties you brought me, nine match the DNA of the Ashwani plants exactly."

I'll admit, it took me a second. Head tilted, I thought over his results. "How many Ashwani plants do you have DNA for?"

"Nine."

Abruptly my spine stiffened and I spun to stare at Thor. A resigned look flickered through his ebony eyes as I dropped his hand and confronted him. "Your people are not indigenous to this planet, are they? You're colonists from Ashwan."

CHAPTER 19

"Were you ever going to tell me, or where you just going to let me go on thinking this was your planet of origin?" I couldn't stop the glare I shot him. Damn it, it hurt knowing he didn't trust me.

He lifted a hand to touch me, but I dodged. With a sigh, he lowered it again. "It is not you we don't trust, but the others of your kind. And yes, I would have shared this knowledge with you when it was safe to do so."

"The Ashwani tapestry. You recognized it, didn't you? That's why you reacted the way you did."

"Yes. It belonged to my sire. It depicts my grandsire and his sire on Feastday. The last time I saw it, it hung in my sire's great hall. If possible, I would wish to have it returned."

"Take it up with the Galactic Federation's Alien Artifact Museum." I squeezed my eyes closed briefly in disgust. "I suspected you were descendants of the Ashwani, but it never occurred to me you were physically *from* their planet. All the clues were there, I just didn't put them together. Ashwan has a heavier gravity. That's why you're so big, why your bones are denser."

"Yes."

"Wait." Suddenly my mind was racing in fifteen different directions. "How long have you been on Orpheus Two? For that matter, how did you get here? Max found no trace of a spaceship."

"Come." He turned and stepped through the door.

I grabbed his arm to stop him. "Come where?"

"With me. It will be easier to show you while I explain." He kept walking, forcing me to either let go or get dragged. I hesitated a second and then raced to catch up.

By now, it didn't even surprise me when he headed toward the mountainous area the Buri had previously banned me from entering. Even in the dark his steps were sure and confident, as though he'd trod this path so many times he knew every leaf and stone by heart. And he probably had.

We walked in silence, staying close the sheer bluff that loomed over the village, and at one point I recognized the fissure leading to the cave with the giant geode, where I'd been taken to prepare me for the mating ceremony. From there, the rock wall began a gentle curve to the right, and fifteen minutes later we came to another opening. This one was larger and showed evidence of tool marks on its face.

Flickering light spilled from inside, almost blinding me after our walk through the night. In its brilliance a moving shape took form and I realized it was a Buri male I'd never seen before. He physically blocked the entrance with his spear held across his body, until Thor shook his head.

Uncertainly, the male lowered his weapon and moved aside. Thor and I stepped across the threshold together, but then I came to a screeching halt, not believing what my eyes were showing me. Deliberately, I blinked twice. The action didn't help. It was still there.

Part of me had expected a ship. More than part, really. What I hadn't expected was a SHIP, capital letters. The entire interior of the mountain was hollow, and if the vessel had been two feet longer, or another inch taller, that mother of a ship never would have fit inside.

Back in the days when Old Earth had first started colonizing other star systems, they'd built big ships to travel in. But they'd built them in space, not dirt side. It would have taken more energy to pull them free from Earth's gravity than could be generated. To see one nearly as big, here, inside a mountain, stunned me silent.

I took a hesitant step forward, then another. When I was close enough, I put out a hand to touch the hull, still not trusting my eyes. My palm hit warm metal, but even as I watched, the color shifted, changed from iron gray to copper.

And suddenly I remembered the report Max had given me while we were in orbit. He'd said there was an anomaly in these mountains. Veins of metal that seemed to change from copper to iron, and then to zinc.

As a camouflage device, it was sheer genius. Neither Max nor I had even considered the possibility that it might be an alien ship. Worked metal wasn't supposed to change properties all by itself. Whether it was deliberate or accidental didn't much matter. It had succeeded in hiding the ship from our scan, and Dynatec's too.

Lowering my hand, I stepped back and looked as far along the side of the ship as I could see. The majority of its bulk vanished into the distance, but torches lined the walls of the cavern so the front of the ship was clearly visible. That's when I noticed the scars and burn marks on the hull.

Now that my brain was finally functioning on all cylinders again, it wasn't hard to put two and two together and come up with four. There had been no meteor angling across the planet, burning all the vegetation in its path. It had been this ship, and obviously something had gone wrong, something that made it crash.

Thor had been standing patiently beside me, waiting for me to accept what my senses were telling me. Now he moved farther down the ship and put his hand on a panel set into the hull. Silently a door slid to one side, letting artificial light spill out of the opening. No wonder the technology on board Max hadn't awed the Buri. They were used to it.

Come. With the one-word order, Thor stepped through the hatch, and I followed him, the slightly metallic scent of canned air assaulting my nose. Behind me, the door slid shut with a faint whirring noise.

The area we stood in was an airlock, but the inner door was wide open. Through it I could see what had to be the command center. It took up the whole front section of the ship, and every wall was lined with electronic equipment. Thor moved confidently to a console filled with blinking lights, paused a moment to survey them, made a slight adjustment to one of the controls and then glanced over his shoulder as I joined him.

"This is the ship that brought the last of my people to this world. We arrived fifteen of your cycles ago, after hundreds of cycles traveling through space. But the ship had suffered damage from space debris, and instead of going into orbit as it should have, it crashed. The Limantti kept the ship from disintegrating, and managed to protect it by hiding it inside the mountain, but part of its programming was destroyed. It did not awaken me until it detected the approach of another ship."

"Awaken you?"

He turned to another console and pushed something. A screen sprang to life, and a gasp escaped me as I stared at the image it showed. Row after row of Buri-sized deep-sleep units hummed and gurgled quietly as they went about the business of keeping their occupants alive.

Here, finally, was the source of that bright clump of

strands I hadn't been able to identify. Great Goddess. At one point I'd actually thought the clump might be more Buri and then got distracted by the individual strands. Talk about not seeing the forest for the trees.

I swallowed hard, twice, before I could speak again. "How many?"

"Three thousand made the voyage. It was all the ship could hold."

"How many females?"

"Half."

Abruptly, adrenaline shot through my veins, hard on the heels of a wild surge of elation. With a whoop of excitement, I grabbed Thor and did a fast jig on the metal deck. "Do you know what this means?"

I didn't wait for an answer. "It means that Dynatec can't file Chapter Twenty! You aren't the indigenous species. You're colonizers. Dynatec can't touch Orpheus Two, because when it comes to an unknown planet without a sentient species in residence, by Federation law, it's finder's keepers. The Buri found it first, so the planet belongs to them."

My feet took off on another exuberant dance before I got them under control. "I can't wait to see the look on Dorn's face when she finds out. You have to wake them up. All of them."

Thor had remained silent throughout my antics, his expression inscrutable. Now he merely shook his head. "No."

"No?" I stopped bouncing and glared at him. "If it's housing you're worried about, the boss can have a load of Quonset huts here in three days, as well as enough food to support them until you can get more crops ready to harvest."

"No, I will not wake them. Not until I know it is safe, or unless a particular skill is needed now. And only the ones who possess the skill will be awakened."

"But—"

"You believe the others will attack my people," he interrupted me. "You said our weapons are no match for theirs, and you're right. But as long as most of my people are here, safely hidden, the others cannot destroy us. The ship's program has been repaired. If a code is not entered once every four sevendays, it will awaken my second in command."

"So the village is a decoy?"

"It was, yes. I needed to know how your people would react to us. But it is also our home, and we will fight for it. If those of us now awake die, then my second will set the ship to only awaken him again after a hundred cycles have passed. And so it will continue until he deems it safe to bring out the rest of my people."

I put my hand on his arm and spoke earnestly. "Thor, there's no need for these elaborate plans. The second we leave this cave I'll contact Max. He'll let the boss know what's happened. Dr. Daniels will then arrange to have Dynatec's application for a Chapter Twenty denied. If necessary, he'll send Federation troops to forcibly remove them from the planet. Dorn can't take action against you after that or she'll end up spending the rest of her life imprisoned on Inferno. By this time next week, everything will be over and your people will be safe."

He didn't bother taking the time to think about his response. "Then next week, when the others have gone, I will reassess the situation and make a decision based on the new circumstances."

The man's middle name was *stubborn*. Come to think about it, *stubborn* could have been his last name for all I knew. Not that I blamed him. If the only members left of my species—assuming I *had* one—were in deep sleep on a spaceship, I'd be a tad overprotective too.

Good grief. The things I didn't know about him and the Buri were legion. The very thought of everything that had brought them to this point was staggering. Add that to the information I wanted on the Limantti, and I didn't know where to start.

We will start by returning to the village. I will answer your questions there.

"All of them?" Okay, call me suspicious, but he hadn't exactly been forthcoming up till now.

"Yes, all of them."

He ushered me back into the cave, then turned to seal the hatch closed. I noticed the unfamiliar male staring at me, so I waggled my fingers and gave him a big smile.

"Hi there. I'm the new Shushanna."

He just looked blank until I said *Shushanna*, and then he glanced at Thor, one brow arched in question.

"She is Shushanna and my bond mate," Thor confirmed.

Immediately the new guy bowed his head in acknowledgment. Oh, yeah. That was much better than being stared at as if I were a dangerous and exotic critter on display in a zoo.

I strutted the rest of the way to the cave's entrance even though I could feel Thor's amusement. The guard followed us and took up his previous stance as we exited.

As soon as we were clear of the cavern walls, I relayed everything I knew to Max, told him to get the information to the boss, and then continued my questioning. "You said you'd traveled hundreds of cycles. Do you know exactly how many?"

"No. The chronometer on the ship was part of the program destroyed."

"Interesting. Humans discovered Ashwan two hundred and fifty cycles ago. The atmosphere was gone and the buildings were covered in a massive layer of ice. It takes ages for that to happen. You must have been in deep sleep for thousands of cycles, instead of hundreds."

He winced. "I do not wish to think of it."

Couldn't blame him for that. It was giving *me* a headache and I hadn't lived through it. Or maybe I should say slept through it.

Shaking off the image of thousands of Buri, sleeping in those boxes for a seemingly endless number of cycles, I changed the subject. "Did you deliberately head for this planet, or was it an accident you landed here?"

"The Limantti chose this planet even though it was a great distance from our home. She indicated this world had everything we needed to survive and prosper."

"So the rock told the Shushanna—" I stopped and grimaced. "That sounds like the beginning of a really bad joke. Maybe we should wait until we get back to the village, and then you can tell me the whole story from the beginning."

"Without interruption?" He was smiling when he spoke.

"Hell no." I shot him a glare for knowing me so well. "If I have a question, I'm asking."

"Yes." He sighed. "I know."

We walked the rest of the way in silence, brushing against each other occasionally, either by accident or intentionally. When we reached the village, Churka was leaving the communal kitchen, heading toward her house, and it reminded me I hadn't arranged for Claudia's clothing.

Since Lurran had already gone to bed, we stopped Churka and explained what was needed. With a yawn, she assured me she'd get together with Lurran first thing in the morning and work something out, although she seemed a bit puzzled by Claudia's desire for a covering. For that matter, so was Thor, but I could tell he just chalked it up as an unexplainable female mystery.

Apparently males were males regardless of species.

As soon as we entered the stone building, I mentally checked Claudia's status. She was sound asleep, but I could still feel satisfaction oozing from her, and I smiled.

With his palm resting on the small of my back, Thor ushered me past her room to our own. Once there, I took a jug of wine from a shelf and poured two wooden glasses full before joining him at the small table. Just to be on the safe side, I took the jug with me.

He'd lit two of the oil lamps, and in their dim glow we made ourselves comfortable on the pillows. From the doorway to the terrace a gentle, fragrant night breeze wafted, making the lamp flames dance gracefully.

"Okay," I said quietly. "Tell me how a people whose most advanced weapon is a sword can build a spaceship complete with computers and deep-sleep chambers."

"The swords are our primary weapon," he told me absently. "But we normally keep them in storage because they aren't needed on a daily basis."

Taking a drink of wine, he leaned back, resting an elbow on a bright yellow pillow. "Our lifestyle is from choice, mate, not necessity. As you will learn if you let me continue."

Chagrined, I zipped my lip and nodded.

"My people are an ancient race. Some of our scholars believed that at one time we were as small as your people are, and that we lived under a different star, a brighter, warmer star. I only know that we lived long cycles without knowledge of the crystals, and that the facts of their discovery and learning their uses are lost in the past."

He took another drink of wine, his gaze distant, as though he were seeing the things he told me. And, I realized, I could see them too, through the mind bond. Mesmerized, I closed my eyes and let the images roll through me.

"But use them we did," he said. "And the power they gave us was unimaginable. With them, we built a technology that ruled our world. Great cities sprang up everywhere, and our population exploded. Life was good. Until our growth began to outstrip our resources.

"Even then our sun was weak and dying. The planting seasons were short, the cold intense. And as the cities grew, they took more and more of the land once used for crops."

This time, he gulped the wine, and I didn't blame him. I'd caught a glimpse in his mind of what was coming. Silently, I refilled his glass, and then closed my eyes again, the better to see what he was showing me.

"We call it the Age of Darkness." His voice was low and deep, as if it hurt just to say the name. "The crystals were turned into weapons of horror as people fought for every scrap of ground, every morsel of food. Families turned on families, brother against brother, and sister against sister. It was during this period that the great ships were created. From above, they rained down fire and ruin. The cities were destroyed and our blood soaked the places where they had once stood."

From down the hall, I felt a sudden pulse of something I can only describe as remorse from the Limantti, and I blinked in surprise. Apparently the stone was eavesdropping on our conversation. The intrusion reminded me of something, and I opened my eyes to gaze at Thor.

"I thought you told me the Limantti had never hurt anyone before?"

"It hasn't. What occurred was due to our own innate greed, our need for power. We didn't even know the Limantti existed. And while the Limantti knew of us, it was alien. It didn't understand what was happening, how the crystals were being used."

From the little I knew of the Limantti, that made sense. It was the most alien intelligence I'd ever encountered before, and working for Alien Affairs, I'd encountered a lot. "So what happened to change things?"

He sighed and gazed down into his wine. "A young girl, badly wounded in battle, escaped from the fight and sought refuge in a cave out of sight from those hunting her. She had lost her whole family, and the pain from her burns was so great she merely wanted a quiet place to die in peace. Instead, she found the Limantti."

Thor wasn't the only one I was getting images from now. The Limantti showed me a young Buri female, blood and debris coating her ebony hair. Her dirty face was streaked with tears and it was obvious she was in shock from the horrible burns covering her body. Slowly, every move a study in agony, she dragged herself into the welcoming darkness of a small cave, where she collapsed and went still.

And then her wounds began to heal. Gradually, at first, as if the Limantti wasn't quite sure of what it was doing, then faster as the stone learned.

Several days went by, but eventually the girl woke, whole and completely healed. At least she was physically healed. It wasn't until she touched the stone that the Limantti discovered the extent to which the crystals had been used, the pain they had caused. What the stone considered a gift had been employed as tools of destruction, and the Limantti was appalled.

Immediately, the Limantti took back control of every crystal on the planet. From that day to this, she made sure the crystals could only be used on a small personal level. Never again would she allow one of her colony to become a weapon.

Thor was watching me, and I knew he'd shared the information the Limantti gave me. The image of the girl stuck with me, and I realized she was one of only a handful of Buri I'd seen with black hair, if you counted the ones on the tapestry.

"She was your ancestor, wasn't she?"

"Yes." His lips curved in slight smile. "She was our first Shushanna. When the crystals stopped working and the bloodshed ended, she gathered what was left of our people and they began anew. It was then, in disgust and pain over so many unnecessary deaths, that we swore an oath to never again use weapons that could kill from a distance. We also decided to keep our lives simple, to concentrate on preserving our planet for future generations. And, except for the Rellanti, we decided not to use the crystals at all."

Curious, I tilted my head to one side and studied him. "Did you have a lot of children in those days?"

"No." He straightened into an upright position and put his glass on the table. "During the Age of Darkness, females fought just as fiercely as males. Bearing children interfered with their ability to wage war, so they used the crystals to inhibit the process. By the time it was over, it was too late. None of our females was able to conceive, and the knowledge to change them back had been lost. Only through the Limantti, with the Shushanna's help, were the females able to bear young. Since then, a new Shushanna was born during each generation, and so it continued until our sun began its final death throes."

I leaned across the table and took his hand. "You revived one of the ships."

"There was only one left." He toyed with my fingers as he spoke. "The others had drifted from orbit and were pulled into the sun. With the Limantti's help, we restored it, but there was only room for three thousand. It was decided that only the youngest and strongest would go, with a few elders who were in good health to serve as teachers and advisors. I was named by the Limantti to be leader."

He took a deep breath. "As the day of our departure drew nearer, more and more of my people chose to die so there would be enough food for our families to see us on our way. By the time we left, most were gone. I can still see my sire and dam, standing together as Churka and I boarded the last shuttle to the ship. I knew that as soon as we were gone, they would return to our home and end their lives, but they were smiling, happy that their children would be saved. It was the bravest thing I'd ever seen, and it broke my heart. Not just for them, but for all my people who sacrificed so much to insure our continued existence."

Tears filled my eyes and spilled down my cheeks as his emotions swept over me.

"Now do you see why I cannot wake the rest of my people?" His ebony eyes were intense as he looked at me. "Their future, their very lives, was entrusted to me. I can do no less than our parents to protect them, even if it means some of us must die."

I wiped my cheeks dry with the backs of my hands, and then stood and moved around the table. With a soft *plop*, I landed on his lap and put my arms around him, my head resting on his chest. "Of course I understand. And I don't suppose it really matters. They've been asleep this long, a few more days won't hurt them. Once the troops arrive, they'll be able to verify my report with their own eyes and document the ship's existence. When you feel it's safe, then we'll wake them. No matter what else happens, this is your world. As its leader, you can handle this any way you want. But I hope you'll decide to join the Galactic Federation. They could do so much for your people, and you have so much to offer them in return."

His head dipped down to rest on top of mine, and I felt him smile. "First I must understand what this Federation is and how it works. Luckily, I have you to teach me."

"Thor," I leaned back enough to see his face. "You know I'll do what I can, but I probably won't be allowed to stay here long, whether I want to or not. Alien Affairs owns my indenture and I don't have the money to pay it off. Until I do, I have no choice in the matter. I'll have to go where they send me."

"Then I will go with you, as I said I would."

Slowly, without breaking eye contact, I shook my head. "You have to stay here."

He started to protest, but I put my fingers against his lips. "Don't. We both know you can't leave. These are your people, and they need you. More now than ever before, since the Federation will be involved. If you left with me, you'd spend all your time worrying about them. And sooner or later you'd start to resent me for forcing you to choose me over them. I couldn't live with that, Thor, especially when I can pick up everything you feel."

His arms tightened around me convulsively, and moisture filled his eyes. "And how am I supposed to live without you? How can I stand and do nothing while I lose someone else I love? Wasn't once enough for a lifetime?"

"I'm sorry." I choked, my voice nearly a sob. "I'm so sorry."

"It won't happen," he whispered fiercely. "I won't let you go. Somehow, I will find a way—"

His mouth crashed down on mine, and I lost myself in the kiss, barely aware of him standing, carrying me to the sleeping platform. If my time with him was coming to an end, I would make the most of it.

Considering the desperation we were both feeling, I expected our lovemaking to be wild and hard. Instead, it turned slow and sweet, with each of us giving everything we had to give. For the first time in my life, sex wasn't about self-fulfillment. It was about bringing the greatest amount of pleasure possible to the one I loved and valued above all others.

It seemed to go on for hours, each of us reaching peaks we'd never touched before, then descending slowly, only to begin the climb anew.

"Tell me," he growled near the end.

I knew instantly what he wanted, and knew I shouldn't. It would only make it harder for us when I left. But I couldn't deny him, or myself.

"I love you," I whispered.

"Again."

"I love you."

His final climax was explosive, and triggered my own. Together, we rode the crest of the wave until it faded into quiet repletion.

Afterward we lay exhausted, wrapped around each other tightly, each hanging on as though our lives depended on it. And maybe they did.

I had no idea how the mind bond worked, what would happen if Thor and I were separated. Would it stretch over such vast distances, or would it break? And what would happen to us if it broke?

Thor seemed to think the only way to end it was death, which didn't bode well for our chances. I turned to ask him about it and realized he was asleep.

Maybe I could coerce the boss into giving me jobs that kept me in the vicinity. And if I pulled a lot of overtime, I might be able to pay my indenture off faster. Plus, Dr. Daniels was always after me to take more vacation time, which I could spend anywhere I wanted. It wasn't an ideal solution, but it was better than never seeing Thor again.

Thinking about the boss reminded me of the news I'd sent earlier. "Max, have you heard from Dr. Daniels yet?"

"Yes, just a few minutes ago. He's very excited to hear the Buri are colonists from Ashwan. Unfortunately, the news reached him too late in the day. The court is closed and won't open again until morning. However, he said to tell you he'll have all the documents ready to go first thing. By tomorrow afternoon, Dynatec will be notified that their

Chapter Twenty has been denied and they'll be ordered to vacate Orpheus Two."

"Excellent." I let out a loud yawn. "Let me know when they're about to get the news. I want to be in their camp when Dorn and Frisk find out."

I was already asleep before he had time to answer.

CHAPTER 20

I woke to a strange sensation the next morning, and it took a second for me to realize the pressure on my bottom lip was, in fact, due to my own personal dragon bird. He was right in my face, gripping my lip in one small talon for balance.

While I blinked in surprise, he trilled a happy greeting, and then glanced over his shoulder at the sound of a chuckle.

"He likes you."

I rolled my eyes toward Thor and spit out the tiny foot. "Ya think?" Reaching up, I dislodged my new alarm clock, depositing him beside me on the sleeping platform. "Have they ever shown any interest in the Buri?"

"Not to this degree, although they are curious. There's always a flock around watching, as if they don't understand what we're doing, and want to figure it out." He tilted his head toward the foot of the sleeping platform.

I looked in the same direction as two more of the small creatures, apparently inspired by mine's bravery, strutted across the bed, chittering quietly to each other as they eyed Thor. One of them, a brilliant scarlet lady, was feeling quite possessive toward him.

"I suspect they're fairly intelligent, in a dragon bird kind of way," I told him. "At least, I can pick up elementary emotions from my guy and some of the others."

From outside on the terrace, a loud squawk sounded, and all the dragon birds in the room took to the air in a whirring rush of wings and feathers. A second later, they all swooped through the open doorway and were gone.

They had barely disappeared when the reason for all the excitement stalked into view. After a quick glance into the room to assure himself I was there, Crigo commenced pacing the length of the terrace, an occasional rumble issuing from deep in his chest.

I frowned as I watched him. The big cat was feeling distinctly uneasy about something, and seemed almost hyper-alert. His tufted ears were erect, swiveling constantly to catch any unusual sound.

With a flick of my wrist, I tossed aside the light covering and rose to look outside.

"Is something wrong?" Thor questioned, joining me.

"I don't know." Quickly I scanned the village, but nothing looked out of place. Two of the Buri were bathing in the pool near the waterfall, and across the clearing Poe sat, sharpening his spear, Junior beside him, watching and offering the occasional comment. From down the hall, I could hear giggles as Lurran and Churka tried to design clothing Claudia could live with, and the scents of breakfast cooking drifted in on the air from the communal kitchen.

All in all, it looked like a typical peaceful morning in the village. And yet . . .

"Something's made Crigo nervous, and I trust his instincts. Let's get dressed and check the village, just to be on the safe side."

We dressed in record time, and I finished off my braid as we went down the hall. Pausing at Claudia's door, I stuck my head inside and surveyed the chaos of material littering the sleeping platform. The two Buri females had Claudia decked out in a lemon-yellow kechic that did wonders for her skin tone, and a matching strip of cloth, fastened in front with one of the wooden clasps.

"How do I look?" She held her arms up for my inspection.

"Great. But it would look better with your blaster."

"My blaster?" A startled expression crossed her face.

"Yes. Do me a favor and keep it close."

"Sure, if you say so."

Good enough. I trotted on down the hall to catch up with Thor. Crigo was inspecting the edge of the jungle as we stepped outside, and both Thor and I stopped to look around. It was still peaceful, but by now I'd caught the cat's nerves and it felt like ants were crawling over my skin.

"You go that way, and I'll go this way," I gestured to Thor. "We'll meet at the kitchen. And don't forget to check back into the trees."

He reached back inside the building and picked up the spear he'd leaned against the wall. "Be careful."

"You too." I started a slow walk in my chosen direction. "Max?"

"Yes, Kiera?"

"Is there anything going on at the Dynatec camp?"

"Not really. Most of them went out with the survey team early this morning. There are only a few crew members left in camp, and they appear to be playing cards."

A sudden chill crawled over my skin. "Dorn and Frisk?"

"They went with the survey team."

That was so out of character that my alarm increased to a new all-time high. "Can you see the survey team?"

He hesitated a split second before answering. "Not really. The satellites that usually cover that area are the ones I'm having problems with."

"You haven't had any luck fixing them?"

"No. I need to go up and replace them as soon as possible."

Abruptly, I had a quandary. I really, really needed to know exactly where that survey team was located. But that meant sending Max into space to replace his eyes, and he was our best defense. I wanted him close enough to help if it became necessary.

"How long will it take you?"

"A few minutes to get there, a few more to place the new satellites in the correct orbit, and then a few to get back. Maybe ten minutes total."

I had to make a decision, and I had to make it fast. "Okay, go, but do it as quickly as you can. Something's up, Max."

"I'll leave now."

The words were still echoing in my ears when I saw a streak of gray flash across the blue sky above the treetops. I watched until he was out of sight, and then continued checking the perimeter of the village. So far, so good.

Thor, have you seen anything?

No. Everything is quiet. Almost too quiet. Even the dragon birds are silent.

He was right, I thought, glancing around the village. Normally, flocks of the small creatures darted in and out of the waterfall at all hours of the day, not to mention the bunch that stayed near me. Now, there wasn't a jeweled form to be seen.

Two doors down, Redfield stepped out of his quarters, one hand clutching his head, eyes so red it looked like they were bleeding. He was wearing his blaster. Unlike Claudia, he was a GEP, trained to never let his weapon out of his sight.

"Who won?" he asked when I got close enough.

"Brownie—"

A strange crackling noise erupted from the implant behind my ear and my entire body went tense. "Max?"

His reply almost deafened me. "Pirates! Under attack! Mayday, may—"

The words were cut off mid-broadcast, and my blaster was in my hand so fast there wasn't even a blur. Mentally, I grabbed every strand of life force that wasn't connected to a Buri in deep sleep, and gave them a hard yank. From all over the village they spilled into the open, and I spotted Thor charging out from the trees.

"Into the caves! Get them into the caves! We're under attack!"

Roaring orders, Thor sent the Buri scrambling toward the jungle edging the sheer bluff wall, but it was already too late. From above, the air groaned with the high-pitched whistle of a laser cannon.

Going into overdrive, I grabbed Redfield, took five running steps, and threw us both to the ground, covering his body with mine. I'd barely completed the maneuver when the house he'd just exited exploded. Dust and debris shot everywhere, and I felt a hot stinging in my shoulder. I ignored it, knowing any wound would heal faster than I could check for damage, but I dropped back to normal speed in order to conserve energy. Then I was up and moving again.

Claudia. Damn. She was nowhere to be seen, so I swerved toward the stone building, screaming her name at the top of my lungs.

She came out at a run, blaster in hand, and I pointed toward the fleeing Buri as another building, this one on the far side of the village, disintegrated. "Go!"

By now, the first Buri had reached the trees, but there seemed to be some confusion. Those in the back were milling but going nowhere, and I saw Brownie's mate looking frantically for her child, her face etched with fear as she screamed his name.

The blue of a crew uniform caught my attention and I looked around in time to see one of Dorn's men step from the protection of the trees. A blaster was in his hand, and it was aimed right at Brownie's little boy while the child stood frozen in fear.

I wasn't the only one who'd seen them. Both Brownie and his mate were charging in their direction, but they were too far away. There was no way they could reach him in time.

Anger mixed with fear went through me like a nuclear flash fire, and before the emotion could settle, I was in overdrive, passing Brownie as though he were standing still. I could literally see the man's finger tightening on the firing mechanism; see the hazy beam of energy erupt from the end of the blaster. And I knew there was only one thing I could do.

With an unprecedented burst of speed, I put myself between the child and the blast, felt it sear my side right above my hip. Then I was on the man, my fist hammering into his unprotected throat. The flesh gave, then the bones beneath as I crushed his windpipe.

I came out of overdrive as he collapsed to the ground, hands clutching his throat as he gasped for air and died, wondering why I wasn't on the verge of shock from so much expended energy. And then realized the Limantti was feeding me a steady stream of power.

Grateful in spite of my previous reservations concerning the massive crystal, I turned and scooped up the child, ignoring the trickle of blood staining my jumpsuit crimson. I wasn't dead, so I knew it was only a matter of time before the wound closed.

That didn't stop it from burning like hell, though, and the

soothing noises I made were almost as much for my own benefit as they were for the child, who clung to me so desperately.

All my protective instincts on high alert, I held him tightly until Brownie arrived, then winced as I handed the child to his father and pressed the heel of my hand to my side. Clutching his child forcefully to his chest, Brownie's eyes widened as he took in the blood on my clothes. His head dipped in a bow, and even over the din of battle I heard his murmured "Shushanna."

Didn't look like Brownie would be giving me any more trouble, assuming we all lived through this attack.

I was turning to help the others when, out of the blue, Crigo streaked by us, gave a mighty push with his powerful hind legs, and went airborne. When he came down inside the jungle, I heard a man scream. I knew that voice. Crigo had finally taken his revenge on Frisk.

The sound of the man's death broke off as quickly as it had started, but it told me what I needed to know. The survey team was blocking the Buri's exit, keeping them pinned in the village so the pirates could finish the job for them. There was no other choice. We had to fight.

Thor had reached the same conclusion. Over the melee, I heard him shouting directions, and suddenly it seemed as if all the Buri were holding spears or swords.

Well, almost all. A man wearing the Dynatec uniform staggered from the trees and fell, an arrow embedded in his chest.

A blaster beam flickered from behind a tree, and the Buri holding the bow screamed.

Again, I reacted instinctively. My blaster was aimed at the tree before the Buri's mouth opened, and I pulled the trigger. The laser drilled straight through the bole and nailed the man behind it.

All around me the fight degenerated into small islands of chaos as the Buri engaged the crew members one on one. Why the hell hadn't Dynatec stayed in the trees and picked the Buri off one at a time? I paused to break the neck of a man about to plunge a knife into Junior's back, then kept going, doing what I could for the Buri, who were weakening.

It had to be because they weren't expecting the Buri to charge into the jungle so quickly. And they wouldn't have, if not for Max's warning.

Grief, hollow and black had welled inside me since the ship's abrupt silence, but there was no time to mourn. I had to protect the Buri, if possible get between them and the crew members still taking cover in the jungle. They were the ones capable of doing the most damage with their blasters.

I fought my way closer and closer to the trees, noting both Redfield and Claudia were making good use of their weapons. Claudia was using hers to disable; Redfield was gleefully shooting to kill. Crigo was doing his part too, picking his targets and then pouncing before they knew he was there.

But the Dynatec crew members weren't the only ones dying. I'd already felt two life force strands wink out, and others were weakening rapidly.

Dropping the woman in front of me with a well placed blow, I dove into the jungle. Where the hell was Thor? His strand was intact, but I realized I hadn't heard or seen him in a while now.

Stay back. His voice echoed in my head. *It is a trap. The Dorn female is waiting for you. There are three males with her.*

Yeah, like that would slow me down.

Tell me exactly where they are in relation to you. I'd already pinpointed his approximate location from his lifeforce strand, and began to move stealthily in his direction.

*The Dorn is behind me with a weapon pointed at my back.
She is as fast as you, wife.*

*That's impossible. She'd have to be my kind of GEP to
move like—*

A buzzing filled my head. Sweet Goddess. She wasn't
merely a clone, she was a GEP.

As I crept closer, circling to get behind them, I did the
math. Zander Dorn had ordered her cloned through the black
market. If there were enough money involved, Gertz would
have jumped at the job. And there had undoubtedly been an
obscene amount of money offered.

Add that to the file she kept on him, and I'd bet dollars to
donuts Gertz had created her. And he wouldn't have stopped
at making her a GEP. The man was constitutionally unable
to leave well enough alone. He would have tinkered with her
DNA, just as he had mine.

This meant I had no idea what she was capable of doing.
She was at least ten cycles older than me, though, so I could
only hope Gertz was still perfecting his technique when he
made her.

Where are the men? I asked Thor.

Hiding in the jungle around us. He sent me a mental image of their approximate locations.

Piece of cake, I decided. As soon as I was in range, I
stopped to listen. It only took a few seconds for my extra-
sensitive ears to detect the slight noises each man made.

Taking a deep breath, I replaced my blaster in its holster
and began to move. Before I could take another breath, I was
in overdrive. To any Natural watching, it would have looked
like all three men just spontaneously died.

But Dorn wasn't a Natural, and I realized the trap too
late.

"Impressive. I suggest you stop now, or your mate won't
last another second."

When I halted, she was staring right at me. Her blaster was pressed against Thor's spine at an upward angle. If she pulled the trigger, he was dead. And if she could move even a fraction as fast as me, I wouldn't be in time to keep it from happening.

"Nothing to say?" She smiled. "Don't you think it was clever of me to post those men nearby so their deaths would warn me of your arrival?"

"Let him go, Dorn."

"And lose my advantage? I don't think so."

"It's all over anyway. Your Chapter Twenty is being denied. The news would have been delivered this afternoon."

Her smile turned feral. "Well, golly gee. Isn't it too bad you and the Buri won't be around to celebrate? And with all of you gone, the planet will be up for grabs again."

Thor was watching me intently and I read his intention to act, to die so that I could take her out. Panic roared through me.

No! I sent him a mental shout. *Don't do it. Give me time. I'll find a way out.*

His expression remained calm, but he gave the slightest nod of agreement and I turned my attention back to Dorn.

"If you kill us, Alien Affairs will lock you up and throw away the key."

"Me? Now, why would I kill you? *Au contraire*, most of my crew died trying to save you from those nasty pirates." The weapon never wavered in her hand. "And unfortunately, our ship is too old and out of date to be of any help."

Realization hit me too late. "You had this planned from the beginning, didn't you? That's why you used an outdated ship, why Max's satellites kept going out. You used a disrupter on them to give the pirates a chance to hide behind the moon without him seeing them." Inside I was praying harder than I'd ever prayed before. I needed something, anything to distract her. Just for a split second. "How are you going to explain the bodies with blaster wounds?"

"What bodies?" She gave one of those shrugs she'd mastered so well. "They were all destroyed by the pirates' laser cannons."

The horrifying thing was, it could have worked. If not for the Limantti. And the Buri ship. And the thousands of Buri currently in deep sleep, all of which Alien Affairs knew about, but Dorn didn't.

As it was, we were all going to die for nothing unless I came up with a plan.

From the over-canopy, I heard a faint rustle and caught a glimpse of jeweled feathers in my peripheral vision, but I didn't dare look away from Dorn. One second of inattention and she could shoot me, then finish Thor off at her leisure.

I had to keep her talking.

"So what happens now? If you shoot Thor, I'll kill you. If you take the blaster off him long enough to shoot me, I'll kill you. You may be a GEP, but I'm still willing to bet I'm faster than you."

"Oh, you finally figured that out, did you?" She snorted, a most unladylike sound coming from her. "Took you long enough. Yes, I was one of dear Dr. Gertz's first experiments, although certainly not his last. Gave my 'father' a rather nasty surprise when he discovered he'd gotten more than he paid for. Of course, by then it was too late for him. He died screaming. As for what I'm going to do, one of my crew will be along soon. Then I'll take great pleasure in having you killed. I believe it takes a head shot, correct?"

My hand hovered over my blaster, muscles tense and ready. From the limb above Dorn's head, my dragon bird peered down at her, his eyes flashing the blood red of fury. And he wasn't alone. Every tree branch held one of the glittering creatures.

Silently, they were creeping ever closer.

Frantically, I searched for a topic that would keep her attention on me. "What do you mean, you weren't the last?"

One of her perfectly shaped brows arched. "You didn't really think you were the only one Gertz toyed with, did you?" She studied me, and then smiled. "Yes, I can see you did. The truth is, there are hundreds of his creations running loose. And I imagine he's still at it."

"Gertz is dead," I told her. "He killed himself when he realized my boss was onto him."

She laughed. She actually laughed. "Don't be ridiculous. A man with an ego the size of Gertz's does not kill himself. He simply killed one of his own clones and made it look like suicide."

"How do you know?"

"Because I've been in contact with him. He's the one who gave me copies of your records. After all, what good is being a genius if you can't brag about it, and he was very proud of you."

Another rustle sounded, this time from behind me, and Dorn heard it.

"Here come my men. Sorry, Smith. I really have nothing personal against you."

There must have been some signal I missed, because suddenly the air was full of shrieking, diving dragon birds, all bent on ripping Dorn to pieces with their sharp little talons.

With a scream of surprise, she threw her hands in the air, instinctively trying to protect her face. It was all I needed. She was dead before she knew I'd moved. But her finger must have been tight on the trigger.

In a blast of heated air, Thor collapsed, blood welling from a gaping hole in his bronze skin.

"Thor!" His name was ripped out of me as I dropped to my knees beside him, pulled him into my arms. Already, the bond that linked us was growing thinner, dimming as blood pumped from the wound in his back. I pressed my hand against it hard in a futile effort to stop the flow. "Don't you dare die on me, damn it!"

Tears spilled down my cheeks as I stared into the face I'd come to love. "You can't die," I pleaded. "You're the only one who's ever loved me. Please don't leave me all alone, Thor. I don't want to live without you."

His lips curved, just the tiniest bit, and his voice came to me faintly through what remained of the bond.

You will survive, mate. You are the strongest person I know. Promise me you will care for my people, make sure they are safe. His eyes closed, and his breathing slowed to a gurgling rasp. *Never forget I loved you and part of me will always be with you.*

"No!" The word ripped from my very soul. Gently, I laid him down and rose to my knees. His people? Right now I didn't give a gergian's ass about his people. He was dying and there was only one way I could prevent it.

Above me the dragon birds swooped and circled, chittering wildly as I slowly lifted my hand, palm out. Thor's blood covered the black outline of the stone, but I ignored it. Teeth tightly clenched, my voice was more growl than words.

"Of my own free will, I accept you. Take me."

Instantly, blue-black light exploded inside my head, flowed throughout my body, and my mind spun away, flung through space. Galaxies turned, stars were born and died. But this time, I didn't just go with it. This time I fought for control, and I could feel the Limantti urging me on, showing me what to do. But I needed time, more time than I had before Thor was lost to me.

The thought was barely formed when the movement around me slowed and stopped. The wildly swooping dragon birds hung suspended in midair, and the leaves moving in a gentle breeze froze. Even the sun halted in its orbit.

With all my strength, I focused on one star system, and abruptly I was there, hanging in the darkness above it. I backed off and tried it again, and this time it was easier.

I needed something that would take more delicacy before I tried to help Thor, something that would require more from me than just strength. And I knew just the thing.

In a split second, I was hovering over Alpha Centauri, the home of the Galactic Federation and Alien Affairs. I formed a picture of the boss in my mind, and there he was, in a small courtroom, a judge signing the stack of documents the boss had given him.

I studied him in great detail, and noted his back was bothering him from staying so long at his desk the night before. With only a flicker of thought, I fixed it.

His hand went to his back and he straightened, looking around the room as though he sensed my presence, and I wondered if I could do more.

Pirates hired by Dynatec have attacked the Buri, I sent him. *Max was hit. People are dying.*

He stood so fast his chair tipped over and hit the floor with a crash. Then he rushed from the room without a word to the surprised judge.

Okay, if I could do that, I could concentrate on the problems closer to home. With minimal effort now, I was back in the Orpheus system, looking down on the pirate ship. Its cannons were still firing, but the beams were frozen in space, and I was a bit shocked to realize how little time had gone by since the first beam had hit the village. To me, it felt like hours, but in reality it had only been minutes.

As tempted as I was to grab the ship and toss it into the sun, I couldn't. The pirates would be needed as witnesses before they were sent to Inferno.

Drawing on the power of the Limantti, I shut down all their equipment except life support. The cannons went dead and the ship hung dark and still above the planet. And then I disabled the blasters of what remained of the Dynatec crew members.

Now for the most important task of all.

I don't know when I'd closed my eyes, but I opened them and looked at Thor, concentrated all my attention on scanning him right down to the cellular level. There. Rapidly I repaired damaged cells and grew new ones to replace those already dead. With a single thought, I knit vessels together, closed the hole in his lungs, strengthened his heart and poured energy into him.

He would live.

Joy sang through me. Not only did I accept what I'd become, I embraced it. I wasn't just a genetically created freak. I was Kiera Smith, Agent for Alien Affairs, GEP, mate of Thor, and Shushanna to the Buri.

I was doing exactly what I'd been designed to do, even though Gertz hadn't known the extent of what he'd created. In spite of his machinations, I was human where it counted the most. In my heart. It had just taken Thor and the Buri to teach me that. It had taken Dynatec, too, and Crigo and Redfield and Claudia. It had taken Max—

Max!

I paused in my cavorting long enough to seal the breach in his hull and repair his fried circuits. He came online in mid-bellow.

"—day! Mayday!"

Abruptly he went silent, and a second later queried me in a confused tone. "Kiera? What happened? Where are you?"

"I'll explain later, Max. But it's all over and you're fine. You can come back now."

"What about the pirates?"

"Take my word for it, they aren't going anywhere."

A soft touch on my cheek yanked me back into the here and now, and I opened my eyes to see Thor kneeling in front of me, a look of such love in his eyes that I wanted to weep again.

"You joined with the Limantti," he said quietly. "For me."

"Yes."

"Do you regret it?"

I gave him a luminous smile. "Not for a second. The stone is part of me now. Just like you're a part of me."

He stood and offered me his hand. The blood still streaking his skin was the only sign he'd ever been wounded. "Come. Our people wait. It's time to go home."

Home. Damn, that sounded good. I took his hand and together, we walked back to the village.

EPILOGUE

Thor and I sat on the terrace of the stone building outside our sleeping quarters and watched the bustle of activity in the village. It had been a week since the Dynatec attack and there had been lots of changes, some painful, others exciting.

A hard knot formed in my chest when I thought of Poe, the gentle giant who had been killed in the fight, along with four other Buri. I'd never lost anyone I considered a friend before, so this grief was new for me. And it was only a fraction of what Thor was still going through. Not only had he lost his home and family, now he felt responsible for the tribe members we'd lost. How could I let him leave with me after that?

But there were things we needed to get worked out, urgent questions that needed answers. Dr. Daniels was preparing to leave, and as far as Alien Affairs was concerned, my job here was done. Yet Thor refused to talk about it. Whenever I tried he got a stubborn look and walked away. And to make matters worse, the boss was doing the same thing. I couldn't get a straight answer from either of the males in my life and it was making me slightly crazy.

I'd learned a lot from the Limantti in the moment we'd joined, things I'd never dreamed she could show me. Like exactly how the mind bond worked. I could now wall off my thoughts from Thor at will while still maintaining contact, which was a relief. Even when you feel as close to someone as I felt to Thor, you don't want them privy to all your innermost thoughts.

I also knew how to slice through his mental shields like a hot knife through butter without him suspecting a thing. But privacy is a two-way street, and I wouldn't do that to him any more than I'd want him doing it to me.

She'd taught me one final thing, something I wasn't sure I wanted to know. She showed me how to sever the mate bond without hurting either Thor or myself.

I glanced at him just in time to see Rayda, a scarlet-feathered dragon bird, land on his shoulder and then squawk warnings at two others who tried to follow suit. Thor belonged to her, and she was making damn sure the others knew it. Emitting meek little *cheeps*, they darted off to find other, unowned Buri.

Gem, my own guy, was striding up and down the length of Crigo's back, chittering to the cat in dragon birdese. Whatever he was saying looked pretty intense, and I smiled in spite of my mood. Gem seemed to be laboring under the impression that he'd single-handedly saved me from Dorn, and now had the right to rule me and everything attached to me, including Crigo. The cat wasn't happy about it, but he knew I'd frown on his making a meal of the dragon bird, so he sighed and put up with the indignity.

We weren't the only ones with dragon bird issues, either. Even as we watched, a young Buri female with Ghost's silvery hair and eyes stopped in front of a ruined adobe building, looking confused as four of the small creatures vied for roosting space on her shoulders. They had apparently de-

cided en masse that if Gem could own me, then they de-
served their very own people too, which was how Thor had
ended up with Rayda. As for the young female, turned out
she was Ghost's cousin.

It had been a hectic week for all of us. We'd returned to
the village after the attack to find Claudia and Redfield holding the remaining fifteen crew members prisoner. Nearly all
the surviving Buri were injured in some manner, a few seriously. I'd moved from one to the other, healing them with
the Limantti's help.

The village didn't fare as well. Only three of the adobe
houses were intact, along with the stone building, which the
Limantti assured me she had protected during the battle. The
communal kitchen was damaged but still useable. And it was
a good thing. With the prisoners locked in one of the remaining adobe huts, we needed all the space we could get. But
being crammed into our few remaining buildings was fine.

To my surprise, Federation Troops weren't the only ones
who arrived two days later. Dr. Daniels showed up at the
same time in his own ship, shouting orders and taking charge
of the soldiers. And he'd brought supply ships carrying large
quantities of food and Quonset huts. How he managed to get
that organized, that fast, I'll never understand.

The prisoners were rounded up and sent off on one the
Federation ships, along with the pirates and the remains of
Dorn and Frisk. Although there wasn't much of Frisk left
after Crigo finished with him.

The second the first Quonset hut unfolded, Auntie Em
marched inside and punched in the combination for Panga
ale on the food unit, but Junior and Elder went straight for
the amberberries with chocolate sauce.

As soon as things were under control to Dr. Daniels's
satisfaction, he dragged Thor off for a long talk. Seems
Max had completed a language program and the boss

now spoke fluent Buri. Claudia and I immediately took advantage of the program. One of my biggest problems after that was keeping her pried off Ghost until we could have the mating ceremony, which had of necessity been delayed.

By the time Thor and the boss emerged from their conference, the Buri were the newest members of the Galactic Federation. A little dazed by the boss's zeal, Thor had even agreed to awaken the rest of his people.

Upon hearing the news, I spent the next eight hours feverishly studying Max's medical files with Redfield's assistance. When I was done, I knew everything it was possible to know about the hypothalamus. I then went from female to female, including the ones still in deep sleep, permanently restoring the gland to full functionality.

When I got to Auntie Em, she glared and informed me that if I touched her, she'd break my fingers. All the Buri thought that was quite humorous.

The silver Quonset huts were now scattered through the jungle from the bluff to the plains. They would gradually be replaced as the Buri built their own homes, but for now they worked very nicely.

Even Redfield and Brownie had settled their differences. Since Redfield had killed a crew member who was intent on burning a large hole through Brownie's forehead, the Buri considered all debts paid in full. Now Redfield was scheduled to return to Alien Affairs with Dr. Daniels for retraining and reassignment.

I glanced at Thor again. He was watching something over my shoulder, but I didn't turn to look. "We have to talk."

His chin got that stubborn slant I was becoming all too well acquainted with, but he didn't speak.

"Talk about what?" Dr. Daniels's voice came from behind me, and I swiveled to see him better.

"The future."

"Ah." He smiled and gestured to one of the cushions. "In that case, may I join you? I believe I have a stake in the outcome of this discussion."

"Of course." I poured him a glass of wine while he got comfortable. "I'm just trying to make Thor understand that I can't stay."

"I see." He smoothed a wrinkle in his suit pants and then reached for his drink, sipping thoughtfully. "Do you want to stay?"

While I hesitated, Thor answered for me. "Yes, she wants to stay. This I feel through the bond. She is Shushanna. My people have become her people. She cares about them. But there is part of her that wants to go, also. This part I do not understand."

The boss arched a brow at me. "Why don't you explain the part that wants to go? I'd like to understand too."

Sometimes being connected to Thor even minimally through the bond sucked. I rubbed my forehead to give myself a minute. "It's not that I want to go, because I don't. I don't want to leave Thor or the Buri. But, there's my indenture. I'm legally and morally obliged to pay it off, and I don't have the credits."

Dr. Daniels turned his questioning look on Thor. "May I?"

Thor nodded as I looked from one to the other. "What's going on?"

"Your indenture is taken care of, my dear. The Buri paid it off three days ago."

My mouth dropped open and I reeled with shock. "What? How could they pay it off when they have no credits?"

"They have something better than credits. They have Orpheus crystals. The Bureau was quite happy to accept an amount equivalent to the remainder of your indenture. I would have mentioned it sooner, but Thor wanted it to be a surprise. Actually, I believe his intent was to give you the freedom of choice."

Was that your intent? I asked him.

Yes. He stared at me, his features schooled into a mask. *If you stay it must be because you fully want to be here, with me. And if you go, I'll know you were not forced to leave.*

Dr. Daniels was watching us, and he gave a slight nod, almost as though he knew what had been said. For a Natural, the man could be downright spooky. "Now that your indenture is off the table, why don't you tell us what the real problem is?"

"Okay, I will." I slugged down the rest of my wine and straightened my back. "Gertz created me the way I am and I accept that, accept myself. But part of that is accepting that I was created to do a job, a job I've done my entire life. If I'm not an agent anymore, what will I do? In spite of what Thor thinks, the Buri would survive just fine without me. I've fixed the females so they'll reproduce normally. Eventually, another Shushanna will be born. The truth is, they don't *need* me. If I stay here, I'll spend the rest of my life twiddling my thumbs and being useless."

Thor started to speak, but Dr. Daniels stopped him with a raised hand. "You're afraid you'll be bored."

I nodded. "Out of my skull." *I'm sorry,* I told Thor. *I love you, but I need something to do. It's not in my nature to just stand around looking gorgeous. I'd be a gibbering idiot before the month was over.*

"Weren't you bored with being an agent, too?" The boss continued.

"Well, yes. But at least I had something to do, something to keep me busy and feeling like I was making a difference."

He swirled the wine gently in his glass. "So if you were offered a challenging job that kept you on Orpheus Two, you'd be interested?"

Excitement mixed with hope began a slow trek up my insides to tighten my throat, but I kept my voice level when I answered. This was exactly what I'd wanted to talk him about when he was avoiding me. Now he was offering the chance I'd only dreamed of.

I sat up straighter. If there's one thing I know it's how to negotiate a deal to my advantage. "I might. Did you have something specific in mind?"

My calm tone didn't fool the boss for a second, though. A smile lifted the corners of his lips as he answered. "As a matter of fact, I do. I've asked that you be appointed director of Orpheus Two. The Buri are going to need a lot of help to become productive members of the Federation, not to mention protection from unscrupulous people who'd love nothing more than to take advantage of them. There are also trade negotiations, and the crystals are going to be a large part of that, which will complicate matters enormously."

His gaze met mine as he continued. "I can't think of anyone more qualified for the job than you, my dear. And the truth is, I've been selfish. You should have been promoted several cycles ago and your indenture commuted. I knew you were becoming bored with the job, but you were the best agent we've ever had and I didn't want to lose you, so I kept putting it off."

"I'm getting a promotion?" I was so dazed at the idea I could barely blink. To think, I'd actually been hoping for a job as the new director's assistant. "I didn't know I was qualified to be a director."

"All of our best directors were once agents," he told me. "Since it's the same duties on a larger scale, being an agent is the perfect training ground for the job. Shall I assume you're interested?"

I narrowed my eyes and tilted my head. "Does the job include a raise?"

Thor looked downright smug, waves of love and satisfaction rolling off him, and the boss was smiling again. "A substantial one."

"And of course, I'd need a ship so Thor and I can attend the Federation council meetings."

"Of course. You'll be happy to know that Max has volunteered to stay with you."

"Excellent." By now I could hardly breathe, I was so excited. Ideas and plans for the Buri's future filled my head. Abruptly, I thought of Claudia. I *had* promised her a job, after all, and I'm a woman of my word.

"I'll need a staff, too," I happily informed the boss.

This time it was the Dr. Daniels who narrowed his eyes. "You're allowed three paid employees, based on the Buri population."

I cut my eyes at him. "And a new office building paid for by the Federation."

He scowled. "Fine, and a new office. Hasn't even accepted the job yet and already she's a politician," he grumbled.

With an exuberant whoop, I leaped on him and hugged him hard. "I accept. Thank you. Oh, wow, thank you so much. You have no idea how much this means to me."

"Oh, I think I've got the idea," he choked, untangling my arms from around his neck. "If you have to strangle someone, strangle your mate. He's younger, and can withstand your enthusiasm."

But he was smiling when he said it. "Now tell Redfield good-bye so we can be on our way."

Thor stood when I turned to the GEP, who had just arrived. Impulsively, I leaped to my feet and hugged Redfield, too. "Thomas, I'm going to miss you. If I had a brother, I'd want him to be just like you. Promise me that after your retraining you'll come back and visit us."

He returned the embrace, his voice husky when he answered. "I'll miss you too. And a herd of wild gergians couldn't keep me away. If the boss ever gives me any time off, I'll be heading your way."

"I'm sure that can be arranged," Dr. Daniels said as I released Redfield and moved to stand by Thor. He draped an arm around my shoulders and pulled me close as we watched the men walk away. At the edge of the jungle, they both turned and lifted a hand in farewell.

I waved vigorously and called "Good-bye, Dr. Daniels, good-bye, Thomas!"

"Happy?" Thor asked me.

"Ecstatic," I answered. "I get to stay here with you, *and* keep working."

He gazed down at me, a smile curving his lips. "Did I not tell you there would be a new purpose for you?"

"Yes, you did. You're a wise man, mate of mine."

"Like the Yoda?"

"Exactly like the Yoda. Only you're taller and better-looking."

Suddenly he got serious. "Would you really have left me and our people?"

A smug feeling went through me. "Guess I finally got one over on you, huh? I thought for sure you'd notice how well I was shielding my thoughts."

His brows snapped together as he gave me his best "I-am-the-leader-you-will-respond" stare.

"No," I told him quietly, letting all my love for him pour through the bond. "I never intended to leave you. If you'd talked to me when I wanted you to instead of avoiding me, you'd have known that I only wanted to discuss ways to make this work."

His emerging smile was brighter than Orpheus's star. "I love you, mate."

"Like I said, you're a very wise man." I reached out and took his hand. "Shall we?"

Together, we turned toward our home, where a large tapestry of an Ashwani Feastday now hung on the wall in the great room. Our people were waiting, and we had a mating ceremony to prepare for.